All The Days After

Noah & Eve

⟨⊪⟩ ⟨⊪⟩

Erin FitzGerald

Thank you for reading the work of a local writer. I hope this brings joy, hope & a temporary escape into a fictional world.

♡

Erin FitzGerald

Contents

Give sorrow words; the grief that does not speak knits up the o-er wrought heart and bids it break. - William Shakespeare, Macbeth

ONE

Noah

‹‹‹›››

Avery was running around the kitchen like her ass was on fire. It was an impressive display of stamina and dexterity, since my girl was seven months pregnant and though I'd never have said it out loud, she actually resembled a beached whale when she collapsed butt-down onto the sofa.

I couldn't say something like that because she'd shave my head in my sleep, and I have really awesome hair.

Or feed me pubes of unknown origin in my breakfast and tell me after.

Or slip ghost pepper oil into my coffee and let me figure that one out for myself.

I probably deserved any one of those things on the average day, but I did dumb shit for laughs and Avery was just as much of a childish prankster as I was. That was why I loved her. I mean, there were other reasons too, but that was the one I could tell people about without getting into trouble.

"You shouldn't have let me sleep so late!" she squealed, throwing things out of the fridge and onto the counter. "Now you're going to have to make your own breakfast, because I have to be at work in half an hour. There's no way I have time for a shower--I'm going to have to rush just to get dressed!" She paused, leaning over the counter and taking a deep breath.

"Whoa, babe. You okay?" I was instantly concerned. She'd been experiencing some cramping the past couple weeks that the doctor said were Braxton-Hicks contractions, but I called bullshit on that. I'd put money on my girl being put on bedrest at her next doctor's visit.

1

My oldest brother, Thomas, liked to tease that if anything was going to get us down the aisle, or to split up for good, it was having a baby. He was probably right, too. Pregnancy made Avery meaner than usual, a genetic legacy from her scary father.

We had been together since high school, but both of us came from weird family dynamics, so neither of us really felt like getting married was high on the priority list. I loved her and she loved me and that was a hell of a lot more powerful than any piece of paper, even though it made her dad spit with anger every time he saw me. I hadn't yet made an honest woman of his baby girl, he always yelled, and it seemed to be the only time he was interested in Avery at all.

"You've been so tired lately," I argued with her while I started a pot of coffee. "I didn't see any harm in letting you get a few extra minutes."

"A few extra minutes," she muttered, shoving a hand into the unfolded laundry pile on the sofa and pulling out a pair of horribly wrinkled leggings. "Try forty. Do you have any idea how long it takes to get Mount Vesuvius ready in the morning?" She gestured toward her belly and I grinned at her reference.

"This is like running a marathon uphill the entire time. I'm exhausted by the time I get to work on a *good* day."

That may or may not have had something to do with the gestational diabetes, and the doc had a pretty close eye on her. Because of it, she had to be pretty careful with her diet and she got crazy-mad when I ate Oreos in front of her.

Or pizza.

Or even carrot sticks.

Basically, eating in front of her was a bad idea, and eating was something I could do like it was an Olympic sport.

"Go get dressed," I told her finally, crossing the room to kiss the top of her head and pat her butt. (She hated it when I patted her butt.) "I'll pack some healthy snacks and drive you to work."

We both knew I was the better driver, even though I had a lead foot.

I was filling a travel mug with coffee when she rushed back into the kitchen, her hair in a crazy pile on top of her head. It made me grin at

2

her. She was tiny to my huge; short and petite to my tall and broad; and hugely pregnant with our baby, whereas I was still just tall and muscular. I didn't like doing sit-ups or push-ups, or lifting in the cold garage every day after work, but I made some sacrifices to keep in decent shape, because I liked to have a beer or two in the evenings. I understood the concept of the trade-off.

We were going to be a family--just us--and she would be my forever, not like the rotating roster of women my father kept cycling through his house as "wife." The average life cycle of a relationship, for him, seemed to be about three years, whereas Avery and I were going on twenty-three.

"Jenny's going to be on her own with all those little crazies...and we're doing the Thanksgiving play rehearsal today…" Avery was getting herself all worked up.

Her class of kindergarteners adored her, as they did every year, which was never surprising. She'd been teaching for fourteen years already, straight out of college, and the woman practically had a certificate in herding cats.

At least she'd gone to college, which was something her sister would always hang over my head. I wasn't good enough for Avery, because I'd barely made it through high school. I'd completed all kinds of on-the-job certification courses, but I was not a college man. Just the thought made me break out in hives.

Instead, my training had been on the job and I'd been working since I was eight, learning from my father's team of men how to wire, plumb, drywall and tile. I could demo with the best of them, but it was my patching work that could make experienced contractors weep. I was whatever level was beyond expert.

Avery struggled to wrap the seat belt around her body and she growled at me as I turned over the engine on my old work truck. "You are never knocking me up again, Atholton. You put this monster in me and it's going to take a buzz saw and a crane to get it out." She wiggled down in the seat, trying to shift the baby's position so she could take a full breath.

"We're having a whole football team of babies, Aves." I grinned down my shoulder at her. "The combination of our exemplary genetic material is a gift to this world. Besides, you'll make the prettiest babies." I leaned over to peck at her cheek and she swatted at my shoulder, her hand bouncing off harmlessly. She was smiling despite being irritated.

I broke the sound barrier to get her to school on time and she took the lunch bag I'd packed for her, shaking her head at me. "One baby, Atholton. I don't think I can handle any more of your monster spawn. Not if you want into Vegas ever again." She gestured vaguely toward her lower body.

Yeah, I'd nicknamed her lady bits. It made leaving places and uncomfortable situations really simple: *Babe, we should get going--we're going to miss our flight to Vegas.* People had no idea what they were overhearing was our own innuendo signaling I wanted to head home to have crazy monkey sex.

She leaned over to kiss me quickly, waddling across the walkway and up the steps and I watched her go, admiring the sway of her hips. I loved that pregnancy added extra pounds to her boobs and butt. She'd always been curvy, but now she was like a funhouse of squeezy toys, and I was probably wearing her out with my eagerness over all the new goodies.

I sighed, throwing the truck into drive and pulling away from the curb. Work, for the next couple weeks, was just a little farther downtown. The crew and I were working on new construction, a block of condos that were already a hot commodity. We were two months out from completion, but all the units had already been snapped up, mostly by investors living overseas, from what I'd overheard. China seemed real eager to buy us up, almost as hot a real estate market as Vancouver.

We'd just broken for lunch, my crew's favorite time of day, since all the girls working in the offices sashayed down the streets to pick up sandwiches or salads. Some days I think they leered and catcalled more than they ate, but they were pretty polite as far as most crews went. They saved the catcalls for the shortest skirts.

Suddenly a sound rang out, like a thousand cannons going off all at once, and the building shook so hard I could hear glass tinkling somewhere on one of the lower floors. It startled me enough that I dropped to my stomach on the floor, a vicious ringing in my ears.

Not a minute later a cruiser went howling past, light bar ablaze, and I watched it with interest from my eighth floor vantage point. He was moving at a pretty good clip for being in the inner city.

Another streaked past, four more on his tail.

I had a bad feeling about this.

In the distance there was a long, low wail winding up and it took me a minute to realize it was more responder units--bigger ones: fire trucks and ambulances.

The noise was deafening as five fire engines rumbled past and a long line of ambulances trailed after. Fourteen, fifteen, sixteen...something jumped in my stomach. Something really big was going down, and I pulled out my phone to check out the home page of one of the local news stations. Nothing yet.

The units left the same way they came, the ambulances first, screaming past only moments later, even as more were on their way in.

"Noah!" It was Brad, one of my dad's foremen and the guy I usually reported to. I looked up from the panel I'd been working on, nodding at him in greeting. "Son..." His fingers on my shoulder were gentle. "Doesn't your girl work at Lafayette?"

I nodded stupidly, something cold and hard stabbing at my gut.

"You'd best get to the hospital," he said gently. "There's something gone wrong at the school--a lot of hurt kids."

I slapped the button for the buck hoist before I realized I'd blacked out on my feet and run forty yards without recollection of movement. Come on, come on, come on...I could rappel down the side of the building faster.

I frantically punched at Avery's contact information on my phone and after four rings it went to voicemail. Again and again and again. *It's ok, it's ok--breathe. It's lunchtime and she's probably wrangling those little monsters...she's ok.*

My truck was parked in the small lot next to the site and I threw myself in, grinding the starter and shooting gravel across the lot as I tore out onto the street.

Damn it. A lot of the roads were blocked off by cruisers and traffic was being redirected. I went up one road and down the next, completely incapable of forming a comprehensive route in my head although I knew this city like the back of my hand.

Finally, I pulled right up to one of the officers and rolled down my window. He eyed me warily as he moved closer. "No getting through this way, sir." His voice was clipped and authoritative, like he was ex-military.

"I need help," I finally said, scrubbing my hands over my face. He saw that I was distraught and he moved a little closer. "My boss said something happened at Lafayette...my girl works there...she's pregnant." I swallowed hard and my throat made a weird noise. The man's eyes softened sympathetically.

"Lieutenant Jackson!" he barked, and another officer hurried over. "Get your cruiser and give this man an escort to the hospital. Stay with him until he finds his woman."

"Thank you, sir," I stammered, pins and needles prickling over my skin.

"Godspeed, son," he said, dropping a sharp salute in my direction before he turned and walked back to his station.

Jackson drove like a bat out of hell, siren howling, lights flashing, and I pushed my old tank to keep up with him even while I willed him to drive faster.

It couldn't have taken more than a few minutes, but it felt like forever before he screeched to a stop near a long line of cruisers outside the hospital, and he threw open his door, shouting to the few officers standing nearby. "Boys, move the truck for him; we're here on urgent business. Bring the keys to me."

Someone grumbled about being a valet wanting his tip as he slid into my truck and Jackson's fist wound into my shirt, dragging me along behind him as we ran toward the sliding doors of the ER. I was really glad this guy took his charge so seriously.

The waiting room was like the seventh circle of hell, filled with gurneys and wailing kids. There was blood everywhere, something I'd never been able to handle, and my stomach lurched with nausea as I scanned the room for any familiar faces.

"Avery MacGowan!" I roared over the din, and for only a second the room quieted.

"Sir." It was Jackson again. "We should check in with one of the attendants. I'm sure there are more already in the back--perhaps she's in there."

Satisfied he had a better plan, I had just turned toward him when I heard the tiniest voice.

"Noah?"

I spun quickly. It was Avery's aide, Jenny, lying on one of the gurneys with a wicked gash across her forehead. Both of her hands were covered in blood--they looked burned. I hurried toward her, dropping to my knees beside her.

"Jenny. Tell me. Tell me what happened. Where's Avery?"

She hiccuped and her pale face folded in as she began to cry. "I'm so sorry...I wasn't...I couldn't...she sent me to get something from the classroom and I was on my way back when it happened. I…" She was fully sobbing now and the look on Jackson's face told me I already had my answer. My stomach lurched.

"Have you seen her?" I asked, suddenly oddly calm despite my churning guts. My brain had drowned out all the noise and isolated everything but Jenny and her response. "Do you know if she was brought here?" She shook her head again and again.

"Sir?" There was a woman standing next to me. I'd watched her out of the corner of my eye since hollering for Avery and she'd begun weaving through gurneys in our direction. "I'm Rosalie, executive assistant to the principal at Lafayette." She stood there like she was waiting for me to say something and I nodded dumbly.

"There are teams still at the school," she said softly, "making sure as many are rescued as possible."

Jackson's shoulder microphone crackled and I saw his face pale even though I couldn't make out the words. "Ma'am," he said shortly, addressing Rosalie, and she turned to him with wide eyes. "Can you tell me where Ms. McGowan's class was at the time of the blast?"

Oh please, God, no.

"Ms. MacGowan and Ms. Vargas had Thanksgiving play rehearsal in the gym today, sir. I believe they were just about to break for lunch."

A terrible sobbing sound echoed through the large room and Jackson and Rosalie turned to look at me in alarm.

It was me.

"The gym..." I finally managed to croak, looking beseechingly at Jackson, who quickly swiveled a chair under me as my knees gave out. The words from the microphone had just unspooled in my brain, processed slowly to remove the crackling interference and the din.

"Suspected gas leak in the cafeteria, adjacent to the gymnasium. Both portions of the structure leveled."

"Nurse! Someone, please! We need a nurse!" Rosalee started shrieking as the edges of my vision began to turn black.

Just like that, my whole world was gone.

TWO

Eve

◄‖►

What kind of special hell was this?

I'd been called in by my supervisor, who insisted she needed all hands on deck and she'd be willing to put me in for time-and-a-half, since this was an emergency situation. *Willing, my ass.* I was already over for the pay period.

As it was, I was coming off a shift of four twelves, since I'd pulled an extra, and I'd crashed into bed at 12:30 the night (morning?) before, up in time to feed Jared a super nutritious breakfast of boxed cereal and orange juice, shove his books in his backpack and drag him off to school.

I'd been running full-out the past week, between work and Jared's Thanksgiving program at the school. I was trying really hard to help out with his class when I could, as a kind of room parent, even if it wasn't in any really official capacity. But Jason, my ex, had filled up the rest of the week with his nonsense. He'd complained that I was negatively influencing Jared against him and so again, as was his annual tradition, I had a court date to contend with.

Truth was, I made an ok living as an ER nurse. But it would have been a much better living (house instead of condo, maybe) if I hadn't had to keep a lawyer practically on retainer since Jason had walked out on us when Jared was four. Not that Jason wanted any sort of custody, mind you--he liked to play head games, so dicking me around was his idea of a good time. Since he didn't actually have to raise his son, he had all the time in the world to scheme and plot, and since he was the sort of person who thrived on conflict I was the easiest target.

I barely had time to call Jared's babysitter--thank God she was available, since I was supposed to have today off. I really needed to look into some subsidized after-school programs, but I'd heard scary things about them from my girlfriends, so I hadn't exactly been in a rush.

The truth of the matter was that we didn't live in the best part of town, though it was far from the worst. The schools we were zoned for could be called a little rough around the edges, depending upon your standards and socioeconomic status. And that meant the after school programs were sometimes a little sketchy, run by graduate students and high school kids looking to make eight bucks an hour to sit on their phones when they should have been providing oversight and direction.

There was a squealing noise when I swung the wheel to tuck into a tight space in the parking garage and I winced, patting the steering wheel. I'd needed to take my car in for service for some time now. I was almost eight hundred miles overdue for an oil change and she was starting to groan and creak and screech in some kind of scary ways. I had a feeling the damage was going to be extreme--more than the price of an oil change, anyway, and that was *after* the mechanic lectured me about maintenance. That was a lecture I'd pay almost anything to avoid.

Rushing into the staff area, I clocked in and tossed my hastily assembled lunch bag into the communal refrigerator. I prayed my food would be there later when I got to it--if I got to it. Then I swung the door open, into the main hallway.

Chaos.

There were gurneys everywhere, most of them filled with children and my eyes swept the gurneys wildly with the instinct of a mother, looking for Jared. *What in the hell happened?*

"Hey!" I shouted to the orderly running down the hallway and he turned quickly, a look of absolute panic on his face. "What's going on here?"

"You didn't hear?" He looked incredulous. "Gas leak at Lafayette-- leveled the cafeteria and the gymnasium. At least forty-eight dead that we know of and the rescue crews are still working. In the meantime we've got easy two hundred kids, teachers and God-knows-who-else to patch up. A couple of the other hospitals got hit just as hard--we couldn't handle all of it."

Lafayette was huge. It serviced a lot of the inner city kids, a monster of a catch-all in the city's educational system. I shuddered, thankful I lived just outside that district: Jared wasn't in this group and that meant I could focus.

"We're moving them as fast as we can," he called back as he turned and began to jog down the hall. "Go get more from the front--triage is up there already."

The wave of collective panic hit me as soon as I opened the door into the waiting room. The air was thick with wailing, sweat and blood. The room was filled with little kids, and I could see a blue line outside the doors trying to hold back what was probably a mob of panicked parents.

"Beth." I sank to my knees next to one of the triage nurses on duty and she looked up at me in surprise as she held her fingers over the neck of a truly giant man.

Bear.

The word came to me unbidden as I looked at the huge man slumped in his seat, his beautiful features slack as he struggled to regain consciousness, his warm brown eyes blink-blinking slowly, and I watched as a huge tear rolled down his cheek.

I didn't think for a second. I reached up to brush it away and took his face in my hand. Beth stood then, moving quickly away but I stayed, waiting for his eyes to focus on me.

"Sir." It was my voice. "Let me help you. Where are you hurt?"

His big hand slapped over his heart and his upper body collapsed across his knees, silent sobs shaking his huge shoulders.

Something stabbed at my heart. *This guy lost someone to this...* I wished for the thousandth time that I'd gone to school for counseling rather than nursing.

"Shhh, hey...it's ok." I knew I was wasting valuable time, but I couldn't walk away from him and I didn't even know why. Something about this guy kept me anchored firmly to his side, watching him fall apart, hoping there was something I could do to help.

11

"Oh god, she's gone," he moaned, slumping forward and I caught him as best I could, pushing my toes into the floor to try to catch him and push him back into his seat. *You're a caregiver, Eve. Act like one. You aren't personally involved; turn off your heart and turn your brain on.*

"William!" I shouted over the big guy's shoulder. "I need help!"

William stepped in quickly. "Eve, hey, it's ok--I got this." He braced himself into the big guy's weight and pushed him back into the chair.

"Hey," I said softly to the man as his eyes focused on me. "What can I do to help?"

His face crumpled again. "I need her back, lady. We were gonna be a family, and I need them back." He leaned forward and William almost folded in half trying to keep him up.

"William," I said softly into the man's ear, and I felt him tense. "Let's get this guy a bed somewhere. He's not fit to leave. He needs rest and probably an IV and definitely some sedatives. Can we do that?"

William was a charge nurse and he could definitely do that. He liked me and had asked me out several times, which meant I was unduly influencing him, but I had absolutely no qualms about doing so.

"Yeah, I got this." William stood up, bracing the big guy's weight carefully as he lifted him. "You get to the kids and I'll take care of this."

Nodding, I moved slowly, carefully past the two of them.

I wanted to stay.

I wanted to put the man on a gurney and wheel him into the back and tend to him myself. *Why?* But I knew the answer already: This man loved someone with every fiber of his being, something I had never known. And if I was being honest, I wanted to stand close to him and absorb the knowledge of what that person had done to be this man's air.

THREE

Noah
◄╫►

"Bear, come back..."

The voice was low and sweet, lips just barely tickling my ear. It had to be Avery, I figured, because once they got to heaven angels probably got new voices. And now that we were in heaven...

Wait.

There was something beeping and I could hear swooshing noises. This was definitely not heaven.

"Oh, thank God."

My eyes opened slowly, taking in the dark red hair I'd been seeing in my dreams. I frowned, because it wasn't Avery.

"It's ok, Noah." Her sweet voice faltered a little. "Let me know what you need."

I looked up, my gaze fixing on the clock on the far wall. It was already well past three, which meant I'd been out for a long time.

When I didn't answer, she squeezed my arm gently and turned to leave, her red hair swishing behind her, and my heart ached when I remembered why I was here. I was a pansy. A pussy. Unable to handle the fact that my girl had been hurt--taken from me--and I'd required sedatives and electrolytes to keep me from dying of anguish.

"Let me out!" I yelled, pulling against the IV until the tape snapped and the needle popped from my arm, a few drops of blood spilling on the blanket. "Someone. Get in here and let me go!"

Howling wouldn't get me anywhere and I knew it, but I didn't know how long I'd been out. I needed to put on real clothes and get to the school. I needed to talk to people who knew things. I needed to know what had happened.

"Hey, man." The face with the calming voice wasn't happy with me, and it wasn't the voice I wanted. I could see it in the way he looked at me, his jaw tight. "We'll get a doctor to check you out and then you're free to go, but you gotta wait."

I sat waiting, rubbing the hand I'd ripped the needles from, and when the doctor returned with the guy I assumed was my nurse, I asked: "Was I dreaming? Where did the other nurse go--the redhead?" They looked at me like I was crazy, and maybe I was. She was a leftover fog from my dreams.

They exchanged looks and didn't answer, mumbling to one another about a psychiatric hold and the doctor gave the other man a tight shake of his head. "No go," he said quietly, and started reading my chart, then checking my vitals manually. I didn't much like it, but I didn't have much of a choice if I was going to get out.

Billing spit me out onto the sidewalk and I tried desperately to remember where I'd been when I left my truck with the cops.

My phone was dead. I hadn't charged it in who knew how long, and I hurried toward the spot I remembered Jackson having jumped out of his car. My truck had to be close, and it had a charger. If I could just find it, I could charge my phone, and then I could head to the school. Just maybe she'd been taken to a different hospital, I thought, clinging to that small amount of hope. By now, surely she'd gotten my message...she would be frantic, wondering what had happened to me.

The sun disappeared behind a cloud as I found my truck and fitted the key to the old, rusting lock. I climbed in and turned over the engine, plugging in my phone and waiting until it charged enough to turn on. I had fourteen new voicemails, most of them from my family, but I was looking for one from Avery.

I dropped my head onto the steering wheel and sucked in a few deep breaths, a feeling of absolute despair washing over me, because there were no voicemails from her. She was gone.

14

FOUR

Eve

◄▮►

The hospital was so overrun, I ended up working a straight seven days that week. My supervisor cut me off at eighty hours, just to keep me on the right side of the legal cap and it was going to make for a great paycheck, but I was completely exhausted.

As little patients began to be discharged and the hospital settled into a slightly more normal rhythm, William caught up with me late in the afternoon the last day I was on. I'd asked him to find out where Bear had been moved. (Yeah, that's what I was calling him. Don't judge.). It made William look at me funny, so I made up something stupid about thinking I might know him and I wanted to make sure he was ok.

He'd been knocked out for a while, thanks to a powerful combo of drugs--enough to take down an elephant, because he'd been so frantic with grief the doctor feared he'd hurt himself or someone else.

I waited until my break to go find him. There was something about him that pulled me with magnetic force, and I hated it, because I knew it meant I was crossing a professional line. That I'd already given him a nickname meant my subconscious had already crossed that line in a *big* way, betraying me with someone I didn't even know.

He wasn't exactly conscious yet when I found him and I looked up quickly to make sure we didn't have any observers, hoverers, or general trouble headed our way before I ran my fingertips over his cheekbone and up, over his ear. There was hurt here, and I wanted to fix it--and that scared the shit out of me. It scared me because I could understand his loss and I knew how it would continue to wreck him for a long time to come.

"Come back, Bear, you're going to get through this," I whispered, even though I had no idea why I'd said it.

Like I was his sister.

His mother.

His girlfriend.

His lover.

His eyelids fluttered and I sucked in a sharp breath, saying something stupid about wanting to help him in any way I could before he slipped back into dreams for a moment and I took my chance to leave the room, alerting one of the nurses he was awake.

By the time my break was over, I was very nearly off the clock and I hurried to complete some charting and chatted with the nurse coming on duty before handing off my patients. I didn't like anyone to go in cold, learning things strictly from a chart, and I'd developed a good standing with most of my colleagues as a result. (Turned out they liked the human touch better than tablets, too.)

I was able to pick Jared up from school, since he'd stayed late in the tutoring program. It was something I didn't usually get to do. Usually I let his sitter pick him up and spend a few hours with him while I took care of the grocery shopping, the dry cleaning...all the things I would have loved to split out with the partner I didn't have, because the partner I *had* been with turned out to be a completely unreliable asshole.

Jared's father was in the military and had been since he was eighteen. We'd met when Jason was twenty-three and I was twenty, and Jared went from being a twinkle in my eye to a very real infant in all of ten months. Of course, Jason was furious. He'd wanted time with me as "just us," and when my traitorous and evolutionarily-primed uterus betrayed me, he very begrudgingly asked me to marry him. I didn't think for a second that he'd done it for any reason other than that his mother pressured him.

What's the worst thing a pregnant, single girl with no support network can do? I'll tell you right now: Marry the idiot who refused to suit up, knocked her up, and would never accept the responsibility.

Jared and I would have been better off without Jason from the start.

Of course, he insisted upon a paternity test once Jared was born and was furious with me once paternity was confirmed, because he no longer had an out. I knew then that he could never be trusted to love our son unconditionally.

We held on until Jared was four, probably only because Jason was deployed for two of those years, and eventually he left because he'd found some young, dumb new girl to take my place. Although...maybe she wasn't as dumb as I'd been, because she'd insisted he wrap the submarine before they got busy. (Yeah, he told me that and he thought his analogy was hilarious. He was *that* much of an asshole.)

Miraculously, that next week I was off for a three-day stretch that actually included Thanksgiving and as I rushed home Wednesday night, I waited impatiently at the drive-through. The line was interminable, but I needed up the caffeine that would carry me through dinner, homework, laundry, tidying...and *maybe* a few stolen moments with Aidan Turner and the BBC. Nah, I knew better: I'd be folding laundry and basting a turkey in my sleep.

It was nearing eight and I parked in my rented space and hurried toward the condo. I was a few minutes late and Maggie, although extremely patient with me, was already studying for her upcoming finals and would need some serious time to herself. I was cutting into her time now.

Dropping the grocery bags onto the counter and hurrying into the living room, I wasn't surprised to see her quizzing Jared with flash cards. He needed a lot of extra help with math and since Maggie was studying to be a teacher, she was the perfect person to help him with homework and studying during the afternoons he wasn't in the tutoring program at school. Thankfully, it also largely let me off the hook when it came to homework--possibly the only break I got.

While she gathered up her things and briefed me on the few things Jared had left to complete, I Venmoed her wages for the week. I was remarkably adept at listening and processing while completing things, multi-tasking being a skill I'd perfected in the ER.

Jared wanted mac and cheese for dinner, so I chopped up a quick salad to go with it, in hopes that it was enough to make up for what was probably a nutritional shortfall of late. And while I did that, he finished his Social Studies and Science homework at the kitchen table.

"Mom," he asked quietly, and I stopped stirring just long enough to look up at him. "I heard a lot of kids were hurt last week in an explosion. Do you think that could ever happen at my school?"

"It could happen anywhere," I answered, with maybe a little more brutal honesty than I'd wanted to display. "But…" I tried to take the edge off. "It's very unlikely. You can bet inspectors will be out to all the schools this week to make sure everything is safe."

"What about our house?" he asked, his forehead crinkled with worry.

"We don't have any gas lines in this building," I answered confidently. "I checked before we moved here." But I didn't tell him why I was a freak about natural gas. It had been banned in new construction in the area, but not for safety reasons, and I wondered if dead kids were going to be enough to promote code changes.

He seemed satisfied with my answer as he gathered up his books to put in his backpack and I heard him shuffle out of the room to drop it in the entryway, so he didn't have to search for it come Monday morning. He was a planner, an organizer, a generally quiet, thoughtful kid who didn't take after Jason at all.

My lawyer had left a voicemail while I was at the grocery store and I waited until after Jared was in bed to listen to it. I didn't want him to see me upset with his father, which was becoming harder and harder to pull off. Jason was already such a shadowy figure in his life, I tried to let him cling to whatever tiny shred of positivity there was to be had, because my kid was a damn optimist. Life hadn't quite beaten it out of him yet. His linings were silver, whereas mine were distinctly grey.

I called Daniel back the instant I listened to the voicemail, although it was already after nine. As expected, he answered on the first ring--of course he did, because he was still in his office, even the week before Thanksgiving.

"Eve." His voice was incredible, a rich baritone that was so soothing, I had a hard time focusing. It had been a long time since a man said my name the way he did, drawn out just a little too long, like he was licking the consonant. I tried to tell myself he treated all his female clients the same way: that he was just personable and couldn't help it.

"I was starting to worry I wouldn't hear from you tonight." Was that a hint of disappointment in his voice?

"Hi Daniel," I said with a sigh. My temples ached just a little with the threat of a headache. "I knew your message was nothing good, so I listened to it just now, since Jared is finally in bed. I called back right away."

Daniel broke down Jason's latest filing, not only accusing me of negatively influencing Jared against him, but demanding more visitation. It made me scoff when I knew I'd have been better off holding my tongue. "More visitation? Is he high? So he'll take me to court in order to get more days on the calendar with Jared--*more* days that he *won't* show up, and I'll have to explain to my disappointed kid that maybe Dad got busy and forgot to call.

"Or maybe he shipped out.

"Or maybe he's too deep in the flavor of the week to be bothered with his son." I stopped myself before it became a full rant. "I'm sorry, Daniel, I shouldn't have said any of that. It's just…" I let a weary sigh escape as my eyes began to throb--this headache was coming for me fast. "It's just that he gets to be the fun parent. His input is exactly what he wants it to be, which means it's little to none most of the time. Then when he does show up, he's the hero--yay, it's Daddy.

"The rest of the time I'm picking up the pieces and trying to convince my son that his father's absence doesn't mean he's not important. But come on, I feel like a liar."

Daniel made a sympathetic humming noise and I reminded myself I needed to stop talking, because my words were costing me--literally--and Daniel's time was not cheap.

"The fastest route to resolution in this case," he responded quickly, "is to agree to increased visitation provided the parameters previously laid out remain in place. Presently Jason is allowed one visit of two consecutive overnights--so a weekend, really--per month. When this was established it was determined he couldn't be more involved, due to his career and frequent travel. If that information has changed, it will need to be updated. Also, you may want to consider revisiting the child support arrangement and requesting a deduction order since you can't count on him to make regular payments. We haven't pursued updated salary information or enforcement for some time."

I snorted before I could help myself and pain rocked my sinuses. "What's the point? That's just throwing money into a pit. The only kind of support I've ever seen from him has been the occasional odd gift for Jared, when Jason feels badly enough that he tries to buy our son's affection with a game console or a new pair of shoes."

By the time Daniel signed off, I'd racked up several hundred dollars in fees for his time and I'd earned myself a stellar headache. Talking about Jason and his lack of involvement always did it. In fact, just *thinking* about Jason, or hearing his name, often did it and I moved carefully to my bathroom to fish around in the cabinet for painkillers. If I got lucky this wouldn't turn into a full-blown migraine, which could sometimes render me entirely useless for a full day.

"Mom?" It was Jared, standing outside my bathroom door. "Is all that stuff about Dad true?"

Oh, crap. I knew I should have called Daniel back from behind my closed bedroom door instead of sitting in the living room.

"Um…" I took a few extra big chugs of water before I answered. "Your dad and I have different ideas about how involved each one of us should be in your life and sometimes I get upset because I know it hurts you."

"You're right," he said softly and I clicked off the bathroom light and guided him back down the hallway to tuck him in again. "You can give him more time with me, but he won't show up."

I could hear the dejection in his voice.

"The way someone treats you is not a reflection of you, honey," I said gently as he climbed back into his bed. "It's a reflection of them--of their true selves."

"I know," he said pensively. "It's just hard not to feel like I disappoint him, or I'm not enough, because if I made him happy then he would want to spend more time with me."

Dropping to my knees beside his bed, I crossed my arms on his pillow and rested my cheek so that our faces were very close. "If your daddy can't see how special you are, he's cheating himself. Because someday you'll grow up to be even more amazing than you already are, and he's going to realize he missed out on all that time with you. And I'm sorry, because I know it hurts and it's hard not to take it personally, but you are *so* loved."

He let me squeeze him and I dropped a kiss on his cheek before crossing the room and only partially closing the door as I walked back down the hallway.

I had laundry to fold and dishes to put away.

If I started working on breakfast now, tomorrow's main meal prep would be easier.

But I couldn't do it. The pounding in my head threatened to bring me to my knees, and I collapsed face down on my bed and prayed for oblivion.

FIVE

Noah

◄II►

Da told me to take as much time as I needed, and since I could barely function, I took him up on the offer.

I barely made it out of bed the first week.

The second week, I finally showered but it was only so I could make it to the grocery store and once I got there I couldn't figure out what to buy. I ended up dumping most of the freezer section into my cart and wedging it into my freezer at home.

Avery hadn't been a gourmet cook, but she kept us from going hungry even if it meant bagged salads and pasta five nights a week. I didn't complain, as long as I could get some beef and potatoes thrown in here and there. Generally I kept my mouth shut, because if it was up to me we'd have starved. I hadn't met any kind of food I couldn't incinerate when I tried my hand at cooking. Avery had said it was because I was too distractible: I'd put something on the stove to warm and wander off to fill a few moments, only to set off the smoke alarm half an hour later when the food had been reduced to something resembling a smoking lump of charcoal.

Since I could hardly bring myself to eat, TV dinners suited me just fine. It didn't matter whether I put them in the oven for five minutes and had to chip through the permafrost, or forty-five minutes and had to eat rubber. I couldn't taste anything anyway.

Sleeping didn't go so well. First I tried p.m. painkillers, figuring it was better than booze. But when those didn't work I resorted to bourbon, which had about a fifty percent success rate. The problem with that was that just because the stuff put me to sleep, it didn't keep the nightmares away.

Avery's mom had been by a few times to clean up a little and to take a few little mementos with her. She always brought me something nice, like cookies or a casserole and I knew she was struggling too, but she didn't show it in the way I did, with my uncombed hair and weeks of beard. I couldn't remember the last time I'd done the laundry and the bedsheets had lost Avery's smell, so I'd taken to sleeping on the sofa in the living room.

I guess we all struggled in our own way, but obviously my struggle had no shame, because I took to wearing the same clothes for four or five days in a row, even though I definitely smelled like a herd of dirty-assed goats by the second day.

Avery's family started planning a memorial service. We had no body to bury, so there was no hurry, but there was also a great gap between fantasy and reality in my mind. I wasn't sure I wanted closure, and while everyone else moved forward, I kept waiting for Avery to walk through the door.

To tell me to get my giant sasquatch feet off the coffee table.

To tell me the living room smelled like the primate house at the zoo and that homeless encampments had cleaner facilities, would I please go scrub the toilet?

It had been almost four weeks when Finn showed up. My only sister, the youngest of all six of us, I knew Thomas had sent her. She lived in San Diego with my sweet little nephew, Griffin. But she'd gotten away from her idiot husband, Magnus for even a second, I had no idea. Dude had serious control issues and I worried that one day, if Finn didn't grab Griffin and run, he was going to hurt them both.

But Finn? She didn't listen.

She made excuses for him.

She told everyone who worried that it wasn't that bad.

I knew better.

"Hey, big guy." My sister wrapped me up in a huge hug and she took an admirably deep, choking breath as I held her a little too long. I released her and she composed her face, trying not to shudder, and I loved her for it.

"Sorry," I said, holding the door to let her walk into the house ahead of me. "I'm not doing real well with...uh, normal human stuff these days. Like showering."

She nodded and headed for the kitchen, sifting through the batch of groceries Helen, Avery's mom, brought for me a couple days earlier. Since my own mom was dead, I was more grateful to Helen for her care than she could ever know.

Finn set to work right away, clearing the counter and wiping it down, dumping dishes into the sink. She sorted the dishwasher and put things away, then reloaded it and set it to clean while she pulled a plate from the cupboard.

"You're here early," I finally said, the island barstool creaking under my weight. "The service isn't until Friday."

"Thom's flying everyone in tomorrow," she said gently, and I swallowed hard. My brothers and I hadn't always gotten along great, but we were growing closer in our adulthood and I knew this meant a house full. They would all insist on bunking with me in my little two-bedroom house, to show "support," although if you knew my family, you knew that word had a very loose interpretation.

In Aaron's case, I suspected he was staying with me because he was broke. Rumor from Asher was that it was because when Gillian left him, she cleaned out their bank account.

In Asher's case, it was because he was too fucking lazy to get a hotel. His excuse would be that he traveled too much for work and hated hotels.

Thomas would stay to act as the father figure, keeping order and seeing to things like transportation and food.

And Finn? She was our mama bear these days, the master maker of sandwiches and a crack barista. To her credit, she'd put summer jobs, schooling and personal passion to use and she was the personal chef for a MLB player. I mean, she probably didn't have to work since Magnus came from shipping magnate money--his family owned the largest commercial fleet in Sweden--but I don't think she trusted him to provide for her and Griffin since he was known to snort his way through piles of cash.

I watched her assemble a huge turkey, lettuce and tomato sandwich and my stomach grumbled a warning. The thought of putting anything into my mouth made me want to vomit. I'd lost almost twenty pounds in the last month, thanks to my almost non-existent diet. I often forgot to eat altogether and I was aware I didn't look so good.

"Gerry said she'll come after I leave," she said softly, glopping mayonnaise onto the top slice of bread. She knew I liked my turkey sandwiches gooey with mayo. "I sent Griff to her since I can't trust Magnus to do basic things like feed and supervise his own kid." She rolled her eyes. "So I'm staying with you through next Wednesday, and then Gerry will be here."

"What?" I half-heartedly joked. "The family's pulling suicide watch on me?"

That my family had summoned Gerry, the first in a long line of stepmothers, did not bode well. She was the only one of them with a higher education, and it happened to be in behavioral therapy. That meant she could read me and my simple mind as easily as a Dick and Jane book.

"Not funny, Noah." Her nostrils flared and she jammed the sandwich together with a wet slap before pushing the plate across the countertop. "You've been with Avery for twenty damn years. You were with her for more of your life than you were without and it's going to be really, really hard to adjust to…" She looked around for a moment, her eyes filling, and she waved her hands helplessly. "This."

I took a bite of the huge sandwich, not surprised I could hardly taste it. But I kept chewing, just because I knew I'd feel sicker if I didn't eat soon.

Finn opened the freezer and her mouth dropped. "Seriously, Noah? *This* is what you're eating?" She pulled the bin from beneath the sink and started tossing the frozen rectangles into the trash. I wanted to protest, but I hardly had the energy. I just wanted to struggle with my sandwich and then take a nap.

I wouldn't have been mad about some Oreos.

Pulling out a blender and dumping in ingredients, Finn stared at me disapprovingly while she whirred the blender, and chopped up some vegetables right on the countertop. Then she plunked a handful of celery and carrots down on my plate and added a huge glob of fresh hummus. "Eat it," she commanded. "Then you're taking a shower while I wash a load of laundry."

I made a sound of protest and she shook her head with a tight little jerk. "The other option," she warned, "is to stand out in the yard and I'll drag out the garden hose. You can't live like this, Noah, and things will look a little better after a shower and a nap."

When I emerged from the shower in what was probably my last clean pair of underwear and sweatpants, Finn had changed the sheets on my bed. I wanted to thank her, but irrational anger boiled up behind my eyes and threatened to leak out in a wave of allergies. The last person to change the sheets had been Avery, and now something she'd done was lost to me forever. Something so small and routine. But this felt like another big loss.

I closed the bedroom door and pulled the blinds. Then I sat on the edge of the bed and cried until I was empty.

SIX

Eve

◄II►

Jason brought his latest girlfriend to court, which worked out in my favor when she bent over to retrieve something off the floor and the judge got an eyeful of the Promised Land.

It was impressive, really, how unaware she was of the fact that her skirt was so short, I could see the back of her neck even when she was upright. That, I leaned over to whisper to Daniel, took dedication to her craft, and he smirked. He was equally sure it wasn't an accident at all.

Lucky for me, the judge wasn't at all impressed by the wares and he rolled his eyes obviously when Jason tried to claim that he was due more visitation to "undo the negative influence" I had brought about. Daniel squeezed my knee under the table to keep me from running my mouth, and I clamped down on the Irish that wanted to fly out of my lips about how he was creating the negative influences all on his own.

"Mr. Stanton." The judge sighed heavily, and Daniel smirked at me with a quick movement of his lips. "I would like to discuss the level of...ah...stability within *your* household. I understand you are still considered active duty and you may be gone for long periods of time?" It wasn't really a question.

Jason's face went flat. He wasn't what I'd call quick, but even he knew this was going nowhere good. "I *am* still on active duty, your honor. I will be for the next five years, at which point it is likely I will retire from the military."

Somehow he'd managed to climb only a few stations in all the years he'd been employed by the government. By now he should have been sitting behind a desk, not playing in sandboxes.

27

"It is possible you might be reassigned at any time." That was not a question, either.

"Yes, sir." Jason was uncomfortable. "I could be reassigned to a new location or shipped out, but Eve has always been willing to work with me when it comes to visitation."

"You are blessed with an accommodating partner," the judge commented wryly as he stared down the hooker sitting next to Jason. "However, I have in front of me a record of the number of times you have utilized your visitation rights within this past year."

It was my record.

Jason paled.

"You have seen your son four of the available twelve times in the past year, which leads me to believe that gifting you with more time is pointless, as you have not utilized that which you already have."

The woman next to him huffed and Jason held up a hand to silence her. She rolled her eyes at him and the judge's lips tightened perceptibly. "Would you care to disclose the role of this woman within your household, sir?" he asked next, and Jason's eyes bugged out.

"Um, Your Honor...sir..." He scratched his face nervously. "Rebecca is my fiancee' and will be a permanent fixture in my life, and my son's, going forward."

I had a really hard time hiding the snort that wanted to rocket out. Becky looked just as surprised by the fiancee' pronouncement as did Jason's lawyer, and Daniel clamped down on his lips to fight the smile that threatened to wreath his handsome face.

The judge sighed heavily. "If Ms. Ryan wishes for you to spend more time with your child, I will allow it." He looked at me significantly. "However, I would first like to hear her feelings on the matter."

Daniel squeezed my leg again, under the table, and I cleared my throat. "Your Honor," I said, and I thought my voice sounded timid. "I too would prefer that Jason first meet the visitations established, prior to discussing anything additional. Although he spent four weekends with our son this past year, that meant eight were missed. Those were eight terrible, depressing weekends for our son, who worries that he is not enough to keep his father's attention.

"Each time Mr. Stanton backs out of plans, I am left explaining to our son that something has come up. I am exhausted, trying to convince him that it's not his fault his father has other priorities."

"Bitch." Becky's nasally voice was just loud enough that even the judge heard her.

Leaning back into my chair with a heavy sigh, I felt Jason boring holes through me with his eyes. I didn't care. I didn't owe him anything. The jerk couldn't even be bothered to provide regular child support for his son, so I owed him less than nothing.

"In this case," the judge said heavily, "I am predisposed to agree with Ms. Ryan. I would like to have an appointed social worker meet with the child in question to determine how he is affected by the current situation, and whether he would benefit or suffer from changes. However, at the present time I am not inclined to approve any increased visitation. I would first like to confirm that the full visitation schedule is being utilized." He fixed Jason with a weighted glare. "And in my courtroom, all parties are respectful of one another. I suggest a muzzle and wearing something more appropriate than a handkerchief in my courtroom for your next attendance." His gaze drifted to Becky.

He slapped his leather folder shut, banged the gavel, and his chair squeaked across the floor as he stood, causing the rest of us to push back our chairs and jump to our feet. We all waited as he left the room and Daniel quickly took my elbow to guide me from the room, whispering into my ear, "No eye contact. Just walk."

He hauled me all the way out of the courthouse, right to the door of my car, and blocked my view of the sidewalk with his large body. "That went well," he said quietly, and the smile on his handsome face was warm and triumphant. "Can I interest you in a celebratory drink?"

"Uh…" my brain was spinning. "Are you going to bill me for your time?" If he didn't, surely this was a violation of ethics.

He threw back his head and a booming laugh echoed through the parking lot. "I never know what's going to come out of your mouth." He smiled a smile that crinkled up his pretty blue eyes. "I'm asking you to have a drink with me; I won't bill you for something that's at my invitation."

"Huh." I tucked a strand of hair behind my ear and fumbled with my keys. "I don't know about that, Daniel. I don't want to cross any lines and I have to be home by six, when my babysitter absolutely has to leave."

"Westside Tavern," he said with a smile. "You can ride with me or meet me there."

I fumbled with my keys a little more. I'd have been lying if I said I hadn't fantasized about Daniel a little. For a lawyer, he was impressively warm and genuinely personable. It wasn't an act. He was also startlingly handsome, with dark hair and ice blue eyes. He was a little older than me, by my guess, but he'd taken good care of himself over the years and he filled out a suit in a way that suggested he was packing more muscle than fat. So I wanted to say yes, I really did, but this felt like a grey area.

"I promise to have you home by six." His smile was easy, and he squeezed my arm reassuringly. "I also have some information I think you'll find not only highly entertaining, but extremely useful...I had my PA run a little background on Becky."

The bar wasn't all that far from the courthouse and it was still early in the afternoon, which meant traffic hadn't yet really begun to pick up. It also meant I was able to find on-street parking after a ten minute drive, and I dug into the center console, hoping I had a handful of quarters hanging around for the parking meter. I came up with nine and I plugged six into the meter and set the alarm on my phone.

Daniel was already tucked into a booth when I walked in. It looked like he'd been there for some time, but he drove an expensive Mercedes I was surely paying for, and it undoubtedly had an easier time making the trip than my little Camry, which had been on its last legs for the past three years.

"You found the place, then!" His face lit up with a warm, genuine smile. I remembered why I found him so attractive.

"What are you having, love?" called the bartender and I tossed my bag into the booth, stepping closer to the bar.

"Whatever you have on tap. I'm not fancy, and I'm Irish. If you can brew or distill it, I'll drink it."

The bartender grinned at me and grabbed a tall glass, pulling on one of the taps and sliding it down the bar toward me. He looked over my shoulder and angled his chin upward, grinning at Daniel. "Lucky bastard."

Daniel, for his part, was the perfect gentleman. In fact, maybe a little too perfect. He was intelligent and witty, kind, caring, even sarcastic when the mood called for it. It was what I'd have considered the perfect date, had it been a date, and had it not been with the man I paid to represent me in family court.

"How are you holding up, Eve?" Daniel's expression was concerned and it pulled me up short, realizing I was about to hit the bottom of my glass.

"I'm managing," was about all I could get out.

I couldn't tell him about the migraines I'd had the past week, stressing myself out over seeing Jason again. Every time I saw that man, something hurt inside of me that I wanted to rip out and stomp all over. I hated him for what he'd done to us, Jared and me, leaving us to fend for ourselves while he went on with his life.

Carefree.

For the love of God, the man didn't even have a pet--best for the animal, too, because he'd have forgotten to feed it.

"Seriously." His pale blue eyes were intense, a kind smile on his face, and I let out a sigh I hadn't realized I was holding in.

"Yeah," I said. "Just managing." I tucked my hair behind my ear. "It's been a little more rough than usual lately. I've been pulling a lot of extra hours.

"Jared has been having a tough time with school and Jason hasn't been very reliable when it's come to his visits, so there hasn't been a lot of downtime for me, but there's been plenty of hardship for Jared. I mean…" I started tracing random patterns at the bottom of my glass, where the condensation was nearly gone. "Jason is just an added complication at this point. Life is harder with him in it."

I looked up at Daniel, a little warmth flooding into my face. This was why I didn't drink: it didn't matter whether it was beer, wine or hard liquor, it was my truth serum. In fact, a whiff of a strong cleaning spray was probably enough to make me spill my guts.

Maybe he did it purposely and maybe not, but Daniel ordered me a second glass before he decided to tell me he had it on good authority that Becky wasn't actually Jason's fiancee, yet, but that she *was* pregnant. It was enough to make me choke on a mouthful of beer and I very consciously coughed and gagged and swallowed, rather than spit it all over him. Then, once I was no longer in danger of dying in front of him, he produced a few pieces of paper and I lazily brought my eyes into focus on a series of mugshots.

Becky, it turned out, had been picked up for solicitation no fewer than four times in the past two years and had mysteriously been cut loose each time, though her fines and jail time should have been significant in each instance.

"You need another one?" Daniel gestured toward my beer and I realized I'd pounded the second glass.

"Erm, no." I brought a hand up to my forehead because I felt hot. It was fairly likely I was going to have a problem driving back to my place, and when Daniel gestured toward the bartender, I smacked his hand back down onto the table.

"Stop it," I moaned, dragging a hand down my face. "I haven't eaten since breakfast because I've been hyped up on adrenaline all day. I'm a lightweight with two pints in me. That would be inadvisable even with a full stomach, and you're trying to order me a third while my meter's about to run out in…" I pulled out my phone. "Oh shit, three minutes. Daniel, I gotta go." I hadn't heard the alarm go off.

"I'll walk you," he offered, rising smoothly and leaving a very large bill on the counter as we walked past. I let him too, figuring I'd probably earned a few drinks for the exorbitant fees I paid him.

We stood awkwardly outside my car as I fished in my bag for my keys and for a moment Daniel was not cool and suave, fidgeting with his tie and then the buttons on his jacket as I turned my handbag inside out looking for the keys to my car.

"Aha!" I exclaimed triumphantly, and it made Daniel startle. I fished the keys out of the tiny cell phone pocket and dangled them in the air. How they'd landed there, I'd never know.

"Ah, Eve...Miss Ryan..." Daniel looked really nervous and it freaked me out. Daniel was *never* nervous. In fact, he kind of looked like he was about to throw up on my shoes. "Would it be ok if I took you to dinner sometime?"

I stood there staring at him for a full minute, waiting for my brain to process the words that had just come from his mouth. After all, the man who represented me in court was asking me to dinner and though I found him quite attractive, I wasn't entirely sure what to do with this new information.

"Um, Daniel...what?" I felt like an idiot, my words completely failing me.

"You know." His confident grin returned. "That thing people do when they go to restaurants and eat together. I enjoy your company and the fact you speak your mind. I would like to take you to dinner, whenever you're available, *if* you're available." He looked at me significantly.

Was I available? Well, I supposed I could make arrangements. So I nodded. "Yeah, ok. That might be nice. But...won't you get in trouble?"

"You let me worry about that," he answered, his confidence back.

I hadn't been out to dinner with a man in a long time.

I thought back.

Almost five years, if memory served, when I'd decided after a bottle of wine to be brave and post a profile on a popular dating site. It had been disastrous, too. Three dates with three different men, none of whom looked like their photo, all of whom expected to "go back to your place." I hadn't invited any of them up, despite their wheedling and cajoling, and after the third disastrous date, I deleted my account. *That* guy had asked me if I would be willing to stash my dirty underwear in Ziploc bags, to bring to him on our next date. (I didn't just turn my back and walk away--I grabbed my coat and ran like hell.)

I quickly unlocked my car, aware the meter maid was making her way toward my car, and Daniel held up his phone as he crossed the street, a grin on his face. I imagined that meant he was going to call me, and I thought he was seriously hot, so that was...good...right?

I called in an order for pizza as I drove, and I picked it up on my way home. I ordered enough to feed three, just in case, and when I burst through the door carrying two enormous pies, Maggie was quickly packing her bag.

"Mags!" I tossed both boxes onto the counter, stifling a hiccup. "You have time for a few slices?"

"Thanks, Eve." She blushed a little and I looked at her closely. "I'm...ah...well, I have a date tonight and I'm already running a little late."

How did this girl do it? I grinned at her. She had a full class load, she babysat Jared, yet she made time to date. I was impressed, seeing as I could hardly manage clean underwear.

Jared helped me pull dishes from the cupboard and the two of us settled on the sofa after Maggie left. Since it was a Friday night, our designated movie night, the two of us could relax together and stuff our faces.

I let him choose the movie we would watch and since he was ten, of course it involved a superhero. I wanted to roll my eyes, but I didn't, only on account of the fact that Thor was really quite the looker.

Feelings?

Not hurt.

While Jared watched the movie wide-eyed, I tried to remember the last time I'd really appreciated the male form. I had to think back, back, back...all the way back to my junior year, when I'd briefly dated the center on the high school football team. He'd been held back a year, so he was an adult where the others were boys, and his muscles had muscles. (It hadn't hurt my feelings at all then, either.)

There was very little to appreciate in my life, but I had appreciated him, all right.

In the back of his truck.

In the basement of his parents' house.

On the beach.

In the boys' locker room.

That relationship had lasted all of four months and there hadn't been a whole lot of talking involved, so when he graduated and went off to college on a scholarship, neither of us expected anything more to come of it. It had been mutually beneficial, as much as it could be, and we went our separate ways without so much as a backward glance.

Then I met Jason. The man who'd knocked me off my feet and knocked me up before I had a chance to catch my breath. (I blamed it on hormones.) He was cute and I was a sucker for a well built blonde. (See aforementioned poor decision; I'd been on a tear.)

To say I was more selective these days was a bit of an understatement. I didn't date, because dating meant there were expectations. Expectations were messy and difficult to coordinate. And sex was out of the question, because chances were good that Jared, who was a light sleeper, would walk in halfway through the deed.

That was a therapy bill neither of us needed.

Jared was asleep before the movie ended and I sighed heavily, tossing the old maids from the bowl of popcorn into the trash before turning off the TV and grunting as I lifted him in a desperate attempt to carry him to his bed. These days were numbered: I was tall and strong, strength due to lifting bodies all day long in the ER. But my son was built like Jason, all muscle and sinew, and he was far heavier than he looked.

I turned out the kitchen light, leaving on the light over the oven in case Jared wanted a glass of water in the middle of the night. Then I checked the door to make sure it was locked, took a few supplements, and shuffled down the hallway to my bedroom.

There was really nothing to draw me there, I thought somewhat woefully, pulling my shirt over my head and dropping my pants to the floor before hurriedly washing my face and brushing my teeth.

There was no warm, sleepy, muscular wall of man waiting for me in my bed.

There wasn't even a flabby, pot bellied man with cold feet waiting for me in my bed.

There was only my sadly neglected vibrator, probably dusty with disuse, tucked out of sight in my bedside stand.

I was too young for this, I thought as I slapped a little moisturizer on my face and mourned the death of my vagina. It was downright atrophied from disuse, but more than that, it was my life that felt neglected.

I had Jared, and I loved him more than anything, but I needed that from someone else, too: to be loved more than anything by someone else. But for almost as long as I could remember, there had been no one.

As usual, I was on my own.

SEVEN

Noah
◄||►

The only reason I made it through the service was because my family kept me on my feet. I was flanked by Finn and Thomas, surrounding me with all the love they could possibly spare. And though I'd tried to write something nice to say about Avery, in the end I couldn't do it. Instead, Thomas took the notes from my hand and walked to the front of the church where he delivered my eulogy in a firm, clear voice. It was what I'd wanted to be able to do for Avery, but when it came down to it I was a pansy. My knees buckled every time I tried to stand.

Thomas took care of flights for everyone again, or maybe it was his ridiculously capable Swedish assistant who handled everything. I thanked him for it before he left, pulling him in for a hard hug. No one in our family was as well off as he was, and he'd always gone out of his way to take care of each of us when he knew we were too proud to ask for help.

So Aaron caught a commercial flight back to wherever he was based out of these days--I didn't know much, just that he'd been going through some shit with his wife Gillian. He was headed into a tour in Afghanistan and wasn't real big on talking.

Asher flew back to California with Thomas, since they shared similar destinations. Ash was the Information Tech Director for a tech company based out of San Francisco and Thomas ran his own tech development company out of Palo Alto. Both of them were doing very well for themselves, but I'd never been jealous. I didn't have the mental stamina to sit behind a desk or a conference table all day long.

Finn was the last one to leave. She had turned down Thomas's offer to hitch a ride on his private plane, and I knew her employer had graciously booked her a return ticket. Although we'd had a long, boozy talk about her relationship with the man who signed her paychecks, she hadn't admitted to a whole lot. The woman was a vault, even with six drinks in her.

I'd teased her that I was willing to bet he'd asked her more than once if she'd let him taste her cookie and she'd turned the craziest shade of purple I'd ever seen, right before she slapped me.

Her husband, Magnus, would have flipped shit if he suspected anything was going on, not because he loved her but because he was an arrogant son of a bitch. But it sounded like he'd been sticking his fingers in a few other pies lately, so if Finn wanted a little snack on the side, I wasn't gonna look at her cross eyed. Besides, I hated Magnus--couldn't wait to see him get what was coming to him.

She hugged me hard before she walked out the door. "I am always available," she admonished me, pulling her hair out of my beard. She was tall for a woman, but she was still a good eight inches shorter than me, her platinum blonde hair catching in my scruff each time she leaned in for a hug, which she did often. She was just as touchy-feely as I was.

"I'm serious," she said gently, notching her index finger beneath my chin. "Anytime you need me, just call. We're in the same time zone, big guy. It's not a problem."

I held her tight, not ready to close the door and return to the loneliness of my empty house. I had been able to pretend for the past week that things were mostly right with the world, since my place was filled with people who loved me and Finn cooked constantly, filling our bellies with amazing food. (I'd even gained back a few pounds.)

Dropping onto the sofa as the afternoon sunlight drifted in through the living room windows, I took a deep breath. I expected Gerry at any moment and though it made me nervous to think of her All Seeing Eyes, I was glad not to be left alone.

Gerry was a trained behavioral therapist and thanks to our mother's early death and our father's marital antics, my siblings and I were greatly in need of the help Gerry provided. She'd even pulled a stint as our first stepmom, managing to put up with Da's bullshit for six whole years before she told him to go fuck himself.

As such, most of us had weekly sessions she cleverly disguised as "chats" with her, well into adulthood, and each of us credited her with being one of the only reasons we weren't heavily medicated or institutionalized. (Maybe a few of us should have been though, especially Asher and Thomas.) Because of her we were all functioning, reasonably well adjusted adults who were largely capable of self care. Except for the depression and drinking, because most of us seemed a little stuck there.

She didn't spoil me like Finn did, but Gerry made me do what no one else could: talk about *real* things. No jokes, no pranks, just serious shit. She knew when to let me be and when to draw me out. She knew when I'd had too much and when I really needed to let something go.

By the time she left I'd been moping around at home for over six weeks, most of that time largely supervised.

I knew it was time to rejoin life.

Da had been checking in occasionally, to "see how you're doing," which I knew meant he was tired of paying someone else to do my job. If I didn't get back to it soon, there was a small chance he would fill my position with the new guy and then I'd really be shit out of luck. Not to say I was destitute, since I'd been smart with my money.

Avery and I were hard workers and we'd bought our house before we were even old enough to drink. We had paid it down hard, renovated it, and then started dumping our money into joint savings and investment accounts. It left me in a pretty comfortable position, but I'd have traded all of it to have her back. I'd have given anything to hold her one more time and make sure she knew how much I loved her.

That night was the first night I'd been alone in the last three weeks and though Finn had left my refrigerator and freezer stocked with meals, I couldn't bring myself to eat anything. Instead, I pulled the enormous bottle of vodka from the island cabinet. It was the cheap stuff, the stuff a bartender would have called well vodka. (I'd have called it lighter fluid.)

It was the stuff Avery used to make linen sprays with her essential oils, and the enormous jug was nearly full.

I wasn't feeling real picky. I grabbed a jar of olives from the fridge and poured a healthy portion of the juice into a glass, then chased it with more fingers of vodka than I had on my hand. I wanted to sleep tonight. I needed oblivion and the only way to achieve that was to pass out.

When that drink disappeared, I made another. Then I stumbled down the hallway to our bedroom and collapsed into our bed, my arm stretched out across the place she should have been.

For the first time in weeks, I really let go.

I broke.

I begged her to come back, pounding the pillows with my fists, soaking them with angry tears and begging God to make the hurting stop.

My phone dinged with a text and I rolled over to read it with bleary eyes. It was Finn, checking in on me and making sure I was taking care of myself. I typed something quick and perfunctory back to her, though it took me longer than it should have since I could hardly see straight.

Slamming the phone down on the nightstand, I buried my face in Avery's pillow and let the room spin.

***

It was midmorning when I woke, an incessant hammering happening somewhere in the distance, and my head was pounding angrily in time. I'd been too stupid to bring a glass of water with me when I'd gone to bed, so I dragged myself to the bathroom and waited for the world to stop spinning while I ducked my head under the faucet and took a few long pulls.

The hammering noise resumed and I blinked blearily as my brain started to creak back to life. I was pretty sure that was what woke me up and I stumbled out to the living room, where the noise got louder.

"Look at ya." Da's Geordie accent became more pronounced when he was angry, and he was obviously angry with me. "Not even nine-thirty an' you're rat-arsed."

I winced, holding the door open for him so he could continue to berate me inside my own home. I had some idea of how this would go, thankful only that he was sober, since he could string together hair-raising curses when *he* was drinking.

While he went after me about how to re-engage with my life, I poured a huge cup of coffee and brought him one. I'd learned long ago that the best way to make him stop was to be as agreeable as possible and let him blow off all the steam in one go.

I didn't remind him that I'd just lost my other half and our unborn child.

I didn't remind him that he hadn't even shown up for the memorial service, which bothered me maybe more than it should have.

I certainly didn't tell him that he could go right ahead and hire on my fill-in on a permanent basis, because I wasn't ready to leave the house, much less return to work.

He glowered at me while I took one of Finn's breakfast casseroles out of the freezer and popped it in to bake according to the instructions she'd left in Sharpie on the tinfoil covering.

He had a second cup of coffee and ate breakfast with me while he complained that my stand-in was cocking up jobs left and right and he'd had to let the kid go, since it was costing him more money to keep him on than it would have to just pause projects until I returned. Ah, so there it was: My time was up. Da needed something, and as he was now being greatly inconvenienced, everyone else had better get with the program.

This, I'd found in the past, was one of the biggest issues when it came to working for family: Da didn't pay me nearly what I was worth, yet I was his jack of all trades. I fixed what others screwed up and met impossible deadlines so he could save face and the money it would cost to extend deadlines.

"It's time to snap out of it, boy," he said, standing and pushing back from the island counter. "When yer mum passed I was back at work after the funeral. Don't suppose I need to tell ya ah'll need ya back come Monday."

I didn't look up at him, pretty sure I was getting the hairy eyeball. Instead I nodded once, into my food, barely able to taste it though I'd nearly drowned whatever it was in hot sauce. An abomination, Finn would have called it.

He clapped my arm again, already on his way back out the door. Obviously he thought we'd had a real meeting of the minds, which wasn't unusual when it came to his approach. Da's world had room for one view: his. Nothing else was accepted, considered, or given any sort of validation.

Thom joked that the only way Mom could win an argument with that pig-headed arse was to die, and though it had taken years, she'd finally gotten the last word.

Yeah, Da knew what it was to lose the love of his life and one could almost be forgiven for thinking that would have made him sympathetic to my plight. But in his case, he sought the soothing balm of other women, and had almost as long as I could remember--probably a contributing factor to Ma's drinking herself to death, really.

In fact, by now I wasn't sure I knew the actual tally on the number of stepmothers I'd had. Lately he'd been rotating through them so quickly that Asher said he didn't even bother to learn their names. Now he just called each one "Mom," which predictably drove the women insane, but probably even more so because most of them were closer to Asher's age than to Da's.

It was peculiar, as Finn put it, but as Da aged, somehow the women kept getting younger. One of them had gotten a little too drunk and hands-y with Thomas a couple Christmases earlier, when we'd managed the true Christmas miracle: all five siblings under one roof for four days without a single death.

Even if Thomas's wife, Lydia, had been there to observe the woman panting all over her husband, I don't think she'd have batted an eyelash. She had never been a big fan of the Atholton boys, with the marginal exception of her husband, so she tended to keep her distance when she could, holidays be damned. But what I'd never understood was that she didn't seem to have a care in the world when it came to Thom. She acted like she was God's gift and didn't seem at all concerned that women flocked to *him* like ants to sugar--and that was *before* they knew he was stupid-wealthy.

Da had an ironclad prenup--the man learned quickly when it came to some things--and a short fuse. That particular marriage was history by Easter. (Lydia, I heard later, thought Thomas's stepmother pawing him was *hysterical*.)

I managed a load of dishes and a load of laundry, then I paid a couple bills online and called Avery's mom back to thank her for all the sympathy cards and flowers she'd redirected to my house. Truth was, I hadn't read a single one of them. They sat in a wicker basket, the one Helen had left on my front porch a couple days before, but I'd moved the basket to the coffee table.

The house reeked of overly perfumed flowers. I hated all the roses and lilies, reminding me of loss with every damned breath.

I looked over at the calendar on the wall, some stupid beefcake Game of Thrones thing one of Avery's coworkers had gotten for her, since Avery had been obsessed with the show. I'd wisely never pointed out that I was eight inches taller than that Snow guy she drooled over, and I was a hundred percent confident there was a hell of a lot more going on under my kilt.

Jon Snow said it was Tuesday, which meant I had five days left to get my shit together.

Five days left to decide whether I even *wanted* to go back to work for my dad.

Five days until I had no choice but to establish some kind of new "normal."

The rest of the week was kind of a blur, thanks to daytime TV and booze. I had finished the cheap, nasty vodka, which forced me out of the house for a trip to the grocery store and while I was at it, I loaded up on beer and some liquor hard enough to melt my teeth.

The weekend was pretty much a giant hangover. I'd drink to forget, fall asleep, wake up sick and drink off the hangover. Even I knew I couldn't go on like this, but right now it felt like my only option.

It was only January, so it was cold outside. Best to stay in, I decided, wrapped in the warped, crazy looking blanket Avery made when she'd decided to teach herself how to knit. The project-gone-wrong looked more like a giant taco than a blanket.

By Sunday afternoon, I had my answer: I was done. I couldn't imagine showing up for work the next morning, acting like nothing had happened and just buckling down and carrying on like everything was normal. The guys wouldn't say anything beyond offering condolences, but I'd feel their pity all day long. I'd catch the sidelong glances and the sympathetic looks. They'd be quieter than usual: Less hollering at each other. Less catcalling at lunch. Less swearing. I would make things weird just by being there.

I typed up a quick resignation email and sent it to my direct superior. I thanked him for being so understanding and for giving me so much time to get my shit together, but I had decided I needed more time than was fair to the team. If they wanted recommendations for my replacement, I had a few.

Since I knew Brad would call my father, and Da would show up on my doorstep, I was determined not to be home. In fact, it was something I should have done weeks earlier: remove myself from the situation entirely.

I tossed a duffel bag onto the bed and filled it with warm clothes, socks, underwear, and a hat. I packed my passport, my concealed carry permit, my handgun, a rifle and my hunting license. It was small game season in Washington and I didn't plan to actively hunt anything, but as far as a bobcat was concerned, things that moved were *always* in season, even if they were human. If I ventured out into the woods, it wouldn't be without my rifle.

Packing up some provisions, I brewed one last pot of coffee and took out the trash before putting the bedroom light and the living room lamp on a timer. Then I made sure all the dirty dishes were loaded up and the dishwasher was humming away before I filled my giant travel mug with coffee, slung the duffel over my shoulder and locked the front door.

44

The drive to the cabin, not all that far outside of Vancouver, really didn't take that long. As it was, the last time I'd been there was just this last summer.

It already seemed like a lifetime ago.

Avery and I had spent a week there, blissfully cut off from the world as I fished and she read baby books and tried to settle on a name.

I had argued with her that Everly was a dumb name, that our kid would grow up sounding like some emo tween vampire, but she told me if she had to grow my monster spawn in her tiny body, she got to pick the name.

At night I cooked whatever I'd caught that day, rubbed her feet and made a campfire so we could roast marshmallows. Then each night I gathered her up into my arms and carried her into the cabin, where I loved her the way God intended.

It had been the perfect week.

I hadn't counted on the strength of the memories as I pulled up to the cabin and sat there in my truck, afraid to go inside. Avery was just as present here as she was in our house--what was I thinking?

My stomach grumbled angrily, probably because I hadn't been putting much more than booze into it for the past week, and I finally grabbed the bags I'd loaded into the bed and carried them up to the small porch.

The door hinges complained loudly and the screen door echoed its protest, the dark interior stinking of stale air and dust. I set one of the bags just inside, to prop the screen door open while I carried the rest inside. Thankfully I'd had the good sense to pack a camping lantern, since there was a small generator but no real electricity to speak of. I fished it out of my bag and used it to help me locate the kerosene lamps we'd stowed in a cabinet before leaving last summer.

There was a squirrel's nest under the sink and I found the small dustpan, scooping up the collection of twigs and leaves and tossing it out the front door. Then I grabbed the pack of steel wool I kept for just such an emergency and performed a full perimeter sweep, stuffing steel wool into even the tiniest cracks, holes or gaps I could find.

That night I ate beef jerky for dinner and washed it down with beer. Then I cleaned both guns and locked up the cabin for the night.

It was raining again, typical for a Washington winter, and though it took me a while to get a fire going in the huge fireplace, once it was good and crackling it definitely added some cheer to the room.

I had already trekked out to the woodshed to bring in enough to last me into midmorning the next day.

Avery always hated that part, constantly feeding the fire to keep the cabin warm enough. Even on summer nights, we usually had a fire going.

I couldn't even look at the bed in the far corner. She had made it up with clean sheets and blankets before we'd left, hauling the dirty linens home to launder and bring back when we came out for deer hunting season.

But we never made it back for the deer, because by then she'd been diagnosed with gestational diabetes. She was already considered high-risk, at thirty-six. In fact, her doctor had no qualms about telling her that hers was a "geriatric pregnancy," and I'd wanted to hit him for being such a dick.

At that point we were keeping weekly doctor's visits and since she was due in December, the staff kept a close eye on the size of the baby. She'd been growing faster than the doctor would have liked, and chances had been good Avery would be scheduled for a C-section several weeks prior to her actual due date.

Sinking onto the sofa, I let it really hit me: I wasn't supposed to be here right now. I should have been at home, helping Avery with diapers and feedings and buying her that special cream for her boobs, since she'd insisted she would breastfeed the baby.

The fun bags are off-limits until the baby's weaned, Noah.

I debated grabbing another one of the beers I'd brought with me. Honestly, I'd brought more beer than food. But I decided the last thing I wanted to do was get up at two in the morning to take a piss in the

46

woods, so I grabbed the blanket off the back of the sofa and curled up, hoping I could sleep without nightmares.

EIGHT

Eve

◀┃▶

A week after our court appearance, Daniel sent flowers. They were waiting for me on the kitchen table when I got home and Maggie had a knowing smile on her face as she plucked the small card from the arrangement and handed it to me. "I take it these are not from Jason," she whispered, well aware of how his bid had gone down in flames.

Honestly, at first I didn't know who they were from. It had been my birthday a few weeks earlier and it was possible my brother had just now remembered. Also, William had sent me flowers once, after he'd asked me out the second time.

Eve,

A delicate flower, you are a radiant and captivating woman, truly God's original creation.

Affectionately,
Daniel

Maggie made a gagging sound over my shoulder and it startled me. I hadn't realized she'd been standing so close as to read the card with me and I jammed it back into the envelope with a lot more color in my cheeks than I'd have liked.

"That's not even original," she complained, tossing a thick wave of blonde hair over her shoulder. "He ripped off some old poem."

As far as I was concerned, the gesture was pretty damned romantic, but that was coming from someone who was starved for it.

"Wait…" she dropped her voice quickly. "Daniel…your *lawyer*?"

I sighed.

She sounded judgy.

"I'm not…dating him, Mags. We had a celebratory drink after the last hearing, maybe because Jason files something petty annually, like clockwork, so it was like a 'Hey, see you in a year' kind of thing."

Maggie raised an eyebrow at me. "This is more like a 'Hey, see you Saturday night--hope you'll be under me' sort of thing." She seemed to have forgotten she was late for her own date and she popped one hip out, her hand coming to rest. "Besides, you're hot. I'm just not sure why it took the guy so long--must have been at the bottom of his class. Good thing he's gorgeous--you know, for an old guy."

I had a pretty good idea why Daniel was single, and it had something to do with the words "ex" and "wife." I didn't pry or ask for details, but I knew that particular dissolution had happened since the last time Daniel and I had been to court. I had definitely noticed he was no longer wearing a wedding band.

Shoving a few things into her bag, Maggie leaned in to give me a quick squeeze. "All I'm saying is that it's about time. I know you don't have a lot of time to spare for extracurricular activities like…" she coughed significantly, looking over her shoulder for Jared, "horseback riding. But you know, no time like the present--especially with that stallion. Bet you he's got some experience in the…stables." She wiggled her eyebrows suggestively, and I shot a look over her shoulder, to make sure Jared wasn't listening to our conversation.

"You're an idiot. There will be no horseback riding," I said firmly. "Dinner maybe, but I'm not inviting anyone back to the stable for private lessons."

She grinned, slinging her bag over her shoulder.
"Mmmhmm...whatever you say." Then she threw a hand up in the air to wave to Jared and she hurried out the door. Swear to God I heard her whinny like a horse on her way out.

Maggie had been the one to save me from myself more than once. She'd been babysitting Jared since he was four years old, all through undergrad and now her graduate studies. It had been six years that had gone by in a blink between work and Jason's constant racket, and I knew that soon I was going to have to face the fact Maggie was graduating. She'd probably have her own classroom in the fall, filled with kids who needed her even more than Jared.

Over the years, Maggie had become my friend, one of the few who knew what was really going on, and I could always count on her for the appropriate amount of snark. I could also depend on her for an occasional Friday Night Girls Night, during which time we ordered pizza and sat in the kitchen to eat and drink wine, gossiping and quietly talking trash while Jared watched a movie in the next room.

My phone lit up with an incoming call and I shook my head.

Lauren.

Which probably meant Maggie had just called her to relay the fact there were flowers *from a man* sitting on the table in my condo.

My friends were telepathic, nosy bitches.

Lauren and I had gone to school together, then worked together for years, and we were thick as thieves. She was married and had four kids though, so her participation in Friday Night Girls Night with Maggie and me was pretty hit-or-miss. When we were together though, watch out. We'd been told by more than one group of men that we were the Testosterone Trifecta. Apparently something about a petite blonde, a curvy brunette and a tall redhead really melted male minds.

"You gotta tell me quick if you're doing the dirty with this guy," she hissed into my ear even before I'd had the chance to say hello.

"Babe," I chuckled. "Are you hiding from the kids in the laundry room with vodka again?"

"Coat closet--gin this time," she confirmed quickly. "The baby's working on another tooth and I'm not sleeping, so I may as well sneak a drink here and there so I don't give away my kids to some random stranger at the supermarket. Now give me the goods or I'll get the less-than-satisfying details from Maggie. We both know that girl can't get the details I need for shit."

"Nothing to report yet," I sighed, and when I heard a muffled little voice on the other end of the line Lauren stifled a groan.

"Which one was that, Andrew?" I asked and she grunted back at me, which meant she was tipping back for a swallow.

"Fuck my life. Kid just asked me how to get poop out of a rug."

I snorted so hard, my sinuses burned. "That sounds like an important life lesson, Mom. What's the answer?"

"You know don't get shit out of a rug, stupid. You throw the damn thing away."

Our shifts had been all over the place lately, since Lauren had moved to the PM shift in the Psychiatric ICU and I was still on Days in the ER. There wasn't as much overlap as we'd have liked--absolutely none, in fact--and we had to make a concerted effort to see one another, so sometimes she left for work early and I took a late break so we could meet up in the cafeteria. It was only ever enough time for a rushed coffee, but it helped keep me sane.

"The instant there are salacious details, you'll be the first to know," I told her. "So far I've only had a drink with him, and he's invited me to dinner. But he just sent some really pretty flowers, so I imagine he's softening me up to re-extend that dinner invite in the next couple days."

"Mmm, I miss those days." Lauren sounded a little wistful. "There are things to be said for proper courtship and sex that takes *time*."

I tried to keep the laugh in--I really did. Because the last thing Lauren believed in was taking her time. When she started seeing Alex and he assured her he would take their relationship slow--because he was an old fashioned Italian boy who'd been badly burned--she conspired with his partner to stage a traffic stop and she jumped him in his patrol car.

"Whatever, you tramp," I teased. "Let's ask Alex about how *you* courted *him*."

"Hey." She kept her voice low. "Ain't no shame in my game, and Alex is a *very* happy man because I make sure he gets it more on the regular than he ever did before. It's just a little more drive-by than a full frisk-and-cuff these days."

I gagged a little at the thought, because she was definitely not above using her husband's handcuffs against him. That they were probably work issued grossed me out.

I wasn't jealous of Lauren, even though her husband was panty-dropping hot. I didn't really enjoy thinking about other people having sex when I couldn't seem to get any for myself. Clearly I was setting the bar too high, or I simply wasn't adventurous enough because I would never have been bold enough to jump an enormous cop in his own patrol car.

"You're coming for the twins' birthday party on Sunday, right?"

Crap. That was this Sunday? I needed to go buy gifts.

"Yeah, of course. You need me there early to help with setup?"

"Bring Jared around eleven and he can entertain the kids while we blow up balloons and drink mimosas."

"Done."

I hung up and sighed, glancing again at what I knew was a very expensive bouquet. It made me a little jumpy inside, knowing it meant Daniel was actively pursuing me--or at least he was throwing down a gauntlet, right? His intentions seemed pretty clear.

Jared had finished all of his homework with Maggie, so I told him to shower and then he could watch TV for a while if he folded laundry for me. That way I had a minute to prep dinner.

I made a huge portion of chicken and tucked most of it away for easy meal prep later in the week, then assembled a salad and roasted some asparagus. Jared wasn't a big meat eater, but he didn't turn up his nose at chicken, and he was one of those weird kids who'd liked both asparagus and broccoli since he was little.

After dinner he helped me clean up, and he took the stacks of folded laundry to each of our bedrooms while I whipped out the vacuum and gave the floors just enough of a pass to keep the dust bunnies at bay.

By eight we were settled into his bed as I read him another two chapters of *Eragon*. He was perfectly capable of reading it on his own, but this was the only quiet time we really got together in a day and I tried to read him at least one chapter of a book of his choice each night.

It was getting more and more difficult to convince Jared he needed technological downtime, and telling him to get ready for bed almost always brought on a fight. The stupid tablet Jason had gotten for him seemed to be taking the place of anything else in his life and sometimes I hid his charger just to buy an hour or two of semi-quiet when the damn thing died.

There was a harsh buzzing and I jerked awake. Jared was curled up next to me, sound asleep, and the book was facedown on my lap. It was the second time this week I'd fallen asleep while reading to him.

I snatched my vibrating phone from the bedside table and flicked off the lamp, partially closing the door as I hurried from the room.

"Daniel." My voice was husky with sleep and I could hardly stifle the yawn that tried to creep up.

"Eve, I'm sorry to call so late--I'm so sorry, you were sleeping."

I chuckled. "Let me sit down for thirty seconds in your office and I'll fall asleep in that rock-hard chair right across from your desk. I'm a single mom. My prettiest fantasy involves ten hours of uninterrupted sleep in a bed I didn't have to make and waking to find thirty ounces of hot coffee waiting for me."

He laughed softly and it made the butterflies jump in my belly. I liked Business Daniel, so I was pretty sure I'd like Personal Daniel too.

"Maybe that's something I can work up to. I thought maybe I could start with dinner?"

"Oh, right. Yeah. Thanks for the flowers, by the way. They were beautiful, and the card was..." I struggled for a second, my cheeks flushing. "Erm, it was sweet."

"I'm glad everything met with your approval. Look, I know you probably need to make arrangements for Jared, and I don't know what your work schedule looks like...does Saturday afternoon work for you?"

I thought about it for a second. Maybe I could convince Lauren to let Jared spend the night, as a sleepover of sorts. Her oldest son was two years younger than Jared and they adored one another.

"I am actually, probably, available Saturday. I'll see what I can do about getting a sitter for Jared. What did you have in mind?"

Daniel was quiet for a second and I thought maybe he hadn't heard me. Then, "The Pink Door. I thought I could pick you up around five. It makes for an early dinner, but it gives us plenty of time to get there and back, no rushing; plenty of time to talk."

"Tell me right now if you're not actually a guy," I joked as I closed the door to my room. "I don't know any man who would willingly spend his Saturday night *talking* to his date."

When he laughed he sounded a little nervous. "I'm a lawyer, Eve. Talking is what I do."

Well, he had me there.

We confirmed he would pick me up at five, at my place, and made a little more awkward small talk before he wished me sweet dreams and rang off. Then I sent a quick text to Lauren, to ask whether Jared could spend the night Saturday.

Her response was smart-assed, as usual: **For God's sake, get your toes done. Have the hedges scalped, or at least trimmed, buy a cute outfit, and of course Jared can spend the night. I promise not to let him interrupt sexy time.**

Both of us knew there would be no sexy time. I wasn't so desperate that I'd jump the first viable candidate I'd had in years.

I was a girl of mystery.

Of intrigue.

Only, there was nothing intriguing about the terrifying situation going on in my pants.

Immediately I set up an appointment for a wax.

***

Maggie teased me all week long about my date with "Man o' War," my "fine, fine thoroughbred." It made Jared look at her funny a couple times and I shot her warning glares, which drove her further into the deep state of secret hand signals and nonsensical code words. It made her look unhinged and all I could do was laugh every time she tried to sneak more salacious commentary to me.

On Friday she told me to go straight to the salon after work because she'd stay with Jared, and I went a little crazy with a mani-pedi and a haircut--not a lot, just a trim, because even I was aware my hair was my best feature.

Initially I'd only booked only the full wax. Even if I had no intention of showing the guy the lady garden I could still manage the shrubbery, right? For myself.

Definitely for myself.

I hadn't been on a date in so long, I wasn't sure what to expect. But I was nervous--and a little excited. It wasn't like I was going to marry him, but it had been a long time since I'd felt...well, female, quite honestly. So as I dressed on Saturday, the condo strangely quiet since Jared was already at Lauren's, I tried to calm the nervous flutters in my stomach.

There was one advantage to being run ragged, and it was that at thirty I was still in good shape. Everything was high and tight, relatively toned and trim. I looked *really* good in the amethyst sheath dress and I knew it, which was why I'd spent a little more on it than I should have.

Applying a soft lipstick and fluffing my hot-rollered hair, I slipped into the caramel trench and matching heels, setting tiny fake diamond studs in my ears before I peeked out the window.

Daniel was already there, pacing up and down the sidewalk three stories below, looking nervously at his watch. It was cute, I thought with another flutter, to know he was just as nervous as I was. Especially when it came to someone so successful and self-possessed, because surely he was a man who was used to getting what he wanted.

The bell rang at five on the dot and I slipped my phone and lipstick into one coat pocket, cards and cash into the other and opened the door just as he looked up, his eyes registering something I thought might be disbelief. "I'm sorry, I'm...Eve...wow." I had never seen him so tongue tied. He ran a hand through his dark hair, looking me over from head to toe and back up again. "You look incredible." His jaw was working like a fish's, flapping frantically for oxygen intake.

"You're looking pretty nice yourself." I grinned as I locked the door behind me, sure to give him the same head-to-toe perusal he'd given me, and two little pink spots started to burn in his cheeks when he realized what I was doing.

Daniel was an attractive man, in case I hadn't mentioned that before. We stood at an even height, since I was 6' in heels, and though he had broad shoulders and was well defined, he wasn't overly muscular. He was lean and athletic, with the wide shoulders and lithe body of a swimmer. (Yeah, that was secret code--good catch, you: His ass was *fantastic*.)

He solicitously took my arm and tucked it under his, escorting me to the elevator, then to his car where he'd parked in the garage across the street. He started the engine before we got to the garage and I sank into a warm interior with heated leather seats, grateful since the air was cold and sharp with the promise of more rain.

Soft classical music played as he drove and while conversation wasn't quite easy, it wasn't awkward either. We had known one another in a single capacity for years and stepping outside of that box was bound to be a little weird.

The drive from Olympia to Seattle took just over an hour, enough time for me to observe him when I thought he wasn't looking.

I liked the sure, easy way he drove with one hand on the wheel.

He had sure, purposeful movements and I liked that he didn't fidget or twitch, and when he smiled the corners of his eyes crinkled a little.

By the time we arrived at the restaurant, I knew several things: Daniel had been divorced for eight months after being married for fifteen years. He had one child, a thirteen-year-old daughter who lived primarily with her mother, but Daniel had visitation every other weekend and he *never* missed it. Also, he smelled really good, like old saddle leather and vetiver.

We laughed our way through drinks and appetizers.

We discussed false starts, goals and ambitions over dinner.

He took my hand over dessert and flipped it in his, to rub his thumb against my palm as we flirted, and it was...nice. There were no fireworks happening in my belly, but it was comfortable and easy.

Which was exactly what Lauren said the next day, with far more sarcasm: *"Nice?* Come on, Eve. Things were either fireworks-hot or they weren't. Don't give me this *nice* crap." She tied off the balloon she'd just blown up and her face was still red from the exertion.

I didn't know what else to call it, because it had been a wonderful evening. And honestly, if there was anything I wanted to hide from Lauren, it was my powerful disappointment. I'd been hoping for wild fireworks.

Daniel held up his end of the conversation and was funny and polite.

He insisted on picking up the bill and wouldn't hear of me contributing.

He drove me home and saw me to the front door of my building, but said goodnight there because he didn't want to be presumptuous or make me uncomfortable.

"He's gay," Lauren said flatly, plopping a stack of napkins down on the long table already filled with cut vegetables, chips, juice boxes and cupcakes. "You were smokin' last night, Eve." She raised an eyebrow at me and I regretted sending her a photo just before I'd slipped into my coat. "Any red-blooded man wouldn't have been able to resist you."

Alex sauntered past with one of the three-year-old twins dangling over his shoulder and Lauren patted his enviously firm butt. "Right, babe?"

Alex turned to look at her suspiciously, but she'd been completely distracted by his butt and looked like she'd forgotten her train of thought.

"Don't mind your wife," I said with a sigh and Alex grinned at me, snatching a juice box off the table to hand to his newest personal appendage.

"Lauren told me you had a hot date last night," he commented, watching my face carefully. I was pretty sure the guy thought I was either a lesbian or destined for a convent, considering this was the first date I'd been on in almost as long as he'd known me.

"Yeah," I said, fiddling with the stack of forks that were driving me crazy the longer I looked at them, jumbled and pointing in all different directions. "It was nice."

"*Nice?*" Alex's eyebrows shot up into his very thick hair.

Damn Italian men and their good hair.

"Right?" Lauren crowed, nudging him in the ribs with her elbow before patting his butt again. "See? Exactly what I said. There is no such thing as a *nice* date. It's either hot or it's not. The guy has to be gay."

"I don't think he's gay--he has a kid," I protested weakly, but I thought back to the chaste kiss on the cheek before he bid me goodnight and I didn't have anything better to offer. All the signs he'd been sending to that point indicated he was passionate about some things: sailing; rowing; collecting vinyl records; going to the symphony. I was ok with all of those things, though it occurred to me that perhaps none of his pursuits were things I'd have considered particularly manly in a chest-beating sort of way and since that tended to be the sort of man I'd been attracted to in the past, I hoped this meant I was finally on the right path. Maybe I could put an end to my unlucky streak.

My end of that conversation hadn't been nearly as exciting, since I hadn't had time to develop hobbies in the past ten years, between school and raising Jared. I could very honestly list folding laundry as an interest these days, just to fill an extra blank. My life was truly that thrilling.

"Maybe he realized he's just not that into me," I admitted quietly as I reached for the mimosa Lauren had kept topped up since I stepped through the door. I knew she hoped if she boozed me up, I'd spill all kinds of details but honestly, this time there was nothing to spill.

Alex snorted. "Whatever, Ryan. I got three guys down at the station who'd take a battering ram to your door if they thought they stood a chance in hell."

I blushed a little. I'd attended a benefit with Alex, Lauren and one of Alex's colleagues some six months earlier: a benefit packed with police officers. Apparently Alex had been harassed ever since for my phone number. He'd never given it out, telling me he was running interference on my behalf and none of the guys were worth my time.

Lauren patted my butt. She really did have a thing for butts. "It wouldn't hurt to fatten you up a little," she mused, shoving a cupcake at me with her other hand. "You work too hard and most boys like a little extra in the..." She pinched me and I squeaked.

"My ass is just fine," I said a little too loudly and I clapped a hand over my mouth. "I'm...willowy." That word felt weird and stupid and I blushed. "It's the way I'm built. I don't need any extra...luggage, thank you, because then my proportions will be off."

Lauren let the butt conversation drop, but throughout the afternoon she pushed me to call Daniel.

Reminded me I wasn't getting any younger.

Pointed out that Jared needed a real father figure.

By the time Jared and I escaped the party, I was exhausted. I hadn't slept well the night before, having analyzed every word; every movement; every blink from the night before.

If Daniel really was all that into me, why hadn't he even tried to kiss me? He'd pecked me on the cheek and walked down the hallway without so much as a backward glance. It had confused me terribly, as I'd thought we had a delightful evening. I mean, I wasn't going to invite him in, but I wouldn't have minded a kiss or two. After all, Daniel had very nice lips, and I was curious as to just what he could do with them. And his tongue.

When we arrived home, there was a small wrapped package lying outside the front door and I unwrapped it cautiously, unlocking the door so Jared could go inside.

The two leather bound books were old, their pages delightfully heavy, yellowed with time and deliciously crackly.

I had mentioned to Daniel that I had studied to be a grief counselor for a brief year in college, before switching to nursing, since I knew I didn't have the time to obtain the education the job required. I'd needed to be employable as quickly as possible once I found out I was pregnant with Jared.

Over the years I'd kept up with the career in a parallel, hit-or-miss fashion by reading articles and subscribing to academic journals. There were several expensive texts I'd always meant to read, always on an interminably long wait list at the library, and now those books lay in my hands. They were so new, they smelled like the glue in their bindings, the hard covers glossy and unblemished.

Swallowing hard, I flipped the front cover of the second book open and a thick card was pressed into the binding between the cover and the frontispiece.

Eve,

I very much enjoyed spending the evening with you. You should be proud of the woman you are: beautiful, witty, curious, intelligent, driven.

These books are something I recall you wished to read and it is my hope they will bring you joy and thoughtful reflection. Perhaps we can discuss them soon, over dinner?

-Affectionately,
Daniel

Pulling out my phone to text Lauren, I felt a little swoony over the gesture. Maybe I'd misinterpreted the chemistry between us and I was being too hard on the guy. This one was actually trying to get to know the me "up top," not just my lady bits.

I renewed my hope that I was in so much trouble.

NINE

Noah
◀▯▶

The little fucker was back.

I rolled over carefully on the sofa and the noise under the sink stopped when a spring groaned and popped.

Obviously I had missed a crack, a crevice, a crease, or a downright hole somewhere, because I could hear frantic activity that told me I was not alone in the cabin.

The fire was low and I grunted as I stretched out, a solid five inches too big for the large sofa, and my body protested the cramped position I'd been sleeping in for what must have been several hours.

Tossing on a few more logs and stirring things up a bit, I grabbed the flashlight from the coffee table and headed into the small, open kitchen.

Flipping open the cabinet door under the sink, I muttered a few curses under my breath about the industrious nature of squirrels when I discovered a new nest half built in the space I'd cleared only hours before.

Sonofabitch, that quick little shit.

Shining the flashlight into the deepest corners, I could see the tiniest hole in the far back corner and with a triumphant "Aha!" I grabbed another pad of steel wool and shoved as much of the damn thing into the hole as I could possibly fit.

Then I grabbed the dust pan and tossed the new nest out into the yard.

Take that, you little asshole. You got a cute little fluffy tail, but you still don't get to live in my house.

After that, I couldn't sleep. According to my watch it was only 3:30 in the morning and that seemed an ungodly time to be awake, but it wasn't too late to have another beer, especially since it was way too early to make coffee. So I had three and fell into a sort of dream-like slumber for a while before dawn.

Come back, Bear.

I jerked awake and something in the air smelled like hot rubber and flowers. Stupid damn squirrel probably chewed through a wire somewhere.

In the foggy recesses of dream memory I felt a warm hand on my cheek and sweet smelling hair softly brushing my face. Red hair, my brain screamed, not like Avery, whose hair had been a mahogany color (her words, not mine--I'd have called it brown).

Sitting up, I scrubbed a hand across my eyes and realized I needed to take a mighty piss. It was enough to launch me off the sofa and I cranked open the screen door, threw the latch on the heavy outer door and yanked down my zipper as I stumbled down the few porch steps and into the dense thicket of pines.

It was cold and rainy and I took care of business in short order, hurrying back into the cabin to pump water up to the kitchen sink. I could hear Avery's voice in my head: *Noah Atholton, you might have the equipment to pee outside but you will still wash your dirty caveman hands every time you come into this house!*

For the first time in weeks, I grinned. For a minute. Then I heaved a huge sigh and my old friend, crippling depression, threw an arm around my shoulders again.

I couldn't fucking shake this guy.

Aves, I can't do this by myself. I miss you so much.

I held a hand over my eyes, not caring that my hands were wet.

Stumbling over to the sofa, I eyed the half-blazing fire before I collapsed again, hoping I could drop back into sleep for another hour or two. The alternative was to sit up with my memories until the morning light crept through the small cabin windows, and I didn't want to wait that long to be able to breathe.

Thankfully, I did drift off for a while, and when I finally came to again it was because the fire was low and smoking. It was low enough that the room was growing cold and I stretched out my stiff limbs again, wicked thirsty and feeling no less tired than when I'd gone to sleep the night before.

It may or may not have had something to do with the drinks after midnight.

I got up slowly and fed the fire, stirring it again before filling the coffee pot at the sink and dumping an indiscriminate amount of grounds into the filter basket. I drank my coffee black anyway, and I wasn't careful about measurements so more often than not it came out like tar. Not that I could taste much of anything, if I bothered to pay attention to it at all. It was all just sustenance of one sort or another--another way to keep going.

Spending the day on the sofa seemed like a great idea, and it was the last thing I wanted. So I ate another handful of jerky while heating water over a propane burner, then washed the jerky down with a huge cup of coffee. Then I grabbed a handful of bullets to drop into my pocket before I grabbed my rifle and headed out into nature.

Nature didn't much like me. It was rainy and cold and I thought for the millionth time that maybe Thomas and Finn had the right idea when they'd both moved farther south, to California.

I wandered aimlessly through the woods until my stomach started to rumble again, and I headed back to the cabin only because my stomach drew me there.

That night, I slept in the bed Avery and I had shared the summer before and though I could stretch my legs all the way to the bottom of the bed, my body ached. I pulled her pillow into my arms, hoping it would lull me to sleep, but I'd slept next to her for nearly two decades. I hadn't acclimated to an empty bed, and it didn't seem very likely I ever would.

I missed her sass, the woman I'd teasingly called my Tiny Dictator.

I missed the way she'd come home each day, frustrated by parents who were pushing their expectations on their kids.

I missed the way she'd pretend not to notice when I got home and I'd chase her around the house for a kiss, like a puppy who was trying to hump her leg.

I missed the way she'd push me back onto our bed and demand I do whatever she wanted. (I wanted what she wanted, so I had no fight to put up.)

By the time day three rolled around, the rain let up and I woke to some weak rays of sunshine. It was enough to get me out of bed and I brewed coffee and gagged down more jerky, for the third morning in a row. *I'm going to have to seriously start cooking for myself.* Then I grabbed my gun and headed out into nature.

With no intention of actually hunting anything, I tried to enjoy the crisp air and the faint warmth of the sunlight. It was peaceful and quiet, the silence interrupted only by the occasional breeze stirring the pines and the call of birds.

It allowed me to shut out the rest of the world, to forget about work or the crew of guys who were undoubtedly pissed at me for quitting.

It allowed me to stop thinking about Avery's family, about my dad, about what I was going to do now that life had handed me a crap sandwich.

I spent just over a week at the cabin and didn't turn my phone on once.

I went into town twice for supplies, but other than that it was just me and nature. And though I wanted to be able to say that it had helped to settle me, helped me find peace and answers and direction, when I packed up the few things I'd brought and headed for home, I didn't feel much better than when I'd arrived.

***

It was no surprise to find Da in my house when I got home. I'd locked the place up tight, but he was a damn stealth ninja when it came to breaking and entering, and he sat at my table with a cup of coffee and one raised, hairy eyebrow. He was obviously waiting for me.

It turned out I had a new roommate, at least for a couple weeks, since the latest bunny he'd married had kicked him out of the house. He was confident he could win her back and the guy in me figured it was worth it to him, because she had a pretty great rack--and other skills he alluded to that made me want to puke, especially at his age.

She was batshit crazy, in my opinion, and I didn't know how or why he'd put up with that as long as he did--let alone put a ring on it. He had to be getting damn tired of buying a new ring every couple years.

I also suspected family interference, on Finn's part. Because while it was possible Da needed a place to stay, he could more than afford a really nice hotel. My money was on him being appointed my babysitter.

All of my siblings had flown the coop as soon as possible, probably because the never ending rotation of progressively younger stepmoms became unbearable after Ma died.

Gerry, my first stepmom, left Da when I was seventeen and though she stayed close and kept pointedly in touch with each of us, losing her was hard. She'd brought stability to our home and our daily routines, and that fell apart when she left. Part of me wondered if Da had been searching for her equal ever since, though it seemed he'd kind of lost the narrative with the brainless little plastic girls he kept bringing home.

Maren, the oldest sister, was married by nineteen and moved to Sonoma.

Thomas was off to college at eighteen, which meant he was effectively out of the house.

Aaron didn't even make it out of high school--he was in the Army by the time he turned seventeen.

Asher stayed until he was eighteen, when he went off to college, and Finn was pretty much out by fifteen, living with friends since she didn't get along with any of the women Da paraded through the house.

That left me.

Thomas was in Palo Alto and Sonoma; Aaron was in upstate New York; Asher was in San Francisco; Finn was in San Diego.

I was the only one who hadn't completely abandoned our roots, having elected to remain in the city my father lived in. I'd even worked for him since graduating high school.

Da ran a huge construction business and had been wildly successful, even more so in the past ten years thanks to the fact there was a real estate boom happening on the west coast. It afforded him enough money to get into developing. Rather than having to take on investors, he could bankroll an entire project from start to finish and walk away with a tremendous profit.

I wasn't jealous. I didn't have the same world domination ambitions he did. I just wanted to do what I loved, surrounded by the people I loved. I was pretty simple that way.

Da was never going to admit that I was a charity case, and I knew he was insanely pissed at me for up and quitting on him the week before. But to his credit, he really didn't say much of anything; just made sure I was ok, which was a little weird. Because if there was one thing that man *always* had, it was an opinion.

We didn't talk about my moping for the first week.

I could generally count on him to be out of the house by six-thirty and back some time after four, so I did make an effort to at least have something ready for dinner when he got home. The rest of the day I was usually on the sofa, watching bad daytime TV, wondering if that stupid squirrel had managed to find his way back into my cabin.

The second week Da told me I'd better find a hobby or he'd start dragging me into work with him anyway, even though he made no promises to pay me. It wasn't really enough to light a fire under my butt, but it did encourage me to clean out the garage, so there was that.

By the third week I think he was at his wit's end and he finally convinced his dingbat wife to let him come home.

I really couldn't have cared less, since I couldn't stand her. Bunny or Kitten or Fluffy or some dipshit name like that--not a nickname, but her real name. She was such an idiot, I wasn't sure she could have remembered something more complicated without writing it on her hand. (Like I said, Da was in it for the rack and the sack.)

The night he left, I finally sat down with the basket of sympathy cards and read my way through some of them. I made sure my trusty pal Jack was on hand, right at my side, and every time I felt a tear or a sniffle creeping up, Jack would chase it away with his steady burn. He was reliable like that.

I made it through most of the basket. There were only five cards left at the bottom, and when I recognized Jenny's familiar handwriting--the writing Avery always had all over papers and notebooks since Jenny was her assistant, I had to quit.

I couldn't do it. I didn't want to know what she had to say or how sorry she was or how much she'd been praying for me. All the words meant nothing.

I threw the basket across the room and Jack and I settled down on the sofa, the lights out, the TV on.

My buddy was gonna help me obliterate my sorrows tonight.

TEN

Eve
◄╫►

Over the next three weeks, Daniel and I went out five times.

He was thoughtful and attentive, our conversation was easy and, finally, at the end of our fourth date he kissed me goodnight at the front door of my building. It was...nice. Nothing that made angels sing or the heavens shift or my panties combust, but it was sweet and a little fumbled and maybe there was even a little tongue, but that may have been an accident because I was definitely rusty.

Like I said, nice, but I was starting to get the impression that the hesitation wasn't exactly coming from him, but from me. He was reading my cues, because if anyone was an expert on body language and nonverbal communication, it was him...so it had to be my fault he hadn't pushed me yet for anything more.

It was a rare occurrence, but Lauren and I met up for breakfast and coffee the morning after the fifth date. It was stupid-early, since I had to work, but Lauren had the day off and had texted at three that morning to ask if I wanted breakfast, since Henry had been awake for hours with a low fever and Alex was willing to step in and give her a break before he went to work himself.

I knew why she wanted to have breakfast. By now she was hoping I had detailed information for her, like how much heat Daniel was packing and whether he knew how to use his weapon when the situation called for it. (She had never met a situation that didn't call for it.)

Her last text had me rolling my eyes.

Can he handle the weapon and flick the safety at the same time? Tell me he knows how to find the safety.

Lauren was all about "the safety," everything in cop jargon, and she could turn perfectly innocent references into things of smutty genius.

My stories were never as good as Lauren's. She and Alex were like matches and gasoline together and she was a firm believer in TMI, to the point the tips of my ears were often red for the entire day after she confessed something dark and dirty. Of course, this was probably why they had four kids and though she claimed that she was done, now that Henry had turned one and she'd *finally* "got that little junkie off the funbags," I had a feeling she'd be knocked up again in no time. After all, no one did pregnancy like Lauren.

She glowed.

Her boobs looked amazing.

She was always perfectly rounded in all the right places.

Obviously, Alex liked his woman pregnant--probably made him feel like a chest-thumping, cave-dwelling, virile man. And of course, Lauren's hormone levels were through the roof, her Fuck Dial set to a fourteen on a scale of ten. It was like hitting the lottery on Christmas day, as far as Alex was concerned.

It was no surprise that Lauren looked disappointed when I told her we'd been out five times and hadn't yet graduated to a full-on makeout session.

"Ridiculous." She shook her head at me, chomping down another piece of bacon. "You're just gonna have to tell him you're going back to his place, no questions and no excuses. Or rip his pants down in the hallway--your building is always so quiet, you could absolutely get away with it. Clearly needs some encouragement and a good blowjob is always a great icebreaker."

"Oh!" Her eyes sparkled with trouble. "I know! The next time you go out, don't wear any underwear--Alex loves that. Then I let him know at some point and he spends the whole night trying to get up my dress. In fact, when my parents were in town for the party, they watched the kids while we went to dinner at the restaurant..."

The restaurant in question was a rustic Italian kitchen owned and operated by Alex's parents.

My ears began to burn in preparation for the story.

"Kid you not, he made me come *at* the table in the restaurant. Twice! I told the waiter I was having a hot flash." She smirked and fanned herself, clearly having an actual hot flash this time, though I wouldn't put it past her to have perfected the art of the spontaneous orgasm.

"When we got home I made him park in the garage so I could remind him of my…" she paused, clearing her throat significantly and licking her lips suggestively. "Skills...before we went into the house."

I heard a snort behind Lauren and looked over her shoulder to see an older woman mopping up the coffee she'd spit all over the table. Clearly her code words were no secret code at all.

Shaking my head at her, I took a bite of the huge lumberjack skillet in front of me. I would never have her wild sex life, and I was probably more than a little jealous. I very much doubted I'd have more kids, and that all came down to the fact I was certain I would never have another husband--certainly not one like hers. That man worshipped the ground she walked on and literally kissed her feet. (I'd heard the kinky stories to prove it.) Lauren was very free with all the details.

"Not all of us are as sexually combustible as you and Alex," I said quietly, not sure the poor woman sitting behind Lauren had recovered yet.

"It doesn't have to be combustible all the time, sometimes it's just sweet," she said, tucking a huge helping of omlette into her mouth and talking around it. "But you do need to *have* sex for it to get better."

Like I didn't know that. And it's not that I was unwilling, but I hadn't met anyone in a long time that interested me in that way. I mean, I was genuinely interested in Daniel, but he was clearly fine with taking it slow and I was one hundred percent on board with that thanks to the fact we both had kids. I wasn't eager to parade strange men through Jared's life, as I was certain his father was doing with any number of women.

One of us had to be mature.

"How about I keep Jared on Friday night so you can go out with your scrumptious man? You two can have dinner and go back to your place or his. Take your time. Pick Jared up Saturday afternoon, so you have some time to really...you know..." She wiggled her eyebrows. "Review some case notes, if you will."

I told Lauren I'd think about her offer and as I drove to work, I voice-texted Daniel to thank him for a lovely evening, tell him I had a great time, and ask if he wanted to grab dinner on Friday night. He didn't answer right away, and I decided that was ok given that it was still early, putting my phone in my locker.

There was something in the air that day. We were busier than usual, and I won't say an ER ever has a "normal" day, but this was definitely not even close. I had two kids brought in from a local school, one with a raisin up her nose and the boy had broken off a pencil eraser in his ear. Then a morbidly obese guy who'd suffered an anaphylactic reaction from seafood and a homeless lady who insisted she was having a miscarriage. Which wouldn't have been entirely crazy, but she was easily seventy.

A few more regulars drifted through from the local homeless population, a guy banged up from a car wreck, and a construction worker who'd suffered a pretty nasty burn on-site.

I didn't even think to check my phone at lunch and by the time my shift was over and I clocked out, I quickly changed and dropped my phone into the back pocket of my jeans.

I needed to pick up groceries and Jared needed a few supplies for an art project he had coming up next week, so I pointed the car toward the supermarket and prayed I could find everything I needed in one stop.

"Mom!" Jared greeted me excitedly even before I'd set down the bags in the kitchen and I looked up to see a huge smile on his face. "Dad called! He wants to see me this weekend--he says we can have the whole weekend together if that's ok with you."

Was it ok with me? Not for a damn second. But did I really have a choice? Because obviously Jason was calling me on my bluff.

"He says we'll go to the kids' museum, and maybe even go sailing!"

I tried to look excited, but a hard knot of dread settled in my stomach. Jason was a daredevil and a risk taker. He wasn't careful, cautious, or even logical. And that was when he showed up.

"That's great, honey." My voice sounded strained to my ears. "It sounds like he's planned some really fun things. I guess that means you want to go?"

"Duh." He shook his head at me and I gave him the side eye for what might have been disrespect.

Maggie drifted quietly into the room and packed up her bag to leave, silently observing the dynamic between Jared and myself. When he hurried off to his room with his new art supplies, she stood looking at me expectantly and I knew she'd overheard the whole thing. But I didn't engage, so she started. "You let me know if you need help this weekend. I remember what happened last time."

Of course she did. I'd taken on an extra shift a couple months before, since Jason had sworn he would arrive on a Friday evening to pick up Jared. But by the time eleven-thirty rolled around and there had been no sign of Jason--who was no longer answering his phone--I called Maggie to ask if she could babysit Jared the next day while I worked the day shift.

So much for getting ahead.

Maggie squeezed my arm before letting herself out and I ran a hand across my face. I needed to start dinner and a load of laundry. I also needed an hour on the treadmill, a stiff drink and a solid seven on the orgasm chart to take the edge off. But since none of those things were going to happen, I fished my phone out of my pocket to pull up a favorite food blogger's site and get some quick dinner inspiration.

Daniel had responded earlier that morning and I hadn't seen it, confirming he would love dinner on Friday. Did I have preferences?

I refrained from responding that my place would be just fine, since that was clearly where we'd end up. (We really weren't at that comfort level yet.) Instead, I asked if he wanted to try the new Greek place that had opened just down the block from me and he quickly responded that he'd love to and he'd pick me up at seven.

Well then, that was that.

Jared was high as a kite the rest of the evening and I had no problems getting him to shower, brush his teeth or put away his fresh laundry. I noticed he'd already pulled out a small bag and had begun to pack things for the weekend and I said a little prayer that Jason wouldn't let us down again.

***

Lauren was on stand-by in case Jason didn't show, and I'd really upped my game for the night: my toes were freshly polished, everything had been waxed or shaved, I was wearing a hot new bra and panty set, and I'd packed a couple condoms in my bag, just in case. It was laughable, really. It had been so long, I wasn't entirely sure I remembered how to use one.

The doorbell rang at 6:43, and though Jason said he'd show up to collect Jared at six, I decided not to take him to task. As it was, I'd seen Jared's eyes watching the clock, his expression slipping downward a little with each minute that passed.

"There's my buddy!"

Yup, there was Jason, blowing into the room like a cyclone: Larger than life. Completely gregarious. Loud and fun and goofy. It had been fun at first, until he'd turned bitter and sullen and withdrawn. It was almost like a switch had been flipped and he'd started saving his good moods for other people.

Jared already had his bag over his shoulder and I snaked out an arm to drag him into a hug as he rushed past. We went through the list: toothbrush, deodorant, underwear, socks, phone, charging cord.

Jason was silent and I could feel his eyes on me, moving from the expanse of exposed collarbone, past my knees, all the way to the high heels on my feet.

"Wow, V," he finally said once Jared was out of earshot, sitting by the door to lace up his shoes. "Maybe if you had tried this hard while we were together, I'd have stayed interested."

My lip curled in disgust. The arrogant asshole thought this was for him.

"You decided my efforts weren't enough a long time ago, when you started tripping dick-first into other women."

He looked mildly amused. "All I'm saying is that if you'd gotten out of the scrubs a little more often, maybe I'd have tried a little harder too."

Asshole. I wanted to shoot laser beams out of my eyes and incinerate him, but instead I forced down the anger and smiled with saccharine sweetness. "The best thing you ever did was leave. At least I can count on myself to get off."

"Dad?" It was Jared, interrupting the hateful glare Jason leveled at me. He had rarely been patient enough to get me off, and now he knew it. That was sure to knock his pride in his performance.

"Have him back by five on Sunday so I can keep him in routine for school."

Jason waved a hand over his shoulder, a simultaneous *Yeah, I heard you,* and *Go fuck yourself,* as he hustled Jared toward the door. I closed it behind them, unsure of whether I felt relief or concern, anxiety or plain old fear. Jared always had a good time--Jason got to be the fun parent-- but I was a natural worrier.

Daniel showed up five minutes later, probably having crossed paths with Jason and Jared in the parking garage, and he stood looking around the condo while I rushed back to my room to grab a sweater.

"Great place," he commented as I hurried back into the kitchen, and I smiled with effort. He'd been here before, though briefly.

"Thanks. It's not exactly spacious, but it's enough. I bought it after the divorce because it was something I could afford and with housing prices going the way they are, there wasn't much that was in my range."

As Daniel shepherded me out of the building, his warm hand at the small of my back, my cheeks flushed when I remembered Lauren telling me I should take his pants down in the hallway. It made me turn my head a little so Daniel couldn't see my face, since with my pale coloring it was very easy to see when my cheeks went pink. I wasn't ready to share those thoughts with him just yet.

The restaurant was close enough to my place that we could walk, and I insisted, even though Daniel would have happily driven there and gone through the hassle or parking all over again.

Dinner was delicious and Daniel seemed relaxed. He was funny, sweet, and when we both fell to talking about our kids, he gestured for the check.

I realized at that moment that walking to the restaurant had definitely sent him the signal I'd be inviting him back up to my place after, as now we had to walk back together.

I hadn't tried out any of Lauren's tricks of seduction over dinner, and I was most certainly wearing underwear. I guess I'd been waiting for him to make some kind of move that gave me the butterflies that landed somewhere in the vicinity of my lower body, but though he held my hand under the table and now, as he had his arm around me as we walked, I didn't feel that zing. It was warm and comfortable, but it felt a little more like I was walking home with a close friend than with someone I wanted to invite into my bed. That was hugely disappointing, as I'd worked hard to build up an unrealistic expectation of him in some late night fantasies. You could say I'd been working really hard on selling him to myself.

"Is it ok if I come in?" he asked softly, waiting for my permission, and I realized we'd been standing outside my door for a beat too long.

"Uh…" My brain churned frantically. Maybe I should give it a try. "Yeah, sure. I could see if I have some wine hidden somewhere…"

His lips turned up into a smile and I got the feeling he'd drink anything I poured for him, but that wasn't what he wanted tonight.

I kicked off my shoes just inside the door and tossed my bag onto the kitchen counter, dropping down to dig through the lower cabinets in search of the bottle of wine I was pretty sure Lauren had given me at Christmas. I had hidden it way back, behind the gigantic slow cooker I never used, a gift from the late mother-in-law who hadn't been able to stand me.

Daniel was quiet as I retrieved two dusty wine glasses, rinsed and wiped them, and he fished the corkscrew out of my silverware drawer almost as if he'd known where it was. He opened the bottle and poured carefully, lifting his glass to me. "I wish I had a clever toast," he said, seemingly at a loss for words for the first time since I'd known him. His voice was scratchy. "But I don't. I've just...had another lovely evening with you and I don't want it to end." He reached across the space to cup my face in one hand.

I bumped his arm as I lifted my glass to take a nervous sip, and he stepped back again, taking a sip of his own. Then he set his glass down and moved toward me, taking my glass and setting it on the counter, sifting his fingers through my hair as he moved closer. His intention was unmistakable and while my feeling wasn't one of revulsion, it worried me that I felt a little apathetic. I was nervous, but it wasn't a good kind of nervous.

Everything Daniel did, he did well, including kissing. He was an expert when it came to pressure and timing. He was in tune with my cues, patient, slow to part my lips and slip his tongue inside with firm pressure and soft strokes. And though this was the first time he'd kissed me with any transparent intent, I couldn't help but think that it was still just...nice and comfortable.

Still no fireworks.

An obnoxious sound filled the kitchen, a blaring horn coming from the general direction of my handbag and I jerked back so quickly, I nearly knocked over my wine glass.

Crap, that was Jason's ringtone.

I scrambled for my bag without caring Daniel was looking at me in surprise and I held the phone to my ear, the sound of wailing plain in the background.

"Jason? What happened?"

"Chill out, Eve." His voice was impatient, as it usually was. "Me and Jared went e-bike riding and something went wrong with his. I don't know. He rolled it somehow and got banged up, so we're at the ER getting him checked out. Scared the fuck out of the rental dude."

I closed my eyes, one hand lifting to my forehead. "You took a ten-year-old out on rough trails on an e-bike. Jason, your son has never been on a bicycle in his life."

"Yeah well, now you tell me."

"You've never been there to teach him and you didn't fucking ask!" My eyes flew open and I knew my expression was enraged. I'd forgotten for a second that Daniel was there, watching me, listening to every word.

"Forget it. Are you at my hospital?"

"Yeah, you should probably come get him." He sounded disgusted. "He wants his mommy." He said the last word condescendingly.

I hung up on him, shoving the phone back into my bag.

"You need to go," Daniel observed quietly, and there was disappointment in his eyes.

"Yeah...I'm sorry. It's not exactly a great end to the evening."

"I'll drive you."

"No, it's ok. Really, Daniel. You live in the opposite direction and if you drive me there, then you'd probably also want to drive me back, and..." I tried so hard to ignore the elephant in the room. "Really, it's ok." I was weirdly relieved the date was over.

"Then I'll walk you out to your car and you text me when you get home, so I know you're safe." He tucked my hair behind my ear, his eyes warm and gentle. I really wanted to lean up and kiss his cheek in gratitude, but I was afraid it would send the wrong message.

"Ok, I can do that. Thanks."

He saw me out to my car, then kissed me swiftly before tapping on the roof. I backed out of the space and tore out of the garage like a bat out of hell, because for all I knew Jared was in traction by now.

Stupid Jason. He may as well have taken him parachuting.

I had my hospital ID in my bag and although the ladies at the front desk recognized me, I didn't pause. I waved at them as I hurried past, buzzing in quickly and rushing into the large space.

My eyes darted from one curtain-partitioned bed to the next, most of the curtains open, and I located them quickly. Jared was lying in the bed, a bandage on his forehead, a small gauze wrap around his right elbow.

My heels sounded unnaturally loud on the floor and Jason's head shot up as I crossed the room.

"I'll see you, buddy." He held up his hand for a fist bump and Jared slowly formed a fist with his left hand.

"K, Dad. Sorry."

Jason didn't say anything, just looked away as he brushed past me and I wondered for the millionth time what I had ever seen in such an arrogant, cold-hearted piece of work.

I sank into the small chair next to Jared's bed and waited for the doctor to show up while I fussed over my son. He had thirteen stitches on his forehead and a nasty gravel rash on the arm covered in gauze. Other than that, it seemed he hadn't broken any bones, he hadn't dislocated anything, and thank God he'd been wearing pants or the rash would have been all down his right side.

"I cannot imagine I need to provide you with instructions for his care." Dr. Pradith smiled at me as he signed the release papers. He was one of the doctors I actually liked to work with.

"Son, there is no one better to care for you than the emergency room nurse, and you are blessed this one is your mama." His voice dipped and lilted in a cadence that spoke of a lifetime before the one in an ER in the States, and he smiled at Jared, the golden edge of one of his teeth glinting in the light.

It was late and suddenly I was bone-weary. I helped Jared up and though he whimpered a little, he held it together pretty well as I collected his things and draped his sweatshirt around his shoulders. He was clearly tired and emotionally drained.

There was a low sound of pain in the bed next to us, mere feet away, separated by a flimsy piece of fabric. It made the hair on the back of my neck stand on end and I held out a hand to Jared, indicating he should stay put while I peeked around the curtain and into the next space.

There was a nurse I didn't recognize hooking up a new bag of saline to the stand, followed by a bag of blood. I let my eyes drift down to the form in the bed. A huge man all but spilled out of it, his left arm wound tightly with gauze, the IV feeding into his right hand.

"Bear." It was out of my mouth on a whisper. I recognized the huge man from the day of the blast and I knew without a doubt why he was here when I saw the gauze. It made my heart hurt.

"You know him?" Jared asked quietly, and something passed between us that I couldn't have put into words if I tried.

"He probably needs his mom, too," Jared mused with a sweet grin and I swallowed hard, the pull to the huge man almost visceral. He needed someone, yet no one was here--again--and Jared squeezed my hand gently. "I'll be ok with Auntie Lauren, Mom. You're...at work."

It was almost as if he'd read my thoughts and was giving me permission.

I took Jared out into the waiting room, where I called Lauren. She was there fifteen minutes later, her eyes full of questions as I hustled my son off with her, giving her quick instructions. Jared had been given enough painkillers to take down a horse, I assured her, and I would pick him up the next morning. He'd be out the instant his head hit the pillow.

None of those facts would save me from the crippling guilt that I knew was coming.

I couldn't have told Lauren the truth if she'd asked why I needed to stay, since I didn't even know. I knew it looked bad. It was reckless and irresponsible, but something about the giant man pulled at me in a way that told me he needed someone right now, but he had no one.

Passing my card over the sensor again, I let myself back into the ER and sought out Dr. Pradith to ask about the man. He confirmed what I'd feared, and I thanked him quietly before walking into the man's space and slumping into the chair next to his bed, watching the monitors.

The nurse was in again, checking the bags on the stand and her eyes flicked to me, accusation in her gaze. "He yours?"

Like this had been my fault.

I shook my head slowly. "I helped him once before...I'm usually on Days here." She raised an eyebrow while I tried to sort my thoughts. "I was here to pick up my son and I saw him and I...I don't think I can explain it."

She gave me a strange look. "He's been pretty out of it. He lost a lot of blood and they had to pump his stomach. He'll be out for a while, and in the meantime, you know the drill: If you're staying, pretend you're the girlfriend.

"Once we're sure he's improving, he'll be moved to a room. For now he seems stable, but he'll definitely end up in the Psych ICU."

Didn't I know it, though. I'd seen this happen hundreds of times, but this time it was oddly personal.

I spent the next several hours with him, my hand on his arm or my fingers linked through his thick, still ones, wishing I could somehow give him the will to live. Because I had lived this despair. I could recognize it in his desperate action.

By three in the morning it was deemed safe to move him, and I followed along as he was moved to his room, noting the number to myself so I could come visit him later. Then, as his room emptied again, I tucked the blankets up around him and smoothed the dark hair off his forehead. He was pale, though I doubted that was normal, and I couldn't help but appreciate that he was gorgeous. He had long, thick, dark eyelashes and full, soft lips. His cheekbones were high and his nose straight, his eyebrows dark and winged.

It seemed unlikely he was suffering for female company, I thought, considering just how many nurses had already drifted past and stuck their heads in through the door with expressions of concern. *Thirsty bitches,* I'd thought jealously. Irrationally. Because I was behaving like one, too.

I sighed finally, wrapping my sweater tighter around myself and lifting out of the chair. He would be under Lauren's watch by tomorrow afternoon and I could get details from her then. But now, I needed to go. It was already after four and I'd been a terrible mother, sending my injured son home with my best friend because I'd been inexplicably incapable of leaving.

Smoothing his hair again, I checked his IV, his catheter, the line feeding more blood into his veins. And for a second, I forgot myself. I leaned over him, my hair falling around his face as I kissed his forehead.

"Sleep well, Bear," I whispered. "I hope your heart heals before you wake."

Driving home slowly, I let myself into the condo and kicked off my shoes.

I stripped off the dress and the lacy underthings.

I set my alarm for eight and, without bothering to wash my face or brush my teeth, collapsed into bed.

ELEVEN

Noah

◄II►

Being dead couldn't possibly hurt this much, could it?

Rolling my body just a little, to ease the pressure on my back, I heard a sharp intake of breath and my eyes opened slowly to find my oldest brother at the side of the bed, his face creased, his eyes exhausted.

"Thomas." My voice was scratchy. My throat hurt like hell.

"You trying to leave me to deal with Da's crazy all on my own?" He was trying to joke, I knew, but neither of us laughed.

I looked down at the bandage wound tightly around my left wrist.

Damn it, so doubling down hadn't done the trick.

"Yeah...nice try." Thomas grabbed my hand and held on tight, which was weird for him, because our level of demonstrative affection was usually limited to whaling on each other. "The paramedics barely made it in time, bro."

Vaguely, I remembered calling Thomas.

When I'd hit the bottom of the bottle, Jack had whispered in my ear that I could make everything stop hurting. I liked his idea--he was a smart guy--and I lurched down the hallway and into the small half bath, where there was an assortment of medications in the small under-sink cabinet. I had some powerful painkillers in there somewhere, thanks to an injury on the job a few years earlier. There must have been twenty pills left in the bottle and since they were old--expired, in fact--I figured it would be most effective if I took all of them.

But then, to be safe, Jack reminded me I should probably also see what could be done with the straight edge razor I found buried in the organizing bin.

Always thinking ahead, that one.

I think I called Thomas to say goodbye before running the razor over my wrist, because he was the one who would take care of things. I doubted anyone else would care.

Hallelujah, no more days without my girls.

"I don't ever want to get a phone call like that again." Thomas's voice was hard, and he scrubbed a rolled up shirt sleeve over his red, tired eyes. "But thank God you called *anyone*, bro. They almost couldn't save you."

I was a little angry I was here to have this conversation, if I was being completely honest with myself. I'd hoped to turn the lights out forever, or to wake up to find Avery waiting for me, our sweet little girl in her arms.

The door creaked just a little and I looked up to see a gorgeous, curvy brunette watching us with a smile on her face. "Well," she said, and I thought she sounded happy. "I know it's not the paradise you had in mind, but there are a few people who are awfully happy to see you in this dimension."

Thomas pushed himself to his feet, working the kinks out of his back and neck with a long stretch.

I saw the brunette's eyes sweep over him appreciatively before I noticed the ridiculous wedding set on her left hand. Some guy had *really* marked his territory with this one, no mistaking it.

There was a vase of flowers sitting on the table to my right and the woman's eyes followed mine. She grinned. "You have some admirers, big man." Then she moved quickly to check my vitals, noting something on the tablet she carried and moving to the white board to update some information.

"I'm Lauren," she said finally. "I'm just coming on shift, so you'll see me for the next twelve hours or so."

I could think of worse things. At least this one was really easy on the eyes.

"You my admirer?" I asked Thomas with a voice that sounded like it had been dragged over glass, grinning at him as I pointed to the flowers.

"Dumbass." He rolled his eyes at me, but he was smiling too. "I saw a woman bring them in really early this morning. She was wearing scrubs, so it was definitely one of the nurses. She checked your vitals and tried to get me to sleep in the chair over there." He pointed to the corner. "She was very pretty. Very...attentive toward you." His face twisted into a funny expression and I told myself to ask him what that face meant later, because it was obvious the nurse was listening in.

Thomas stayed with me until I was discharged the next day. In fact, he was the one who signed me out to his own care, because I'd been placed under a mental health hold for seventy-two hours.

He waited with me while the doctor explained how to care for the wound on my arm and to take it easy on my stomach for a while--under no uncertain terms, no more alcohol and no more pills, and easy on the fried foods. It was a miracle, he said, they'd been able to pump my stomach as quickly as they did, or the pills would have eaten through the lining and I'd have been a goner.

I didn't point out the obvious: that very thing had clearly been my intention.

Thomas drove me home and insisted I rest on the sofa while he called a cleaning service to have the house dealt with.

Then he placed an order for groceries through a delivery service and swept my house for booze.

Then he called Gerry and had a hushed, whispered conversation and when he came back into the room he had a slip of paper. "Gerry agrees with me that this is out of her depth, bro."

I swung my eyes to his.

"You need help--a lot of it. You need to talk with someone who can help you through what you haven't been able to deal with on your own. You can't continue to avoid people and self-medicate with booze. I know you don't want to be here, but there are an awful lot of people who'd be wrecked if you decided not to stick around. Your secret is safe with me and Gerry--for now. But only if you get your shit together." He swallowed hard, and for the first time I felt just a little bit guilty.

Thomas set up an appointment for me with one of the counselors Gerry recommended, and he stayed long enough to drive me to my first appointment. I wanted to fuss and complain the whole way there, but I knew it wouldn't do any good. If he had to, Thomas would drag me into the guy's office in a headlock.

By the time he left to drive home, he'd been with me for a week and I was more thankful to him for his tough love approach than I could ever put into words, mostly because he'd been there when I needed someone to push me. I wasn't even going to try voicing what it meant to me that he'd dropped everything and rushed to my literal bedside, as that would be risking the handing in of my man card. I'd definitely cry and that was not gonna work, so I just made sure to give him a real good hug before he left and I promised no more foolishness--at least for the foreseeable future.

The look he gave me could have singed the hair off my eyebrows.

I decided once he left that I should make an effort.

I cleaned the house and donated a bunch of crap to charity.

I started watching cooking shows, because my skills were real rusty, and I started putting together not-too-inedible meals for myself. (Okay, maybe I started watching one of them because the lady always wore low-cut tops and she was smokin'.)

I started working out again, just a little bit, every day.

I made sure to get plenty of sleep, which worked out just fine with my depression and shitty energy levels.

I attended meetings with my counselor three times a week.

So while I didn't feel like I'd necessarily turned the corner, with my new routine I had less time to sit and think. I kept myself busy, engaged and actively doing and learning new things, because I knew I had to.

It was about a month later that I finally ventured out to go grocery shopping, finally foregoing the delivery service Thom had introduced me to. I was tired of the shoppers consistently delivering the wrong brand of bacon and always substituting my laundry detergent with something that smelled like a freaking field of flowers. Mountain streams, that was where it was at. I didn't need to smell like a little girl with pigtails, skipping down a mountainside in that stupid dirndl thing.

My arm had healed up pretty well, so to look at me you'd never know what a mess I still was on the inside, especially if I wore long sleeved shirts that hid the long pink scar across my left wrist.

I was a little lost in the supermarket at first. Avery had done most of the food shopping when we were together, so I made a list and went slowly through the store, reading the signs, the labels, often backtracking to find something. It was frustrating, but it wasn't like my options weren't great.

"Oh! You're ok!"

There was a gorgeous redhead grinning at me from ear to ear when I turned around, and I looked quickly behind me to see whether there was anyone else in the produce section with us. Something about her seemed a little familiar, and I squinted at her while I tried to remember.

"Ah, I'm sorry..." I shuffled my feet a little closer, because she smelled weirdly familiar. "I know you, right?"

Two bright pink spots popped up in her cheeks and her smile faltered a little. "Um, I'm sorry--no, not really, and the explanation is a little weird. I was on duty at the hospital when...when it happened. The first thing." Her voice trailed off and she looked terribly guilty.

I knew I'd paled a little when I felt the blood rush from my head, and for a second the huge room went fuzzy.

"That's probably why you look so familiar." I smiled weakly, eager to get away from her and her reminder of the worst days of my life. "Thanks for...you know...that."

Her cheeks flushed even more pink, something I hadn't thought possible. "I sat with you for a while that night...and this last time, too. I was worried. I..." She looked down at her feet and stopped talking for a second, chewing on something. "I'm sorry, I'm just making this weird. I'm just glad to see you're ok." With that, she turned and started to slowly walk away, but something had piqued my curiosity. She had been worried about me and had sat through the night with me while I was knocked out, because...why?

"So you were there the last time, too?" I called as I grabbed a clamshell of spinach and tossed it into my cart, waiting for her to turn around. She did, slowly, but didn't look back up at me when she nodded.

Soft, red hair brushing my face and warm lips on my forehead.

"You know what happened then, I suppose. What I did...and probably even why I did it."

She stepped closer and set down her shopping basket. "I understand." She pushed up the sleeve on her right arm and ran a finger along a thin, almost imperceptible white scar that ran upward from her wrist to the inside of her elbow. The mark of a thin blade.

"Foster care," she said quietly. "You know you're desperate when this is your only way out. For a long time I was really angry with people who told me I was 'lucky' to have made it, because I didn't feel lucky at all; it would have been easier to die with them."

I wanted to reach out and drag her close, but the moment was already deeply fraught with emotion and something more that I couldn't name. It seemed a pretty sure thing she didn't talk about this with many people.

"Foster care," I said slowly, forgetting for a moment that we were standing in the middle of a supermarket. "You lost your family, too."

She nodded and she looked at me as if she was carefully weighing her words. "Natural gas leak," she finally said, so quietly that I almost didn't hear her, the words traveling through my body like a shockwave. "I was fourteen and my brother was twelve. My bus had already picked me up for school and my brother was at the stop down the street, waiting for his. Our parents hadn't left for work yet...he was the one who saw the fireball." She shivered. "Natural gas explosions happen with alarming regularity in the winters in Bayonne."

She wiped at her eyes and I swallowed hard. This woman knew almost exactly my experience--she knew *more* of it than I did, as it had displaced her as a child. It made me feel like a big jerk, like I had insisted upon acting like I was the only person who knew what it was to suffer.

"Anyway..." She swallowed so hard, I heard her Adam's apple drag. "I'm sorry, I guess I sort of made some assumptions that we had some things in common, and it made me feel like I knew something about you.

That's definitely weird. I'm not usually…" She looked up at me uncomfortably, finally meeting my eyes. "I'm not usually this awkward."

"You're not awkward."

Every instinct I had was screaming to back away from this woman and the black cloud of hurt she was stirring inside of me, but I couldn't help myself. My hand shot out to hold the side of her face. It was an intimate gesture and I knew it, but I couldn't have stopped myself if I'd wanted to--and I really didn't want to. "You have a kind heart," I said, incredibly grateful the universe had sent me someone who could understand. "I'm glad you were there to watch over me when I couldn't…you know…watch over myself, I guess," I ended awkwardly. "So, uh…thanks."

She nodded, my hand rubbing across her cheek as she did, and I finally let it drop. I missed the feeling of her warm skin immediately and the realization made me feel incredibly guilty. It had only been a few months--I wasn't ready to feel the little zings of attraction tightening in my gut.

"Well…" she shuffled a little, clearly out of words now that the moment had been broken. "I'm holding you up. I suppose I should let you get to your business."

I nodded too, unsure of what to say. There was still something hanging in the air between us.

"Okay then," I said finally. "Thanks for, um…checking on me."

Her smile was sweet and I was struck again by how pretty she was. It was a chance meeting, yet I wasn't sure I wanted her to walk away. But I let her, watching her, kicking myself for being an idiot.

Kicking myself for touching her and making her uncomfortable.

Kicking myself because for the brief seconds I'd had my fingers against her skin, something had flared inside my chest. It was something that felt scary and overwhelming and almost impossible, like touching sunshine.

It felt like hope.

***

In the weeks that followed, my cooking skills improved drastically.

My body felt better thanks to good food and exercise, and my head felt better thanks to the therapist I was seeing.

I was sleeping, not great, but sleeping, and I hadn't had a drink in weeks.

Every time I went grocery shopping, I found myself looking for the redhead out of the corner of my eye. I had no idea what I'd do if I ran into her again, but on some level I wanted to. I had more questions for her, some of them about the time she spent with me, and some of them about her own experience.

To keep myself busy, at night I'd been puttering around with a business plan. Da had been on me to "get something solid" in my life, and since I wasn't going to be the next Top Chef, and I sure as hell wasn't going to go pro with bodybuilding, I'd begun toying with the idea that just maybe I should go into business for myself.

Da liked the idea of me getting back to work, and though I didn't want him to have a hand in my success, I knew he would sub out more jobs to me than I could handle, because he knew I'd do them right. But this way, he'd be paying *my* rates, which would be considerably better than what I'd been making before. He would undoubtedly rationalize that he could afford the higher price point, since I was no longer pulling in benefits.

Over the next few days, I registered my business, then applied for a federal identification number and a surety bond. Once I had general liability insurance in place, I printed business cards and started tacking them up all over town. Gaining traction was going to take me a while, I knew, and I could afford to wait, but I really didn't want to. I was eager to get out there and throw myself into new projects, things to tire out my body and my mind so I could come home at the end of the day and fall into my bed, sleeping through the night.

I needed to get out of the house before I watched another episode with Gordon Ramsay screaming at someone, or a show involving scary creations concocted from leftovers. (That one had been enough to make me clean out the fridge, and all those damn leftovers went right into the trash.)

Lucky for me, I'd been driven as a kid. I'd obtained licensing for a number of things, including appliances, carpentry, closets, boilers, concrete, demo, drywall, electrical, everything related to plumbing, floors and countertops, insulation and the general capacity of "handyman." It was a pretty impressive list, if I said so myself--and I did--and I knew it was just a matter of time and a few of the right connections to really get me started.

No surprise, my first job was a sub for Da. He'd purchased a teardown house on an oversized lot and had decided he would demo the building, clear the lot, and start a fresh build. He brought me in on the planning, in order to offer my opinion on what was needed, how long it would take and what it would cost. Then he tasked me with project management and told me to hire as many guys as I needed to make it happen in a six-month window. It was ambitious, given the market, but if we worked hard it wasn't entirely impossible, provided the inspectors could keep up with us.

Every day I drove to the job site, passing a huge rundown Colonial-style home that just begged to be renovated and cared for. Something about the building spoke to me, set back on a huge, overgrown lot with a long drive.

It was something Avery and I had talked about when we found out she was pregnant, buying a big house with an even bigger yard so the kid could run wild.

The house's leaded glass windows were wavy in the early morning or late evening light and I could see the need for new siding, a new roof, new fascia...but I needed a project. I needed to fall in love with something again, and when Da mentioned the house had been foreclosed upon and he was considering buying it, I cut him off at the pass.

"Nope." That was how I started my argument. "That's my house. You can bid against me if it goes to auction, but I'm gonna find out which bank owns it. Then I'm gonna call them and I'll make an offer before it even hits the block."

Da's bushy eyebrows hitched up like two freaked out caterpillars. (I'm telling you, English men really know how to do eyebrows.)

"You have a house, boy."

"I do, but I think we can agree it's maybe not the best place for me anymore. If I don't start over...make a clean break..." I couldn't finish the sentence.

He didn't say anything, but he looked at me thoughtfully and finally nodded. "You've had worse ideas, grant ya that."

It took me a while to find the bank, and the representative I spoke with referred me to the realtor who was preparing to list the property. Turned out they wanted to try their luck before going to auction.

I called the realtor and told her I wanted to see the house and put in an offer. She was surprised, since it hadn't even been listed yet, but she agreed to meet me there the next day. Since my crew was done by three, it was easy for me to make the drive over after work.

"Careful," she admonished as she climbed the porch steps. "I have a feeling some of the porch will need to be replaced." She swung a leg sideways and tested a squishy spot. "Big guy like you could go right through this thing."

She fitted the key to the old lock and swung the door open. It smelled like dust and decay, old and decrepit, but it had a center staircase and the large, gracious rooms on either side boasted a heinous wallpaper that had probably been put up in the eighties, all flowers and ribbons and birds. Absolutely hideous shit.

"I would imagine there's hardwood under all of this," she said, tapping her foot against carpeting that really didn't have a color, it was so filthy.

The kitchen was another eighties special, and each of the six bedrooms were a horrifying shade of clearance rack paint.

The eggplant purple bathroom in the hallway was probably the least scary, and my jaw dropped when we came to the last bedroom at the end of the hallway. The small space boasted a wall of windows, the walls a neon green with chalkboard paint squares that made my eyeballs ache.

"Travesty," she clucked, shaking her head, and I was glad I wasn't the only one questioning the prior owner's choices. "This could be such a gorgeous house. It's going to take a lot of work, but you seem like a capable guy."

Me? I was more than capable. The problem was that I was only *one* guy. I could handle a lot of this on my own, but if I wanted it to happen quickly I was going to have to hire some of my guys under the table. Nights and weekends would be full, giving me no time to think or to wallow.

I put in an offer that afternoon. I followed the realtor into town and sat at the table in her office's small conference room, signing where she indicated and initialing where told. Then I shook her hand, thanked her again for her time, and walked out to my truck with butterflies in my stomach. I hadn't felt that way about something in a long time: excited. Nervous. I was ready to start a relationship with a new and demanding project.

It was something like the way I'd felt when I'd asked Avery to go to Homecoming with me, our freshman year of high school. I'd been so scared she'd say no, in much the same way I was scared the bank was going to reject what I knew was a very good offer. I knew exactly what it would cost to rehab that house and the figure was considerable, which I took into account, and I knew the realtor would champion my cause.

That night I went home and cooked a simple dinner.

I did a load of laundry and dishes, vacuumed the house and, hoping to invite some good luck, dragged out a couple boxes and started packing up a few things.

My offer on the house was cash. The bank could answer me tomorrow if they chose, and I could close immediately. It didn't mean I was ready to move, but it did mean I should think about preparing--and maybe, eventually, I would list the house Avery and I had lived in for the last fifteen years.

I showered, thinking as I washed, that Avery's family would undoubtedly be upset if I sold the house. I didn't think they could begrudge me trying to move on, though I knew they wouldn't understand why I was going from a 1,300 square foot home to something that was well over 4,000. It was just me and I was a big guy, but I didn't need *that* much space.

The rundown house was mammoth, with several acres of neglected landscaping, a derelict shed, and a crumbling deck out back. If I wanted to, I could spend years working on the project.

It was getting late and finally I crawled into bed, for the first time feeling like there just might be something to look forward to.

Sleep claimed me with dreams of a warm, beautiful home filled with the laughter of the people I needed most: family.

TWELVE

Eve

◄►

    I didn't see Noah at the grocery store anymore, but that was my own fault: I'd started going to a different store, terrified I'd see him again and it would fuel the dreams that had been plaguing me at night.

    Dreams that made me feel guilty.

    Dreams that heated my blood and, more than once I'd awakened in such a state, I'd had to dust off my vibrator.

    Times were clearly desperate.

    I couldn't have explained my pull toward him if someone had put a gun to my head. That something in my psyche recognized something in his was the best I could come up with.

    Jason was really stepping up his efforts when it came to visitation, and though I was hesitant to let Jared go with him after that fun-filled trip to the hospital, I really didn't have much of a choice.

    Daniel had noticed and commented upon my "reticence" toward him during our last dinner out. I'd tried to deny it, but he leaned across the table and cut me off mid-sentence with a kiss, like he needed to prove a point. And while it was obvious he was affected by it, when he pulled away long moments later, it was plain to both of us that I wasn't. I made the lame excuse that I had a lot going on, which was always true, but we both knew I was trying to let him down easy: he felt the spark and I didn't.

    I think the thought of giving up made me almost as sad as it seemed to make him. He hugged me and said he would still see me in a professional capacity when I needed him, but I had just made it abundantly clear that I wasn't interested in seeing him in a personal capacity.

94

I could have argued, but we both knew that was pointless.

Lauren was furious with me. She blamed it entirely on my "unhealthy obsession with that guy you'll never even see again." She'd jokingly given me a basket of sex toys and told me to "get him out of your system."

I didn't tell her I'd run into Bear at the store, or she'd probably have gone into hysterics. She was still one hundred percent Team Daniel, and she couldn't understand why I felt a connection to someone in such obvious mental distress.

"You can't have someone that unstable around Jared," she started out accusingly when we met up on a rare, shared day off. We'd met for coffee, and though Lauren's energy levels suggested her body could synthesize caffeine from oxygen, the woman was always in search of another cup.

"What if he doesn't have his shit together yet? It's way too soon," she said, pouring an ungodly amount of half and half into her tall paper cup. "What if you end up being a placebo for the woman he lost? And did you know she was pregnant? He lost the baby *and* his fiancee'."

I hadn't known she was pregnant. Though I'd gathered his name from his chart, I'd purposely avoided plugging his name into a search engine or reading anything further about the accident. I just hadn't been ready to know.

"I don't even know him, not really," I sighed, swirling a biscotti in my coffee.

"Exactly my point." She took a slurp of her coffee and smacked her lips. "That's why this is so unhealthy. You need to patch things up with Daniel and have *actual* sex with a real human being. A *relationship*, Eve. Your fantasies and the basket of toys don't make up for that."

I must have blushed, because she paused and looked at me suspiciously. "You know when it's with yourself, it doesn't count as a relationship."

That made me blush more.

"Oh, come on." She rolled her eyes at me. "You're not a nun. God knows some nights Alex has to work late and I…"

I shoved my fingers in my ears and started shaking my head at her. "I can't hear you. I have no idea what you're saying. La, la, la, la..."

She swatted me. "I'm just saying no one would blame you. Alex's dick is absolute magic and sometimes when he's not there to play with, I have to take matters into my own hands." She cleared her throat, not an ounce of embarrassment to be found. "As one does."

Wrinkling my nose, I wondered if I'd ever be as sexually confident as Lauren was. God knew I hadn't had an easy start of it, thanks to a creepy foster dad, bad decisions in the boyfriend department--then the worst luck of all when it came to choosing a husband. He hadn't exactly been reliable, dependable, trustworthy, faithful, or a great boost to my self-esteem. Certainly not when he openly ogled other women or told me I should dress sexier.

Lauren switched topics suddenly, confirming exactly what I'd suspected: Alex had gotten his way. Having come from a large Italian family, he'd convinced Lauren to try for "just one more baby," and she knew that secretly he was hoping for twins again. I suspected she was simply enjoying the process, as she was all about the "research."

Lauren seemed awfully eager to relieve Alex of his babysitting duties, and I grinned at her, shaking my head. "You'll get home around morning naptime, won't you?"

She smiled coyly. "The baby's a champion napper, and he'll sleep through until lunch. The twins will give me a solid hour, maybe an hour and-a-half, and Blake doesn't get home from school until twelve-thirty. So..."

She didn't even have to finish the thought. I knew she'd be on Alex like a bug on sticky paper the instant she was through the door, and I doubted very much that he would complain. She was a woman obsessed with her husband, which was exactly what *her* husband needed.

Lauren hugged me in the parking lot, glancing quickly down at her watch. "I just wanna see you happy, Evie. You know that. I'll support you in whatever decision you make, so long as you stop punishing yourself."

I wanted to see me happy, too. The problem was that just maybe I didn't know what that looked like.

Lauren ducked into her car and turned over the engine, waving at me through the windshield as she reversed out of her parking spot and peeled out of the parking lot. She was clearly on a mission.

I sighed, digging into my bag to fish out my keys. Just once I wouldn't have minded going home to catch up on some sleep. Jared was with Jason until tomorrow night anyway, but I knew better than to waste this precious time. Instead, I promised myself an early evening with a filthy movie and a tall glass of wine.

It was my first day off after working a five day stretch, which was somewhat unusual for me, and I had a lot of things on my To Do list: Jared was growing like a weed and I needed to get him new pants and shoes.

The grocery shopping wasn't going to do itself, so I wanted to hit the market before lunch to beat the rush I usually dealt with in the evenings.

Again, Old Faithful was due for an oil change, so I'd scheduled an appointment at my regular garage and was bracing myself for a dressing down.

"Well, if it isn't my guardian angel. You been a little scarce lately, Angel."

The voice came from behind me. It was warm and deep and teasing, and I knew who it was even before I turned around because I felt the flutter in my damn ovaries.

"Noah." I knew the smile on my face was huge and stupid, butterfly wings hammering against the insides of my chest. I was going to have a heart attack.

"You know my name." He grinned back a little warily, a carrier tray slammed full of coffee cups in his huge right hand.

Truthfully, I knew a lot more than his name. I knew he was 6'6", his middle name was Charles, and he weighed 285 pounds of solid, delicious muscle. And though his eye color was listed as "brown," they were the most delightfully warm eyes shot with threads of molten caramel. It was a color I'd never seen and it was the magical color that could melt off my underwear.

"Yeah..." I swallowed hard and stepped away from my car. "Some of your other stats, too. Your chart gave away most of your secrets." I was trying hard not to come across as creepy, and failing.

He opened the door and set the carrier tray on the seat before closing it again and rounding the truck. We met in the middle, standing in the empty parking space between our two vehicles.

"Suppose angels don't have much need for eating, do they, Eve?"

I loved the way his voice curled around my name.

Wait...how did he know *my* name?

"Maybe," I said, immediately aware he'd noticed my absence at the supermarket. I felt a furious flush start to creep up my neck.

"You were gettin' too attached, huh?" he teased, stepping a little closer, and as a breeze kicked up, he smoothed my hair behind my ear. He looked a little surprised that he did it too, like he'd had no control over that hand.

Oh, if only you knew, I thought guiltily as electric shocks tingled across my skin, afraid that if he looked too deeply into my eyes he'd see the truth. He'd starred in a few of my fantasies in the long weeks since I'd seen him last, and a few of those fantasies ended somewhere right around me screaming his name. That definitely made me a creep, one who had it bad for a total stranger who probably wasn't half the man I'd made him out to be in my head.

"If I was?" popped out of my mouth before I could stop the flirty comment, and his eyebrows lifted in surprise while the blush crept the rest of the way up my neck and flamed in my cheeks.

"I'd say whoever gets your attention is a lucky man," he said softly and he wasn't smiling anymore, but I wasn't sure why.

Immediately, I felt guilty. I was obsessed with a guy who'd lost his family only six months earlier. I'd been present to witness the immediate fallout from that, and maybe it was officially time I had my head examined.

"So now that I've run into you here, we can safely assume you'll never come back to this coffee shop too, right?" He was teasing, but his voice was gentle and when I looked up, his eyes were completely serious. He absolutely knew I'd been avoiding him.

"How do you know my name?" I finally managed, and he took a step back to lean easily against his truck, the warm smile back on his face. He seemed more at ease with additional space between our bodies.

"Because I called your work and told them I wanted to send something nice to the nurse who'd taken such great care of me."

I hadn't gotten anything--what was he talking about?

"I sent flowers to Lauren, with my number on the card. Her husband responded--sent me a real kick-to-the-balls text." His grin grew wider. "I got the feeling he didn't like another dude sending his woman flowers. Got all jealous and possessive and showed up at my work site in his squad car. I didn't ask how he found me, cuz it's something I would have done too."

I just knew Lauren had benefited from Alex's hot, possessive streak. She liked to push him sometimes.

"I told him I just wanted to thank his wife for her superior care, but I was really interested in finding out more about the redhead who brought me flowers. Wasn't sure at first that I wasn't making things up...like you were an apparition.

"Funny thing was, Alex seemed to know right away who I was talking about. Wouldn't give me your number, though. Seemed a little protective of you."

He pushed off his truck and closed the distance between us in two large steps, leaning over me again so that I could see the golden threads in his beautiful eyes.

"This is me." He held a business card out to me and I took it slowly, noticing my hand shook a little as he pressed it into my palm. "This way you can find me if you decide you wanna do it. Then you can continue avoiding me, or you can call me and I'll find some way to thank you properly for what you did. Seems like I owe you, and I always make good on my debts."

I hadn't done anything. I'd done more than what was expected of me as a nurse, but somehow I felt I'd done less for him than was expected as a human. I'd wanted to help, but I had no way to really do so.

"Things are good," he said slowly, and I realized I couldn't look away. The pull of his eyes was magnetic. "Things are...better. I'm getting help. I've sold the house and bought another." He gestured toward the truck and laughed. "That coffee is for me and the crew I've got in today, helping me get the last of the drywall in. It's been a lot of work--a real project--and I have a long way to go, but it keeps me busy and I've needed that. This way I don't have a lot of time to mope...and end up in hospital beds."

His eyes were boring holes into me and I remembered suddenly that I needed to take a breath, sucking in a long breath through my mouth.

"Okay then," he said softly, in what sounded like a way to extricate himself from the conversation.

He brought up one big hand and curled it under my chin. I thought he might kiss me and I leaned forward a little in anticipation, his face moving slowly toward mine. But when his lips landed, warm and soft on my cheek, disappointment settled in my heart even as a bolt of energy shot straight between my legs.

He didn't say anything more. He just stood there for a moment, and I could feel him looking down at me like he was deciding something.

When I remembered to open my eyes, he released my face and stepped back, rounding his truck again and crawling into the cab.

He waved a small wave as he pulled out of the parking lot and I stood stupidly in the empty space, trying to sort through my thoughts and what had just happened.

The only thing I could think was that I needed to call Lauren. That bitch had been holding out on me.

***

I'd be lying if I said the card wasn't burning a hole in my pocket. I had tucked it into the back pocket of my jeans and my fingers itched to pull it out and dial the number at the bottom. I pulled it out and slapped it on the kitchen counter as I put away groceries, all the cupboard doors hanging wide open.

You're being ridiculous.

You're just bored.

You haven't been attracted to someone like this in a really long time and you could use some fun. He'd probably be a hell of a lot more than just a little fun.

Yeah, I probably was bored. That had to be it. It did nothing to explain the pull I felt, but I wasn't about to examine that in depth right now.

Despite all the groceries, I really didn't feel like cooking and I hit the button to preheat the oven, pulling out one of the frozen pizzas I kept stacked up in the freezer. Then I poured a glass of wine, leaving the bottle uncorked on the counter. Because obviously, I was tired of being responsible. For one night I wanted to get good and silly, eat total crap, and watch something that would sear my retinas, the sex scenes were so steamy. A job for the BBC this was not, but my tolerances weren't much higher than that.

I was appreciating the kitchen table chemistry between Anastasia and Christian when my phone clattered across the countertop in the kitchen. I'd left it there purposely, since I had a bad habit of scrolling through my phone even when the TV was on--in the rare moments I watched it, anyway. *Shit, it's probably Jason again.* I jumped up, almost knocking over the wine glass, since I'd pushed the coffee table way too close to the sofa so I could put my feet on it.

The number didn't pop up as one of my contacts and I waited until it went to voicemail. My motto had always been "If it's important, they'll leave a message." And sure enough, a minute later the phone buzzed again, indicating I had a new voicemail. I unlocked the phone and put it on speaker, steeling myself--calls from unknown numbers were rarely a good thing in my experience.

"Eve...um, it's Noah. I'm not very good at this, so I was kinda hoping you'd call me first, but I'm the guy and Alex told me that's my job. Told me I'm a big pussy." He chuckled, making a high-pitched noise, and blew out a big puff of air. "I don't really know what I'm doing. I just...well, it's easier to explain if I'm talking to you, so give me a call back when you can."

I sat there staring at the phone. What did he want? What did he mean? He'd seemed so eager to get away from me earlier in the day, he'd almost tripped running back to his truck.

Already I'd had more wine than pizza, so I probably wasn't in the best frame of mind to be making any serious decisions. Instead, I did what any rational woman would do: I called my best friend.

"You have two minutes to tell me what's wrong and then I'm hanging up on you." Lauren was out of breath and I winced, looking at the clock, realizing it was getting late.

"You're a nympho," I accused laughingly, because I knew exactly what she was doing.

"There are *very few* people in my life that I will answer the phone for during sex," she told me and I heard a snort in the background that I knew came from Alex. "Ok, the only other one is you, baby, and that's when I need you to talk me through it." She made a kissing noise and I just about gagged.

"Spill it, woman. What's wrong?"

I told her quickly about running into Noah at the coffee shop, about our awkward exchange and how he'd given me his business card. I left out the part about him touching me and causing fireworks to go off in my pants, but I did tell her he'd just left me a voicemail.

"Of course he did," she said matter-of-factly. "I had an epiphany today, right after I came home and jumped my husband."

There was a sound in the background that made me suspicious Alex's patience had run out and he was resuming activities whether Lauren actively participated or not.

She grunted.

"What was this brilliant insight?" I asked, hoping to hurry it out of her before I had to hear her husband moaning.

"I called him and told him that I didn't approve at all, given his situation, but you were never going to make the first move and you had a thing for him."

"Oh, of all things holy--you didn't." I wanted to crawl into the sofa cushions and hide until the world ended. Hopefully that would be soon.

"Well, maybe I wasn't quite that blunt."

Yes, she was.

"I told him that your experiences with men had been largely unsatisfactory and I didn't know why, but you seemed to be drawn to him. And that if he was even a little bit interested, he should give you a call and see where things went."

"Don't meddle, Lauren!" I exclaimed angrily, and there were a few seconds of shocked silence on the other end.

"Evie, you and I both know there's no harm in helping things along. You're just wasting away all by yourself when you should be having the time of your life. What do you stand to lose?"

Everything. The fantasies that get me through the monotonous days and the boring nights.

"Ok girl, I gotta go." Her voice was breathy, and I rolled my eyes.

"Tell Alex it's really rude of him to be doing that while I'm on the phone with you." I was spitballing, pretty sure I was right.

"Trust me, babe," she laughed, and her voice hitched a little. "The last thing I'm thinking about his tongue right now is that it's rude."

I hung up.

I'd spent the night on her living room sofa once, when Jared had been really little and Jason had him for the weekend. The plan had been to go out and get shitfaced, but Lauren had just found out she was pregnant with Blake, so we stayed in and she made virgin margaritas for herself, adding her measure of alcohol to mine. I'd been knocked completely sideways, being a total lightweight, and that was the night I'd learned that Lauren was even more of a psycho hornball when she was pregnant. An absolute zero on the Sneaky scale.

I'd buried my head in the pillows on the sofa to try to muffle the sounds drifting through the house after lights out, because I was not eager to hear *either* of them come.

Again and again, for the love of God.

Taking the phone with me into the living room, I grabbed another slice of pizza and sat chewing it while I debated what to do. The answer, it seemed, was obvious: more wine. Then I couldn't be embarrassed by what came out of my mouth when I called him back, because I was intrigued, which obviously meant I was calling him back.

"Eve, hi." The phone hadn't even rung and it was obvious from the tremor in his voice that he was nervous.

"So, I have to apologize for Lauren," I started, taking another healthy gulp from my rapidly emptying glass. "She likes to stick her nose where it doesn't belong and since *no one* gets it as much as she does, she thinks she's going to be like the Mother Teresa of orgasms and just benevolently hook me up. Because she says everything looks better when you're getting laid." I hiccuped. "Oh no, I did not just say that out loud." *Stupid, stupid wine...I need more.*

His laugh was warm, like he wasn't *exactly* laughing at me. "Oh you sure did, but I bet you didn't mean to. The Mother Teresa of orgasms, huh? Now there's a saint I'd be interested in learning more about. Those things are scarce these days."

"Telling me," I scoffed, and there was no one there to see the wicked blush spreading up my neck, but I could feel it creeping toward my cheeks. This was *not* how the conversation was supposed to go. These were supposed to be my *inside* thoughts.

"My best friend is very...happily...married," I said slowly and I heard him chuckle.

"I've gathered as much."

"I am very happily divorced," I chirped. That felt pretty positive for once.

"I see."

I gave up all pretenses and emptied the rest of the bottle into my glass.

"So, what did you want?" I asked suddenly, and he was quiet for a long moment.

"Your friend called me tonight and told me if I'm interested in you, I have to make the first move. Says you're determined to live your life single and alone, with no one tending to your needs--direct quote."

He didn't sound like he was making fun of me. His tone wasn't all judgy like Lauren's usually was, even though I always forgave her because I loved her. She definitely had my best interests at heart.

"How do you know what my needs are?" I asked, quickly setting down the glass and pushing it far away from myself. I needed to cut myself off *now*, as it clearly gave me a vicious case of verbal diarrhea.

He was quiet again and I waited, remembering that most people are uncomfortable with silence and will rush to fill it with words.

"I *don't* know, and it bothers me I wanna figure it out," he answered finally, and I felt a cold rush of adrenaline leave pins and needles in its wake. "Makes me feel guilty, 'cuz there's this *thing* when I'm around you, and I can't think straight. And I'm...not supposed to feel like this, right? I mean, I see red hair and can't even *breathe,* just hoping for a second that it's you. Fucked if I know why...don't even know you."

I briefly considered letting him in on the fact I routinely fantasized about him, before realizing that was the wine talking and I'd best keep that dirty little tidbit to myself.

"I think it's probably simpler than that," I said, a little disappointed with myself for what was about to come out of my mouth. "I think the broken places in our souls recognize one another and maybe that's the draw."

"Hmm." He sounded thoughtful. "Yeah. Nope, that's not it. Good one, though, Socrates." He pronounced the name like Keanu Reeves in the Bill & Ted movie, which made me giggle.

"Ok, Freud," I teased. "Then what is it?" I ended on a hiccup, and I swear he giggled like a little girl.

"I think it's a lot easier than that--maybe evolutionary," he answered. "More like you're beautiful and kind, and you think I'm big and strong and handsome." There was an infectious silliness in his voice.

"I do?"

Damn straight I did, and I wanted to lick the man like a lollipop, which horrified me.

"Yup." I could hear the smile in his voice. "Look, even just a couple months ago I wouldn't have even *considered* another woman attractive. I didn't want it--don't want it--and I know there's folks who'll tell me it's too soon.

"There's a lot of people who'll be mad at me for deciding to move on, but this whole thing has pretty much turned me into a woman." He snorted. "I'm doin' some work on myself and figure days spent without people you love in your life are just more days lost to what might've been."

"Wow." I swallowed hard. "You just out-philosophized me."

He laughed a delightfully warm, low laugh. "Don't be gettin' used to it.

"Would like to spend some time getting to know you, Eve. You sat by my bedside so I wouldn't be alone, and you didn't know me at all." His voice broke. "I wanna spend some of my awake time not feeling alone, too."

It was raw and honest and I could hear the shards of his heart rattling around in his voice. How could I say no to that? "Ok," I whispered. "Now what?"

He made a sound that made me think he was relieved. "Now I pick you up tomorrow for breakfast. Then if you want, come see the place I bought and I'm renovating. I spend just about every spare minute workin' on it and I wouldn't mind a woman's eye on it to catch the details I'm missing."

So that was it, then. It felt like a flimsy excuse for...something...but I had a breakfast date. I quickly walked the wine glass over to the sink and dumped it out, hardly eager to start the next morning with a hangover.

"Deal," I said, "but only because you're a sweet talker."

"Angel, I'm sweet at *everything*."

I let the pet name slide. He was a confident one once the pressure was off.

"Yeah, well..." I couldn't help it. "I suppose you'll just have to prove that with time." I only half-didn't mean it *that* way.

He laughed a deep, genuine laugh before telling me to be ready by eight, because he'd pick me up.

Lauren, it seemed, had also pre-vetted his plans and thoughtfully provided him with my address. (Freaking fairy of something, all right, and my guess was trouble.)

Immediately after hanging up I rushed to my closet and threw just about everything on my bed. Chances were good I'd end up in a sweater and jeans, but I hadn't had a case of the butterflies like this since...well, maybe never, because Noah Charles Atholton was a giant mountain of manly, walking sex. And damn it, I was here for it.

This time I didn't have to consult with the butterflies in my stomach. There was no question that whatever happened with Noah would blow "nice" right the hell out of the water.

THIRTEEN

Noah
❦

I was nervous.

I didn't sleep well and woke up way too early, cursing the pre-dawn light and the garbage sleeping pills I'd broken down and taken after calling Eve. The pills had guaranteed she had a starring role in my dreams, even if they were a little weird, and when I finally dragged my sorry ass out of bed I tossed the whole damn bottle into the trash.

No kidding, I was in Eve's parking garage by seven-thirty and I felt like an idiot that I was so keyed up, I couldn't even stay away any longer. It was some kind of nervous energy that had me out of the car and pacing around the garage, probably freaking people out.

I was a big guy. Common descriptive words attributed to my appearance were Moose, Monster, Hulk, and Drax. That last one was ridiculous. I did *not* look like the muscle-bound wrestler who played the character, but when one woman shuffling through the garage looked up from her phone and gasped in horror, I wondered if maybe I looked like a hit man stalking my target. (All signs pointed to that one when she dropped her phone and started running the other way. I felt a little bad, once I stopped laughing.)

By a quarter to, I couldn't handle it any longer and I marched into her building, lifting my hand to knock just as her door flew open.

"Holy mother of…" I didn't even know how I'd intended to finish the sentence, because the words just died right there on my lips when I saw her standing there.

Now let me just say, I always thought I had a type: short, curvy brunettes with plenty of ass and sass. But this was a whole new set of expectations. She was solidly 5'10", most of that being long legs and a great backside, as her form-fitting jeans told me. She was much smaller and tighter than I knew what to do with, but damned if I wasn't willing to figure it out.

"I didn't know what to wear." She gestured toward herself, and I grinned. Her dark jeans and fitted navy blue sweater were showcasing her glorious assets and she didn't even know it. She was long and lithe, with the body of a ballet dancer, everything about her taught and small and firm, her glorious hair falling in wide curls down her back.

"You look great," I said, leaning in to kiss her cheek and feeling sparks travel up my nerve endings as my lips touched her cheek. Telegraphing the most inappropriate messages to my dick.

My hand landed near her waist and the cashmere was feather soft against my rough fingers. Shit, now I was gonna spend the whole morning wanting to pet her like a cat. That would really set my pants on fire and I wouldn't be able to get the blaze back under control.

She was quiet all the way out to the car and when I clicked the fob to unlock the sleek black Audi R8, her mouth visibly dropped.

"My brother bought it for me," I rushed to explain. "He's some big, fancy guy in the tech world and he decided my beat up old truck was great for the everyday, but I should also have something reliable--and a little fun." I grinned. The beast had some juice under her hood, which was definitely fun. It was why I'd named her Elizabeth Taylor, after the original hellcat. (Thomas thought it was hilarious and moronic that I'd named the car.)

"I definitely would not have pegged you for an Audi guy," she said hesitantly as I opened Liz's passenger door and helped her in.

"Me neither, but Thom decided it was a little more under the radar than a McLaren. Besides...I don't think I could have fit into one of those. I can barely squeeze into this one." I grinned at her, pushing the button to start the engine. My seat was already pushed back as far as it would go to accommodate my long legs, and I was aware I probably looked like I was about to burst out, like a can of biscuits under pressure.

"The truck would have been fine," she said softly, and I looked at her in surprise. Avery had loved the R8--said my truck was too shabby--and jumped at every chance she got to drive it, though I wouldn't let her drive it to school, considering Lafayette was in a bad part of town. And that was where her beat up little Scion had come in real handy. (It was beat up because she was a shitty driver, if we were being honest.)

"That old girl?" I grinned over at her. "Nah...that big old tank ain't nothin' to take a woman out in."

She shrugged. "You don't have to impress me, Noah."

I was the one who was impressed.

The place I planned to take her to wasn't all that far away and I parked in the lot, hurrying around to open her door and help her out of the car.

"It doesn't look like much," I warned as she took in the yellow and green paint job, "but you won't be hungry for the rest of the day after you eat here."

She smiled at me and my heart skipped a beat. "I know that was meant to be a ringing endorsement, but it *could* be taken the opposite way," she said with a sweet smile.

We were seated quickly and she ordered the Hangtown Fry *and* an extra order of toast and hashbrowns. I looked at her suspiciously, seconding her order, right down to the sides, as I always ordered extra hashbrowns and toast. But where was *she* going to put it all?

"There's no way you can eat all that." I had to say it.

"Watch me," she grinned and, since she was inviting me, I did just that.

I watched her drink four cups of coffee.

I watched her pack away every last bite of her breakfast.

I watched her lips move as she talked, and for the first time in months I felt lighter and happier than I'd felt in a very long time, like maybe my jokes were coming back. It was almost enough to override the guilt churning in my gut.

Almost.

Whether Lauren was truly the Mother Teresa of orgasms--I snorted to myself--I probably wouldn't find out, but I was willing to nominate her for sainthood for paving the way with the beautiful woman sitting across from me.

"So, what do you want?"

Eve's question pulled me up short. I tore my gaze away from her mouth and looked into her bright green eyes.

"What do you mean?" I tripped over the words a little. I hadn't been ready for her to just come to the point.

"I mean why are we here, Noah?" Her question was valid and her voice was gentle. "I'm not jumping to any conclusions, but I think you're suffering from a great deal of guilt, on both sides of this thing." She paused to swipe her napkin across her lips. "I was there when you were in a bad place, and now you're acting like you owe me. And I think you feel guilty, like you're stepping out on the love you still carry around your heart." She bit her lip, tapping her chest, and I shook my head. But before I could respond, she launched into a sentence that made my blood run cold.

"In the interest of full disclosure, let me tell you right now how this is not going to go."

Uh-oh, buckle up, because here it comes.

"I'm a single mother with a ten, almost eleven-year-old boy who doesn't need any more instability in his life.

"I have a job that I enjoy, most days, and I spend entirely too much time there, putting in overtime so I can make up for the fact that my son's deadbeat father stopped even pretending to pay child support when Jared was six.

"My idea of a wild night is folding *two* loads of laundry while having a glass of wine and watching 'Poldark.'" She flattened her lips into a thin line and looked at me like she was waiting for me to say something. Then she tacked on, "I don't do casual, and I'm not stupid enough to think you actually need more friends."

My eyebrows must have disappeared into my hairline. That was a valid assumption, but it was cold.

"Angel," I teased, and her lips flattened even further. "You think that's what I'm here for, an inaugural run with a new girl? Trust me, I'm even less acquainted with casual than you are, I'd be willing to bet."

She fixed me with a stare I'd have called "The All-Seeing Eye." It was the look perfected by my stepmom, Gerry, when she knew I was lying to her. (Which was most of the time.)

"I have a child, Noah. That puts most men off right away. On top of that, I refuse to expose him to things he's too young to learn. He needs to have one stable, responsible parent who's not parading their sexual conquests in front of him." Her words gained heat as she went on. "So I don't have sleepovers.

"I don't have men over to spend the evening with us, having dinner or watching TV.

"I need Jared to know that when I bring a man into the picture, that man is there for *both* of us. For good. And so far..." She held her hands out, palms up.

I shifted uncomfortably. I hadn't actually known about the kid until just now, but she seemed sure the news would chase me off. I had to respect that her standards were high and she was putting it all out there up front, though. She'd probably shot down a crap ton of pointless advances by putting it all out there this way, eliminating time and emotional investment wasted. But there it was, behind her eyes--I could see it. She was terrified of being hurt, and watching her child get hurt was something she'd never forgive.

"Like I said," I cleared my throat and took another long draw of my coffee. "I'm not familiar with casual, but I wouldn't mind having a friend as feisty as you."

Something in her face fell at my use of the f-word, and it wasn't "feisty."

She finished her coffee and the last triangle of toast, then crossed her utensils over her plate and scooted back in the booth.

Whatever hurt I'd seen flash across her face, it was gone now. She'd hidden it away, composing herself while she finished her breakfast, and I wondered if she had a lot of experience doing that: hiding her feelings.

I refused to let her pay the bill and I placed my hand on the small of her back to steer her out to the car. She jolted a little when I first touched her, like she hadn't expected it, but she didn't look at me funny or insist I keep my hands to myself.

"So..." I'd waited to speak until we were all buckled in and I'd turned over the engine.

Liz purred like a mountain lion, all deep and throaty, while she awaited commands from the accelerator, the transmission, the brakes.

Eve turned to face me and it knocked the wind out of me for a second. She had a small smile on her face and something, a premonition maybe, flashed before my eyes: Eve here, with me, her hair blowing in the breeze, laughing as I said something stupid, her hand on my thigh as I drove down the road.

Daggers of guilt speared my conscience immediately, because what the fuck was I doing, imagining something with her when I still belonged to Avery?

"Would you like me to take you home?" I finally managed to spit out, hoping to God the answer was no, despite the guilt rolling in my gut. "Or can I show you my therapy, and what's been totally wiping me out the last few months?"

She didn't say anything, the small smile still on her face, and she nodded.

It made something in my chest tighten and squeeze and I had to swallow hard, because it felt like my heart was coming up my throat. Indigestion from too many greasy hash browns, maybe.

I was proud of the work I'd done on my house. The last several months had been utterly exhausting, mostly in a good way, and when I fell into bed at night I was so wiped out that I didn't spare the time to dream, because it was straight into deep sleep for me.

Paying some of my crew under the table to work nights and weekends had turned an insurmountable task into something a lot more manageable. Most of the dense overgrowth had been scraped, peeled and hacked back. A few new hedges and baby trees were in place and the crumbling old drive had been painstakingly jackhammered up and repoured.

"Oh!" Eve exclaimed as I flipped the blinker and turned into the drive. It made me look at her quickly, unable to keep the proud smile off my face because I knew the house was majestic, backlit by the early morning sun.

The roof was new, the fascia had been replaced, the porch almost completely rebuilt and the siding had been fully swapped out.

I had yet to replace the windows and in a house with thirty-nine windows that was going to be one hell of an expensive undertaking, even if I did manage to get them at cost.

Putting Liz into park, I killed the engine and risked looking over at Eve again. Her eyes were sweeping over the roofline, taking in the leaded glass windows, admiring the fresh new porch. Someone had even planted a row of hydrangea bushes out front--I'd had to look them up once they started flowering, because I didn't have the first clue what they were.

"Noah, this is incredible." She unhooked her seatbelt and climbed out of the car.

From where we stood in the driveway, I could hear noises coming from inside the house. Someone was running a circular saw to make quick cuts, and from an open bedroom window I could hear the squeak of a drywall hoist.

"We did the exterior and the big structural stuff first," I explained, leading her toward the porch and swinging open the front door. "I made a few changes to the layout: knocked down a couple walls and stuff. The drywalling is finished down here." I gestured with one arm toward the living room where Nikolai was on the floor, putting up new base trim. His eyes widened a little and I knew it was on account of the bombshell standing in my entryway, so I did my best to give him a stealthy hairy eyeball.

"Finally," Nikolai laughed, his thick Russian accent revealed with a single word. "You have found woman to make this real home. What you have promised her?"

Eve's cheeks went pink and she looked to me quickly, so I decided to downplay it, sighing: "Nikolai, this is Eve.

"You'll want to steer clear of this one, Angel."

"What, big man?" Nikolai scoffed, quickly setting down the brad nailer. "You are afraid woman is not immune to the charms of Nikolai?"

"He's from North Caucasus," I told Eve. "You know what they say about those guys."

"Big, strong men." Nikolai puffed out his broad chest, grinning at Eve like he was going to win this stupid pissing match.

"I've heard that too." I was feeling just a touch agreeable. "But you know...tiny little dicks." I grinned, holding up and squeezing my fingers together for emphasis.

Eve snorted, turning her head over her shoulder as Nikolai's face crumpled in disbelief. "Who is saying this?" he demanded, shoving off his palms to stand quickly. "I prove them wrong!" His hands were at his belt buckle and I quickly spun Eve in the other direction, calling over my shoulder to Nikolai.

"Keep your pants on, Niki. This lady works in the ER, so she's probably an expert. Don't embarrass yourself with Exhibit D."

That thought sobered me a little: Eve probably really did see dicks all day long. I wasn't sure I liked that, even if it was no business of mine.

"Sorry," I mumbled as she climbed the stairs in front of me, my eyes glued to her ass. It was a miracle I could form coherent sentences. "I like to rile him up because he's such an easy target."

"You aren't serious very often, are you?" she asked over her shoulder. "Probably always the big goofball because it's easy, right? Smoothing the way?"

That felt like an accusation of something not altogether positive. Maybe she was calling me shallow and silly, and I didn't have an answer for her that I liked, so I followed her to the top of the staircase and we stood in the hallway looking down the hallway broken up by bedroom doors.

I *was* always the big goofball. I'd been the class clown, the practical joker, the butt of a few jokes and the creator of many more. I was a good time *all* the time. Avery was the only person who'd ever seen me serious, sad, quiet or down, and that hadn't been often because I'd always felt it was my responsibility to be the life of the party. I considered it my job to make people laugh, and as a result I *knew* a lot of people, but I didn't have many close friends other than my siblings. (I probably didn't trust people enough to let them get that close.) It was easier to just be the overgrown dumbass everyone could count on for a laugh.

"Probably," I said, and she slipped her arm through mine and leaned in close, her side pressed up against mine. It was enough to freeze me in place, and I looked down my shoulder at her. She was tall, but I was still quite a bit bigger than her. She couldn't have been more than a buck thirty or so, and for the briefest second I wondered what she would do if I turned just a little and wrapped my arms around her.

Would she melt into my arms the way Avery had?

Would she disappear into them, dwarfed by me?

An intense ache clawed at my trachea, because I kind of wanted to find out.

I still missed Avery so much; the loneliness was eating at me and the need to feel a woman's touch, something as simple as a hug, was turning me inside out.

"Who's there to lift you up when you get tired of carrying the burden by yourself?" she asked, and I knew we were talking about more than the face I put on for the world. I tried to plaster on a smile but her words cut deep, like she saw right through me and was calling me on my shit. *Fuck me.* I sucked in a big breath, 'cuz my eyes felt dangerously prickly.

Her fingers trailed down my left arm, her thumb rubbing gently back and forth across the pink scar on my wrist. "I've seen sorrow before," she said, her voice low. "I see it every day, and God knows I've lived enough of it that even if the rest of my life was sunshine and rainbows, it wouldn't erase the painful memories." She paused, lifting my wrist to her lips and placing a soft kiss over the scar.

My heart and my dick jumped at the same time and I shifted a little uncomfortably, completely freaked out by my reaction to her, hoping she wouldn't notice.

"You two gonna get your fuck on in the hallway, or you gonna come see another fine job?" A voice bellowed out of one of the bedrooms at the end of the hallway and I let my head drop, my right hand coming up to cover my eyes in shame. Because of all the guys from my crew, I had two of the most insensitive assholes under my roof today.

Eve raised her eyebrow at me, her lips quirking. "Well?" Her voice was soft and teasing. "What'll it be?"

For the first time in months, I was sorely tempted. The guilt wasn't any less, but I desperately wanted to back her up against the wall and find out what those soft pink lips really tasted like. Because this was more than fantasy. This was in the flesh, a potentially willing, engaging party.

I stepped back quickly, lowering my gaze before she could see the shame in my eyes. *Twenty-two fucking years, Atholton. You were with Avery for twenty-two years and now you're going to throw her memory over after just a few months, for someone you don't even know?*

I could have sworn the voice in my head sounded like her sister. That bitch had never liked me, not even for a minute, not even when I was fourteen and she was ten. As far as she was concerned, I still had boy cooties.

Not surprisingly, Amanda's girlfriend shared her suspicion, their hatred of me intensified because somehow Amanda blamed me for Avery's death.

Eve removed herself from my side, letting my hand fall, and she didn't touch me again. Instead, she followed me from one room to the next as I talked her through progress while most of my guys did their best to hit on her, to brag about their prowess, professional and otherwise. Even some of the married ones.

Pissed me right off.

It was just before noon when I drove her back to her place and though I suggested lunch, she politely declined. I needed some quiet time, she told me. I needed to go back to my house and kick the crew out; maybe spend the day painting or whatever else it was that brought me calm.

It was like she'd crawled right inside my head and saw all the broken parts I had rattling around in there, and I did go home and tell the guys they could head out early.

Nikolai was still mad at me, still willing to disprove my joking theory about North Caucasus men. I told him I'd only been teasing to ruffle his feathers, but he didn't understand the saying and he left muttering something under his breath about turkeys and feathers. I suspected it might be a vicious Russian curse.

Maybe it was an odd choice, but I started painting the smallest room, the one nearest the master bedroom. Maybe at one time it had been a closet or a dressing room, but in my mind I could see it as a sweet, cozy little nursery where a baby slept only steps away from his or her mother. I painted it a very soft lavender color because I don't know what came over me, but the instant I set foot in that room I'd envisioned pale purple walls and a white bassinet. It seemed a sort of premonition, and I wasn't one to argue when Fate presented her demands.

When I finished painting the room, which was quickly since it was so small, I sank to the floor and sat looking around. My eyes burned and my heart was heavy, and I knew then that the room was for the daughter I'd lost.

There was no one in my house but me. I didn't need to crack a joke or put on a brave face. So I folded my knees up to my chest and let the hurt run down my face.

FOURTEEN

Eve

◄╫►

Noah's brokenness was visceral, a pain sharper than stepping on Legos in the middle of the night with bare feet: sudden and stabbing, the message relayed frantically to the brain in frantic, white-hot bursts.

He didn't call or text me that night, and I wisely put my phone in the refrigerator, just to keep myself from texting to make sure he was ok. Because the man had *Damaged Goods* practically stamped across his forehead and I didn't need the complication. Today had shown me just how complicated it would be, because he was still bleeding from a wound that hadn't closed.

Noah still ached for Avery and his unborn daughter, and I didn't blame him at all. I mean, I was a little jealous, but it was unfair of me. I knew what grief was and how long it took to sort. To impose a time limit was the mark of a fool.

Something about his brokenness called to me and that was terrifying. I stupidly confessed it all to Lauren that afternoon, not long before Jared was due to arrive home, and for the first time since I could remember she kept her mouth shut and just listened. She let me vent, and I went on and on about shitty timing and bad circumstances and...well, I may have mentioned that I'd been burning through an obscene number of batteries lately. It made her squeak a little and I knew she was laughing, because she knew I was cycling through the offensive goodies in her gift basket. But what could I say? Noah was gorgeous and sexy and it had been a long time--a really, really, *really* long time. In fact, my dry spell had gone on for so long, my son had been in diapers the last time I'd had sex with another human being.

Well, that was sobering, especially when we considered Jared was already in the fifth grade.

"I'd throw Alex your way," Lauren's chuckle was low and throaty, "but I couldn't share that magic for love or money. There's just no way. Besides, once you go old school Italian, you won't ever go for anything else. He's ruined me with his magic..." I snorted to cut her off.

There was a noise from the front door and I knew Jared was back, so I told Lauren I would text her later and I shoved my phone under my pillow to pretend I couldn't check on Noah.

His business was none of mine.

Not my place.

The man was hurt and angry and despairing and confused, and I knew it had been a mistake on his part to ask me to breakfast. He may have implied he was looking for a friend, but I'd caught a glimpse of what happened when I kissed his wrist in the hallway--a stupid move on my part--and I knew he wasn't ready for that. Physically, maybe, but his heart was still in pieces.

I was ready for the physical pull, though. His reaction to me kissing his scar told me he was a big man all over, and I'd entertained visions of him stretched over me, his huge body covering mine. Would he be rough and angry and demanding, or gentle and sweet and loving? I shivered, imagining both delicious options. I wanted both.

I reminded myself that most men have an easier time separating sex from emotion, but I had a feeling Noah wasn't one of those men. Not if he'd been with his girlfriend for even half as long as I suspected.

No, Noah was loyal through and through. He was the labrador retriever of men: loyal, loving, sweet, accepting, with a thick layer of goofiness. The layer that hid the black hole of need in his chest. The one that wanted to scream "Love me and I'll be yours forever." Because that was exactly the vibe I'd picked up from him today, the one that told me he was a serial monogamist.

I didn't know many of those: serial monogamists. In fact, other than Lauren and Alex, and maybe my brother and his wife, I didn't know anyone else who had honed in on "The One" and stuck joyfully and purposefully to those narrow parameters over the years. I suspected though, with some concern, that I might be one too, and that was really damned inconvenient.

Jared was all smiles. He dropped his bag in the living room and I met him halfway into the hallway, where he threw his arms around me and told me he'd had a great time with his dad, but that he'd missed me. I kept quiet, as I'd missed him terribly but I was afraid I'd say something negative about Jason accidentally. Jared had been really sensitive lately about the things I had to say about Jason, even though I was always cautious.

The two of us had pizza again that night and we watched one of Jared's favorite movies before I sent him off to shower before bed.

I'd finally given up and fished out my phone, which buzzed with a text at 9:45, long after Jared was in bed and long after I *should* have been in bed.

Thank you for spending time with me today, I know you don't have a lot of extra.

It was nice to feel normal again for a while, so thanks. It's dumb, but I don't feel like I gotta be so "on" with you, cuz you don't expect it. So...thanks, friend.

I made a face at that last word.

If I was even a little honest with myself, I'd made up a man inside of my head and foisted the image upon Noah. This imaginary man was similarly built like a tank, thank you very much. He was seriously tall and muscular, his thighs probably the size of my torso.

And his hair? That was where fantasy bled into reality, because the guy in my head was *definitely* Noah. The man had thick, dark waves that, if he let grow out any longer, would make me call him Absolom after the Biblical character. He was a character study my strict Methodist mother always used to make her point: *Beautiful men cannot be trusted, sweetheart. They are vain and selfish.* Probably why she married my very plain, redheaded Irish father and nagged him to the end, God rest his unfortunate soul.

It would be unfortunate if I had the same effect on Noah as he had on me, because his fantasies couldn't be nearly as pretty. I took after my Dad in the looks department, so nothing particularly special. He'd been tall and thin, his hair tending more toward a rust color, his eyes such a bright shade of green they didn't look real.

For whatever reason my dark haired, beautiful German mother found him irresistible and followed him to the dockyards of Bayonne, New Jersey, where they lived for nineteen years, until...well, you know.

This man I'd made up...he shared a lot of characteristics with the father I'd had in my life for too short a time: gregarious, silly, big hearted, warm, a tender soul, loyal to a fault, a man with a solid work ethic and a kind word for everyone.

What worried me a little was that Noah was proving to be *all* of those things. Checking every box. The trouble was, he tried to profess himself ready to move on, but I knew without a doubt that he wasn't anywhere close. Perhaps I had come into his life at the wrong time, and wouldn't that just suck?

What had come over me today? Why had I kissed the scar on his wrist? Was it to comfort him, or to comfort myself? Because I could feel his sadness, rising around us like the tide, ready to suck us back into a sea of grief and remorse. And I couldn't go there with him--not yet. I wasn't strong enough for him to lean on, of that I was certain, and with the uncertainty I knew he was experiencing, he needed someone stronger than myself to hold him upright.

What scared me most was that of the things I'd imagined about him-- the things he'd let me see--he was *more*. He had a deep appreciation for beauty and effort and perfection, with a protective streak a mile wide, a little shy and a lot insecure, since he'd been completely unmoored.

He was someone who would love with his whole heart, of that I had no question.

He had dropped me off awkwardly, asking if he could text or call sometime, and I'd tried to remain somewhat noncommittal.

But here he was, texting me--not so late at night as to be obscene, but late enough to make me wonder if I was going to learn some deep, dark, maybe drunken secret.

So I don't get any jokes? I texted back, feeling just a little guilty because I didn't want to push him into feeling like he needed to be "on" near me either.

I don't think you like jokes. His response was almost immediate.

I sat there staring at the screen for a moment, unsure of how to respond. He was right, I didn't have much of a sense of humor these days--it had been beaten out of me over the years.

Setting my phone facedown on the nightstand, I moved to the bathroom to brush my teeth and wash my face. I needed a moment to think about what I wanted from this man, because though it was obvious he wasn't ready for me, I was pretty sure he was trying to take baby steps toward something he thought might be healing.

It occurred to me briefly, as I brushed my teeth, that he was the sort to make everyone laugh, but he didn't speak of any close friends other than a brother and a sister. That was surprising to me, since according to Lauren he'd been with his girlfriend for decades. Maybe there wasn't much room in his heart for others, because he was the sort who kept a select few and held them close.

Men like him, I knew, were rare. I wondered if that was why I'd been so drawn to him from the beginning, because my heart recognized something in him that it craved but had never found in another human before. That made me feel guilty, I thought as I spit into the sink. It was unfair to expect him to fix anything in me that was broken, damaged, cracked or bruised. That wasn't his job, it was mine, and I hadn't been seeing to it.

It made me feel terribly guilty, to envision him as I crawled into my bed, imagining him in the yawning, cold spot next to me. *What was my deal?* And still I ignored my phone, hoping to shut out the reality for a minute with the fantasy. But something deep inside could envision his warm, sleepy smile, his arms held open to me as I crawled in and scooted to him.

123

The problem, I thought sleepily as I tried to talk myself out of it, was that I was all wrong for him. I was shy and quiet.

Too tall.

Too boyishly built, with my small butt and smaller chest.

Too redheaded.

Too much of everything the woman he'd been with for decades *wasn't*.

I was a poor substitute at best and just a sad, lonely, neglected single mom with an ugly past when it really came down to it. There was no way he'd want to step into the role my life required.

How could someone parent a child who wasn't their own?

How could he look at me each day as something better than what had been in his life before?

When I woke the next morning, the alarm on my phone making it clatter across my nightstand, I wasn't exactly surprised to find there were no more texts from Noah. He had to be scared, I thought, at least as much as me. He had even less experience with dating, with flirting, than I did and I couldn't decide whether that was a good thing.

Considering the obituary Lauren had forwarded to me--and I was still mad at her for that--he had been with Avery since they'd met in high school. They'd moved in together when they were of legal age and they bought a house together at twenty. If that wasn't pragmatism and "forever" all wrapped up with a nice, neat bow, I didn't know what was.

Jason and I had never owned a house together, but in hindsight perhaps that had been a blessing, since it meant there was less to argue about. Since he was in the service, we were in military housing for the duration of our relationship. In fact, the condo had been my first purchase. *My* purchase. The first big thing I bought on my own. The home that I chose, and painted, and decorated...Jared and I had been here for the last four years, as I'd purchased it just after starting my job at the hospital. Up until that point, after moving out of military housing, Jared and I had been living in apartments of questionable safety, sanitation, and honestly, some of the spaces were not even legal apartments.

I wanted to hate Jason for the turmoil he'd put us through. The upheaval had been tremendous, until I'd been able to afford the downpayment on the condo, and though Jared could remember hardship and gunfire late at night, and cockroaches sneaking in from the neighbor's apartment, he still seemed surprisingly well adjusted for a kid who'd seen more than he should have at this point in his life.

The guilt I felt was incredible. Sometimes, in fact, it was crippling. I'd have replaced his memories of childhood with idyllic farm scenes, swinging in the park or walking along the beach in a heartbeat. But at the time I'd done the best I could, even if it had been barely enough to keep our spirits united with our bodies.

Not that Jason had helped at all. He'd been sent on a covert mission to Egypt during the Arab Spring--something I would learn only much, much later--and when he returned, he was ready to end our marriage.

It took me a while to deduce that I'd been thrown over for a woman in his unit, one with dark hair and a short, stocky build. But that didn't last long, as none of the rotating cast had.

In the meantime, our divorce played out in the courts for months because he couldn't begin to understand why he should help support the son who still needed diapers and three decent meals daily, a roof over his head and clothing. His reasoning was that since I'd been the one to file, it absolved him of any responsibility.

That was when I'd vowed to myself that I would never be dependent upon a man. Not again. I'd let myself slip into complacency while he'd been overseas, away on one mission or another.

Having learned the hard way that men couldn't be trusted, I knew I was an idiot to even consider that Noah was the sort who just might break this rule for me. He was a fantasy, someone who might be a positive male role model for my son while being someone who was a really good distraction when I couldn't fall asleep at night.

I freaked out after chasing the thoughts around my own head all day long. By then it was late and the last person I needed to text was Noah, so I texted Lauren.

Since Alex worked early shifts and Lauren's suffered from perpetual TMI, I knew her husband liked very early morning sex. In fact, she was probably playing Hide the Magic Wand right now and I wasn't at all worried about waking her.

Lauren, I think I like him more than he likes me. I think he wants to be my friend because he doesn't know what to do with me. He's...lonely.

It took a long time for the bouncing dots to show up, which proved that she'd either been sleeping, or...well, you know.

Of course he's lonely. Do you think it matters why? If I were you I'd capitalize on that loneliness. He appears to be a very *capable* man, if you know what I mean. A real man, and it's about damn time you found one of those.

I rolled my eyes. It was typical of Lauren to go straight for the sex.

I need someone who's capable outside of my bed too, and I'm not interested in holding auditions and subjecting Jared to a parade of manwhores.

I was lonely too, but it wasn't the same thing. I wasn't trying to get over losing the love of my life to a tragic accident.

Love of his life. A cold rush of adrenaline washed over me at the thought, because I wasn't ready or willing to be anyone's second choice.

Lauren didn't respond and I knew what that meant: she was otherwise occupied, and probably not with one of the kids.

So I tucked my phone in my pocket and got ready for work.

***

The days blurred together, and it was Thursday before I'd even determined which end was up. Jared was out of school for the summer in just a few short weeks and I'd have to change up my morning routine a little, so I'd scheduled him for a summer day camp since Maggie wouldn't be available for much longer. She had graduated in April and had already been offered a job at a private school in Utah and damn, I was going to miss her. She made my life easier and she filled it with laughter when she joined me for our Friday night bitch fests.

I grabbed the overstuffed bag from my locker and changed quickly into clean clothes, putting my dirty scrubs into a plastic bag to tuck back in, to take home and wash. Then I fished out my keys and my phone, retrieved my empty lunch bag from the other hook, and headed out to the parking lot.

There was a text from Noah. The man had left me alone--had been completely radio silent--all week. It had bothered me, though I knew I'd been the one to initiate the silence. I hadn't even answered his last text, and my heartbeat picked up a little faster as I unlocked the screen.

I asked my German friend if he knew the square root of eighty-one. He said no.

What the hell? I thought about it for a second, then snorted and texted him back, because I couldn't help it.

That was a horrible Dad joke.

The bubbles bounced up immediately and I wondered if he'd been waiting all day on my response.

I've got Dad jokes for days, Angel. Besides, you wanted jokes.

That wasn't the reason I hadn't answered his last text and we both knew it, but he was letting me off the hook. I thought for a moment before responding.

Angel?

He'd been calling me that for a while, and suddenly it was all I could focus on.

Yup, it's what I'm calling you because you watched over me when I had no one.

I wondered how hard it had been for him to type that, and I sucked in my breath at the admission. There was nothing silly or funny about that, only raw, painful honesty.

There was no response coming to mind. The admission had reached inside and stolen all my words, and I sat there in my hot car for another moment, staring at the screen. I wasn't going to ghost him again, but I didn't know what to say back.

The phone buzzed in my hand and I turned over the engine and cracked open a window.

"Ms. Ryan?"

I hadn't looked at the screen before answering and the female voice took me by surprise, as I knew I'd been hoping it was Noah.

"Yes," I responded, and I heard Jared's voice in the background.

"It's ok." He sounded far away. "You really don't have to call my mom."

"This is Adrienne Thomas; I'm the vice principal here at Madison Elementary. Would it be possible to come pick up your son this afternoon? I'd like to discuss something with you."

Uh-oh, I didn't like the sound of this. Jared was never in trouble--not ever. He was quiet and shy, maybe not the best student out of all of them, but he typically stayed on task and minded his own business.

I'd been planning to pick Jared up anyway, but I gave the Camry a little extra push and parked in the lot just a few minutes before the final bell rang.

The administrative offices were right up at the front of the school and I was buzzed in immediately, the secretary's expression sympathetic, which was when I knew that I was really in for it.

I could see Jared from where I stood, his back to me, his head visible in the glass window that looked out from the vice principal's office and into the waiting area.

"Ms. Ryan." The woman holding open the door to the office had a voice that could freeze water on a hot day. "If you would be so kind."

My heart hammered in my chest and I was transported to the days of my youth, when I'd seen the inside of the principal's office many, many times.

After losing my parents and being separated from my brother, I'd gone from being a dedicated, straight-A student to being a troublemaker. I was the girl who wore ripped, baggy clothes and too much eyeliner.

The one who rarely brushed her hair and had scary jewelry. It kept people at an arm's length, and that way no one knew I wasn't getting enough food to eat.

They didn't know I was sometimes locked in my room at night, or that in one foster home, the husband had tried to get a little too friendly. When that became a problem I'd packed the few things I had and headed to a nearby church that I knew ran a small women's shelter.

CPS found me three weeks later, at school, and when I told them why I'd run away the social worker hadn't taken me seriously. She'd given me a dubious look, in my grungy clothes and tangled hair, and told me I shouldn't make things up to get good people into trouble.

Jim was not a good person, I told her, but she'd shaken her head at me and told me to go back "home" without noting a damn thing in my file.

I didn't. I stayed at the shelter and prayed my eighteenth birthday would come faster.

The church pastor gave me a job under the table and I cleaned and helped with the cooking for the rest of the summer, saving up enough that I thought I could move to Washington, where my grandparents lived.

Something I hadn't even considered when my grandparents hadn't stepped in to rescue my brother and me from the foster system, was that maybe it was because they didn't want us. That was confirmed when I arrived at the Greyhound station early that fall and called them collect.

"Ms. Ryan?" The woman was staring at me expectantly and it shook me from my awful reverie.

"Uh, sorry…" I giggled nervously and Jared's head swung toward me, his eyes wide and worried. There were so many things I would never tell him. "I guess I was reliving the mistakes of my youth." I gave her a smile that she didn't return. "I spent a lot of time in the principal's office in high school."

"I am the vice principal." Her lips flattened, and I sighed. This one was a stickler with no sense of humor, but weren't they all?

Settling into the chair next to Jared, I took his small hand and waited for the woman to launch into whatever it was that had necessitated this emergency meeting. She waited for a beat, the school bell reverberating throughout the building, and the halls were filled with shrieks and excited chatter as children escaped the confines of the squat building.

"I'm afraid this young man was involved in a bit of a verbal...shall we call it 'altercation,' earlier today," she began, fiddling with a pencil on the desk in front of her. "It seems," she said, even as I turned to look at Jared, "that he was involved in a disagreement with one of the young ladies in his classroom. They've been completing the unit on puberty this week, as I'm sure you know."

Oh, did I ever know. I'd received at least thirteen emails on the matter, and Jared's teacher had called me personally to make sure I didn't want to opt out. (Of course I didn't want to opt out. Why would I put that target on my kid's back? Besides, he had to learn this stuff at some point.)

"I'm aware," I said cautiously, and Jared's hand curled up into a fist inside my own.

"According to their teacher, one of the girls asked a question about reproduction and this young man had an opinion he felt needed to be shared."

My eyes narrowed.

"I do not believe the words need to be repeated," she said, clearing her throat and she swiveled a piece of paper toward me--something that appeared to be an official report, and I knew it was something that would go into his student file. On it, there were some ugly words:

"When Samantha asked about the reproductive rights of women, Jared interrupted that 'Everyone knows women are are only good for cooking and fucking.'"

Oh. My. Sweet Baby Jesus.

My eyes went wide as I stared down at the paper and I realized it was a report quickly compiled by his teacher.

"Where did you pick up that idea? And that *word*?" I whispered to him, but he wouldn't meet my eyes. It was a rhetorical question and we both knew the answer. It wasn't hard to guess what Jason had been filling his head with lately, under the guise of "male bonding."

"I'm sorry." I addressed the woman with a shamefaced expression, the color already bright and hot in my cheeks. "I'm afraid there's been a little more negative influence in his life of late. His father and I are adjusting to some new challenges."

Jared's expression became wild and he jumped up from his chair. "You don't get to talk about my dad that way!" He was standing in front of me, suddenly shaking with rage and I swallowed hard. This wasn't my son.

"Honey, go sit in the main office for a minute while I speak with Ms. Thomas. There are a few things that need to be explained."

He stood there with arms folded across his chest, glaring at me in a way I didn't like.

"Jared," I said, my voice lowering with more authority than I felt. "Now."

He huffed, grabbing his backpack and shutting the door hard on his way out.

"I'm sorry," I said once I heard the latch click. "It would seem he's been obtaining an alternate education during the weekends he's allowed to visit his father." I passed a hand over my tired eyes and I thought I saw the woman's expression soften just a little.

"His father's been more...ah, strenuously observing his visitations and there haven't really been any problems--not of this magnitude--until now. I'm sorry to say that I didn't know his head was being filled with such offensive things and I will discuss it with my lawyer and my son. He knows he's not allowed to speak that way."

"This will go into his permanent file, I'm afraid," she said, her tone only marginally warmer. "I would like to think it is an isolated incident, but there has been an emerging pattern. Prior, slighter infractions."

My head snapped up, because Jared's teacher hadn't spoken to me even once.

"I fear you will see more of this if the home environment differs greatly from what he experiences when he is with his father," she continued, and her voice softened a little. "It is difficult for children to understand, and they often take out their frustrations on the undeserving."

Yeah, I knew a few things about that.

"It may be helpful to seek a counselor for him," she suggested. "I will arrange for him to meet with the guidance counselor each day, for the few weeks of school remaining. However, it may be helpful to find him a professional he can meet with over the summer. This is surely a difficult adjustment for him."

That wasn't the half of it.

I pushed myself to my feet as the words ran through my head, shaking her hand and thanking her for her time. I was seriously disappointed with myself, with Jared, and livid with Jason, but I had the presence of mind to snap a photo of the report, which I would fire off to Daniel later that evening.

Couldn't wait for that strained interaction. Ugh.

"Wanna talk about it?" I asked as we pulled out of the parking lot. Honestly, the last thing I wanted to do was talk about it, but I really didn't need this happening again.

"No." His expression was sullen as he stared out the window, arms crossed over his seatbelt.

"You know why that wasn't ok, right?" I asked, flipping the blinker and turning quickly out into traffic.

"Why does it have to be ok?" he asked angrily, puffing a breath out of his nostrils. "It's true."

"Is that what you think of me?" I asked, a little more sharply than I'd have liked. It was hard to keep my Irish temper and salty streak under control. It had been a real challenge for the past ten years, because I could curse a blue streak without even putting my mind to it.

I could see his shocked expression in the mirror, and then his face cracked into a small grin. "Don't be stupid, Mom."

"Do you?" I asked, the fingers of my left hand going white as I choked the life out of the steering wheel.

"No. You're just...you're Mom. You can't be a...you're not one of those." His voice was defensive suddenly.

Interesting.

"Ok, so tell me what you mean by 'one of those,' please."

I knew what was coming.

"You know..." He sounded plaintive, like he *really* didn't want to give me the definition.

"Apparently I don't," I said, coming to a stop at a red light.

"The desperate b-bitches." His voice dropped just a little with shame and I nodded for him to go on.

"Dad says they're the ones who wanna have babies because they just want your money, so you gotta get them to cook and clean, cuz they're not worth anything else."

"Is that what you think about girls?" I asked, sure my face had just gone even whiter than usual. Jason had just come running full tilt out of my son's mouth.

"The stupid ones, and they're *all* stupid," he said under his breath and I almost had to pull the car to the side of the road.

I drew in a deep breath. Something smelled like burning rubber. Maybe it was the car, or maybe it was my patience.

"The only stupid people in this world are the people who treat others like they are less," I finally said, trying and probably failing to keep the fury out of my voice. "There are a lot of people who are willing to put up with it because they've been told their whole lives that they don't deserve anything better. But how would that make you feel?"

He sat quietly for a moment. "How would what make me feel?"

"If someone told you that you weren't worth anything to them. That you were only good enough to make their food or wash their laundry, but you weren't important enough to them to be treated like you were a whole person with ideas and dreams."

"I suppose I'd be mad," he conceded finally, and I pulled into the parking spot in the garage and killed the engine.

We sat for a moment and I could see he was chewing on something difficult.

"Your dad has seen some terrible things in his life," I said finally, catching Jared's eye in the rearview mirror. "It's messed him up in a lot of ways. And I don't think he'll ever be happy, because he's never going to get the help he needs. He's been to a lot of countries where women and children were treated like dogs, and it changed him in bad ways."

133

I didn't know what else to say, and I was really tired of making excuses for him, because Jason's problem with women had been an issue long before the first time he shipped out. He'd learned from the best, a hateful, abusive father and a weak, battered mother who refused to leave. I certainly didn't believe there was any redemption for him. He'd been a difficult human before he'd been deployed, but he'd been returned to me in pieces.

***

It wasn't until I had tucked Jared into bed and was folding a basket of laundry that I remembered I had never texted Noah back. This new issue I was dealing with, however, did not seem like a job for him.

In a moment of anger and weakness, I called Jason.

"Babe." His voice was full of confidence. "You finally get tired of hanging out with that pencil dick lawyer of yours and come looking for a real man?"

"Watch yourself, buddy," I snarled. Even as the words came out of my mouth I knew I needed to keep a leash on the words I really wanted to say to him. There was a reason all my correspondence with him was conducted through lawyers. "Today I had a meeting with the vice principal at our son's school, who told me our child has been running his mouth at school. Saying offensive things, like that women are only good for cooking and fucking."

There was a low laugh in the background and I became aware of a low, thumping bass beat as I realized Jason had me on speaker. Of course he did. He was partying on a Tuesday night, not a care in the world.

"That's my boy."

"That's not going to be your boy for much longer if the school calls in CPS, Jason. And if it comes to that, rest assured I *will* get full custody."

There was another chuckle in the background and I heard someone mutter something about a bitch getting her panties in a twist and needing a hard fuck.

"No woman with half a brain or any sense of self worth would fuck any of you losers," I announced angrily and after a burst of laughter I heard Jason swallow something before responding.

"Guess you're one of those women, babe, because you fucked me more than once. Didn't seem real upset about it then."

"Once was enough," I retorted. "And if I hadn't faked it I would have ended up with a concussion, Colonel Jackrabbit."

There was an explosion of sound, hoots and hollers, and after a derisive noise from Jason the line went dead.

Lauren would be off work in another two hours, and I knew I wouldn't be sleeping well, Jared's words still bouncing around the inside of my head. So I texted her to call me from her car while on her way home from work.

When the phone rang it was nearly midnight and I looked up quickly from my laptop, my eyes crossing from the strain. I'd been researching therapists within my healthcare network and I'd fired off an email to Daniel that he'd answered almost immediately, a little too eagerly for my taste.

I knew I should have found another lawyer, because going forward with Daniel was going to prove difficult considering our brief personal history, even if it helped that he'd been with us through the whole ordeal with the court system.

Like everything else, it was just one more item on my ever-expanding list: the list I couldn't cross things off quickly enough, so I just kept carrying them over to the next day's column. It was the shittiest kind of accounting in the history of ever, and I was eternally in the red.

Lauren listened sympathetically as I relayed the day's events, uncharacteristically quiet for someone who always had advice and something to say. But she kept her opinions to herself, occasionally offering sympathetic sounds or verbal nods that told me to continue. And by the time I got to the end of my story, she blew out the huge breath I felt had been trapped in my lungs all afternoon.

"Wow, girl. Shit. I mean...I guess maybe we expected this was going to happen sooner, but I thought we'd get some warning signs. This is...it's pretty extreme. You think it'll get worse from here?"

Of course I thought it was going to get worse. Jared's attitude always took a couple days to fully iron out after visiting Jason, and that was why I'd fired off an email to Daniel, requesting he put a copy of the report into our file. It was concrete evidence to use against Jason, but now the question was whether I drag him into court, or let a few more of these situations pile up to make it a sure thing.

The problem was that I had no idea what would come out of Jared's mouth next, or when things would escalate. His attitude seemed to be spiraling lately and the last thing I needed was to receive a letter from the county saying that he wasn't welcome to the sixth grade in any of the middle schools he was zoned to attend.

Jason had picked the worst possible time to decide he wanted to be involved in Jared's life. Jared was just starting to show signs of going through puberty, his need for showers eclipsing his desire for them, and I just about had to tackle him and apply his deodorant myself each morning. So on top of massive hormonal shifts, now Jason was screwing with our routine and with my established methods of discipline, and I freaking hated it.

"You working this weekend?" Lauren asked, knowing full well I was. I had already asked her if I could drop Jared off with her both days, since Maggie was already gone.

"Alex has Saturday off," she said, "and I would never presume to make parental decisions for you, but maybe it would help if I had him talk to Jared? I mean, you know, being a positive male role model and all...one man to another?"

She was right, and I'd been hoping she'd offer just that--I was pretty sure she just *knew*.

"Thanks, babe," I said with a sigh. "I'm sure he'll be more receptive to life advice from Alex than he is from me."

Lauren was really quiet for a minute and I heard her blinker flip on. Then, "Not to make you all suspicious and ask weird questions, but...you're keeping tabs on what Jared does online, right?"

Some kind of spidey sense prickled into awareness in the back of my mind. Jason had given him a tablet for Christmas last year and I'd put some serious parental locks on it, but I hadn't checked his browser history for a couple weeks now just to make sure nothing new and weird was slipping through. Things had just been too hectic. Considering what had happened at school, I needed to get back on the parenting wagon.

"And what about that beautiful mess you've been seeing?"

Lauren totally distracted me, and a vision of the giant man that I wanted to scale like a mountain made me close my eyes in shame.

"Noah? You know I'm not seeing him. I had breakfast with him once, and he took me to see the progress he's made on the huge house he bought on Sunset Drive."

She whistled low. "Fancy. That's a nice area."

"It will be fancy," I agreed, "and it *is* a nice area. He picked up a monster foreclosure and I think he's using it to fill his time. It's good therapy for him, maybe."

"Is this where you come in?" Her voice was teasing. "Redheaded Cinderella is going to fill his shiny new castle with babies?"

I snorted. Loudly. "Whatever. Not all of us want to raise the next Italian soccer team."

"Calcio," she warned with a surprisingly accurate Italian accent. "Get it right, woman, or I'll tell my husband and then you're really in it deep. He'll cut off your access to Nonna's limoncello, and then you're really screwed."

"I'm serious," I told her. "I don't think Noah's interested in me the way you think." *Or the way I want him to be.* Admitting that to myself was a little disappointing. "He's been calling me 'Angel,' and when I called him on it he said it was there because I was there to watch out for him when he had no one. I kind of think that's it. Like he feels that he owes me, or he needs a friend, or..." I trailed off. "Who knows. But he clearly doesn't know what to do with me."

"No." There was laughter in her voice. "I promise you the last thing that man wants is for you to be his friend." She sighed. "Oh, I miss those days...and I guarantee you that he's going to figure it out soon. It will definitely involve freaky, but not freaked out." She let a little fart of a laugh slip out.

I could hear her garage door whirring closed behind her and I knew if she wasn't inside soon, Alex would come looking for her. He was wildly protective of her, all five feet, two inches, one hundred and ten pounds of energy and fire that she packed into her little body. Not that he should have worried, because she was a deadly weapon. The woman should have come with a warning label.

"Thanks for listening," I said quietly. She knew there was no one else I'd call and I reminded her often that it had been divine intervention that placed us in the same nursing courses. We'd been friends for the last ten years, during which time both of us had seen some serious shit.

She promised to text me in the morning and I let her go just as I heard Alex in the background. "Babe, what's taking you so long?"

What would it be like to have a hot Italian husband who couldn't keep his hands off me?

Hell, I'd settle for a kind man who didn't mind the sight of me.

It wasn't hard to admit I was jealous of my best friend for discovering the love of her life; the man who couldn't get enough of her kind of crazy. Anyone who looked at them could see the ferocity of their love for one another, undiminished by dirty diapers, demanding careers and frequent trips to the ER for their oldest, Blake, who was an absolute hellion--just like Alex had been, according to his mother.

My phone dinged with an incoming text as I brushed my teeth and I seriously considered ignoring it until morning, but I knew it would eat at me.

I grinned despite myself when I saw that it was from Noah.

What happens when it rains cats and dogs?

I sat there for a full minute, staring at the screen, blanket pulled up to my chest. Finally, I responded.

I have no idea.

My phone rang and I winced, accepting the call as I turned off the lamp and slid down into my bed.

"You have to be careful not to step in a poodle." Noah's voice was deep and warm, and he dissolved into a fit of giggles. His giggle was the only thing about him that I could say was distinctly unmanly. It was high-pitched and unnerving, like he was possessed by the demon of a four-year-old girl.

I groaned and said some uncomplimentary things about his sense of humor and his delivery, and he tried to act like he was genuinely offended.

"So, what do you want, Noah?" I asked finally, sleepily. It was obvious we were going to have to have *that* conversation, since he didn't seem to be picking up on the fact I was clearly ignoring him.

He sighed. "You thought I was gonna take you to breakfast and leave it like that? Like my debt was repaid? I'm serious about this, woman. I got no clue what I'm doing and I know I'm no good at this, but I gotta take the steps. Some folks'll say it's too soon, but it's none of their damn business.

"I like being around you. Somehow you….help." I heard a deep breath and he stayed quiet for a long time. "It's dumb, but I can breathe when you're in the room...when I talk to you. Makes things seem better."

I didn't know what that meant, but it made me feel all warm when he said it, because I wasn't used to sweet words. When it came to kindness and tenderness and honesty, I'd been starving for years.

He asked what I'd been up to and without meaning to, I let the story about Jared slip out. He listened while I talked and huffed and strung together angry curses with silly cobbled-together words. I called Jason "an ugly, no-dick, red-butted monkey," and he snorted.

"I'm stealing that one to use on my brother," he announced once he was able to stop laughing at my juvenile insult. "It's a huge competition between us, and I think you just came up with the winner." He hooted. "What a doozy."

I calmed down a little and told him about Lauren and Alex watching him for me, and that Alex would talk with Jared.

I told him about their four kids and Alex's desire for another, his and Lauren's chemistry almost as wild as their work schedules.

About Lauren losing her shit with Alex when she'd sent him out to get diapers and wipes a couple weeks ago and he'd forgotten the wipes. He'd shrugged, grabbed a roll of paper towels and changed the twins on the kitchen counter using wet paper towels as wipes, calm in the face of Lauren's complete meltdown.

Then he took each baby up the stairs and tucked them into their cribs, returning to the kitchen to find his wife pouring a glass of wine down her throat with tired, frustrated tears running down her face while she tried to open a canister of disinfecting wipes for the counter.

"I'm sorry," I said, cutting the story short. "I'm tired and I'm on a tangent. My point is that the two of them have been really important in my life. They're crazy and messy and one of the best examples of real, insane, devoted love that I have in my life.

"I'm so grateful to have Alex in Jared's life, even if it's in a small capacity. He already has four boys of his own, so this means a lot to me. I hope to God this helps to straighten him out."

"Definitely," he said gently. "And I know it's a weird thing to offer, and we're not there yet, but I'd like to help too, if you'll let me."

I didn't even ask what that would entail.

"Now, tell me what happened after Alex found Lauren crying in the kitchen?"

My face flamed. I knew Alex had taken the wine glass from her hands and downed the rest in a single chug before scooping her up and carrying her up the stairs and into their bedroom.

I knew what had happened after that, because she'd told me herself the next day, fanning herself dramatically as she bragged about his methods of distraction.

I decided to go for it, because God knew neither of us was getting any, and living a little vicariously was as good as it was going to get for a long time.

Noah was quiet as I finished telling the story, ending with the triumphant grin on Lauren's face when we crossed paths in the parking lot the next day.

"I miss that," he said quietly, and I let the weight of many potential meanings sink in. I didn't say anything though, and he finally continued: "Being the center of someone's world and having the power to fix things, even if it's just for a minute."

I had never known those things, I thought sadly, and I stayed quiet because I was ashamed to put the truth into words.

He let me remain silent, and he didn't push. He lapsed into long moments of quiet himself, occasionally breaking the peace with an observation or a comment that required no input from me, and I realized that he just needed the connection. He needed to have someone on the other end of the phone for a minute, to feel normal and human and like he had *something*.

God knew how well I could understand that.

When he went quiet again, I decided to tell him why I had a scar similar to his.

I rolled over and I picked up the thread: that terrible day in Bayonne. He listened quietly, giving verbal cues occasionally, much like Lauren did, to let me know that I should continue or that he agreed. But not once did he interrupt or try to draw a personal comparison. He just let me talk it out. And when I got to the part where I'd opened up my arm in the ladies room of a Greyhound bus terminal in Seattle, he made a low, pained noise and I knew he understood that level of anguish.

He let me talk until my voice cracked and my words began to run dry, and when I woke at five to get ready for work, the line was still open. I could hear soft snores coming from his end, and my heart twisted a little.

He had stayed with me through my own dark hours.

FIFTEEN

Noah

◀❙▶

Eve was a little different with me after our late night conversation. It was sorta like she thawed. She even started initiating a little, texting silly jokes or calling at bedtime, just to ask about my day. And while I wasn't sure I was out of the friend zone, a place I'd put myself with just a few dumb words, I had some pretty high hopes that there was room for advancement.

Things were going real well at work. My crew had finished the project, even under Da's stupid-tight deadline, and he was nice enough to throw in a bonus for everyone involved since we'd managed to pull it off early.

Things were going well with my house, too. With the steady pay I bought materials for the kitchen and got to work again, gutting it and starting fresh, working toward the pretty picture I had in my head.

The only thing that wasn't going well was that Eve had been so busy lately, she hadn't let me take her out again, and talking to her at night was as good as things got.

I knew she was picking up extra hours to store up money for legal fees. Her ex had been granted additional visitation, despite her objections, and he was actually showing up every other weekend to collect their son. It sounded like he was still messing with the kid's head too, from what Eve said about the way Jared had become quiet and withdrawn, sullen and secretive.

I wasn't usually a violent guy: a lover, not a hater, and at my size that was probably a good thing. But if I was honest with myself, I wanted to open the door for the guy on a Friday night when he came to pick up the kid.

Stare him down with unmistakable intent and a couple clenched fists.

I wanted to get a good, long look at him and make sure he knew I was his worst nightmare and his biggest threat. I was already tired of the way he was jerking Eve around, and he was using the kid to do it.

There had been a few more instances Eve told me about. She'd found Jared a specialist and had been taking him twice a week--like she wasn't already busy enough. And not only had the head doc made her aware of some problematic behavior, but one of the counselors at the summer camp she had him in had as well.

While Alex's talk with him had been well received, there were additional problems to deal with now that were not a simple part of growing up.

There had been a couple late night phone calls during which I swear she'd been crying, and I was pretty sure she'd muted herself when it got real bad, so I wouldn't know. But what bothered her was really starting to bug me. She was good and pure and kind, and this jackass was doing everything in his power to undo all the good she'd done for their kid. So if there was anything I could do about it, I was *going* to.

It was July before she took a moment to breathe.

I hadn't seen her face to face in months, though we'd been speaking to one another on a nightly basis for more weeks than I cared to count, sometimes by text, but usually by video or voice.

I was trying to be patient.

I had thrown myself into another paying project, and my own kitchen was nearly finished. In fact, over the past weekend I'd picked up a clawfoot tub off Craigslist and I was going to refinish it myself, as a master bathroom revamp was the next thing to knock out.

It was the holiday and it just happened to fall near a weekend this year, so I invited her to come to my place. I told her to bring Jared, that it was cool to introduce me as her friend and we'd just spend the day hanging out. I didn't know if she'd do it, knowing how nervous she was about introducing her son to any new men, so I tried to play it like it was super low-key. I even tried inviting Lauren and Alex and their nine million kids, but they had plans with Alex's enormous family.

I'd been to the store the day before, picking up all the things I had no clue how to cook because they didn't involve a grill/Giada hadn't taught me on her cooking show just yet. So to be safe, I picked up some standards: packaged potato salad and coleslaw. Turkey dogs, beef dogs, beef patties, a giant bag of buns, cheese and condiments.

I must have tossed eight different flavors of potato chips in the cart, a case of beer, some juice and soda and sparkling water for the kid, a watermelon, pickles, deviled eggs, a tray of pre-cut veggies and a couple boxes of popsicles. I hoped to God it was enough, since I remembered eating like a horse at that age.

Not that that particular situation had ever changed, really.

She showed up earlier than I expected. I heard the car doors slam in the driveway and I swear my heart skipped a beat. It was only ten in the morning and I hadn't started on anything, since I'd been working in the backyard refinishing the tub.

She was so fucking gorgeous. I'd almost forgotten, in the months since I'd seen her in person, just what it did to me every time I clapped eyes on her. Things that were highly inappropriate for her just-eleven-year old son to see, that much was for sure.

"Noah."

There was a deep emotion in her voice that I couldn't interpret, but I hoped some of it was happiness at seeing me. I wanted this woman to want me in the same way I wanted her--the way that I knew, after many late night conversations, she needed to feel wanted. But she was locked up tight. She wouldn't even listen to compliments, like she was afraid I had an ulterior motive. And maybe I did, because in the months she'd kept me at an arm's length, dangerous things had been stirring in my chest and my brain--and most definitely in my pants, which was damned inconvenient.

"Angel." I couldn't stop the huge grin that spread across my face. I pulled her into me and she resisted for only a second before I planted a big, hearty smack on each of her cheeks. I'd have kept going if she hadn't brought her kid with her.

There was a giggle from somewhere behind her left shoulder and my hand shot out to drag the kid into the hug. "Get in on this, buddy. We're huggers around here." I made sure my voice was friendly, and he cautiously put his arms up around us.

She took over meal prep while I walked Jared into the backyard and showed him the tub I was painstakingly refinishing. He wanted to know why I'd go through such trouble when it would be so much easier just to buy a new one and I started trying to explain to him that I liked history and beautiful details, and I was willing to put in extra work to get those finishes.

The last thing I wanted to tell him was that I was refinishing the tub in the hopes that one day his mother would sink into it with me after spending the night in my bed. That was a sweet and very private fantasy, and there was no way to PG it up for him, so I kept that one to myself.

I had to turn away for a second and pretend to look through my crate of tools for a pad of steel wool, because the sweet vision of Eve lounging naked in my bathtub was enough to telegraph inappropriate messages to my dick, which was receiving the message loud and clear.

"Mr. Noah?"

Shit, this kid was polite. Now, anyway.

"Jared, we're cool." I smiled at him in a way I hoped was friendly and not terrifying, like the way I'd apparently smiled at the lady in the parking garage. "You can just call me Noah."

"Are you and my mom *really* just friends?"

Aw fuck, the kid was onto me.

"Um, well...yeah. We talk a lot--mostly about you."

Horrible and inaccurate distraction, stupid.

"So you're not like...doing The Nasty with her?"

My face went so white, I thought I'd need a transfusion to return it to its normal color. "Where did you learn about something like that?" I tried to keep my voice light and friendly, but my eyeballs were ready to fill up with blood.

"My dad says stuff like that about his girlfriends."

I had to look away for a second, terrified that some completely inappropriate response about Jason might come running out of my mouth and Eve would never speak to me again.

Girlfriends?

"What exactly do you know about The Nasty, little man?"

Eve was going to block my number forever and have me served with a restraining order.

"I dunno." He shrugged, peering over the edge of the tub that I'd scrubbed to within an inch of its life. "I mean, we sorta learned about stuff in school this year, but my dad says I'm not getting the for real stuff in school." His little cheeks went red while mine went whiter. I wasn't sure I wanted additional clarification about what his father told him.

"Dad says there are things I should know about life that I can't learn at school, because they're teaching me the useless shit." His eyes darted around quickly; he knew he'd get in trouble for the s-word.

I looked away for a second, sure there was murder in my eyes.

I'm going to find Jason and fucking kill him.

"You're eleven," I said slowly, not entirely sure where to take this. "You don't need to know how to be an adult yet." I tried to keep my voice light, like I was teasing. "I mean, unless you're planning on getting married next week or something? 'Cuz then this is a whole different talk."

I couldn't believe this was my first interaction with the kid.

Jared was quiet for a moment, his face a little screwed up as he thought, and I ran a pad of steel wool over one of the claw feet. Paint and rust sifted down and I thought I'd never been so invested in cleaning something with such attention to detail in my life.

"I don't think I wanna have girlfriends," he said quietly, watching me work. "He has a lot of girlfriends, and most of them are just mean to me and their kids.

"And I can't say anything to Mom, but I don't like going to his place, because we don't do fun stuff anymore. The other kids are there all the time."

I wanted to cry, because I could remember some pretty shitty interactions with women who were going through the vetting process with Da, trying out for the position of stepmom. I'd been a little older than Jared was now and I remembered some of the fights I'd had to establish a pecking order with other women's children.

Tossing the steel wool pad into the box at my side, I sank down beside him. "Have you even tried to talk to your mom about it? I bet she'd be pretty cool," I said, hoping my voice was gentle because my inside setting was ratcheting up to Kill.

Jared shook his head and I knew I was going to have to take a different tack.

"Right now you're allowed to be a kid. You should be worrying about baseball and your next science test, and what you're learning in school is enough for what you need to know *right now*, and a little bit of what you need to know later. Besides, you're going into middle school in the fall and that's a big change, but it's a good sort of change."

He looked skeptical, so I switched it up a little. "Someday you might want a nice girlfriend of your own, but don't rush it, dude. There is *no* rush to grow up--you got plenty of time. Besides," I made an exaggeratedly grossed out face, "adults have to do all kinds of really boring, awful stuff, like pay bills and do their taxes and mow the lawn. And if someone clogs up the toilet...who do you think has gotta fix it?"

He grinned up at me.

"I promise you something, Jared," I said, trying to think of how I would unspool this for Eve, realizing there was no delicate way to put any of it. This was complicated and I might be betraying a young boy's trust, even if it was--and it definitely was--for his own good. "If he has a problem with just letting you be a kid, you send him to me."

He nodded hesitantly.

"Tell you what," I said, picking up a bottle of spray paint and shaking it until the ball gave that satisfying clackity-clack noise. I was feeling pretty confident. "How about first we talk about how to treat ladies right? Then, when you start getting *really* interested in them, you can come ask me any of the questions you've got. I promise I'll always give it to you straight. I won't blow smoke up your ass." I clapped a hand over my mouth and he giggled. "Shit, don't tell your mom...Shit!" I slapped the other hand over my forehead. I needed to shut up, because he was giggling harder.

"It's ok, Noah." His hand smacked my upper arm. "I won't tell Mom you said a curse. And thanks, maybe I will...I sure can't ask Mom that stuff, she'd freak out." He rolled his eyes before completely blindsiding me.

"You know, I hear Mom talking about you a lot with Auntie Lauren. Usually when she thinks I'm asleep. Auntie likes to tease Mom about being in *looove* with you." He was grinning and his eyebrows were wiggling.

The kid was freaking me out, and I had to clear my throat before I could respond. "I think your Aunt Lauren likes to push your mom a little. She's a pretty wild lady."

"Yeah, she's funny. My dad hates her--he says she's a basic bitch, just like mom."

My eye twitched. "He says she's a..." I had to let it die in my mouth and I pulled in a deep breath through my nostrils. "What do you think?"

"I think he's wrong. Aunt Lauren is a good person, and so is my mom. They both work *hard*. Like all the time, and their kids are important to them."

His voice trailed off and I looked over at him quickly.

"Mom tries way harder than my dad," he said quietly. "Dad just orders pizza when I give up waiting for dinner and tell him I'm hungry. And if I want clean laundry, I have to wait until I go home, so Mom can wash it."

He plopped down on his butt and started chewing his lip. I didn't interrupt him, either. I let him sit and think, ruminating on all his past sins and misconceptions, and hopefully it gave him a little time to realize what a complete asshole his dad was. It had to be tough though, given his narrow frame of reference.

"Your mom is pretty awesome," I said finally, pushing up on one fist and then spreading my fingers to offer a hand to pull him up with.

"You're lucky. I haven't had a mom for a long time. Having one is nice, if she's a good one." I winced--that had been a little too honest and personal, and I hoped he didn't pick up on it.

"She does take pretty good care of me." His smile was apologetic. "I'm sorry, Bear. I just kinda...get confused, going between her and my dad. They're so different and they expect different things. But for real, I know I'm happier at Mom's, even if Dad is more fun. Because Mom is more...I dunno. She's like the *same* all the time. I know what she wants."

"Bear?" I asked, because there was something nagging in my memory. I'd heard this somewhere before, and the memory was hazy and fragmented and painful.

"Yeah, big guy." He grinned up at me. "That's what Mom calls you. She says you're a teddy bear, like you're all cuddly and adorable. I thought she was nuts, because when I saw you I thought you were big and scary, but I guess you're pretty okay. You definitely like hugging." He shrugged, like that was some kind of ringing endorsement.

I was *not* cuddly and adorable, thank you very much. I was big and scary and threatening. Just the way it needed to be.

I was pretty sure he wouldn't be as open and accepting of me when I told him what kind of interest I had in his mother, but at least my plans were much bigger than Jason's narrow scope for his women.

I need to tell her about the shit Jason's filling their kid's head with.

Later, I promised myself. When Jared wasn't around to hear her freak out.

***

Eve was knee-deep in preparation by the time I drifted back into the house and I looked across the counters in astonishment, finding everything laid out, the hot dogs and burgers cooking on the stove. I wisely decided not to start an argument about properly cooking things on the grill.

"I know we were a bit early," she said, and my eyes darted around the room to make sure Jared wasn't closely observing before I pulled her into a tight hug. It was tight enough to make her squeak, and I lowered my face into her hair.

Way over the line.

"You could move in and take over stuff like this," I teased hoarsely, and she laughed a little uncomfortably.

"That might be a little sudden," she protested, but she didn't sound upset. Then she melted against me, her arms coming up to wrap around my back and my body got the memo in the most inappropriate way.

"Sorry," I whispered as she plastered herself up against me and I knew she felt what was happening in my pants. "I'm just really happy to have you here. It's dumb, but I missed you."

Like she couldn't tell.

She held on for a long time, like she was drawing strength from me, and when I looked up again Jared was standing in the doorway, watching us with a little grin on his face.

"You want in on some more of this hugging shit?" I asked, smiling at him and clearing my throat. He just shook his head, still grinning when Eve slapped my back with her open palm.

"Nah, I'm good, Bear."

The little fuck was messing with me.

Eve started to drop her arms, but I refused to drop mine and let her go. I held on tighter. "Nope," I told her, "I haven't seen you in months; you've got a lot of missed hugs to make up for."

And maybe some other things, after all those flirtatious late night conversations.

I knew a lot of things about her I probably shouldn't have known, and wouldn't have if we hadn't talked late at night. I knew that she hated coconut, thought thong underwear were the most unflattering thing a woman could possibly wear, and she missed kissing even more than she missed sex. (Yeah, that one blew my mind too.)

She let me hold her for a long time, and she fit in my arms perfectly, the top of her head tucking just under my chin. Finally, she slipped her right hand under my arm and brought it between us, to rest over my heart. She patted several times and I loosened my grip finally, letting her lean back just a little. She looked up at me, her face so close to my own, and her bright green eyes were dilated, her pupils huge as she stared up at my face. It was a look that stirred my blood and made my heart beat against my ribs like a trapped bird, because she was watching my mouth with that heavy-lidded look.

I wanted more than anything to lean down those few inches and blow the Friend Zone right the fuck out of the water.

Instead, I moved my hands slowly up her sides and cupped her face, bringing my lips down to her forehead. She made a soft sound when I did it, something between a sigh and a pained groan, and the thought of making her groan like that when I kissed her *for real* was enough to rob even more blood from my brain, boarding the express train going south.

I couldn't stop the triumphant grin that spread across my face, and she unconsciously licked her lips as she looked back up at me.

I'm not the only one; she wants me too. Joy bubbled up in my chest and I had to keep myself from doing what would be a completely ridiculous and uncoordinated dance in my kitchen. I had absolutely no sense of rhythm when I was upright, so I didn't chance it.

To be fair, in the months since I'd seen her, whatever we were building was with phone calls and texts, and I had Facetimed her more than once to show her the things I'd been working on in the house. It had been a way to be with her even when I couldn't be *with* her, and I knew that she was busy, so I didn't hold it against her. But I also knew that she wasn't going out of her way to see me--in fact, it felt like she was going out of her way *not* to see me. I didn't exactly understand why, but I hoped that today I could get closer to the bottom of things. I wanted more of her, and that she'd agreed to bring Jared was something I saw as a positive step. There was hope I could pass the test, because I had no doubt that was what today was.

We put together huge plates of food and carried them out into the back yard. It was a warm day, for Washington, in the high seventies and surprisingly sunny. It was the perfect day for a picnic, especially now that the yard looked a little more tended and intentional.

I'd meant to buy a picnic table that week, but I'd gotten distracted. So instead I'd spread a couple big blankets over the ground and we all sat awkwardly with our plates, shoveling food into our mouths while Jared told us stories about his days at summer camp and a couple of the kids he'd made friends with.

I had managed to rig up a swing during the week, just a simple contraption: a wide plank seat dangling from a huge tree branch, suspended by rope. And once Jared finished his lunch, he was perfectly happy to give it a test run for me.

Of course, I may or may not have had ulterior motives. Because the blankets were soft and the sun was warm, and my belly was full and there was a beautiful woman sitting close to me. So I leaned over and nudged her with my shoulder, and her gaze drifted from Jared to me. There was a sweet smile on her face as she watched him swinging gently back and forth, just pushing off the grass and dirt with the toes of one foot.

"It would seem you've got me right where you want me." She flipped the curtain of deep red hair over her shoulder, leaning a little closer.

Her words shocked me speechless, my mind running riot with what I knew she probably hadn't intended as innuendo, and I looked up to see Jared watching us curiously.

"Nap in the sunshine?" I called to him, spreading out my arm to pat the wide open expanse of blanket.

"Nah," he called back. "I'm good. Mom could use one, though. She likes to cuddle." He grinned at her devilishly, and her eyes narrowed at the same time mine did. This kid wasn't very subtle.

I leaned back on the blanket, sure to give Eve plenty of space. I knew she was really cautious about what Jared saw her doing, and I knew she was really hesitant to bring any men into his life who weren't serious about sticking around. And while I hadn't come right out and said it, since I knew she was gun shy, I was still one hundred percent confident I was the right guy for the job.

It was something I wouldn't have admitted to anyone other than Thomas, or maybe even Finn, but when I closed my eyes at night I pictured Eve curled up beside me, warm and soft and sweet, and Jared down the hallway, sleeping like a baby in the bedroom I'd made just for him.

Yeah, there was a bedroom for him. I'd picked a good one, one of the larger rooms with great windows and natural light. I'd painted the walls the lightest blue and I'd bought some of that glow-in-the-dark paint crap and painted the night sky on the ceiling. (That bullshit took me the better part of three nights.)

There was a full size bed, complete with sheets and a manly plaid blanket, a bookshelf and a desk, a nightstand and a lamp. I'd even broken down and put a small TV in there.

Because if anything was going to convince Eve that she had a place with me, in my life and eventually in my house, her kid had to have his own space. And with each passing night that I talked to her, I'd begun to feel that I wanted that more and more.

Was I jumping the gun? Probably, but it wasn't like I gave a shit, since it kept me getting out of bed each morning.

I let my head loll to the side to look at Eve, stretched out on the blanket beside me several feet away, and a cold knot of fear balled up in my stomach. The woman was going to think I was fucking bonkers.

Crossing my arms up over my head, to keep myself from reaching over and dragging her closer, I closed my eyes for a moment and let the warm sunshine lull me to sleep.

Waking to find the sun a little farther across the sky, I had to think hard to figure out what had awakened me. There was a weight across my ribs that hadn't been there before and I looked down to see an arm thrown over my middle. She was pressed tightly to my side, her arm thrown over me, her legs pressed up tight against mine.

This was the stuff dreams were made of.

"Better get used to it, big guy." There was a loud whisper to my right, and I rolled my head that way to find Jared stretched out several feet away, a Calvin & Hobbes book in his hands. He was grinning from ear to ear. "She sleeps like a crazy person. When I was little I'd try to sleep in

her bed when I had bad dreams, but I had to stop 'cuz she's a snuggler."
He shivered a little, probably imagining cooties.

That's what he was talking about.

"Me too." I gave him a big grin, and he rolled his eyes at me.

"You gonna take good care of her?" he asked, his eyes shooting daggers.

Damn, this kid had my number.

"If she'll let me," I whispered back, and she stirred a little, tightening her hold as if she needed to crawl right into my ribcage.

"Good." He turned a page in his book, trying to appear disinterested again. "I'm not doing such a great job; I could use some help."

I couldn't help the chuckle that rolled out of me and I held out my right hand to him for a low-five.

I was definitely up to the task. I had no problem with being the man of the household.

***

The two of them stayed all day and though Eve was flustered to wake practically on top of me, I smoothed her hair back and assured her that Jared had warned me she was a cuddler. It made her giggle a little and she'd relaxed into me for a moment longer, her position seeming more intimate once she was awake and conscious of all the places her body was touching mine, starting a fire I wasn't sure I wanted to get under control.

She didn't make any excuses, but I could tell by the way she shivered when I ran my fingertips down the back of her arm that she was starved for affection: physically, emotionally--you name it. I understood it too well.

"I don't sleep well. Ever." Her voice was muffled because her face was tucked into my side, right up against my t-shirt, and her breath was warm and wet through the thin cotton. "But here I am, sleeping on the hard ground and I think I just came out of a coma. You must have a magic blanket or something."

154

I have a magic something, all right, I wanted to say, but I managed to keep my internal teenage boy quiet. Instead, I slipped an arm under her, to cradle her head. The added bonus was that it pressed her breasts into my side, which certainly didn't hurt my feelings, though I felt her suck in a sharp breath at the contact. *Maybe she felt it too.*

I brought one leg up, hoping to hide the fact I'd been painfully hard for some time now and though it looked like Jared had dropped off to sleep as well, the last thing I wanted was to display my kickstand to her kid. I brought my other hand up to smooth her hair back, off her face, and I let it rest at the base of her neck for a while, cradling her, my fingers woven into the soft, silky strands.

She stayed that way for a long time, seemingly as uneager to break the physical contact as I was, but eventually she dragged herself to her feet. She was thirsty, she said, so I followed her into the house.

We spent the rest of the day together, a lazy, warm afternoon filled with lemonade and games. I taught Jared how to play horseshoes and we cobbled together a cornhole setup. He laughed like a lunatic, tossing the beanbags at me more often than trying to make an actual shot, which ended with me threatening to tackle and tickle him until he couldn't breathe, and when I carried through he didn't put up much of a fight. He collapsed to the ground in a fit of giggles and I could feel Eve watching us as I tickled his ribs and ruffled his hair before holding out a hand to pull him up. The kid was cute, and he was a pretty good sport.

"This is sweet!" I heard Jared's voice drift down from somewhere upstairs, and I had to bite down on the smile, because I knew he'd just discovered the room I'd put together with him in mind.

"Hey Noah," he called and I moved a little closer to the stairs.

"Yeah, buddy?"

"If we ever have sleepovers, I'm totally calling this room."

I looked at Eve, standing near me with a curious look on her face and I brought her wrist up to my lips, kissing the soft skin on the inside part, like she'd done to me. It made her eyes flame and dilate, and real hope flared in my chest.

"I would love to have sleepovers, my man," I called back to Jared without taking my eyes off of Eve. "I'd even be willing to make waffles for breakfast--Giada taught me, so I'll have you know they're excellent." Actually, Giada's cleavage taught me; that I absorbed any of the instructions had been a miracle.

She had moved closer, and her tongue peeked out to wet her lips as I stared down at her.

I wanted to ask if *she* wanted to have a sleepover. The kind that involved a locked bedroom door with the two of us behind it, doing anything but sleeping once we crawled into my bed.

"Do you like waffles, Angel?" I asked quietly, trailing my thumb over her soft lips.

You really, really need to talk to her about Jared...something's not right.

Now was not the time, I told the voice in my head. We had plenty of time for that later...

She didn't answer me. Instead, she put her thumb and forefinger on my chin to pull my face down toward hers and she tipped her face up, bringing her lips to within millimeters of my own. It made my heart hammer as I waited, not wanting to rush her, barely able to breathe when her sweet, soft lips finally pressed against mine. She tasted like cotton candy and lemonade, and I backed her slowly toward the kitchen so the sound of my ragged breaths wouldn't carry up the stairwell.

She pulled my bottom lip between her teeth, pressing down gently and a strangled groan escaped my lips, swallowed up as her mouth opened against mine. She was winding me up tight and I tried to keep myself in check.

Must not snap.

She slid her fingers up into my hair, short nails scratching my scalp as she gripped my head firmly, holding me where she wanted me. This woman knew exactly what she was after and I was more than happy to give it.

Fuck, this was hot.

She was hot.

I closed my hands around her waist and lifted effortlessly, her legs wrapping immediately around my waist as I carried her into the kitchen. I set her butt on the kitchen counter and she pushed forward, bracing her body with her feet on the lip of the lower drawers. It put me between her legs, her thighs spread by my hips and one of her hands left my hair, sliding down my body to squeeze against my ass, pressing me tighter against her hot center.

Shit, I was going to come right here, with only the barest hint of friction, if she kept this up. God knew I fantasized about her like this-- and with far less clothing--all of the damned time. If my shower tiles could talk, she'd be appalled by the things they had to say.

I heard footsteps overhead and Eve jerked back like she'd been burned, her lips pink and wet, her cheeks flushed, her pupils huge. She pressed a hand to my chest and I stepped back a single step, letting her slide down off the counter.

"I'm sorry." She ran her thumb over her bottom lip. "I...forgot myself. I shouldn't have done that." She wrapped her arms quickly around her middle, like she was holding something in.

"It's not like he found us with your legs around my head," I teased, and her face turned almost as red as her hair at the lurid visual I knew was dancing through her mind. "But don't worry," I continued, newly brave, catching her chin in my hand and applying just enough pressure to make her look up at me. "When that happens, I'll be sure we're behind a *locked* door, in an *empty* house."

She darted away from me so fast, I couldn't have caught her if I tried. In a blink she was around the counter, a physical barrier between the two of us as her chest rose and fell with the same deep, desperate breaths I was still dragging in.

She kept a safe distance from me the rest of the evening, and after the three of us grilled more burgers for dinner, I took the enormous watermelon out of the refrigerator, coating the counter with sticky juice as I cut huge slabs off the thing.

After our meal, I gave Eve the official tour.

Jared had already rushed back upstairs to throw himself on the bed and finish watching a movie and when we looked in on him, Eve's face softened. I could see in her eyes that she knew *exactly* who I'd been thinking of when putting the room together. Thankfully, it didn't seem to freak her out.

I was nervous about showing her the master. It was the largest bedroom at the far right corner of the house, with a huge bank of windows and an enormous fireplace. It was too much for me, sleeping in the huge California king bed all by myself, but I'll confess my plan wasn't to sleep there alone forever.

Though the clawfoot tub was still in the yard, rather than installed in the adjoining bathroom, I saw her eyes widen in appreciation at all the smooth marble tile and the huge glass shower enclosure.

She peeked into the smallest bedroom before I could stop her, and she froze in place when she flipped on the light. And I felt her freeze. I'd painted and installed flooring, set up the furniture, added the toys and stuffed animals and books...

"It's not a shrine," I said quietly, as I began to worry that the expression on her face was one of concern.

"In that case, it's awfully...specific." She was taking in the lavender walls and the soft blanket draped over the deep green velvet chair.

The mobile hung from the ceiling, the filmy butterflies dancing through the air.

The "E" hanging on the wall over the white crib was calling me a liar, as this was very plainly the room Everly would never have. Why had I put that stupid thing up? Avery had insisted we use it for Everly's room and I'd told her it was a total waste of money, but there it was, hanging on the damn wall.

Eve got real quiet after that.

I tried to enlist Jared, getting him to help me fill up the silence with loud words and dumb jokes and in no time I had him laughing so hard, there were tears running down his face. (My dad jokes were a real hit with him. Thank God they were a hit with someone.)

Eve didn't laugh. In fact, I wasn't sure she was listening at all. She looked far away, and I was desperate to bring her back.

We put out a blanket on the front lawn and watched the fireworks go off over the lake while Jared snuggled right up into my side like he was cold, and I was surprised by the gesture. Eve seemed to be as well, her eyes widening as she watched him burrow under my arm. But she kept her distance, sitting at the edge of the blanket with acres of space yawning between us even as the night air grew cool.

Jared was half asleep by the time the show was over and at Eve's request I carried him to the car and tucked him in, carefully buckling the seatbelt around him.

"I don't want you to leave." It slipped out of my mouth before I could stop it and Eve looked up at me, biting her lip in the dark. The porch lights gave me just enough light to study her face and I could see turmoil churning in her eyes.

"I'm sorry," I said, shoving my hands deep in my pockets.

I wasn't. Not really.

"I shouldn't have kissed you, and I'm sorry I freaked you out. You're just..." I made a frustrated sound in the back of my throat, my right hand clenching into a fist inside my pocket.

I didn't have words for what I was feeling, because those feelings were bigger and scarier than any words I could come up with. I wanted to tell her that for an afternoon I'd felt like I was part of a family--like they were mine--but I couldn't. It felt too disloyal. Too presumptuous.

"I don't expect you to just 'get over' your family, Noah." Her thoughts were a frighteningly accurate mirror of my own, her voice so quiet, it was almost a whisper. "We can't replace them and we won't try." She made a sweeping gesture that I knew meant her and Jared. "Besides, I would never ask you to give up your memories of them or tell you that I need you to love us more than you loved them. I'm just..." She trailed off, dashing the back of her hand across one eye and I wondered if she was crying. "I have room enough for your sweet family in my heart. I can honor and respect your memories and your love for Avery and Everly. But they are gone, and I am here, and I've never been enough for anyone." Her voice broke and she stopped, looking up at me imploringly, but I couldn't find my words.

She let me hug her before she got into the car and drove away, and as the taillights disappeared down the road, a deep sadness came crowding in.

What a kick in the balls.

I had been so excited about today. I had loved every minute with them, feeling normal for the first time in a long time. And now, I worried, just maybe I had screwed that up.

I went upstairs and turned on the little lamp in the tiny nursery. Maybe this *was* my shrine to my baby girl. I had completed it, shut the door and never gone back in until today, when I showed it to Eve. I'd used it for therapy in a way, and it had served its purpose, not to get me over her but to help give me a part of her--something I could never have.

I pulled the fluffy blanket off the velvet chair and sank down into it to think. The room was quiet and peaceful and without meaning to, I fell asleep, thinking about the heartbroken look on Eve's face when I couldn't tell her she was more than enough.

SIXTEEN

Eve

◄II►

We could have spent the night at Noah's, since I had the next day off, but I wasn't ready to subject Jared to sleepovers. If I'd freaked out at the thought of him discovering us kissing, there was no way I could handle the idea of him walking in on us--even fully clothed--in the same bed.

Noah didn't text or call, and I knew he was hurt. I couldn't explain to him what had happened between us, because I couldn't explain it to myself. Except that I knew what I was up against, and the dead could do no wrong.

They didn't pick fights or leave dirty dishes lying around.

They didn't forget to pick up bread on the way home or say things like "Not tonight, honey."

There would be no "not tonight's" with Noah, I knew that much. Just looking at the man set my pants on fire, and when I crawled into bed that night I thought about the way he'd looked at me when I wrapped my fingers around his neck and pulled him down to me. I had never seen such want in a man's expression before, hot and molten, and the powerful feeling was heady.

I wanted more of it, something of which I'd had so little.

I remembered the sounds that came from his throat when I kissed him, and I gave up. I'd been aching with lust all day long, since waking up in his arms on the lawn, pressed up against his huge body. His muscles had muscles, his powerful shoulders tapering down into a narrow waist that I was pretty sure had those beautiful v-shaped ridges riding his hips.

I didn't even bother with battery operated devices, opting to go old school as I imagined what it would be like to feel his huge body hovering over my own.

To feel him kneeling between my thighs while he kissed me.

My phone rang as the last tremors left my body and I grasped it feebly, my eyes barely capable of focusing.

"Hello?" My voice was a croak.

I hadn't even been able to see who was calling.

"I know it's late, but I had to work...and I want salacious details."

Oh, Lauren. Like she didn't have a wild sex life of her own. Now she needed the details of mine?

"Details of my solo flights?" I teased, my voice still a little raspy, and she snorted, waiting for me to throw her an actual bone.

"Ok, like the part where I attacked the man in his own kitchen? You know, kissed him and ground on him like a teenager? And I fell asleep on his picnic blanket and woke up wrapped all the way around him, like a freaking leech."

"Oooh." She giggled, obviously settling in for the good parts. "Come on, give up the details. Alex is working extra hours tonight, thanks to the holiday, and I need some entertainment. This is as good as my day's going to get."

I told her about seeing Noah and Jared deep in conversation, Noah's forehead furrowed seriously as he focused his attention upon my son.

I told her about the finished room that was obviously for Jared and the silly tickle fight, Jared shrieking with laughter as he clung to the giant man.

I told her about discovering the tiny nursery, and about going a little crazy on him.

She knew about my past--all of it, including my time in foster care and some of the bad situations I'd been in.

The fact that my brother and I had never mended the rift formed when we were ripped apart.

She knew I could have made better choices when it came to the men in my life. In fact, she even knew that I wouldn't have married Jason if I hadn't gotten pregnant with Jared.

Lauren knew the real reason I'd flipped out. The reason I'd kept buried for so many years and had never even admitted to her: I didn't trust anyone, ever, because people had always let me down. So I kept them at an arm's length, preferring to fend for myself even if it caused insurmountable loneliness.

"Did you tell him about your grandparents?" she asked softly, and there was an ache around my heart.

Yeah, I'd told him about my grandparents, weeks ago. He'd been quiet. He'd listened and hummed in the moments a response was called for.

But I hadn't exactly told him the *whole* story. I'd kind of glossed over some parts.

I hadn't told him about the stationmaster busting down the bathroom door in the Greyhound terminal.

Or the part where he'd called the paramedics.

Or the fact it had taken four bags of blood and a frantic ambulance ride to keep me from dying in a public bathroom stall.

The part where my grandparents had refused to come see me at the hospital.

But somehow, I thought, he already knew what he needed to. And not only that, but he understood. He didn't judge me for the weak moment when I'd felt hopeless.

"Lauren, I think I messed things up."

She was quiet.

"I told him that Jared and I couldn't be replacements for his dead family."

She sucked in a noisy breath. "Shit, girl. You've got some lady balls."

"I don't exactly know where that came from."

Yes, I did.

"You sure as fuck do." This was why she was the other half of myself. "There was definitely a better time to do it, but you put it out there. Now he knows exactly where you stand."

Lauren made me tell her all about the kiss in the kitchen and I relived the moment in my memory, lust coursing hot and thick through my veins once more.

I had never experienced an attraction, an undeniable magnetic pull, to someone before like I had to Noah. It was true that I recognized some of my own brokenness in him, but it was something beyond that. There was something far beyond the physical that was a considerable part of the equation. He was built like a mountain, huge and wide, and he was beautiful because he was so different from anyone and anything I'd ever known. But despite his very distracting exterior, all I could see when I looked at him was the man I knew he'd be: gentle, patient, tender, loving. Things that had been desperately lacking in my life for as long as I could remember.

It wasn't just that he would treat me well, I knew.

Tender.

I'd known the instant I saw the room Jared had taken over, that it had been created with him in mind.

Thoughtful.

I'd also watched the way Jared had snuggled up to him during the fireworks, which was something he *didn't* do. He wasn't a fan of physical contact, and I'd have chalked it up to puberty, but he'd always been that way: Hugs from him were few and far between, and reading bedtime stories side by side was about as close as he'd let me get most days.

But he'd had no problem sidling right up to Noah.

Tucking himself right up under his arm.

Staying there until he was half asleep and Noah carried him to the car for me.

Patient.

Their interactions that entire day had been easy and light, and Jared's face had bloomed with joy under Noah's kindness and gentle attention.

164

Kind.

I slept fitfully that night, which was pretty normal for me, and when I woke the next morning I wasn't surprised to see Noah hadn't texted or tried to call.

What did I want from this man, I asked myself all day as I went about my shift.

Oh please, everything.

The thought almost knocked me over in the hospital hallway and I swayed for a second, grabbing for a door frame to steady myself. William was passing me and he eyed me suspiciously. "You ok, Eve?"

"Yeah, thanks." I ran a hand over my face. "I haven't been sleeping well."

His face softened a little. "Yeah, I get that." And knowing he was a divorced dad of young twin girls, I knew he *definitely* got that.

Jared had gone quieter than usual and I kept a worried eye on him, checking his browser history each night after he went to bed. But nothing jumped out at me, and I tried to reassure myself that eventually it would come out, because he was a brooder. He was an overthinker; a ruminator; an internalizer, just like me.

It was days before he voiced what was bothering him, weeks having passed since we'd been to Noah's place.

"Mom?" He pushed some spaghetti around his plate, not meeting my eyes while he waited for my response.

I looked up and he drew a deep breath, setting down his fork. "Do you think Mr. Noah might invite us to come to his place again? I really liked spending time with him."

"Why would he, honey? It was a holiday--that's why we went. He invited us to be nice."

"But he loves us."

I sat up a little straighter. "How do you know that?" It seemed like an awfully big leap.

He grinned just a little, a smear of spaghetti sauce on his upper lip. "Whatever, Mom. Like you didn't see him looking at you."

I was genuinely confused.

He rolled his eyes like I was an idiot and his cheeks pinked up. "It was actually pretty gross."

"Huh." I had no words for my son's implication that the enormous man wanted to eat me up. *What did he know about that?* I didn't know how to respond, but it was a fairly astute observation for a child, if it was true.

"You liked his place?" I asked, desperate to redirect the conversation as I rose from the table to rinse my plate and slot it into the dishwasher.

"It was huge," he said, shoveling another forkful of food into his mouth. "The yard was crazy-big, like a park. And I liked the bedroom upstairs. It was like the size of our living room!" He threw an arm out toward the general direction of our living room.

He wasn't wrong. All the bedrooms in that oversize house were enormous, with the exception of the tiny nursery I couldn't stop thinking about.

That room bothered me in ways it shouldn't.

It bothered me to think of what had sent him to me in the hospital that first day and the reason I'd discovered him there again, later. There was no way he was over that. There was no way he was ready to move on, and I was sure as hell not going to be a rebound, no matter how much just seeing him made my ovaries burst into flame.

It was another long week before I heard from him again--it had been almost a month--and I was surprised he caved first. I'd been fighting myself the entire time, trying not to contact him. But honestly, I'd missed our flirtatious nightly texts.

I missed Facetiming with him. He always had a dumb joke ready for me and I loved the way his eyes lit up every time I laughed, like I'd given him something precious.

It was late but I was still up, folding laundry and packing a lunch to send with Jared the next day. It was nearing his last week of summer camp, as school started again soon and it was a reminder that time waited for no one, and that as I tried to survive one day at a time, life was slipping past.

My phone buzzed and I glanced over at it quickly, surprised to see it wasn't Lauren. That made me chuckle a little, because it was late enough that the last thing on her mind was calling me. I let it ring a few times, taking a couple deep breaths before I answered it with "Hi, Noah."

"Eve." His voice sounded funny. "I guess you got your way."

"What do you mean?"

"I'm ready to apologize for whatever I did that made you go away."

"Noah, it's been a month. You just now figured out you miss us?" I knew it was mean and uncalled for.

"Eve." His voice went low, pleading. "I gave you time because you wanted to push me away that night. I'm not an idiot."

"Why are you calling me?"

"Because I *can't* stay away." He sounded guilty. "You think I haven't replayed what happened in the kitchen in my head a million times? You... want me too, Angel." His voice cracked. "No one has ever kissed me like that. Not even...she never...*fuck*." He swallowed hard and I could hear him breathing raggedly, struggling with something. "I loved her so much. I thought I had everything, and if they hadn't been taken away from me, I would have loved them forever. But things changed. A lot. And I have to start over.

"And then there was an angel who watched over me while I was sleeping, more than once." He hiccuped, and suddenly his disjointed thoughts made sense. He was drinking again.

"I asked my brother about you." He let the words hang, and I heard him swallow hard in a noise that I knew was a swallow of liquid courage. "He told me a pretty redhead brought me flowers. He said she didn't know he wasn't asleep when she checked on me, again and again that day. He said she held my hand and called me 'Bear.'

"It was you, Eve, and when I woke up I thought you'd been a dream."

He had me there. It was all true. The only thing missing was that I'd looked around carefully before kissing his forehead each time before I left. I'd needed some kind of physical connection to the man, irritated by my irrational need to be so close to someone I didn't know at all.

"It *was* me." My voice was strained and unnatural. *Busted.* "But I was there because you needed someone, and I *could* be there. I felt like...well, you know this already. I understood you."

"Yeah." His response was clipped.

I waited.

"My brother Thomas," he said, and I heard him swallow again. "I gave him your name and he dug up a lot of things you didn't tell me about, like disappearing from the system and changing your name."

I didn't owe him anything, and I was half tempted to say that out loud.

"I'm sorry, Angel...that you had to go through all of that when you were just a kid, with no one to protect you or take care of you. And I can't go back to undo any of it, but I can take care of you now.

"I can be the man your son looks up to, and I can teach him how to respect women and work hard and be an adult.

"I'll be more to him than that garbage ex of yours ever was."

I swallowed so hard, my throat made a funny noise. "You're drunk, Noah. Tomorrow you won't even remember we had this conversation." But I liked drunk Noah's honesty, like he'd opened up a window into his heart and let me crawl in.

"I sure will. I remember everything about you, Angel. I remember that you tasted like cotton candy and lemonade, and the way you grabbed me to pull me closer." His voice was dark with desire. "I remember the sounds you made when I kissed you and the way you wrapped your legs around me. How the hell am I supposed to forget those things? You're keeping me up at night and you're not even here."

He fell silent.

I had nothing to say, my face flushed. What *could* I say? I'd been trying to avoid him for a very long time, but he just kept showing up again and again, reinserting himself into my life.

"I talked to Lauren an hour ago--not much of a conversationalist after nine, is she? She was a little busy." He chuckled. "I told her you want what she has with Alex. She said I gotta be the one you wanna come home to." Another swallow, followed by a hiccup. "She said I'm gonna have to be a persistent pain in the ass." His voice went falsetto, like he was mimicking Lauren, and he was starting to struggle with his words. "She says that you're a tough nut to crack, and mostly 'cuz you've never been able to depend on anyone. But you can depend on me. I'm solid as they get."

"You're as hammered as they get," I teased, entirely aware that all the blood had fled my brain and rushed toward the center of my body. His proclamations of tenderness and stability made funny things happen to places that didn't see a lot of action, like my heart.

"We're too young, Angel." His voice was low and adamant. "We're too young to just give up and be sad all the time. These lives got no love; no family dinners; no warm bodies waiting for us in our beds."

His voice trailed off and I recognized the emotion as one of wistfulness and regret.

"Noah, I've been living that life for years. It doesn't mean I don't want more, but it *does* mean that I'm terrified of anything other than the status quo. I can't lose more than I already have. I can't lose *again*, and I don't think I can be what you need."

"I'm a big boy, Eve. Don't try makin' decisions for me."

"I have to go to bed," I said softly. "I have to be up for work in five hours."

"Ah, but you're off the next day. And Lauren volunteered to watch Jared, 'cuz I wanna take you out. Like a real date."

He wasn't wrong. I had an unheard of four-day stretch coming up, something Lauren knew because she could find out my schedule with relative ease.

I agreed to it somewhat begrudgingly, and I told Noah to go to bed. It was undoubted that his morning would be difficult.

I didn't sleep any better that night, and before bed I googled Thomas Atholton. I quickly confirmed he was the tech giant Noah promised, which explained how and why he had been able to uncover my information so quickly. His reach must have been long, as some of my records were sealed, and if Noah knew about those...that scared me.

While I was online, I placed a delivery order with Starlight for the next morning, to save Noah from himself.

His text rolled in at 6:10, thanking me for what he knew was thoughtfulness on my part and I smiled to myself, to think that his first thought upon receiving a greasy breakfast delivery had been of me. *Maybe he really didn't have people in his life who cared for him in the small ways.*

I wondered how many of the words he'd said the night before had been his own, because I feared a great number of them had been Jack's.

SEVENTEEN

Noah

I'd done reasonably well staying away from the booze since the night I landed in the hospital. At least, until that night I called Eve.

To deny that booze ran through my veins was to deny my very heritage. Da was a shameless drinker, but Ma had been the real boozer. She could drink a three hundred pound man under the table and on her bad days, sometimes she did. I couldn't hold a candle to her when it came to my drinking habits, but I had no desire to start the day with a double shot of rum in my coffee or to end it drinking straight vodka, whereas she hadn't been all that picky. After a while she stopped even trying to hide it.

She was even less selective about her poison when she found out Da was cheating on her and really, that was when things really started to spiral. So maybe it was unfair, but I still blamed him for killing her.

We called it cancer. At least, that's what we told everyone around us: sudden, vicious, terrible cancer. But it was the liquor. It made her bleed on the inside, and eventually her stomach had enough.

Asher had been the one to find her, collapsed on her bedroom floor. She was already gone and there was nothing he could have done, but that had completely fucked up my baby brother. That was when he stopped smiling. It was when he lost a huge piece of himself he couldn't seem to get back.

Generally, I wasn't one who drank to escape, though it seemed that had been my way of life since the accident.

Usually I was a happy drunk.

Goofy.

It used to be that I'd go out and drink with the boys after work, but only sometimes, since I didn't want to slip into Ma's habits. And of course, my routine *before* had been to come home and have a beer or two after my workout.

I groaned, swinging my legs over the edge of the bed. Someone was hammering on my door--and Jack was hammering in my head. That fucker clearly wasn't a morning person.

I dragged myself down the stairs and found a young guy on my dark front porch with a big paper bag in his hands. "Atholton?"

"That's me."

"Delivery for you from Starlight."

I blinked at him, aware the fumes rolling off me were probably enough to fill up the backup tank on his little electric car.

Had I placed an order the night before?

"Receipt's in the bag," he gestured dismissively, obviously eager to get off my front porch and back into the little bubble of his car, where things probably smelled a hell of a lot better.

"Thanks," I said, patting the back pocket of the pants I'd fallen asleep in. "What do I owe you?"

"Taken care of." He waved at me dismissively. "Enjoy your breakfast." Then he spun and launched off the porch, muttering something as he went that sounded an awful lot like "You'll need it."

The bag was stuffed with takeout containers and wrapped sandwiches. There was a huge styrofoam cup of coffee nestled into the corner, next to a parchment bag overflowing with buttered toast.

I ripped everything out of the bag, searching for the promised receipt. There were no numbers on it, but there was a note. It was at the very bottom, a little grease smearing some of the writing: *This should make the morning a little better. Take it easier on yourself, Bear.*

That was it, but I knew who it was from and I felt a little thrill run through me at the nickname. It felt like she cared, even though I was getting the very distinct impression that was wildly inconvenient for her.

I settled in at the island in my kitchen and started slowly, coating my stomach with greasy hash browns to stop the rolling that I'd earned so hard, so I could work my way through the rest of the food. And while I ate, I tapped out a text to Eve, thanking her for her thoughtfulness. No one had ever done that for me before, not even Avery, who always teased that if I suffered the consequences of my poor decisions, maybe I wouldn't make the same mistakes again.

It was a busy day and thanks to Eve I wasn't badly hung over, the greasy food and a few ibuprofen enough to fix things. Good thing too, because I had three job sites to visit, things to check and sign off on, and I finished up a wiring job before calling it a day at three-thirty and heading home to clean up.

It occurred to me out of the blue, as I got out of the shower, that I hadn't heard from my brother in a few days. He'd been a little short with me on the phone lately and his calls had been fewer and farther between than was normal for us, which I'd chalked it up to his insane work schedule.

I knew he'd been overseas when I'd tried to pull a runner, and he'd chartered a private flight to get to me as quickly as possible. Maybe he was still playing catch-up from all the time he'd spent on me.

I didn't know much about what happened when he got back, but I knew he'd left something unfinished in order to rush to my side, and he had called in a coworker to take his place. But something had gone wrong--someone fucked up--and he had to fly back overseas to fix it.

Shit of some sort had hit the fan when he'd gotten home and he'd left his company and his homes, suddenly moving his little family to the middle of Bumfuck, Alabama and Gerry had relocated from Seattle to Alabama not long after. I hadn't had a chance to ask either of them why; Thomas hadn't been returning my calls. But to be fair, so much had happened in his life in the last six months that I had to forgive him for being distracted.

That afternoon I decided to dial his number and to my surprise, he picked up. I'd been prepared to leave him a voicemail.

"You never pick up when I call in the middle of the day." The shock was obvious in my voice.

"I had to fly into LA from Milan last night." His voice was hard and clipped and it made me draw up my shoulders a little straighter, because something was going down.

"Lydia was in an accident yesterday and Aden's in bad shape. Responders on the scene said they suspected it was intentional."

I could hear it then, the heartbreak in his voice and how hard he had to work not to break down.

"Tell me where you are. I'll throw a few things in the car and be right there." *Holy shit, had Lydia been trying to kill everyone in the car?*

"No." His voice was sharp. "I don't want you seeing him like this. It's…" He choked on what sounded like a strangled sob. "It's been too much already, and I can't explain it all. I'll call you if things change."

He didn't call. Instead, he texted later that night, and I knew it was because he couldn't talk.

Lydia was seriously injured, but she would make it.

Aden, his three-year-old son, had not. Thomas said he would text me the details regarding arrangements as soon as he could.

I called Alex immediately. I'd only once met the guy face-to-face, when he showed up at my place thinking he'd intimidate me, and I knew he was still a little suspicious of me talking to his wife. But I was about to call in a giant bro favor with someone who owed me nothing, because I needed a lot of help.

"Atholton." Alex's voice wasn't exactly warm and friendly, but he didn't sound like he wanted to rip my head off and shit down my throat anymore. He was playing a little nicer, probably under strict instructions from his wife, who had clearly programmed my contact information into his phone. "What can I do for you?"

"I've had some bad news," I said, trying to control the shaking of my voice as I pinched the bridge of my nose. "I need to go out of town for a few days. My brother's just lost his son."

Alex swallowed hard. Here was something he could understand, having sons of his own.

"I don't think I can do this on my own."

"You want to take Eve with you."

Damn, Alex was like Alexa, a creepy quasi-psychic who read my thoughts along with my browser history.

"If she agrees to it, but I haven't asked her yet. I didn't wanna to expose Jared to something so awful, and I thought I'd ask first if he could stay with you for a few days. I know it's really presumptuous, and I haven't run it by Eve at all."

"Yeah buddy, you might wanna do that. Women aren't usually big fans of decisions being made for them."

"I know, and I will. I'm just...kinda messed up about it."

Alex was quiet for a beat. Then, "Yeah, I get that. I've heard some things about what you went through, man, and I'm sorry. I don't think I could have handled it like you did."

Ah, so he didn't know *quite* the whole story. He didn't know that I *couldn't* handle it, and what I'd tried to do.

"Long as you're after Eve, and not my woman, we're good. I'll help."

I couldn't help the stupid, high-pitched giggle that came flying out of my mouth. I hated that damned thing. It was the surrender of my man card every time. "You've got a real fireball on your hands, but she's not for me. I've got a thing for the redhead."

Alex snorted. "Obviously. Considering that you're desperate enough to use my wife as a conduit, I'd say you've got it pretty bad."

He was right and I knew it. It made me a desperate man, to use another man's wife to get to the object of my obsession, but Eve wasn't about to let me in. I needed all the help I could get.

"A word of advice."

I was all ears.

"She's never really had someone she could depend on, so she doesn't trust easily. Ah...no...actually, she doesn't trust at all. Not ever. Especially men, according to my wife, so I'm gonna guess that was earned.

"You're gonna have to be patient with that one. Keep showing up, because she's a good one, Atholton. By that, I mean don't you dare fuck this up, because I will *find* you if you do. And *I'm* not the one you have to worry about."

He was right. It was his wife I'd have to worry about. I was pretty sure she had top secret training from the Israeli army, and I wasn't about to test that theory. I had absolutely no plans to fuck anything up.

"Jared can stay with us for as long as you need," he said quietly. "He's a good kid. He needs a solid guy in his life. Someone who will be a real father figure and teach him how to be a man--a man who takes care of the people depending on him."

That guy was me. I could teach him how to be a man and how to take care of the people who needed him. In fact, I could teach him a hell of a lot more than just that, and we would start with decency and treating his mother right.

I thanked him, trying to explain that his wife had been very helpful in getting me to Eve, and that I was in their debt. Somehow, I think he already knew that, but he liked to make me work for it.

My next call was to Eve and I'd like to say it went better than my talk with Alex but honestly, she seemed shocked that I would ask her to come with me. I mean, I understood: She'd never met my family and this would be a real crash course for anyone. Especially for someone who seemed to be deciding whether or not I was acceptable to...I don't even know. Associate with? I certainly couldn't call her my girlfriend, because she damn well wouldn't let me be her man.

The fact I'd already cleared Jared staying with Lauren and Alex didn't seem to make her particularly happy. She claimed she was glad I'd thought ahead, but I knew my presumption irritated her, even though she agreed reluctantly. She could give me four days, she said, but she couldn't guarantee anything beyond that.

I told her to pack; that I'd book the tickets and pick her up the next day.

I called Gerry, knowing she'd have a few more details.

Then I texted Thomas that I would be there as quickly as I could, and booked tickets for the two of us on the next flight out, which left just after noon the next day. Of course he didn't respond, and I didn't expect him to, and to be safe I texted Mrs. Jensen, his housekeeper.

Quickly throwing some things into a bag, I texted Eve that I would pick her up by nine the next morning.

Even with her there for moral support--that was huge and I knew I was asking a lot--I didn't know if I could make it through this. Events were still too recent, too raw and fresh.

If anything, this trip would definitely rip off the scab.

***

Eve was quieter than usual the next day. I gave her a little squeeze when she opened her door, being unable to stop myself from touching her. It didn't seem to go over well, because I felt her whole body tense when I pulled her against me. Her hands went up between us almost immediately, pushing against my chest, and I tried to disguise the hurt look I knew passed across my face.

Push, pull. Push, pull. What do you want, woman?

She was quiet during our drive to the airport and through security.

I didn't try to touch her again, afraid she wouldn't speak for the rest of the trip, and I wanted to talk to her. For the first time ever, I had her mostly to myself for the rest of the day and I would have more access to her over the course of the next four days than I'd ever had before. The thought both made me giddy and was completely terrifying.

By the time we boarded the plane, stowed our baggage and went through the safety rundown, I was just about ready to explode. I needed to crack a joke--a really stupid dad joke I'd stored away in my memory that morning.

Her fingers gripped the armrests, her knuckles white as we started to taxi down the runway and her eyes squeezed shut.

"You don't like airplanes?" I asked quietly, finally breaking down and wrapping one of my hands over hers. Her hand completely disappeared in mine and she let go of the armrest, quickly slipping her fingers through mine and squeezing with astonishing strength.

"I've never been on one before," she said a little breathlessly, an admission that left me staggered.

"No kidding." It came out more a comment than a question and as the plane hurtled toward the edge of the runway, engines screaming, I tugged at her a little and she burrowed her face into my shoulder.

"I had a dream, you know," I said, deciding to unleash my joke in all of its cringeworthy glory at once. She mumbled something that I thought was permission for me to continue, so I leaned closer, my words drifting through her hair. "I had a dream that I weighed less than a gram. I was like...OMG." I tinged the ending with my best Valley Girl and it was a beat before I heard her snort--hard.

Then her shoulders started to shake.

Then a tiny laugh erupted from her mouth and she pulled her hand from mine to throw over her face as she leaned back just a little, just as the plane lifted into the air, and moments later the landing gear started to whine and crank.

"You're terrible," she giggled, her expression filled with relief, and I grabbed the side of her face with my free hand.

"I can't stand to see you scared or hurt or suffering," I said honestly, hopeful it didn't break the moment, and she tipped her head down, so I kissed the top. "I'll make an idiot out of myself every time, just to make you smile."

She was quiet again for a long time, but she let me pull her back against my side. In fact, she was quiet for such a long time that the first round of beverage service moved through and when she didn't move, I assumed she was asleep.

"What are we doing, Noah?" Her voice was soft, not at all sleepy.

"We're doing whatever you want us to be doing," I said, swallowing hard, aware that my knees were perilously close to my chest, despite the fact I'd booked a row with extra leg room. And then I tacked on, "What do *you* want this to be?"

She didn't answer, but she slipped her hand beneath my arm, twined our wrists together and linked her fingers through my own. Purposely. It made a wave of hot joy rush through my limbs, tingling and zinging, every nerve ending on fire. It was like being a damn teenager again and I kept my mouth shut, for fear my voice would crack if I tried to speak.

She held my hand for the rest of the flight and I grinned like an idiot the whole time, so that my face was sore by the time the captain announced our descent into Sacramento.

I had expected to rent a car when we landed, but there was Jensen, waiting near the baggage claim. He cracked a devious grin when he saw me, because my brother's Scottish groundskeeper/driver/man about the house and I were engaged in a constant battle of the wits when it came to who could tell the best stupid joke.

According to my tally, I was still in the lead.

Jensen nodded at me as we drew closer and before I'd even had the chance to introduce him to Eve, he launched into it. I could tell he was just bursting with it, which meant he'd been working on this one for a while.

"A Scot walked into a bar after a tough day o' skiin' on the Canadian slopes," he started out, his eyes twinkling. "After five or six good, stiff drinks, he noticed a stuffed animal hangin' over the bar and he asked the barman, 'What *is* the thing hangin' over there?'

"'Ah,' said the barman. 'That be a moose.'

"'Fuck me!' cried the Scot. 'How big are the cats?'"

He doubled over, wheezing, whacking his lower thigh with one hand at his own joke and while Eve's eyes bounced between the two of us, looking somewhat concerned, I joined him in hilarity. I'd always been a pushover.

"Well," I finally rejoined, and the conveyor alarm sounded behind us, the belt beginning to whir. I too had come prepared with an old standard. "When I got dressed this morning, a button on my shirt fell off. And then, when I tried to pick up my suitcase, the stupid handle fell off. So I figured it couldn't get much worse, but when I tried to open my truck door, the handle fell off! So I haven't peed all day."

I could feel the eye roll from Eve, somewhere behind me, but Jensen was purple and laughing so hard that I had to clap his back. "Ach, that's a good one, boy!" he wheezed, turning even redder than usual with the exertion of trying to catch a breath.

Jensen worked on composing himself, which was hilarious of its own accord, considering he was never anything but composed. And while he sniffed and smoothed and chuckled, I grabbed our bags off the belt.

It wasn't until we were in the car that I finally introduced Eve to Jensen, and for the first time he seemed to understand she was there *with* me. His eyebrows shot into his hairline and he slowly extended a hand, taking hers and kissing the back. "Delighted, Lass."

"Don't be too delighted," I warned him with a grin. "Her last name's Ryan."

"Ach then, no harm," he waved a hand in the air. "Yer people took off the O when ye came through Ellis Island. Some did."

She looked like she had no idea what he was talking about, and I quietly whispered to her that his Scottish ancestry was at odds with her Irish background.

"I think we're going to get along just fine," she said bravely, finally finding her voice as she leaned over the partition between the seats and placed a kiss on his cheek. His face flush a mottled red, and I grinned at her as she settled back into her seat. This was exactly who I'd been hoping she was: charming, sweet, intuitive, and downright disarming. She had just wound one of the crustiest old guys I knew right around her little finger.

The drive to Thomas's house wasn't particularly long, and I wanted to settle back into the seat and draw Eve up against my side again. It seemed she had other ideas though, because she sat at the opposite end of the car, arms folded across her chest as she stared out the window at the passing landscape. She seemed lost in thought, the occasional unreadable emotion flitting across her face.

Why was this woman so closed off?

Had I done or said something wrong?

Had I been pushing too hard?

Finally, I reached across the space and tugged at her arm. She relaxed it slowly, dropping her hand to the seat and I covered her smaller hand with my giant one. I was a very touchy person, and I was going to need to touch her a lot for reassurance over the next couple days. I knew what awaited us, but I didn't know how I was going to be able to handle it.

Mrs. Jensen met us at the door when we arrived and I could see Eve out of the corner of my eye, taking in the vast expanse and stunning beauty of what was Thomas's favorite house, previously our sister Maren's.

Finn had already arrived, Mrs. J. said, and was taking a nap in one of the guest rooms. And since I was the only one to bring a significant other, she said, and Eve's right eyebrow hitched upward, she was putting us in the suite over the large garage.

Jensen carried our bags up before I could even get to it, and I clapped him on the shoulder as we passed on the stairs.

Eve looked distinctly uncomfortable. She took in the large, gracious space with the small kitchen, a generous bathroom, a sitting area and a huge bed that backed up against the windows overlooking the vineyard. Her eyes drifted to me, her lower lip tucked between her teeth, and I tried to grin. "It's ok, I can sleep on the sofa."

She said something in response, but it was so low that I couldn't make out the words. I hoped it was something like "I'm not sure I want you to."

I left her to unpack and went in search of Thomas, unsure whether he was at the house or not. He still owned a property in Portola Valley as far as I knew, so it was possible he wasn't yet in Sonoma, where all of us were congregating.

My brother Aaron and I weren't as close as we should have been, and Asher and I didn't put in enough work to understand one another. But we were brothers, and family sticks together. So I'd called them both, just in case Thomas hadn't and they were supposed to be arriving as well, sometime later that evening.

The door to Thomas's main floor office was shut and locked and though I could hear muffled noises on the other side of the door, no one answered when I knocked. I stayed there for a long time, knocking gently, then determinedly, then hammering.

Eventually, Jensen followed the noise and found me, my head resting against the heavy wooden panel. Wordlessly, he produced a key from his pocket and clapped my shoulder with one big hand. He fixed me with a serious look that told me it was bad. I could read volumes in the expression on his lined face: It was really, really bad, and I braced myself for whatever I was going to find on the other side of that door.

I waited until Jensen moved back down the hallway before fitting the key to the heavy lock and saying a quick prayer for strength. Then I turned it slowly, a loud "click" rolling down the hallway as the lock disengaged.

The office was dark and rank. Thomas had obviously been holed up for days, the air thick with the stink of sorrow and scotch and one very large unwashed man. In fact, I didn't see him when my eyes first swept the room and I moved carefully to the large windows, pulling back the heavy velvet drapes. It was then that a movement caught my eye and I turned quickly to see him sitting in the chair behind his desk, a half full glass of something amber colored resting on his knee. His eyes were bloodshot and his hair was wild, his shirt undone by a few buttons.

This was the most undone I'd ever seen my big brother.

"Now I understand," he said, his voice scratchy as he lifted the glass to his lips again.

I didn't have to ask what he meant, because I knew he was staring down the same dark hole I'd found myself in not long before.

I didn't say anything, but left the room to grab a tall glass of water from the kitchen, setting it on the desk in front of him. Then I made sure the door was closed and locked again, before sitting on the sofa against the far wall and waiting for him to talk.

"It should have been her," he said thickly, and my mouth fell open.

"You don't mean that," I said quickly, not even sure I meant it, because I didn't particularly care for my cold sister-in-law.

"I do mean that." He fixed me with an unsteady gaze, his eyes tracking me like I was moving, even though I wasn't. "She's not mine, Noah." He hiccupped. "I lost her a long time ago, if I ever had her." His voice was bitter as he voiced an awful truth about his wife.

I was so far out of my depth.

"How 'bout we get you cleaned up? You could stand to sleep this shit off," I said, pushing myself up from the sofa. I knew I was gonna have to help him up to his room, and probably put him in the shower myself, and I moved across the space in a few big steps to take the glass from his hand.

"Drink," I said, handing him the glass of water and he winced as the liquid started to wash over his tongue.

Digging through his desk drawer, I found a bottle of painkillers and I quickly shook out three. "Take these." I dropped them into his hand and he dutifully swallowed them.

I opened a window before hoisting him out of his chair, and I practically carried him up the stairs, to the enormous master suite at the far end of the house. There I shut the bedroom door and kept him anchored to my side as I reached into the large shower and flicked the dial. "Come on," I said, hardly eager to undress my own brother. "We gotta get you cleaned up."

He was clumsy, and I unbuttoned the rest of his shirt for him and helped him to peel off the undershirt so he wouldn't tip over. I let him undo his pants and carefully helped him step out of them. He didn't even blink, stripping off his boxers, and when he stepped into the shower I lowered the toilet lid and sat, waiting for him to finish. The last thing anyone needed was for him to pass out in the shower.

He wasn't at all coordinated and I'm pretty sure he got shampoo in his eyes more than once, but at least once he got out he smelled clean.

I was waiting, wrapping a big towel around his waist, my eyes firmly affixed to his forehead.

"Brush your teeth," I ordered, half dragging him toward the vanity, and he unsteadily loaded toothpaste onto the brush and made a halfhearted attempt to clean himself.

He dropped the towel and I grabbed it off the floor. "Nuh-uh, Captain Macallan--hold on." He stood as still as he could while I towel dried his hair--too long for my taste, but Thomas had always had longer hair, usually just past his chin. He probably didn't have the time for regular haircuts, I figured. Then again, I had to admit to myself that if mine was that nice, I'd probably keep it longer, too.

He crashed heavily into the bed and I covered him with the top sheet and light blanket. Then I settled into one of the chairs near the fireplace, ready to keep watch.

Thomas had always been the sentinel. He was our big brother and the caretaker in the family. He'd watched over each of us, helping us when we needed it, always in his own quiet way. He was always there, ready to support, making sure each of us got what we needed. Early on the support was financial--often that was the case--but just as often he was just physically there. And now that he needed someone to be there for him, I was going to be that guy.

Hours passed and I dozed lightly in the chair, aware that I was leaving Eve to fend for herself. It made me feel bad, but I was pretty sure she would understand. And if she didn't, I reasoned, I would explain it all to her later, once I had her to myself in the suite over the garage.

The light grew weaker, the rays of the sun becoming longer and longer outside the huge bank of windows. There was a quiet tap at the door and I moved carefully from the chair, crossing the room to find Mrs. Jensen with a tray of dry toast, coffee, scrambled eggs and hash browns, a tall glass of tomato juice resting in the middle, smelling remarkably like a Bloody Mary.

"Hangover cure," she whispered with a sly grin and I took the tray from her, leaning down to kiss the top of her head. She was so tiny, she only came halfway up my chest and she smiled shyly up at me, her face flushing a furious red. "Go on," she made a shooing motion with one hand. "Go help our boy."

The Jensens had been a part of the family for a long time, going back to when our oldest sister Maren lived in the house. They had taken to us, our loud, obnoxious, often rude family right away and I'd always thought it was because they didn't have any children of their own. They cared for us like we were their kids, and all of us loved the way we were spoiled when we came to visit, which had been often for a time.

It took a while to rouse Thomas and I knew he wasn't feeling all that great yet, so I helped him to sit up in the big bed and carefully folded out the legs of the tray over his lap. "Start with this," I instructed, handing him the glass that was emitting some pretty noxious fumes. "Mrs. J's patented hangover cure. It'll help bring you down a little easier."

He took the glass dutifully and sipped, wincing again.

It could be said that one of the Jensens, if not both, were capable of mixing some pretty wicked potions.

"I don't want it." He gestured toward the tray, his voice rasping out like he'd spent hours and hours screaming and was going hoarse. I knew it was probably that very reason.

"You'll eat it if I have to play airplane to get you to do it," I threatened, looming over the bed. He rolled his eyes at me, inhaling deeply and blowing it out as a heavy sigh. He knew when to pick his battles with me and I was quite a bit bigger than him, so starting something half-tanked was a bad idea. I'd have him in a headlock in no time and he knew it.

He kept missing his mouth, so I took over, slowly feeding him one forkful after another of hash browns and eggs. He managed the toast well enough on his own, even though he had to slow down a couple times, the food threatening to come back up.

"I know better, don't I?" He asked me finally, sipping carefully from the tall mug of coffee that sat on the far corner of the tray.

"We both know better," I said quietly. "Grieving badly, with a bottle of something flammable, seems to be in our blood."

The look on his face told me he was remembering the same thing I was: Da on a weeks-long bender after Ma passed. Drowning himself in the very same poison that had taken her from us.

"We sure did learn it from the best," he said wearily, scrubbing a hand over his face and I took the tray, collapsing the legs and setting it on the large bedside stand. I sat next to him, squeezing his knee firmly and waiting for him to tell me to stop touching him or to suffer physical violence--but he didn't.

185

"I don't know how I'm going to get through tomorrow," he said, sucking in another deep breath.

"With all of us," I said, squeezing harder. "We came to hold you up."

His eyes filled and I looked away uncomfortably. Our relationship was built on name calling, inventive curses and half-cocked martial arts moves, generally executed as a sneak attack. We were intentional, but we disguised those intentions with teenage behavior.

It was hard for me to watch my big brother, the man who was the rock in all of our lives, look so human. "No more of the sauce," I warned, shaking a finger in his face. "I'll sleep next to you if I have to, and I'll warn you right now: when I fall asleep I snuggle like a starving leech." (At least, that was what Avery had always complained about; said I chased her across the bed all night.)

He made a face, something halfway between a grimace and a smile. He seemed thankful for the distraction. "Don't suppose your girlfriend would like that much."

"Not my girlfriend," I said quietly, feeling his eyes bore into me. "Can't seem to convince her."

"She's here, right?" he shrugged. "Must mean something."

He had no idea how badly I wanted that to be true.

EIGHTEEN

Eve

‹ǁ›

Noah was gone for the better part of the afternoon and I knew it meant his brother needed him, so I let myself back into the main house to try to help Mrs. Jensen. She humored me for about an hour, letting me help chop vegetables, but when she heard Finn's voice she shooed me out of the kitchen with "Go on, now--more family for you to meet."

"Oh, hi." The tall blonde woman seemed startled when I walked out of the kitchen, nearly running into her in the living room. She was my height and build and she was startlingly lovely, with incredible platinum hair and huge, warm brown eyes.

"I'm the only sister they have left," she said with a sad smile, holding out a hand to me. "Seraphina, but everyone calls me Finn. So I guess you must be Eve--I've heard a lot about you from Noah."

I blushed suddenly, surprised by the adrenaline rush that came out of nowhere. *What did it mean that Noah was talking to his siblings about me?*

"A quiet word about that one," she said conspiratorially, tucking me under her arm like we'd known one another for ages. "He's a big goofball. Always with the jokes and the pranks--just a big kid in an overgrown body, but he's loyal, Eve." She fixed me with a steady look. "If he's decided you're the one for him, you'll have more luck shaking off a puppy who's trying to hump your leg. He may act like a big clown most of the time, but I swear to God he's the biggest Alpha Male you'll ever meet. The jokes, the goofing off: total front. He's..." She paused for a long moment, thinking. "He's the most big-hearted, emotional caveman ever." She grinned.

I swallowed hard. The Atholtons clearly liked to jump straight into the deep end. *Welcome to the family; here are all our secrets.*

"We're just...ah...getting to know each other," I said lamely, watching as her mouth curved into a seductive and knowing grin.

"That's one way to put it," she said, bumping my hip with hers and wrinkling her nose a little. "Considering how long I've had to put up with his stupid stories about 'This gorgeous angel,'" and her rich voice dipped into a deeper register, "my guess is that he wouldn't mind getting to *know* you a little better. And let me warn you now, none of us Atholtons do anything halfway. You're totally in for it." The way she wiggled her eyebrows when she said it made me blush all over again.

The afternoon dragged on, fueled by appetizers from Mrs. J.'s kitchen and drinks mixed by Jensen himself, and Finn and I sat across from one another in comfortable chairs in the living room. We chatted easily, much to my relief, finding we had a great deal in common when it came to unfaithful husbands and trying to keep the wheels from falling off as working single moms.

My phone rang suddenly and I fished it quickly out of my pocket, not surprised to see Lauren's number on the screen. "Babe." Her voice was as throaty as ever. "Thought we'd give you a call so Jared could say goodnight. You doing ok?"

I answered her questions in short sentences, aware Finn was watching me and overhearing every word. Stepping out seemed rude, so I soldiered on.

She nodded as I hung up after a short chat with Jared. "I'll be taking a call like that in about..." She looked at her watch. "Two hours. My son is staying with my stepmom for the next couple days." Her face folded up into a grimace and she smoothed it out just as quickly. "I make a point of *not* sending him to his father when it can be avoided, and there's no way he's ready to deal with what's going on here." She made a vague circling motion with her fingers, near her ear.

I was curious about her marital situation, as she spoke about her husband and their marriage with obvious distaste, but everything sounded very present tense. Yet I didn't dare ask any pointed questions, for fear of greatly overstepping the unspoken boundaries. We didn't know one another that well just yet. I had a feeling it wouldn't take long, though. She seemed warm and welcoming once you got past her icy, aloof appearance.

Steering the conversation into safer territory, I told her about my job, which led to telling her how Noah and I had met. Her eyes softened when I told her how I'd come across him by accident the second time in the ER, his wrist bandaged.

"That's why he calls you his angel," she murmured softly and I thought her eyes looked a little shimmery. "You were there again and again when he needed you and he didn't even know it."

I felt the flush creeping up my neck again. It was obvious Noah had been talking about me with his family for a long time, or at least his sister. I wondered if she also knew how hard I kept pulling back from him, but if she did she didn't say anything.

Eventually Finn told me about what she did for a living, not that she should have needed to work, since her shipping heir husband made stupid money just breathing. But she wasn't content to live the way he did, she said, waking hung over at two in the afternoon and "partying" until he fell asleep again. I kept to myself that I could relate.

"I like my job," she said finally, suddenly unwilling or maybe unable to look me in the eye. She had a cup of tea in her lap and she wound the string around her index finger, back and forth, on and off, until I began to wonder if she would finish her thought.

"I'm a private chef." Her face broke into a slow, proud smile. "The days are long, but the pay is really good and my employer is…" She let the sentence trail off, but she couldn't hide the small, very secretive grin that tried to steal across her face. "Well, I'm part of a team that keeps him in fighting shape for his games. He's very dedicated…regimented." She licked her lips. "He doesn't let himself have an off-season, like some MLB players do." She sipped her tea again and I tried to coax down my left eyebrow, which had been steadily rising as I'd watched her expression while she spoke.

Interesting. There's more here.

"You keeping my girl entertained?" Noah's deep voice made my stomach and my heart jump at the same time as he came up behind me, curling a large hand around the back of my neck while he grinned at his sister. The afternoon light caught his hair, setting the dark strands on fire. *Holy crap, he was really gorgeous.*

"I was just warning her that sleeping near you puts her in the blast zone. Boys are gross." She grinned up at him, and he tried to look menacing.

"But not all of us, right? I bet you'd latch onto Mateo like a tick on a dog, Blondie." He curled his fingers into a claw and made a tickling motion in her direction as she shrank into her chair, her cheeks violently red.

A noise rolled down the hallway, something like a door being shut, and I could hear heavy footfalls.

"I picked up a bum on the way up from San Francisco."

This was a new voice.

"Flew in this morning and dragged his sorry ass with me."

Two tall men came into view, one gorgeous man with dark blonde hair and the other with the same dark hair Noah had, a bit shorter, his face a little less symmetrical on account of what looked like some scarring. This, I thought, must be Aaron and Asher.

"I need a drink, a nap, and a woman," the blonde grumbled, dropping a small bag next to the sofa before covering the distance to hug Finn. She rose from her chair as he crossed the room, wrapping her arms around him tightly and kissing his cheek.

"Behave yourself, Aaron," she said in her low, husky voice. "This is Noah's girlfriend, Eve."

I didn't even try to fight her over the misleading introduction. I simply rose from the chair, accepting the simpler explanation, and extended my hand to the man.

He was shorter than Noah, but everyone was shorter than Noah. He was in great shape though, with broad shoulders and a trim waist. I was pretty sure this was the brother who was in the military, considering if he flexed he might punch me from across the room with one of his biceps.

"Watch yourself, dude." The other man I knew was Asher called to his brother from the other end of the room. "You put hands on his woman and you'll be whistling out your asshole--not that I'd blame him, you're prettier and he's jealous."

Noah chuckled as Aaron shook my hand, a tight look on his face. "Glad to make your acquaintance, Eve," he said politely, quickly backing toward Finn. I was pretty sure he could hold his own, given his obvious physical conditioning, but he didn't seem eager to test my theory.

"I'm the catch," Asher announced confidently as he crossed the room. "I'm trustworthy, loyal, well off--and gainfully employed in a very lucrative position. If my sorry-ass brother can't take care of you, I'm currently interviewing women for the position of girlfriend, and I *like* redheads." His eyes twinkled and he wrapped his arms around me in a tight hug before Noah could get out a single word.

"Whatever, jerkoff, you don't *have* girlfriends," I heard Noah scoff as Asher squeezed the air out of my lungs. He was also shorter than Noah, a little less broad than the other two brothers, still powerfully built and wide shouldered in his expensive suit. This man was dangerous, all coiled muscle and aggression, something rolling off him that I didn't get from the other brothers.

This was the one who joined Thomas in keeping a technological stranglehold over Silicon Valley, I thought, having done a very small amount of reading on the family before my flight.

At some point Thomas shuffled into the room, tucking himself against a back wall, and when he was discovered there were no exclamations of surprise or loud noises of any kind. Instead, each of the siblings filed over to him like they were greeting a mafia don. They took turns, handling him gently with long hugs before handing him off to the next.

I rose finally as Finn made her way back to her seat, crossing the room to introduce myself. "I'm so sorry," I whispered to him, offering my hand. Instead, he pulled me into a fierce hug, whispering in my ear, "Thank you--this will be hard for him."

I blinked. Apparently an introduction had been unnecessary, as the man seemed to know who I was. I threw a look over my shoulder at Noah, who had a weird expression on his face.

"Hands off, bro," he called across the room, a small, teasing smile pulling up the corners of his mouth and Thomas backed away slowly with his palms facing out.

"Not moving in, stupid," Thomas called back, his wedding band glinting in the light of the fire that roared on the other side of the room.

It wasn't long before Mrs. Jensen announced, in her quiet way, that she'd put together some food and although it was late, they descended upon the kitchen like a starving horde.

Thomas hung back, I noticed, and I waited with him as the rest of the family surged through the doorway like they hadn't eaten in months.

"Do you have to go through this all alone?" The words were out even before I realized I'd said them, and immediately I began kicking myself for something so insensitive.

"Alone?" Thomas asked, eyeing me somewhat warily. "You're all here, aren't you?"

I shook my head. "I mean…"

"Lydia's still in the hospital," he interrupted, "and she won't be released for a few more days, so it's up to me to do this."

"I'm sorry," I said, moving a little closer to him. "This couldn't wait, I suppose." I tried to end it as a statement and not as a question, because the look on his face was genuinely terrible.

"No," he said, leaning slowly against one of the chairs. "It couldn't wait. Even if I'd waited another month, she wouldn't have been there. This way she gets to be the victim."

I had no idea what he was talking about, but his expression was terrifying as hate and anger dripped from his words.

"My wife doesn't love me, and she didn't love our son the way I did-- or the way a mother should." His voice was cold, and I felt the chill run through my blood as I watched his beautiful face turn stony, an expression more terrifying than fury. "I learned too late that children were a commodity in her world."

192

"It's none of my business," I said, putting my hand on his forearm, "but I hope you find peace. I know hope is a dangerous thing, but it seems like you've suffered enough. Don't choose to keep living in that place." I tapped the side of my temple. Then, aware I'd hugely overstepped, I moved quickly into the kitchen to find Noah and tuck myself up against his side.

All around them, the pervading sense of this family was one of loss.

***

The siblings ate together, trading inside jokes that Finn tried to explain to me quietly, and when we all moved back into the sitting area in front of the fire, Noah pulled me into his lap as we all sat. It made me tense up and he pulled me across him, one big hand beneath the back of my sweater, his thumb rubbing across the skin of my lower back. I wasn't even sure he knew he was doing it, his insatiable need for touch something instinctive.

The brothers teased and joked and told embarrassing stories about one another, going easy on Thomas but hitting Noah hard enough that he protested several times.

"Sorry guys," Finn said suddenly, her phone lighting up as she fished it from her pocket. "It's bedtime and I gotta take this."

"Pffft, bedtime." It was Thomas, and I was surprised by the outburst. I remembered her saying she'd be taking a call similar to mine, later.

"It's Griffin's bedtime, right?" I asked, looking quickly at Noah and frowning a little because I had no idea what time it actually was.

"More like Mateo's bedtime, but whatever..." Noah laughed a little, and I sensed some hostility in him, which seemed unusual.

I didn't know where to go with this. "So isn't it normal for a man to call his wife before bedtime?"

Aaron snorted so hard, I thought he might have hurt himself. "He *wishes* he was her husband. He's been trying to steal her away from that Swiss dick for years, but she won't go."

Thankfully, she had left the room already.

"She keeps working for him and dude's been trying to seduce her from the start...girl's stupid or innocent--she can't see it. How she hasn't taken the bait..." Aaron rolled his eyes hard and took a long pull from the steaming mug in his hand, something I suspected was tea. "We're all hoping she'll leave the jackass for Mateo, but she just can't seem to make the jump."

Noah's hand had worked slowly, steadily around to my stomach, and from the way he was breathing I knew his light touch was intentional. It made it hard for me to concentrate as each of the siblings debated the merits of Finn's current husband vs. the merits of Mateo, the handsome, wealthy baseball player who was six years her junior.

But they were guys, so of course they didn't say things like "handsome" or "wealthy." They scoffed out words like "pretty" and "loaded," like they were insults. Because even though they seemed to like him well enough, they couldn't be caught saying anything that sounded like they were granting their approval when it came to their baby sister.

Eventually Finn returned and her brothers reigned in the topic, quickly switching over to Asher's dating life, which seemed abysmal indeed. Mostly, it sounded like his idea of dating was for an evening at a time, and I caught myself curling up my nose more than once.

Noah pushed up in a languorous stretch, raising me up on his lap. "I love you all," he called in his deep voice, "but me and my angel have had a long day. Now that I have her all to myself, it's time for a little worship at the altar of my goddess."

There was a whoop from someone in the room and I didn't know whether it was Asher or Aaron.

"Wait a minute." I whipped around to face him, my expression one of shock and fury. "Did you just tell them we were going to go do something dirty?"

Finn's low laugh was unmistakable. "Girl, take it from me: A man says something like that, you let him. I'd be halfway up the stairs already if I was you."

The brothers laughed almost hysterically, even Thomas, and before I could shriek or protest or blush, Noah had scooped me up and was carrying me down the hallway. There was a doorway leading to an enclosed stairwell and he took it quickly, letting us into the apartment above and crossing into the living space before he set me down.

"What the fuck was that?" I spat angrily, not unaccustomed to cursing like a sailor outside of my head, but definitely unaccustomed to being spoken for.

He didn't say anything at first. He stood there patiently, breathing hard, and I took a moment to appreciate how much bigger than me he really was. I was tall enough, but he was huge. I was thin and lithe, whereas he was wide and muscular and bulky. Had it crossed my mind to fight this guy, I had no doubt it would not end well.

"Eve." His voice was low and plaintive and he lifted one big hand to my face. "You've been avoiding me for months: Ignored me; hidden from me; decided not to answer me when I call or text..."

I stepped back a half step and his hand dropped.

"I've tried so hard to be patient." His voice went hard. "I know what I want, and you know what you want, but you won't let yourself have it.

"I'm a faithful man, Angel, and you know that. You chose me *first*, but you're scared of me and what we could be, and I can't let you walk away, not after the way we were brought together." He looked so serious, I couldn't even interrupt.

"Eve, please…" His voice broke and something hitched inside my chest. "I can't be alone in this. Give me *something...*"

The light was low in the room, nothing more than pale rays from the moon and I was thankful I couldn't see his face, because I was terrified by the emotion in his voice. I didn't want to need someone that way, but he was right. I had been searching for that since Jason had walked away from us: Someone who would love my son and raise him to be a man, caring for me as if I were something precious. Protect us. Keep us at the forefront of his thoughts and demonstrate his love with his words and his actions.

How could that ever be this man? He'd been so completely broken after his own loss. How could his shattered heart ever heal enough to hold love again?

I moved slowly across the large room, kicking off my shoes and pulling the pins from my hair. I needed to get away from him and the way his presence pulled me to him. He was dangerous and he'd been wearing me down for months.

I needed to get away from him, before he could process what I was doing, and I shut the bathroom door rapidly because I needed a minute away from his magnetic pull.

Twisting the dial to the shower, I brushed my teeth while the water warmed and then quickly moved beneath the spray, confused and scared and sad while I fought with myself. I hadn't experienced love or support or anything remotely similar in so long... I'd been on my own for too long, and I'd stopped trusting words a long time ago.

I took a deep breath before flicking off the light switch and stepping cautiously out of the bathroom with the towel wrapped around my body, cursing myself for being so shortsighted.

He was standing in the kitchen area, the light above the stove burning, drinking a glass of water. He turned away quickly, but not before I saw his reaction. If I'd been a cruel person, I'd have done it on purpose but for some reason, seeing that hungry look on his face made my stomach explode with a fit of butterflies.

"I forgot to bring this in with me," I said, aware that wasn't exactly an apology as I hurried toward the bag I'd left at the foot of the bed.

The glass thudded on the counter and I turned quickly to see him moving toward me with long strides, his expression determined as he closed the gap between us. It made my heart jump into my throat and my eyes went wide, knees hitting the back of the bed as I stepped away from him. It was a panicked reaction on my part, and his hands went quickly around my waist, steadying me as I threatened to topple backward from my overcompensation.

"Don't run from me, Angel. You know I would never do anything to hurt you." His voice was raw and I could hardly hear it over the blood thundering in my ears. The way he was looking at me was unlike any way he'd ever looked at me before. This wasn't the easygoing, gentle man I knew. This was someone else entirely, someone I suspected he kept hidden a great deal of the time, and this man looked desperate. He looked scared and anxious and the way he was looking down at me, I knew it was because he'd been starving. *For me.* It made a thrill run through me. No one had looked at me the way he was now and, just for a moment, I let my defenses down.

Letting go of the towel I'd been so tightly clutching, I kept my eyes on his as it dropped quietly to the floor. I was tired of fighting this, because I was the only one fighting. I was tired of denying myself. Tired of being alone and lonely and now, tonight, I didn't have to be.

What happens in California can stay here...

His breath caught as he stared down at me, his nostrils flaring when he released it and I could see the fine tremor run through him, his hands releasing me to fist at his sides.

I understood what it meant, that he was keeping himself in check despite my unmistakable signal. He was waiting for me to come to him.

There were only inches between our bodies, but I took the small step closer before winding one arm around his hips and slipping the fingers of my other hand into his hair, bringing his head down to mine. Taking what I wanted.

It made me shiver when his lips touched mine, they were so warm and soft, and immediately I was wrapped up so tightly in his arms that we were sharing the same single breath.

He kept his hands at my waist as I nibbled at his lower lip, drawing a harsh groan from him. It was costing him dearly to keep himself in check; I could feel the tension vibrating through his huge body like an electric current, buzzing, pulsing, crackling.

Opening to him, letting our tongues tangle and fight and taste, I pulled one of his hands from my hips and placed his big palm over my breast, pressing him to me, my fingers curled around his.

"Bear," I sighed into his mouth, and his resolve cracked. He kissed me hard, deep, breaking away from my mouth for seconds to leave a trail of scorching kisses over my shoulder and up my neck.

His other hand had finally drifted to my butt, where he pressed and kneaded, lifting me against himself effortlessly, a rumble in the back of his throat that warned of the coming storm.

Finally.

The singly-worded thought exploded across my brain in technicolor, my body singing from the sensations of his lips, his fingers, his tongue, the rough sound of his breathing and the sounds he tried so hard not to make. I loved this, making him come unhinged, finally tasting what I'd ached for night after night alone in my bed.

Right now, tomorrow didn't matter, because nothing else existed.

My fingers flew down the buttons of his shirt and I tugged it out of his pants, finally getting my hands on his warm skin. It was smooth and soft, a rich golden color that suggested he worked shirtless often and I let my hands drift over his strong chest, his wide shoulders, his firm stomach and the thick ropes of muscle in his back.

"Holy crap, Noah." I couldn't help the exclamation of surprise. He was a sculpture brought to life, rock warmed by blood and softened with flesh.

"What is it? What's wrong?" He lifted his head from my neck, his eyes filled with panic, and I watched the tight muscles of his stomach ripple as he leaned back.

I smiled up at him, a little dazzled. "You're just..." I had to suck in a deep breath. I felt like I'd just won the lottery on Christmas freaking morning. "Magnificent."

His smile was glorious, just before he lowered his eyes bashfully. "Nobody's ever said that before."

I had to tear my eyes away from his biceps and his thick, strong forearms. He'd only ever been with one woman and the stupid little fool hadn't known what she had. Clearly she hadn't appreciated this man, but I wasn't stupid enough to make that mistake. Just getting his shirt off already exceeded my wildest fantasies--I couldn't wait to see what other surprises waited for me.

His gaze was equally heated and appreciative as he brought his hands up to my breasts, covering them gently, protectively, bending to kiss the small swell of each over the tops of his fingers. His eyes lingered, his lips drifted, his fingers warm on my skin.

"I don't have the word for it," he said softly. "But you're...better. Better than what I imagined, and believe me, I've tried." A little shiver rippled through him again. "You were meant to be worshipped, and I will, Angel. I'll worship every beautiful inch of you." He swallowed hard, looking back up into my eyes with an earnestness that stabbed at my heart.

"Slowly."

There was nothing dirty in the way he said it--it was a promise--but a wicked thrill zinged through my body, terminating in a place that made me squirm with anticipation. Why the hell had I pushed him away for so long when I could have had this?

My fingers shook as I fumbled with his belt and he chuckled softly, placing his hands over my own. Maybe he could tell I was both nervous and eager, his own anticipation apparent in the way he looked at me.

He leaned down then, one hand in my hair as he drank in my kisses, his other hand working to quickly unclasp his belt. The sound of it snapping through the loops and clattering to the floor made my heart hammer. I was desperate to feel his huge body against mine, his mouth on my skin, his fingers touching me in places I hadn't been touched by another human in years.

His touch was reverent although his eyes were wild, and I knew he was keeping himself in check. He had to be almost as desperate as I was, his breath coming in ragged bursts as my hands drifted down the back of his open pants to his backside, squeezing, pulling him against me.

I growled in frustration finally, reaching to yank the fabric from his hips and it made him laugh against my mouth. "Where have *you* been hiding this whole time?" he teased, pulling back slightly and kissing the corner of my mouth as he smoothed a strand of hair over my ear. "I've been waiting for you...I was starting to worry you'd never show." His voice dipped a little and I heard the worry behind it. It told me that he'd worried he wasn't enough; that he hadn't felt desired in the same way he wanted me.

"Too much talking," I complained, finally getting back to wrestling his pants down his hips. "More kissing."

He complied readily and the soft, teasing kisses were gone, replaced with bites and nips, the powerful thrusts of his tongue moving rhythmically with my own. The dance that told me exactly what he could do with his body; the heights of madness to which he'd drive me before tipping me over the edge. It made me moan into his mouth as the vision of our joined bodies flashed through my brain and he pushed me gently back onto the bed, bending quickly to pull his pants over his feet.

"No fair," I whimpered as he crawled up the bed after me, still in fitted black boxer briefs that made my mouth water. He was tight and defined everywhere, his legs just as powerful and muscular as his upper body.

"I started at a distinct disadvantage--I only had a towel."

He chuckled, caging me in between the two tree trunks he called arms and leaning down to dip his tongue into the hollow of my throat. "You're dangerous enough fully clothed. I can't think straight when I'm near you, not ever. I'm not even going to try right now." He nuzzled, slipping lower, drawing one tightened nipple into his mouth and I nearly shot off the bed when he began to suck.

A deep noise rumbled from his throat and slowly he moved down the length of my body, his tongue lapping at the center of my sternum, his fingers splayed across my belly as he dropped a constellation of small kisses across it.

"What are you doing?"

I pulled myself up onto the pillows and looked down at him frantically, my eyes wide as he kissed my navel, then an inch lower, and another inch lower, his eyes flicking up to mine.

"Worshipping at the altar of my goddess." He grinned wickedly up at me and my lips tightened into a flat line. I was just on the verge of panicking, remembering that Jason had flatly refused. He didn't like the taste of a woman, he'd said, and I had always assumed that meant I was dirty. Revolting.

The look on my face must have mirrored the panic I felt, because Noah reached up to take my face in one of his big hands, drawing me up toward him as he raised himself on his knees.

I felt so tiny next to him, looking up into his beautiful face etched with lust and concern.

He kissed me softly, then trailed his lips down my neck. "I want to," he whispered, sucking the soft, sensitive skin beneath my ear. "Just like this."

It made me whimper.

"And maybe like this."

The tip of his tongue began to draw small circles on my neck and he moved lower slowly, using the flat of his tongue to lick gently. It made a sound catch in my throat, something that sounded almost like a sob and he pulled back slowly, licking his lips. "I would never do anything to hurt you, Angel, and I'll never embarrass or shame you like he did. Let me treat you the way you deserve."

He hummed contentedly against my skin as he drifted downward again, slowly, pausing to look back up into my eyes. "Trust me," he whispered gently, reaching up for my hand and linking his fingers with my own.

Screw it. I was going to let him do this, right? What happened in California and all that? Only, I was starting to think that just maybe this would be ok to do in Washington, too. I was starting to think that maybe he meant what he said, and maybe I *could* have it all. Finally.

I took a deep breath, lying back. If he really wanted to do this...I shivered a little. I didn't have much experience with it and that experience wasn't good, but Lauren went on and on about Alex's oral skills ceaselessly. It was annoying and obnoxious. And for once it would be nice to have something in my pocket to shut her up with. I was tired of her amazing sex life, and I desperately wanted one for myself.

He kissed up my inner thigh, then the other, with a tenderness I thought might make me weep. My limited experience to that point, aside from the non-starter with Daniel, had been *take, take, take.*

"Relax, Angel," he whispered gently and I heaved out a deep, shuddering breath. If he knew I was tense and nervous and scared, that couldn't be a good thing.

There was a long pause, a pause between his lips on my inner thighs and my brain screeching to a halt as his mouth pressed softly into the center of my body and I lost all control, all thought, all rationale, and all ability to think in any capacity. With a few soft strokes he rendered me incapable of worry, of breathing in anything other than sharp gasps.

My body wanted to move, and I lifted my hips against him, a sigh escaping my mouth. It made him look up at me, a slow smile spreading across his beautiful face. "More, Angel?"

I nodded wordlessly, an aching emptiness throbbing between my legs. I beckoned him upward and he shook his head, slipping one huge arm beneath me. "I'm not done here," he said, watching my face as he teased me with the tip of one finger, his eyes going wide as he eased it into me. My eyes rolled back into my head and it dropped back onto the pillow. And with that he began to suck gently, slipping a second finger inside. He matched the slow thrusts of his fingers to the stroke of his tongue and the sounds coming out of my mouth stopped making any sort of sense, but I didn't care at all.

Pleasure coiled up tight inside my body, ready to release in a fiery burst and I hoped we were far enough from the main house that no one could hear me, because I had stopped being quiet a long time ago. I was calling out his name, over and over, drugged with the power of his body, his control, the way he knew just what my body needed and he gave it to me patiently.

"Noah," I gasped, stars in my vision. "It's...I'm..." I threw my head back as the first tremors began, arching into him and he hummed against my body, a deep, low growl of satisfaction as he watched me fall apart.

He lifted his head as I clenched around his fingers and he continued his rhythm, drawing it out until I couldn't take it anymore.

"I want to see that over and over," he whispered as my chest heaved and I lay gasping for breath, tears standing in my eyes. He placed a soft kiss against my hip before crawling up my body and pulling me into his arms and against his chest. "And I will. I'll be the one to give you everything you need." His voice was deep with satisfaction.

I let him hold me for a long time, his fingers drifting lazily over my skin as if he needed to touch me constantly. It didn't seem to matter where, so long as his hands were on me, and as I began to come out of the endorphin laced fog, I became aware of how hard he was still breathing, his heart hammering against my cheek.

Something else was hard too. It was pressing mercilessly up against my thigh and I wriggled my hips slightly against him, which made him suck in a breath.

"Sorry," he whispered, moving to put space between us.

"Sorry?" I could hardly get the word out, my brain was still so fuzzy. There was a satisfied buzz humming along my nerve endings and I rolled slowly to face him. "For what?"

"I didn't mean to...you know...push you." He gestured toward me with one hand. "You probably need to sleep; you seemed a little dazed." He couldn't help the grin that stole across his lips.

There were suspicions forming in my mind about the woman who'd owned his heart before me and though it wasn't fair to make assumptions about the dead, I was getting the idea he was very good at giving because he'd been trained by a very demanding woman. In fact, I was going to go so far as to guess that she'd been selfish.

Lifting a hand to his face, I saw the briefest emotion flash through his eyes before his lids drifted shut and he let himself nuzzle into my palm.

"Bear," I whispered softly, and the pet name made him smile, something that pulled and ached in my chest. I curled my fingers, stroking his cheek like I was petting a scared animal and he leaned deeper into my touch, swallowing hard.

Moving my hand in long, soft strokes, I eased down his neck and across his broad chest. His eyes were still closed, his expression finally relaxed in what looked like pleasure. I teased one flat nipple, delighted when it hardened under my touch, and I leaned down slowly. The last thing I wanted to do was spook him, but I wanted to taste his skin.

Kissing his collarbone gently, I dragged the tip of my tongue across the sharply defined bone, kissing my way down until my lips wrapped around the hardened point. It made him catch his breath, his eyes going molten. I wanted him to look at me that way all the time, with such deep, raw need. It made my heart skip a beat and I stretched up to kiss him, palming him through the thin cotton.

It was the first time I'd touched him, and it made me stupid.

"Holy shit." I pulled back from him, looking down at the startling erection that strained against his underwear. "Maybe warn a girl you're loaded for big game?"

His smile was almost bashful, and he lifted one shoulder in a shrug. He had to have some idea what he was packing in there was far above anyone's idea of average, and my greedy little fingers worked to ease the black cotton over his hips and down his powerful thighs.

"Noah." I raised myself, sitting back on my heels as I stared at the man in the bed. I had never seen something so beautiful and I knew the awe I felt was reflected on my face. "You're...wow."

Stupid was back, stealing all my words.

"I'm..."

Braindead, apparently, rapidly spiraling toward the need for a ventilator.

"I just want to sit here for a minute and look at you."

He looked slightly uncomfortable, his eyes on mine as my gaze swept over his body, entertaining thoughts of licking every inch of that warm, golden skin, and I reached out to drag a thumb down the ridge of his hip. This was all for me, the thought struck me suddenly, making me almost giddy. This gorgeous man was more than happy to be my personal playground and by god, I wanted to play with every toy available. I wrapped my fingers around him, feeling his heartbeat pulsate beneath my fingers in hard bursts.

I wanted him everywhere: over me, under me, inside me, moaning my name as I took him.

My body began to throb with desire as I entertained the brief flashes of fantasy, my fingers beginning to move and he gasped, his eyes drifting shut.

"Easy, Angel," he bit out, "or this'll be over before we've started." He gritted his teeth.

I'd only just begun to touch him and his admission made me feel powerful, that I could bring this huge man so close to the edge with just a few strokes of my fingers. I wanted more of that power, that heady drug.

"Please," he begged, his body suddenly going rigid. "Eve." His voice sounded strangled and I sat back slowly, unsure what to do next. This was not exactly my area of expertise.

He took my face in his hands, a fierce look in his eyes. "I want *you*." His voice was low and rough and his intent was obvious.

I nodded, stretching out beside him, tugging at his hips to bring him close and he knelt quickly between my legs, my body completely covered by his. I loved it, the feeling of being so completely consumed, his muscles taut with his restraint as he loomed over me.

I reached for him, keeping my eyes wide and focused on his as I guided our bodies together. I needed to see him fall apart too, to know what I could do to him.

He was slow and deliberate, careful to let me adjust as I stretched to fit him. It was the most incredible sort of discomfort, a tight sort of pleasure that just bordered on pain. Yet he was patient, his body quivering with the effort as he held himself in check.

Lifting my hips against him slowly, his body pressed to mine, I smiled up at him lazily. "We fit."

He brought one arm up near my face, his hand curling around my cheek and when he smiled down at me, I felt like I was seeing inside his heart. He was vulnerable, open to me; scared; joyful; almost overwhelmed.

"We do."

I sighed happily, a weird feeling of contentment blooming in my chest as I held him in my body.

He kissed me slowly, smiling down. "So...more?"

I nodded. "Yes, please."

Our bodies moved together like we'd had years of practice, perfectly in sync, smooth and easy. The room filled with the sounds of our labored breaths and moans, soft sighs and whispered words.

"Angel?" he asked, his voice raspy, and I knew what he was asking.

"Yes," I panted back. "Soon."

He gritted his teeth, pushing one big hand under my hips, and it changed my position. My eyes grew wider at the sensation, the way it opened me to him, and I knew he was watching my face intently for every blink and flutter.

I let my eyes drift as my muscles began to contract and release in blinding waves, and I whispered his name brokenly, letting him watch me come completely undone beneath him as I panted and cried and groaned.

"Angel." His voice was rough and possessive, and I opened my eyes to see his expression strained, an agony of ecstasy playing across his beautiful face as he fell apart. It was the most beautiful thing I'd ever seen and I wrapped my legs up, around his hips, to hold him to me. I wanted him here, just like this, half crushing me, for as long as he'd let me.

He held himself there for a long time, nuzzling my neck, kissing me softly, smoothing the hair off my face before he nestled into my side and pulled me tighter against him, a sleepy, sated smile on his face.

I looped an arm over his hip and turned my face into his chest, kissing his sternum before the exhaustion swam up to meet me. "I'm not done with you, big man," I grumbled as I let my eyes drift shut and, content, my body loose with relaxation, I fell asleep in his arms.

NINETEEN

Noah
◄II►

I had never slept with anyone other than Avery, and I had never *slept* with anyone other than Avery. Because of that, it had been astonishing to me how quickly my body knew Eve's, picking up on cues, learning to fit and move with her in ways I'd thought would have to be learned.

Practiced with awkward giggles and adjustments.

But it had been more than I'd expected. It had been so much better, her responses more fevered, her eyes dark with the passion I'd only hoped for.

It was a powerful thing, to feel wanted by this woman. It was soothing and gratifying, and when she'd sat back on her heels and openly admired my body, I'd felt a little stab of something unfamiliar: Avery had never looked at me that way. She'd never commented on the work I'd put into my body over the years, simply seeming to accept that it was something necessary and utilitarian. It was the vehicle for her pleasure, and though she took it on occasion, she had never asked what I wanted.

And so I had learned how to please her.

Well.

Thoroughly.

When I woke in the middle of the night, it was with Eve still in my arms. And for the brief moments before I opened my eyes, my sleep-soaked brain tried to tell me she was Avery.

When I did open my eyes and realized, in the low light of the room that it was Eve, shame coursed through my veins when I knew I was relieved.

Eve stirred in my arms, her hand coming up to rub slow, lazy circles on my chest, and something fiercely joyful hammered behind my ribs.

Mine.

I'd finally won her over, the woman who'd starred in my dreams and fantasies every night for months on end.

Without a word, Eve pushed me onto my back and slid her hand down my body.

Testing me was unnecessary.

My body calling for hers was what had pulled me from sleep in the first place, and I watched the light glow around her as she straddled me, already warm and ready for me, welcoming.

The last thing I wanted to think about while I was inside Eve was Avery, but as she moved over me I couldn't help but remember all the ways in which Avery was different.

Less.

I hated the thought. It wasn't complementary to the woman I'd loved for most of my life.

Avery had loved me in her way, when she felt like it, willing to accept physical affection but very rarely giving any. She had joked with her sister that my need to be constantly touching her was like having a toddler on her hip all the time.

She'd taken me, my body, my loyalty and my patient attention to her pleasure completely for granted.

She had never thanked me for my willingness to give.

She had never pronounced me, or our lovemaking, remarkable or even satisfactory.

And now that I thought about it, the thought unbidden as Eve's hips rolled against my own, she had never woken with me in the middle of the night. She had never wanted *me* enough to take me like this.

I pushed the thought from my mind, letting my hands drift up to cup Eve's breasts as she groaned and rocked against me. This woman was a balm to my wounds, the sweet sounds she made a powerful boost to my confidence.

She tipped her head back then, her fingers twined through mine overtop her breasts. I could feel the rhythmic pull of her body, knew she was at the very edge, and I tugged at one nipple, toppling her over into an orgasm that left her weakly slumped against me, whispering nearly incoherent nonsense about coming so hard, she'd bitten her own tongue.

When she pulled herself upright and began to move again, I tried to still her. That she had come with my name on her lips as she cried out was already enough to make me feel like a king.

"No," she said firmly, taking my face in her hand. "I'm not here to just take. I want to see you lose control, too. I want to drive you at least half as wild as you make me."

I lifted my hips into the rolling of hers, undone by the sight of the flame-haired goddess riding me. She was more seductive than she'd ever know, biting her bottom lip, groaning softly as she gave herself to me.

It was just what I needed, my body responding to her sweet sounds of pleasure, and when I felt my body draw up tight she exploded again, moaning and shaking as I gripped her hips and filled every last inch of her, my vision going black as the powerful waves ripped through me.

"Can we do that again?" I whispered into her hair, my arms going around her back to anchor her body to my own.

There was something dangerous happening inside.

Something that made my heart feel like it was being stretched painfully inside of my ribcage, a rapid expansion to hold the feelings and the panic that were crowding into that cavity even as my body relaxed from such an incredible high. Probably just endorphins, I told myself. Endorphins and adrenaline and everything just had to settle back down where it belonged...not that every part of my body was getting that message.

I shifted a little uncomfortably, still capable of putting someone's eye out, even at half-mast.

"This is impressive."

Eve had lifted herself off my chest and was lying next to me, her fingers trailing lazily up and down my ribs before settling over my favorite body part.

"You really could just go on all night, couldn't you?" She asked, and her light touch was tempting enough to coax more blood away from the Big Brain.

"Don't you need time to reload or something?" She teased, her fingers curling around me.

"Something," I grunted, a little shocked that only moments had passed and I was even capable of another round. At my age, it didn't seem that should be possible.

"Okay, well…" She yawned heavily. "I might need to play dead girlfriend on this one, because I am beat…but I could offer some encouragement."

She rolled so her back was to me, and she reached behind her to pull me onto my side. She hooked one leg back, over mine, and positioned herself before reaching for me.

"One second…push your hips forward…uh…" She grunted as I rocked forward, filling her from behind.

"There you go," she purred, giggling and flexing her muscles, squeezing me pleasantly.

I flexed my abdominal muscles and it made me jump inside her. She made a noise when I did it, a noise that made me think she'd liked it, and she wriggled her hips against me. I took that as encouragement to keep moving and I kept the pace slow, reveling in the feeling of her warm, soft body.

There was nothing hurried or frantic this time, and I slipped a hand over her hip, letting my fingers drift between her legs. There I could take my time, drawing slow, lazy circles while our bodies set a gentle rhythm. We weren't in a hurry. It was more about being with her, being present in the moment, and just enjoying the feeling of one another. The finish line was a distant goal, and there was no race to get there.

Instead, we whispered tender things to one another and she reached beneath her pillow to find my arm under her head. She pulled my hand toward her mouth, kissing each of my fingers gently and that terrifying feeling kicked inside my chest again. Because suddenly I couldn't imagine a single night without her in it. In a flash, I could see her in my house--our house, our son, our children, sleeping down the hall.

I could see her in my bed, her hair fanned out on the pillow, a smile on her face, her belly round with my baby. And suddenly, I wanted that fiercely. I wanted what I'd missed out on, and I wanted it with *this* woman.

Ever so slightly, I increased the pressure and the speed of my fingers, a pleasant pressure starting to build in my lower spine.

She reached behind herself, over my arm, her fingers pressing into my butt so hard, I knew there would be a handprint come morning. I followed the rhythmic flex of her fingers, surging into her when she squeezed, and withdrawing when she released.

I felt her begin to splinter before I heard it. I let the pulsing of her contractions pull me into ecstasy, burying myself deep inside of her, my teeth grazing her shoulder as my jaw locked and the sound that came from my throat was almost pained.

"Noah," she whispered raggedly when our breathing calmed, and I tucked my hand beneath her breast, squeezing, feeling her heartbeat hammer in her chest.

We fell asleep that way, wrapped in one another, legs intertwined, my body still a part of hers, and when we woke in the early morning light, we hadn't moved at all.

***

Eve giggled when she woke to find me still inside her, and on the dawn of what was going to be one more of the worst days of my life, she woke me with a squeeze of her internal muscles.

Slowly, quietly, we started our day by making love again.

Words didn't seem necessary and when we both rose to shower, she folded into my arms for a long moment and rested her head on my shoulder.

We stood there like that for a while, the connection deep and tender, and I cradled the back of her head in one hand, holding her close with the other.

There were incredible smells coming from the kitchen when we let ourselves into the house for breakfast and Finn, sipping her coffee alone at the table, broke into a wide grin when she saw Eve trail in behind me.

"Mrs. J," she called in her husky voice, sounding as if she had a perpetual case of laryngitis. "A cranberry juice for the lady, if you don't mind."

Eve flushed almost the color of her hair, her mouth dropping open just a little. She did look freshly fucked, if I said so myself, and I was pretty sure Finn saw what I did: a content, satisfied woman, even if she was walking a little stilted.

"Is it that obvious?" Eve hissed at Finn, the color high in her cheeks.

An evil smile bloomed on Finn's face. "Probably not...that hickey's pretty obvious, though." Finn tapped the side of her neck, just under her ear, and Eve hastily pulled her hair around her neck and face.

Finn rose from the table, grabbing a plate from the island and digging into one of the many steaming dishes Mrs. Jensen had lining it.

"Good enough." She bumped me out of the way with her hip, her voice low so that it wouldn't carry through the cavernous house. "At least one of us is getting some."

TWENTY

Eve

✦

"Seraphina." Noah's voice was like liquid velvet, and I cast a sidelong glance at him. I'd never heard him use her full name before.

"Is Mateo too busy playing with balls to meet your needs?"

A spoonful of scrambled eggs came flying over the island and Noah's hand shot out to deflect them, keeping me from being pelted with the steaming hot, cheesy mess.

"Don't be a dick," she warned, her voice as close to a snarl as I'd heard yet. "I'm not *that* kind of woman."

"Blondie, your marriage to Magnus was dead before you took vows, but you were young and optimistic. Kinda dumb," he said seriously, and his expression was sad.

I knew his loyalty to his sister ran deep.

"Any man stupid enough to be more interested in that powdered shit more than he is in you..." He gestured broadly toward the length of her body, shaking his head.

It was inarguable that Finn was beautiful. Like bombshell-level beautiful.

"Well, he's hopeless.

"Worse than an idiot.

"A lost cause.

"But Mateo...now, there's a man who's *not* a lost cause. In fact, I think he might *be* the cause." The teasing grin was back on his face, and another spoonful of eggs came flying through the air.

"I have never broken my vows," she hissed, her voice low and angry, like a cat giving a warning growl just before striking.

213

Snatching her towering plate off the island, she stalked back toward the table and I saw the defeated slump of her shoulders when she collapsed into the chair.

"Now you know the truth, Eve," she called over her shoulder without bothering to turn her head. "I've been married for almost ten years to a man who doesn't want me. In fact, he couldn't care less."

I scooped my own plate off the counter and Noah nodded at me, concern in his eyes.

"I know something about that," I said, crossing the large space to sit down right next to her. I drew the chair up close, reaching out to put my hand on hers as I sat, and in the quietness of the room, I knew she was hiding tears behind the veil of her hair.

I kept my voice down, half conscious of the fact I wasn't ready to share my full history with Noah, even as I shared it with his sister.

I quietly told her of my difficult teenage years: of the men who'd tried to take advantage of me because I'd been the underdog in the situation, and of getting pregnant with Jared because I'd been too stupid to protect myself from a man who wanted nothing more than to own my body.

"He's been gone for years," I said finally, most of the food on my plate gone cold. "I've been raising my son on my own for a long time now and his father's not interested in helping--not really--or he'd have shown up before. If he cared he'd have at least made consistent child support payments."

Finn turned toward me and her beautiful face folded suddenly. She put her face in her hands and I caught her, pulling her into a hug. She let me, leaning heavily into my shoulder and shivering convulsively as silent sobs racked her body.

From Noah's teasing, I suspected the tears had to do with much more than just her wayward husband. In fact, I was willing to bet he was a minor factor.

My heart ached for her. There was so much pain in this family; so much suffering. For the first time in as long as I could remember, I didn't feel like the only broken person in the room.

"I'm so sorry," she said finally, pulling herself from my tear-soaked shoulder and running her fingers under her eyes. Even wrecked, she was stupidly gorgeous. "You came for one mess and you inherited four more." She drew in a huge breath. "I know I wouldn't stick with us; we're too broken."

I sighed, hugging her again. I knew a thing or two about messy and broken, and I had seen more than my fair share of both. It didn't scare me anymore.

We sat together at the table for another hour, scraping the cold food off our plates and refilling them from the steaming dishes on the island. The food had multiplied since the last time we'd served ourselves and Finn smiled, shaking her head as we moved back toward the table. "Mrs. J. is like the tooth fairy," she said, setting her coffee down gently. "Almost mythical. You hear the stories and you don't believe it, but in the morning everything is there, all steaming and glorious on the counter."

We sat stirring our coffee and Finn began slowly to open up to me about Mateo, the man she worked for, a young, sought after baseball player based out of southern California. From the way she spoke of him, almost reverently and with no little heat, I knew there were feelings she'd never acted upon.

I laughed a little, considering the ramifications of dating a 23 year old, and not the 36 year old man I'd shared a bed with the night before, because I knew I'd made the right choice.

"I get it," I agreed, nodding as I sipped what might have been my fourth cup of coffee. "You're not eager to raise another child, and that's completely fair. But...it doesn't sound like Mateo has done anything to prove himself immature or incapable."

Finn sighed heavily, throwing a piece of bacon into her mouth and chewing it with a viciousness I was sure she didn't feel toward the animal itself. "He's a better adult than I am," she said, rolling her eyes. "He's mature and responsible and socially and civically minded. He contributes to charities and does things just because they're the right things to do.

"I am legally linked to someone with the emotional capacity of a toddler; a man who doesn't believe in charity because he says it's rewarding the lazy. A man who hasn't worked a day in his life! I mean..." She broke off suddenly, the look on her face convincing me she was gaining ground on hysteria. "What in the actual fuck was I thinking, Eve? I married someone who couldn't be bothered to provide for his own children--he has more than just my son. And I've stayed with him for almost ten years. I'm too young to have stayed with *anyone* for ten years."

Oh boy, didn't I know it.

There was a noise from the doorway and we both turned to find Thomas, his eyes unfocused, his movements indicating he was drunk or disoriented or both, lurching into the kitchen to pour coffee.

We worked together to fill a plate for him and Finn soothed and clucked while I dished food into his mouth, not unlike what I'd done for Jared when he was a baby. After all, we were burying his son this very day; something I couldn't even imagine doing myself.

Finn finally led him from the room, another cup of coffee in her hand and whether it was for her or for him didn't really matter to me. The battle ahead of her, to get him showered and dressed, was something I knew would be downright monumental.

"Angel."

Noah stood in the doorway, tall and wide and powerful, and a brief flash of memory made me sigh, not even remotely embarrassed by how much I wanted the man who stood before me. He had been all the things I needed him to be, and the biggest one was patient. He had dissolved my barriers even while I tried to fight him. And here he was, waiting for me, concern clear on his face when his concern should have been for his brother.

"Bear." I tried to smile back, knowing I couldn't, and he closed the gap quickly, folding me into his arms as his lips came to rest in my hair.

"Thank you for helping him," he whispered, and I knew he'd been sitting in the living room, listening to Finn and me the entire time.

"I didn't," I responded, surprised to find sorrow twisting my mouth downward. I wanted to do so much more. My heart ached for Seraphina and her lonely heart, and for Thomas, who was barely surviving the loss of his only son.

"You did, Angel. And you...you doin' ok?" The question was loaded. He wasn't talking about dealing with Thomas, and when he pulled me into his arms I nodded against his chest. He bent quickly, one arm sweeping behind my knees while the other banded around my shoulders. It was sudden and surprising, and as he carried me through the house, toward what I knew was the staircase in the garage, I gave myself permission to quit the mental struggle. This man cared for me, that much was obvious, and I was going to let him.

Wrapping one arm around his wide back and throwing the other over his shoulder, I knew without a doubt that what happened in California was not going to stay in California. I had been in love with this man for a long while before I had admitted it to myself. The idea of opening myself up to someone enough to love them was what had been holding me back, because it opened me up to heartbreak.

He carried me up the stairs and laid me gently on the bed, kicking off his big boots and pulling me tight against his body, his fingers curling beneath my breast while his lips pressed against the back of my neck. "Sleep, my angel," he murmured. "We have hours yet."

So I relaxed into his embrace and gave the worries over to sleep.

***

When I woke again, the rays of the sun were longer, the sun over the ridgeline of the house and starting to filter into the room. It cast long, golden fingers over the bed and I stirred slowly, aware Noah had fallen asleep wrapped around me.

"Bear," I whispered softly. "My beautiful man..."

He was so beautiful in sleep, it hurt. I knew the ache meant I'd claimed this man as my own: I had taken possession and was to be held accountable for him, his welfare, and the state of his still-mending heart.

217

"Mmm." He grumbled something low, from deep within that broad chest that made me catch my breath every time I saw him.

"We have to get ready."

He stretched slowly, his eyes opening and his lips curving into a sweet smile when he realized I was the one prompting him. "Mmm, my angel. You can wake me up anytime you think there's something important happening--or about to happen." His eyebrows wiggled a little.

"Noah, come on." My voice sharpened. "Nothing is more important than burying your nephew. Get up."

He shot out of the bed, his expression contrite, and when he stepped from the shower all wrapped up in a towel, I was there to pull him close. I felt a little guilty, but mostly just worried. I worried about how he was going to handle the rest of today.

We dressed in our somber clothes and let ourselves into the main house again, the air already thick with tension.

"He's not gonna be fit to carry it." Aaron's voice carried from the living room and Noah charged in, his hands balled into fists.

"Then we hold him up," he barked and both Asher and Aaron's heads snapped up. They exchanged a look and I wondered briefly if they'd been talking about Thomas, or Noah.

"This is the easy part." Noah's teeth were very nearly grinding. "We pull that little box out of the car and we carry it to the grove. I'll carry him by myself if I have to." There was so much heartbreak etched on his face, it hurt to look at him. I reached across the distance to take his hand, linking my fingers through his. Touch seemed to reach him when nothing else could and he turned his head slowly to look at me, his beautiful, warm eyes welling.

"You can't know," he told them. "It's a kind of loss you can't even imagine. It's unbearable and it *never* stops or goes away. You wake up every day with a giant hole in your heart, and you just have to keep going to get through the day, because that hole's always gonna be there."

Aaron's face tightened like he might disagree, but he didn't voice his thoughts.

There was a sound, something between a hiccup and a sob from the hallway, and dread fisted tight in my gut.

Noah spun quickly, hurrying in the direction of the sound and I followed behind, not surprised to see Thomas crumpled on the floor, his arms wrapped around his knees, his forehead resting on them.

Noah dropped quickly down next to him, his hands on Thomas's arms.

"You can't understand it either." Thomas's voice was raw and grating. "You didn't wake up for nighttime feedings. You weren't there for nightmares or bedtime stories or trips to the park. Doctor visits. Trips to therapy. You had an *idea*, not a child. You lost the *idea* of something you learned to love. You didn't have to watch your baby die." His voice broke.

Noah rocked back on his heels, his expression as stunned as if Thomas had punched him in the teeth. He sat like that for a moment, chewing on his lip, his nostrils flared. He lifted an arm several times to run his sleeve across his face and I sank down next to him, pressing myself tight into his side, hoping to absorb some of the hurt for him.

"Who are you?" Thomas asked thickly, and I looked up at him in surprise. After several conversations and feeding him his breakfast like a toddler, I was surprised his memory hadn't yet catalogued my face.

His eyes were bloodshot and unfocused. He laughed a wild, crazy laugh. "Dude...Avery know you brought another woman with you? She'll kick your ass."

He was looking at me again. He meant that Avery would kick *my* ass.

"Avery's gone." Noah's voice was tight and Thomas's face went slack with shock.

"Shit, I forgot. I'm sorry."

I had a strong suspicion that his confusion had something to do with a bottle of heavy-hitting medication, washed down with liquid forgetfulness.

Noah helped Thomas to his feet and I hurried into the kitchen to fill a glass with water. Finn was there already, filling a glass and she looked over her shoulder at me, shaking her head. "Same idea," she said. "Dilute whatever he's already managed to get down his throat today. I don't know where he's hiding it."

It took all three men to load Thomas into the Land Rover sitting out front. Asher and Aaron crawled in on either side of him, while Finn and the Jensens took the back row.

Helping me into the passenger seat, Noah walked around to the front of the vehicle and turned over the engine.

We drove out of the courtyard, through the tall gate and down a long drive flanked by more vines. The drive stretched on and on and when we finally came to a main road, Noah flipped the blinker and turned out, driving silently for several more moments before making another left turn. It felt like we'd just gone in a giant circle and as we bumped along what was clearly some sort of access road, I watched as vines gave way to trees.

We pulled right into a fairly dense grove of trees and I caught my breath at the sight of a black hearse already parked there. Thomas saw it too, and he shrank from it visibly, his face going pale.

Finn and the Jensens got out of the car quickly, walking past the hearse and deeper into the trees. A man with robes and a long sash joined them, the four of them pausing to discuss something with earnest looks on their faces.

"She's left me to do this all on my own," Thomas muttered as a man climbed from the hearse and rounded the car to open the back door. I caught my breath as it swung open, the sight of the tiny white casket sending a shockwave of silent grief through the car.

Noah gripped the steering wheel tightly, his jaw set hard. I could see a muscle ticing in his cheek. "Come on, boys," he said, finally throwing open his door, "we gotta do this thing."

The officiant stood waiting at the hearse and Thomas stumbled as they drew nearer, seeming smaller suddenly, as if he was folding into himself. Aaron stood on one side and Asher on the other as they held him up.

"Aaron." Noah's voice was commanding and Aaron stepped away from Thomas, toward the car. Noah nodded at him, something unspoken passing between the two of them and there was a noise as the driver disengaged something, allowing the casket to roll easily forward and off the back of the vehicle. Noah stooped, bearing the load as it slid from the car and Aaron stepped quickly forward to shoulder the other end.

Asher had his hands full trying to keep the man upright and moving forward, and Noah and Aaron carried the small white box down the path and through the trees.

There were several ornate gravestones jutting up from the ground and a row of smaller markers in front. I had some idea of what that meant, and I moved only slightly closer as Noah and Aaron knelt, depositing their precious cargo gently on the ground.

The minister or pastor or priest, whatever he was, opened a thick blue book and began to speak. There were words coming out of his mouth and I knew this, because I could see his lips moving. But for some reason my brain couldn't parse, sort and reorganize the sounds into anything that made sense. All I could do was watch Noah, his back to me. He had stepped into Asher's spot moments before, physically holding Thomas up as the words went on and on.

There was a short prayer, heads bowed respectfully, and two men I hadn't noticed before slipped slings beneath the casket, preparing to lower it into the yawning hole in the ground. Noah spun Thomas as they did it, mashing his brother's face into his shoulder and anchoring him there with his huge arms as the box was lowered. Thomas's shoulders shook and Noah absorbed all of it, the strain, the grief, the tears, his own face stony as he gazed toward the hole.

Finn stepped forward then. "You don't need to be here for this," she said gently, her hand on Thomas's shoulder, and to my surprise he let her lead him back toward the car. He moved like his own weight was too much to carry, his shoulders slumped, and when I heard the car door shut I slipped my arm around Noah's middle. He looked down at me like he'd forgotten I was there.

Noah, Aaron, Asher and I stood there as the men filled the hole with dirt, our bodies a wall, physically shielding the view from where we knew Thomas sat watching in the car.

The completed marker hadn't been delivered yet and the men finished their task, taking their shovels with them.

Cars started up behind us, the men moving slowly down the road in a pickup truck, followed by the hearse and the officiant's car.

"Take him back," Noah said to Aaron, his voice strained. "Get Finn to feed him something that'll knock him out--her anti-anxiety meds or something. I'll walk back when I'm ready."

I shifted against his side and he looked down at me again, kissing my temple gently. "It's ok, Angel. You can go. I just need a minute." His expression was still tightly controlled and I moved in closer, pressing the length of my body against his. Even if he shut me out now, I could still communicate with him through touch, and that was a language he spoke fluently.

I didn't argue or protest, but I didn't leave either. "You don't have to do this alone," I said softly, and I continued to cling to him like a barnacle as Aaron's footsteps moved slowly away and the car started up behind us, the sound slowly moving further away.

When the engine noise faded and it was just us, a bird singing somewhere in the trees, Noah broke. He didn't make a sound, but his chest began to tremble, his breath growing harsh and frantic as tears started to pour down his handsome face.

This was so much different from that day in the ER waiting room, when I'd watched him splinter in front of me. I'd been drawn to him then, knowing nothing of his struggle. And now that I knew the depth of his pain, I couldn't stand to watch him suffer. He was mine now, and there was nothing I could do or give him to calm him. I felt helpless and angry.

It was just us, far removed from anyone else, and I wrapped my arms around his chest and held on tight, hoping to hold him together.

***

We stayed in the grove for a very long time. There wasn't a single word spoken between the two of us and we sat on the ground while Noah

222

struggled with his grief. I sat with my legs bracketing his, my front wrapped around his back in a full-body hug. I held him in my arms, one hand alternately sifting through his hair or rubbing up and down his back, his arm, brushing my fingers down his cheeks. He let me, his eyes closed as he leaned back into my shoulder, and I tried to fill up the hole I knew was inside him with the things I felt but couldn't say.

It scared me, the sudden intensity of what I felt for this man. I'd kept things shut down, locked up and hidden safely away for such a long time, and now I'd been knocked sideways by a tidal wave of emotion. It was love and tenderness and a fierce desire to protect him from the things over which I knew I had no control. I knew he'd always been the rock, and this time he needed someone to step in and shoulder the burden for him.

It was late when we finally straggled back to the house. It was a long walk through the rows of vines and we walked silently, my arm around his waist, tucked in beneath his arm.

The shadows were growing longer and the large patio doors were open as we walked through the living room and into the large, gracious kitchen and eating area where everyone but Thomas had gathered. The minister was there, talking earnestly with Mr. Jensen while Mrs. J. sipped a cup of tea, her hand on her husband's knee.

Asher and Finn were deep in conversation as well, food spread out across the table, plates empty and wine glasses half full.

Aaron sat at the large table with his chin propped in the heel of his hand, fingers over his mouth, a deep frown creasing his forehead, clearly miles away in his head.

Noah dropped heavily into one of the chairs and I grabbed a clean plate to begin filling with food. I set it in front of him and crossed the kitchen to draw a glass of water, quickly removing the wine glass from his place setting. He pulled me quickly down into his lap, resting his head against my shoulder and closing his eyes.

The movement seemed to startle Aaron from his reverie and he gazed at us thoughtfully, nodding once. "You're good for him," he said quietly. "God knows good women are in short supply these days." Something I knew he'd learned firsthand, as Finn told me a little about what had happened with Aaron's wife.

I curled my fingers into Noah's hair and he lifted his head to press his lips against my neck, tucking his face tightly into the curve between my neck and shoulder.

The late afternoon stretched into evening and Jensen shut the huge patio doors and built a fire in the living room fireplace. Then, while Asher, Aaron and Finn sat together near the fire and animatedly teased one another, Jensen and the man I'd learned was Pastor Willis settled into the library with glasses of scotch and began a lively discussion about the afterlife.

"You're exhausted, babe," I murmured into Noah's ear. We still sat at the table and I was still in his lap, as he'd been unwilling or unable to bear any physical distance. So we sat, and I held him while Mrs. J. buzzed around the kitchen, loading dishwashers and wrapping food, constantly ferrying plates of cheese and bread, olives and cold meats out to the living room or the library. One thing this family could do, with wild abandon, was eat.

I rose slowly from Noah's lap, pulling him up with me and leading him through the kitchen. I hugged Mrs. J. as we went, leading the huge man quietly down the hallway and out toward the garage.

Pushing him toward the bathroom, I heard the toilet flush, the sink turn on, and the sound of him brushing his teeth.

When he stepped from the bathroom, his shirt unbuttoned halfway, my phone was to my ear and I was asking Jared about his day. He hadn't asked me about why I'd gone, though he knew I'd gone with Noah. I wondered if he was pushing Alex to his breaking point with his curiosity, as Alex had let it slip that Jared had been seeking him out lately to talk about anything that popped through his head.

There was a loud noise in the background, a happy chattering of small voices, and suddenly Lauren was back on the phone with me. "He's good," she said quickly. "Kids are dragging him out to play in the yard. Since Alex just got home from his shift, now's their time for piggyback rides and playing in that death trap of a tree fort."

"Thanks for watching him," I said quietly, a little unsettled by the intense way Noah was looking at me as he crossed the room. He knelt at my feet, placing my hand on his shoulder as he leaned over and slipped the flats off my feet.

I hurried Lauren off the phone as he started to unbutton the front of my calf-length dress, starting at the bottom and working his way up. He stood as he neared the top, sliding it over my shoulders and draping it over a chair. My bra was next, tossed on top of the dress and I stood there in just my underwear, trying to read the expression on his face as he looked down at me.

He stepped forward then, his arms going around me and he dropped his face into my hair. He kept one hand wrapped around my back while the other smoothed the length of my hair, again and again, in what I suspected was a repetitive motion he found soothing.

Reaching up between us, I finished unbuttoning his shirt and added it to the pile, followed by his pants. He sighed, wrapping me back up against his chest and I realized with some surprise that his response to the touch of my skin wasn't sexual. He seemed to draw strength and comfort from my nearness. He was comfortable with me.

When I yawned against his chest he took my hand, pulling back the blankets before crawling in behind me and I turned so I could wrap around him, throwing a leg over his, my arm over his chest, my head cradled on his shoulder. He turned into me slowly, one arm beneath me to hold me close, his other hand resting on the arm I'd thrown over him.

Twisting my head to kiss his chest, I nestled back in and waited for his breathing to slow. My ear rested over his heart and the strong, steady beat was a comforting sound.

When I woke during the night, we had shifted. I had rolled onto my side and he had followed, wrapped up tightly behind me, his arms around me. Even in his sleep he had to be touching me, preferably more rather than less, and when I wiggled his arms tightened almost convulsively. He was making soft noises, sounds of distress, and I knew that was what had awakened me: Noah was having a nightmare.

I woke him then, by rolling him onto his back and crawling on top of him. I was slow and deliberate, and I kissed and loved him until the pale light of dawn began to chase away his ghosts.

TWENTY-ONE

Noah

❮❯

Thomas didn't come down for breakfast that morning.

He didn't come down for lunch either.

At two I went up with a tray, determined to break down his bedroom door if I found it locked. Instead I found him propped up in his bed, the shirt he'd worn the day before half unbuttoned and horribly wrinkled. His eyes were bloodshot and hollow, dark circles beneath them.

His words from the day before had been ringing in my ears for the past twenty-four hours. They burned and cut and scraped my insides raw. I felt like I'd swallowed razor blades, the pain sharp in my chest and stomach. I had no idea whether he even remembered saying such things, but my dreams the night before had included a terrible vision of Avery giving birth to a puff of smoke. Eve had been the one to wake me from it, her lips soft and warm against my neck, and I'd willingly taken solace in her arms.

Setting the tray on the bedside table, I sat next to my brother and reached for his hand. I'd have much rathered put him in a headlock, but I wasn't afraid of what this might look like. I was a pretty enlightened guy, I congratulated myself, able to hold another dude's hand when it was really important.

I was able to get some food into him and shove him through another shower, since he smelled like he'd been living under a bridge with feral cats, and while he was in there, Mrs. J. sneaked into the room and made quick work of changing the bed and opening the windows to air the room.

Finn made an appearance with a glass of water and a pill I suspected was Valium. She hadn't said as much, but I was pretty sure she'd been on medications for anxiety and depression for some time. Obviously, she'd been feeding them to Thomas for the past few days.

Thomas popped the pill into his mouth and reached for a glass on the bedside table. Finn snatched it from him, sniffing it quickly and shaking her head disapprovingly before hurrying to the bathroom to dump the contents. "Don't even try playing that," she warned him as she came back out of the bathroom. "I know you don't care right now, but you forget that you still have a family that needs you. Don't you dare risk it by mixing stupid shit. I am not coming back anytime soon to bury your dumb ass."

He glared at her, taking the glass of water she held out to him and chugging half of it before throwing himself face down into the pillows again.

"One of us needs to stay with him," she said quietly as I shut the door behind us. "Maybe we can take shifts; trade off. But we can't leave him like this, because we're going to lose him."

It seemed to be a genetic legacy of sorts: Our family didn't handle grief well, but our drama game was top-notch, and all of us could drink like fish if we so chose. We really knew how to pull out all the stops.

"I can take shotgun; I can shift things around the next couple weeks," I said as we moved toward the stairs. "He did it for me, so I'll stay and make sure he gets the help he needs. He's gonna need a real head doc, and maybe some time in a fancy rehab. I know a few things about that, thanks to him."

The four of us gathered in the living room to discuss the situation while Eve helped Mrs. J. in the kitchen. Soon enough though, she drifted into the room and curled wordlessly into my side, linking her fingers through my own, wrapping them right around my damn heart.

Asher watched her jealously, I noticed. My youngest brother's eyes seemed drawn to the sway of her hips, her long, lithe legs, her beautiful green eyes and the soft lips that always held a sweet smile for me. I didn't feel threatened by him for a second, but I wrapped an arm around her and kissed the side of her head anyway. Maybe just because I wanted to. It was pretty damn obvious that I couldn't keep my hands off her for anything, and finally she seemed pretty ok with that.

The four of us came up with a tentative schedule, each of us pledging two weeks to our brother's care, and fingers flew over phone screens to put together emails and texts arranging to take time off respective jobs.

Me? I didn't ask anyone, but I did text Da to relay my plans. He should've been here anyway, I thought, shaking my head in irritation. The man had always put himself first, and this time his excuse pinged back that things with the wife were too tenuous. He needed to stay and work on his pathetic sham of a marriage, which was clearly more important to him than his kids.

I put my phone on speaker and we called Gerry, the first stepmother to come into our lives, who for six years held our splintered family together until Da finally drove her off. He was a shitty husband, and she'd put up with him far longer than she should have, his drinking and shouting, his gambling and whoring.

Gerry had wordlessly picked up and moved to Alabama shortly after Thomas. Everyone but him knew it was so she could keep an eye on him after his life began to fall apart. She'd always been there for us like that, more dependable than our own father.

She had a thriving practice as a behavioral therapist and though adults weren't her specialty, she'd been treating all of us for years. Most of the time we didn't even know it, she was so good at getting things out of us and helping us to sort them out.

Gerry hadn't been able to attend the funeral, thanks to a speaking commitment at a professional conference in the Netherlands, but she quickly promised to spend the last two-week stretch with Thomas, after Asher's shift was over. It would allow her to gauge his progress from a professional standpoint, and if we needed to reassess his needs at that time, she was just the person for it.

Eve sat quietly as we planned, pressed against my side, the pressure of her body and the touch of her skin a constant reassurance. I held her there, my arm tightly around her, watching Asher's eyes flick jealously between us. He'd been looking at her that way the whole time, I realized slowly, and I'd only just realized it today. It was possible I was going to have to spend some time bringing him to Jesus.

If Eve noticed Asher's hot gaze, she hadn't said anything. In fact, I wasn't sure she'd looked at him at all but his stare was so intense, it was visceral. Maybe he *was* making her uncomfortable.

It was late before we concluded our meeting and the Jensens saw to it we were well fed and libations flowed freely. I stopped after one beer, but Eve had a couple glasses of wine and the color in her cheeks rose a little more with each glass.

Eve knew my plans to take the first watch with Thomas, that she would be flying home alone tomorrow, and I felt a little guilty for so readily agreeing to something that would leave her in the lurch.

I wouldn't be there to soothe her fears on the plane.

I wouldn't be there to drive her home.

I wouldn't be there for several more weeks, and a momentary stab of fear caused adrenaline to rush through my veins.

It might give her enough time to decide this was a mistake.

It was Eve who led me through the darkened hallway and out toward the garage, where I climbed up the staircase behind her, watching the sway of her hips as she led me toward the apartment. A hotly possessive feeling coiled in my gut, because I couldn't get the way Asher had been looking at her out of my head. I couldn't decide whether it meant that I was jealous, or whether I knew he was the better choice.

He was, too: the better choice. He was younger, probably fitter, clearly drank less and made a salary so bloated, she'd never have to worry for money again.

"I can't stand the way he was looking at you," I blurted as soon as the door had shut, and she turned quickly to look at me.

"Who was looking at me?" She asked the question innocently, moving quickly to the sink to fill two glasses of water and handing one to me.

"Asher. Don't tell me you haven't noticed him eye fucking you all day." The words were hot and bitter, and I tried to drown them by pouring the water down my throat.

She stood there for a moment, staring at me with a thoughtful expression on her face before taking several delicate sips of water and setting her glass on the countertop. "No," she said softly. "I didn't notice, because all I can see is you." She moved toward me then, taking the glass and then curling her fingers into my hair. She tugged a little, pulling my head back and she leaned in to kiss the heartbeat hammering in my throat. It made a thrill run through me, the jolt of electricity canceling out the anger and fear churning in my gut.

"This little treasure trove of brothers," she grinned at me, her fingers working to deftly free the buttons on my shirt. "You're all such gorgeous men. But you..." She kissed the hollow of my throat. "I don't think you know that you're the prize. Out of all these men, I'd pick you every time." She ran a finger down my sternum. "That silly, stupid little girl didn't know what she had." She paused then, like she'd said something bad, and I knew she hadn't meant to say it out loud. She looked up at me guiltily, her cheeks flushed from wine and shame. "I should apologize." She hiccupped and I realized for the first time that she'd had several glasses of wine. "But I'm not really sorry. I don't mean to hurt you with that, but you must know she had no clue how to appreciate you."

I stood there, the muscles in my back tensing as I waited for her to finish her rambling thoughts. I was primed for the "but," the thing that hurt, since Avery hadn't been one to give me compliments and when she did they were usually disguised as something hurtful.

Eve bit her lip then, pulling the shirt from my shoulders and running her fingers lightly over my skin. "You just have no idea," she whispered, leaning forward to kiss my chest.

I wanted to know what it was I had no idea of, so I hooked a finger under her chin, forcing her to look up at me.

"I've been trying to keep you away for so long." She hiccupped again. "But sometimes at night, you get stuck in my brain..."

I liked where this was going.

"And I can't sleep because all I can think about is what it would be like to be yours. I dream about your lips and your hands and I..." She trailed off again, focused on getting the clasp of my belt buckle undone. "I fantasize about having you in my bed."

Holy shit, she was really drunk. This wasn't the reserved woman I was used to, the one whose every emotion was held tightly in check. Every thought of hers was labeled "Inside Voice," and she always clamped down hard on her own urges, never giving in even when I could see her struggling with them.

I liked this one with a little sauce in her. It loosened her up and gave her the humanity she tried so hard to stamp out.

She finally succeeded in getting the buckle undone, and with a delighted little laugh she stripped the belt from my pants and went to work on the button and zipper, her tongue poking out between her teeth and her eyebrows pulled together. It was so damned cute.

"It's not fair," she said suddenly, looking up into my eyes, her own dilated and unfocused. "I never do what I want--not ever--I can't. I always have to be responsible. I'm so tired of being responsible." She struggled with the word.

I took over then, wrenching open her shirt. The sound of tearing fabric made her eyes widen just before she giggled. "Ooh, a little impatient are we, Bear?"

It almost made me giggle too, that stupid, insanely high-pitched giggle that would have completely killed the mood. Instead, I snorted and clamped down on it. "Always impatient, Angel," I said roughly, ripping the fabric from her body and pushing her back against the door. "You're tired of being responsible and I'm tired of waiting. I want in here." I tapped a finger over her heart. "Stop overthinking this. Stop worrying. Let me show you what we can be."

She sighed against my skin, a sound of acquiescence, pulling me down to the floor. She drove me wild, made me desperate to win her over, to prove to her that I was worth the risk after the lifetime she'd spent worrying.

To say that I loved her well was the understatement of a lifetime. I brought all my skills to the fore, dominating her with my sheer size, reminding her with my touch that I could be gentle and tender, loving and careful and when she shuddered and moaned my name, I stopped, moving quickly up her body to hold her close.

It hurt.

It was physical agony to deny myself the comfort of her sweet body. But I'd set out to do something: To prove to her that I was worth her time, effort and attention. So while she came down I wrapped myself around her, whispering sweet, gentle things. It made her hum contentedly and she rolled slowly, crawling on top of me and pinning my hands over my head, a wicked grin on her face.

I liked drunk Eve a lot.

"Ok, big guy…" She rolled her hips against me and I clenched my jaw. "Your turn."

***

It had occurred to me that Thomas might move through the stages of grief faster than I had. Given the upheaval he'd weathered in the past months, all in the name of saving his doomed marriage, I supposed it gave him a bit of a head start.

And now he was *pissed.*

"You don't get to make decisions for me," he barked from the bathroom.

I had cranked the shower dial and hauled him out of bed. His first appointment with a therapist was in three hours and we had to drive into San Francisco, but I wasn't about to sit in a car with him or subject any other human to the way he smelled. It was obvious that he'd forgotten how to be an adult, and we needed to have the old Puberty Talk about using deodorant *all* the time.

Jensen had already driven Eve and Finn to the airport early this morning.

Since Aaron was headed to the airport later that afternoon and Asher was hitching a ride with him, it left me to deal with the roaring rage monster that seemed to have taken possession of my oldest brother's body. This guy was being a giant asshole, and I was trying my hardest not to get mad at him for it, reminding myself daily of what he was going through. Because if there was anyone who should understand something of his mental process, it was me.

With Finn gone, Thomas was coming out of his chemically induced haze. There were no more pills to take the edge off or to dull the pain, and when Thomas drank excessively he was known to get mean and do and say stupid shit he'd never have done or said while sober. Drinking canceled out his filters.

I could handle him. I was several inches taller and had a good fifty or more pounds on him. Often that meant he was quicker than me, since he was smaller and in pretty good physical condition, but the booze slowed him down--a lot. Screwed with his coordination.

It worried me to think of what would happen when Finn took her shift if I couldn't get him off the stuff in time. I doubted he'd do anything to hurt her, but he was scary when he'd had too much. He was threatening and intimidating, and God knew she'd had enough of that in her life already. I didn't want her to suffer emotional scarring at Thomas's hands just because she'd done her duty by him.

He was quiet and sullen during the drive into the city, since I'd enlisted Jensen to help me hide all the liquor in the house. I didn't want him to start the day with bourbon in his coffee, and that pissed him off, but I could handle his empty threats and loud voice.

You'd have thought I was his parent, the way he was acting. He pouted like a toddler as I drove, big arms crossed over a wide chest, and I almost chuckled to myself. *One of the most powerful men in the tech world, and he acts like a four-year-old when he can't have his way.* But I understood an awful lot about the ways heartbreak manifested itself and I knew it wasn't fair of me to judge him for the way he expressed his.

While Thomas met with his therapist, I sat in the waiting area and conducted a very quiet phone call with Gerry. I expressed my concerns about getting him off the booze before Finn arrived--and finding a way to keep him off. She suggested hauling his ass back to Alabama, where his access was somewhat more limited and there were fewer reminders. It was a good idea, but it wasn't feasible, since he needed sessions several times a week with this particular therapist. And he needed to be there physically, since I didn't trust him to attend sessions remotely.

Finn called to check in, four days into my watch, and I told her it was like herding cats. I'd been so busy trying to keep him occupied between therapy sessions that I fell into bed completely exhausted each night, completely incapable of taking five minutes to call my girl.

It dawned on me finally, the morning of the seventh day, that I hadn't heard anything from her in a week. I knew she was jumping right back into work and being Mom, but she hadn't texted or called. She hadn't even let me know she'd gotten home safely, and I quickly lifted the phone to my ear to call her.

She didn't answer, my call rolling into her voicemail and the sweet sound of her voice instructing me to leave a message was enough to make me do just that.

I told her voicemail that I missed her, and that the week had been insanely busy, but Thomas was attending daily sessions with the therapist and the Jensens were working hard to help me keep him sober, well fed and entertained. I ended by telling her I missed her and that I wasn't sleeping well without her, which was true. I was waking several times a night to reach for her and realizing she wasn't there was a stab to the heart every damn time. Only a few nights with her had proven to me I wanted her beside me all the time.

Thomas had been such a dick the past couple days, I didn't know which withdrawal to blame it on. I was over him treating me like shit, though, and finally I challenged him to a submission-only match on the mats in his garage.

We'd trained in Jiu Jitsu for a while as kids--Asher was the only one who'd kept up with the practice, having moved into MMA in his late teens. Our matches had always been particularly brutal, and while we joked we'd "fight to the death," we actually meant it when we were really mad.

This time I was really mad.

Thomas had a monster six-stall garage, a real feat of engineering in that it was really just an enormous room with a poured epoxy floor-- plenty of room to throw down some mats and roll around in the few spaces he hadn't filled with vehicles or gym equipment. And since he had more money than God, he had the expensive, professional grade mats. They were rolled up and stored along the perimeter, enough to create a huge padded area when he rolled them out.

Gi was for pussies, I told him. If he could beat me in street clothes, I'd be willing to admit I'd been bested by an old man. (So what if he was only like a year older than me? I made my point and rubbed it in.)

He swept me immediately and I hit the mat with a grunt, the sharp slap reverberating off the walls.

We rolled and sweated and grunted and cursed, not a word exchanged between the two of us, but more angry mutterings to ourselves, for the next ten minutes.

It was an eternity. An eternity during which neither of us could seem to get the upper hand and finally, thank sweet Jesus, the buzzer went off.

"You're out of practice," he laughed finally, and I struggled to gain traction on the sweat-slicked mats so I could sit up, but he had me pinned good. "Physical exertion has been my life since Lydia left me...did you know the second ranked heavyweight in the world lives in the middle of nowhere, Alabama? Sometimes I train with him. He fell in love with a local girl and moved there for her." He laughed bitterly. "Got him wrapped around her damn finger."

"Oh get off it," I snarled. I was tired of his self-indulgent pity party, like he was the only one hurting. His marriage had been circling the drain for years and he'd been the last to realize. He'd given up his job, his social status, and very nearly his sanity to save it. And still, he'd lost his family, sold all of his own real estate holdings and his car collection and he was living like Salinger, isolated and alone. The sick fuck preferred it that way.

He released his grip on me--a good thing, since he was only a few seconds away from choking me out--and sat back on his heels.

"What's with you?" He looked confused, running a hand through his too-long hair. "You've been bent out of shape all week."

"Bent out of shape?" I asked incredulously, barking out a short laugh before rocking back on my heels and launching myself across the space.

He hit the mat with a loud grunt.

"You told me that my loss was *less* than yours because I never knew my daughter." I got the words out, but barely. They burned my throat like bile.

"The fuck you talking about?" He popped back up quickly, rubbing at his jaw, and I realized I'd knocked him with my shoulder while taking him down.

"You don't even remember it! You were so fucked up, I'll bet you don't remember anything of the last two weeks, do you?"

"Not much." He hung his head, looking remarkably contrite.

"You remember Finn was here? Your brothers?"

"Yeah, sorta. I remember you throwing me into the shower and I wanted to throat punch you."

I swallowed hard, sitting back on the mat and rubbing a forearm across my face to keep the sweat out of my eyes. "Yeah, well...you're lucky my girl was with me. She kept me calm. She..." I couldn't finish the sentence. There was a terrible feeling in my gut and I leaned over to the side, afraid for a second that I might throw up.

"Bit early for a new woman," Thomas said, his upper lip curling with disdain. "It hasn't even been a year, bro. How are you already over that?"

I wasn't, I knew that. But I also knew I wasn't willing to live there forever, moping and pining and crying myself to sleep after a bottle of something that would kill me slowly. I had to choose something better: life, hope, and maybe I had the chance to start over.

Lifting myself from the mat, I held out a hand to help Thomas up.

"You're leaving tomorrow, Thom."

He looked completely confused.

"Gerry has been in touch with your therapist, and the two of them have agreed that if you're going to advance at all, you have to cut out the drinking first."

He grunted at me angrily, his jaw setting firm.

"Hear me out," I begged. "You got me addiction counseling, and I'm telling you that what I'm seeing you go through is the same damn thing. I can't leave here knowing that I haven't helped you address that...and I won't let you keep doing this." I swallowed hard. "So tomorrow I'm driving you upstate and you're checking into a facility. You'll be there for forty days, unless you decide to extend it.

"Dr. Modrahni will make the trip up from San Francisco three times a week to meet with you and when you're released, Finn will be here to stay with you for two weeks, then Asher. Gerry said she'll take the last shift. Then she's putting you on your plane to Alabama, to get away from this." I drew a circle in the air over my head.

He looked completely flabbergasted, his jaw working but with no words coming out. He shook his head then, stalking off the mat and letting himself into the house through the side door.

I rolled onto my back on the mat and lay there for a while, staring up at the bright overhead lighting. This had to be the right thing. This was the best thing I could do for him, and to make sure Finn was safe when it came time for her to take over the watch.

Eventually I straggled back into the house. After all, I didn't feel I could leave Thomas alone for long. The alcohol stash may have been ingeniously hidden in the Jensens' personal quarters, but it wasn't above Thomas to have something hidden away somewhere. He was a man of intelligence, cunning, and substantial means.

We ate dinner together, but in a strained silence. Even Mrs. J.'s incredible chicken pot pie couldn't smooth over the angry words and hurt feelings.

Jensen wisely mixed virgin drinks for us, quite probably under the watchful and hairy eyeball of the all-seeing Mrs. J., and both of us headed off to our respective bedrooms at an early hour.

I was still in the apartment over the garage, the baby monitor that provided a feed from Thomas's room sitting on my nightstand. It felt wrong to watch him like a toddler, but I wasn't taking any chances. Thankfully he hadn't discovered it yet--I knew he wasn't looking for it-- or my time with him on the mat would probably have ended with two black eyes and a broken arm.

Definitely a missing dick.

There were no new messages from Eve and there was an uncomfortable catch in my rib cage when I let myself think maybe I'd done something wrong.

Maybe I'd pushed her too hard and she hadn't been ready.

Maybe I'd said something.

Maybe the fact I'd let her find her own way home had pissed her off.

If I didn't get an answer soon--hear her voice and let her calm the fears spiraling out of control in my head--I was going to end up hitting the stash in the Jensens' apartment myself, and personal history indicated that was a very slippery slope. So instead, I dialed her number, my heart in my throat.

Again there was no answer, and this time I didn't leave a message, hanging up and staring at the screen in frustration and disappointment. I didn't want to come across like a stalker or a creep, but right now I didn't have many options when it came to reaching her.

I pulled my legs up onto the bed and leaned back against the headboard, closing my eyes and letting my mind drift over the last time she'd been in this bed with me. The memory was sweet and I replayed it again and again, terrified that I was already forgetting the way her hair smelled and what it felt like to hold her in my arms.

Just before the panic spiraled out of control, the phone buzzed in my hands and my eyes snapped open. My heart was in my throat as I looked down at the screen, relieved and disappointed and concerned when I saw the screen said "Eve's Lauren."

Like I knew any other Laurens--the woman was unforgettable.

She dispensed with all the niceties. "Have you heard from Eve lately?"

That caused something cold to squeeze in my chest.

"She seems to be ignoring me," I admitted slowly. "I've called and texted, but I can't seem to catch her, and she's not getting back to me."

Lauren heaved a heavy sigh on the other end of the line. "I was afraid of that. The stubborn little shit thinks she has to handle everything on her own."

Wait. What was "everything?"

"Look Noah, I know you've got your hands full right now, but Eve's a mess. She's never going to ask you for your help or support, but she needs you. Jared was signed out of school five days ago by someone the idiot receptionist thought was his father. It wasn't Jason's weekend, and Eve hasn't been able to get a hold of him since. He's not at his house and he's not answering calls. She thinks he's running."

Oh, hell no.

"Where is she?" I asked, my voice trembling a little.

"Alex and I made her come stay with us. This way we can keep an eye on her and she has the benefit of an inside source, thanks to Alex. He can feed her any info he gets at work, which sucks, but it's better than nothing."

"Can you put her on the phone?" I asked, and Lauren blew out a long breath.

"Noah, I can't even get her to eat. There's no way she's going to be able to handle talking on the phone--she can't stop crying long enough. She's a mess, big guy." Her voice went soft.

I dragged a hand over my face, trying to fold my thoughts into a shape that made sense. If Jason had picked up his son on a Friday and hadn't returned him that Sunday, he had an easy head start on anyone looking for them, providing he picked Jared up and ran. And though I knew next to nothing about the man, I knew he'd been in the military long enough to have connections both acceptable and unsavory.

"Why would he do this?" I said aloud, asking myself more than I was asking Lauren.

"I don't have an answer for that," she said slowly. "But I have a suspicion. Jared said something weird to Alex while he was staying with us that's being followed up through proper channels."

"You need to explain," I said shortly, and she heaved out a sigh.

"So...Jared was talking with Blake while they were playing video games one morning and Alex came down to make coffee. He overheard Jared saying he was so glad his mom had let him stay with us when she left, instead of taking him to his dad's, because he doesn't like the other kids there."

"I'm sure yours are much better company," I said in a voice that told her to get on with it.

"Well, Alex just kind of innocently asked why Jared didn't like going to his dad's, and he said it was because the lady who lived there now was mean to him."

My knee started bouncing nervously as I recalled a conversation with Jared while I was scrubbing away at the bathtub. *Girlfriends and their kids.*

"Jared told Alex that sometimes a man comes over late at night and he gives something to Jason, and Jason gives him money." Lauren's voice cracked. "And the crackwhore he claims to be engaged to...she's got five kids living at his place, and on the nights this mysterious man comes over, he disappears with her into one of the bedrooms."

My head was spinning and I grabbed my duffel bag to start throwing things in before it struck me that I couldn't leave until I'd dropped off Thomas.

"The last time Jared was there, he said there were only three kids, and one of them he'd never met before. When he asked about it, that bitch had the nerve to slap him and tell him to mind his own business."

"Do you think…" I couldn't finish the sentence.

"Alex thinks so," she answered. "He had her checked out and she doesn't *have* any kids. Her medical records are patchy, but there was one miscarriage earlier this year and there were drugs in her system.

She drew a deep breath. "The PD thinks there's a cell operating locally to traffic children."

Panic flared.

"You think he'd traffic his own kid?" I couldn't stop the thought from slipping out.

"I think he'd pick up and run if he suspected his cover had been blown, and take any witnesses with him."

"Eve has, understandably, completely flipped her shit," Lauren continued. "That lawyer she was seeing came over to our place to draw up paperwork and he's filed an emergency injunction. I mean, it's too little, too late, but we have to keep her busy or she'll go crazy."

Lawyer she was seeing? We were going to come back to that.

Guilt flooded me as I thought about my conversation with Jared, when I should have asked better questions.

I should have questioned my own suspicions.

I should have said something to Eve.

I should have known he was being subjected to awful things.

This was all my fault.

"Did he file the injunction right away?" I asked, my voice hoarse.

"He did," she answered flatly. "Eve has requested full and permanent custody of her son, due to suspected corruption of a minor. Gross sexual impropriety. Involvement in criminal acts--all of it. Whatever they could throw at him. And if we ever find them, she'll press charges."

"Oh no," I breathed, completely incapable of telling Lauren of what little I knew. It made me feel incredibly guilty, and I dropped my head into my hands, letting the phone rest on the bed beside me.

After hanging up with her I sat staring at my phone for a long time. I couldn't even pretend to get to Eve until after I'd dropped Thomas off at the rehab facility, which meant I couldn't be there until the day after next.

I packed everything and confirmed my flight, and before bed I agonized over a short, simple text to her.

You can lean on me; I can take it.

TWENTY-TWO

Eve

◄►

I hadn't slept in days.

Everything I tried to swallow came back up.

I was stressing out Lauren and Alex something fierce; I was a tougher case than Henry, who was going through a patch of insomnia and nocturnal screaming, thanks to new teeth coming in.

I didn't have that excuse.

For the time being I was out on family leave, spending my days talking to detectives and conducting searches online.

I sat in my car on the street while detectives went to Jason's house with a search warrant, threatening to bust in the door if it wasn't opened.

A woman, one I'd never seen, answered the door and let them inside. She stood on the porch, nervous and twitchy, watching the sidewalk as the place was ransacked. I believe the official term was "searched," but by the time they left, Alex assured me, it looked like it had been hit by a tornado.

They left with box after box of DVD's, and baskets filled with something that looked like bed linens.

Someone pulled records from his internet service provider and another pulled phone records. It seemed there was little to go on, as he'd been just smart enough to use a randomizer for his personal surfing and, sifting through the numbers list on his phone record, nothing jumped out at anyone.

When Noah's text came in, I knew Lauren had finally made good on her threat to get in touch with him to let him know what was going on. I'd been angry at first, when she'd threatened it. I'd told her to stay out of it and that it was my decision, as to just how involved I would let him get.

"Oh, he's involved now," she snapped at me, her eyes fiery. "The instant you decided to send Jared home with me so you could watch over him all night, you decided to involve him.

"When you decided to introduce your son to him, you involved him.

"When you spent four days holding him together so he could help bury his nephew, *you* got involved. You made that choice, and you doubled down when you started sleeping with him--about damn time, too. You thought I wouldn't notice." Her words were furious, but there was a small smile on her lips.

I hadn't said a thing to her about sleeping with Noah, but my stupid face had probably given it all away.

To his credit, Daniel had been a saint. I'd called him, hysterical, and he'd dropped everything to come to me. He'd shown up at Lauren's place with his phone, his laptop, and reassurances that we'd get the filing in immediately.

Thanks to Alex, the police were all over it...and I was completely helpless.

Daniel had been back to see me every day since, and each time Lauren opened the door to find him on the other side, I watched her mouth turn down a little further. If I hadn't known better, I'd have said she was disappointed to find him there.

I didn't respond to Noah's text because I didn't know how to lean on him. I wasn't good at depending upon or trusting anyone else. We were too new, if we were even really a "thing" yet, and I had learned early what stress did to relationships, especially those new and fragile. Given the things we'd already seen together, there was no way I was going to pile more onto the heap.

Two days after Noah's text, and still with no leads, I sat on the sofa in Lauren's living room with Lauren on one side and Daniel on the other. As we dissected what we knew for the four thousandth time, there was a booming knock at the front door. It sounded like someone had taken a battering ram to it.

Alex answered the door and I heard low voices conferring before Alex came through the doorway and Noah, towering over him, rushed in close behind.

He hadn't shaved since I'd seen him and the thick beard on his face made him look wild, intimidating and feral.

I saw Lauren's eyes widen as she got her first real good look at him-- upright, anyway--and I had to admit to myself that he was a startling presence, dark and menacing.

He stalked across the room, his eyes focused singularly on me, like no one else existed, and I felt Daniel draw in an involuntary breath as he shrank to the side.

Noah's eyes flicked to him quickly as Daniel unwound his arm from my shoulders and I saw confusion, jealousy and rage flash through his warm brown eyes.

Lauren let go of my hand, pushing me up from the sofa, and Noah stopped inches away, staring down at me with such an intensity I thought I might burn. The world went into slow motion as he wound one arm around my back and the other hand fisted in my hair.

"Angel." His voice was deep and raw, and in that single word there were questions and fears, promises and anguish. It stole my breath and I didn't remember to draw another until his lips touched mine. A soft, sweet kiss that conveyed his own intensity and suffering, and when he pulled back to look into my eyes, his own were flooded and threatening to spill over.

It was like he'd given me permission, and I collapsed into his neck with a sob, breathing him in, my fingers slipping beneath his jacket to dig and knead into the hard muscles of his back. Holding on for dear life.

"Holy fuck," I heard Lauren whisper behind me and I wanted to swat her, but I couldn't bring myself to let go of Noah.

"Baby," she whispered sotto voce to Alex, "if you looked at me like that, I'd already be pregnant again."

Alex barked something short and lyrical at her, in Italian of course, and she answered back sharply. Whatever it was, it made her purr and move toward him, leaving Daniel trapped in No Man's Land between

Noah and me, and Lauren and Alex. He looked distinctly uncomfortable, fidgeting with his tie, then his watch, and then I stopped watching because Noah was looking down at me with no little heat.

"Whatever this was..." Noah's voice was rough as he gestured between Daniel and me. "It's over."

It was a warning for Daniel.

"I think you know by now, Angel, that I don't share." His nostrils flared a little and I cast a quick glance at Daniel, who looked uncomfortable and terrified.

"Oh, trust me..." Lauren's throaty laugh filled the room as she disentangled herself from her amorous husband. "There's nothing happening there that Eve doesn't want to happen."

Poor Daniel. I cast him an apologetic look at him over Noah's shoulder, and he nodded at me quickly.

"I should go anyway," he said, his voice betraying his discomfort. "I'll keep you apprised of progress, Eve," he said, and he reached over to squeeze my shoulder.

There was a sound low in Noah's throat, something vicious and savage, like he might bite.

In hopes Daniel didn't hear it, I smiled brightly at him and thanked him quickly. He had helped me hold onto sanity this past week I told him, and though I'd meant it only to comfort Daniel, I felt every muscle in Noah's body tense as he absorbed my words, spent on another man.

Lauren murmured something to Daniel as he slipped his laptop into his bag and when I heard the front door shut, I turned to liquid in Noah's arms. He had to hold me up, his arms slipping under my own.

"Baby." It was Lauren's voice, but she wasn't talking to me. "Let's head upstairs; we'll let them catch up."

I felt her hand squeeze my arm and I heard a sharp slap that my skin didn't register. Instead, Noah winced in surprise.

"You know what to do, big guy."

There was no question as to what she meant.

Alex probably breathed a huge sigh of relief as Noah led me from the house. I'd been camped out in their guest room since Saturday, and I knew they'd been keeping themselves in check out of respect for me--well, that and they knew I couldn't sleep. They weren't trying to rub anything in my face.

He tucked me into the car and clipped the seatbelt, since I was almost completely useless. It was a miracle I could remember how to breathe on my own.

"We're going to find him, Angel," Noah breathed into my ear, kissing my temple gently. "There's no question about it. Alex will leave no stone unturned; he's got a good team. And you and me, we're gonna sit down and go through every step together. Somewhere he fucked up, and we're gonna figure out where that was."

I sat mutely, hardly seeing the landscape as it flashed by, and it wasn't until we pulled into the huge circular drive in front of Noah's house that I realized where we were.

Noah pulled a bag from the trunk that I recognized as my own and I didn't ask how he'd gotten into my place. It was enough to know he'd been coordinating things while I'd been falling apart.

He made dinner and he hovered over me, making sure I put at least a few bites into my mouth when all I wanted to do was push the plate away.

Then he led me out to the yard and settled me on the swing, pushing gently, saying nothing as the sun set and the stars began to twinkle in the sky. The air was cooling rapidly and when he decided I'd had enough, he stopped pushing and helped me up, gathering me into a long, silent hug. He held me there, one hand smoothing my hair, the other pressing me tightly against him and I took the deepest breath I'd been able to take all week. He helped to calm and center me and maybe if I could talk myself down a bit, I could think straight. I could figure out where Jason had messed up.

It wasn't yet late, but eventually he led me into the house and made a cup of tea, which he watched me sip while he cleaned up the kitchen around me.

I liked it, the domestic actions familiar and soothing, and watching this big man complete such mundane chores was somehow endearing.

He cared for his house.

He liked order and routine.

He was steady and reliable, consistent and thorough.

A lot can be learned from how a man wields a kitchen sponge.

He waited patiently while I finished the tea, leaning against the counter with his arms crossed over his chest, watching me. It made me a little uncomfortable, since I knew I looked like hell. My hair was in a ratty pile on top of my head and I didn't have a speck of makeup on my face, since I'd cried it all off. My eyes were bloodshot and swollen and I was pretty sure my nose was bright red.

I ducked my head as he took the empty mug from me and slotted it into the dishwasher. Then he flipped off the lights, leaving only the one above the stove burning, and I heard him moving through the house, checking window locks and shooting the bolts on doors. It made me feel so weirdly safe and cared for--I had always been the one to perform that nighttime routine--and I sighed heavily just as he walked back into the kitchen.

More than anything I wished Jared was in the bedroom at the top of the stairs, the one Noah had clearly put together with him in mind.

Without a word he bent over my chair and gathered me up in his arms, carrying me carefully through the hallway and up the staircase.

There was a small lamp burning in the master bedroom and I took in all the progress he'd made since I'd last visited his house. The bed was neatly made with soft linens, and gauzy curtains hung over the windows.

There was a fire log burning in the fireplace, and without a word he set me down on the edge of the bed, dropping to his knees to untie my shoes.

He stood then, gently unwinding the band I'd used to secure the knot on top of my head, and he ran fingers gently through my hair before smoothing it back over my shoulders and lifting my sweatshirt over my head.

I felt like a small child being helped to prepare for bed, but I didn't fight him because I didn't have the energy to do it on my own.

248

When he'd peeled off the last scrap of my clothing, he bent over again and scooped me up.

I didn't have the energy to let out a startled squeak, and I looped my arms around his neck as he carried me into the bathroom.

His beautifully finished bathtub was the crowning glory of his bathroom, the room lit and glowing with a few candles. It was humid from the warmth of the bath and I could smell something flowery.

He dipped a finger into the foamy water, testing it before lowering me gently into it.

I thought he'd leave me to my own devices, but he stayed put. He knelt beside me and washed me gently, from head to toe. Then he grabbed a cup, filling it with warm water to pour over my head, and he washed my hair.

His actions, his gentleness, were enough to reopen the floodgates and while he rinsed my hair again, I closed my eyes and let the scalding tears run down my cheeks. I was terrified, afraid to eat or sleep or even breathe, because in every moment Jared needed me and I still hadn't found him. Every moment spent felt like another one lost, like he was drifting further away, and the thought of never seeing him again filled me with hysteria.

"I can't do this," I whispered, leaning my head back against the solid cast iron tub. "I can't handle the idea that I might never see him again." The sentence ended on a sob.

Noah nodded but he didn't say anything, and instantly I felt like a heartless idiot. If anyone knew what I was experiencing, it was him, only there had been no hope for a happy outcome in his case. There had been nothing for him to hold onto. The thought made me clap a hand over my eyes and I choked out an anguished "I'm sorry."

He didn't say anything, pulling the drain from the tub and helping me to my feet. He toweled me dry and squeezed the water from my hair, then handed me a packaged toothbrush and left the bathroom.

I brushed my teeth and stole some of his deodorant.

I found a small tub of lip balm in one of the vanity drawers and I smoothed some on before flicking off the light and walking out of the bathroom.

It was a given I'd sleep in his bed, and somehow I got the feeling he needed to hold me just as badly as I needed to be held. So while he hurried through a shower and brushed his teeth, I curled up in the big bed and tried to calm my roiling thoughts.

I was of no use to anyone in my current state. I hadn't slept in days and I'd hardly eaten. I was weak and exhausted and my thought process wasn't even remotely coherent.

When he slipped into the bed behind me, he curled his big body around mine and I relaxed into the warmth that seeped from his skin and into my own. Being held in his arms was comforting, and he kissed the back of my head gently. "Sleep, Angel. Tomorrow we will find him."

I closed my eyes and said a prayer inside my head.

I prayed Jared was safe and healthy; that he was getting enough food and he had a comfortable bed.

I prayed he wasn't scared or hurt, and that he knew I was looking for him.

I left God hanging.

I fell asleep halfway through my rambling requests and when I woke halfway through the night, shivering from a terrible nightmare, Noah pulled me back into his arms and shushed me softly.

He must have been dreaming too, the way he made a contented sound as he wrapped around me once more. It sounded as if he sighed with relief, and his voice was warm with love and joy and tenderness when he uttered a single, soft "Baby," his voice curling possessively around the intimate word.

It made my body go rigid with distrust, because this word was new, and I swallowed hard, against the sick feeling crawling up my throat. Because never, not once before, had he ever called me anything but Angel.

***

Noah was a much better cook than me.

When I woke, it was to the smell of waffles cooking, bacon crisping, and coffee brewing.

It was enough to lure me from the bed, and I dug through the bag he'd left near the fireplace, pulling out leggings and a sweatshirt before running a brush through my hair and padding down to the kitchen on bare feet.

He turned as I entered the kitchen, a spatula in one hand, a smile on his face. It made my heart squeeze in my chest. *This is what I want every morning.*

"Coffee for my girl," he said, quickly pouring coffee into a mug and sliding it down the counter. He hadn't noticed yet that I hadn't touched him, and I wondered if he had been aware of my movements during the night.

When I'd separated our bodies after he called me another woman's pet name.

A ding sounded from Noah's back pocket and he loosened one arm so he could reach in to fish out the phone. He held it up over my shoulder and I watched his eyes widen. "Sonofabitch," he muttered under his breath and I pulled back slowly, turning my head in hopes I could see the screen of his phone.

Noah spun and flicked off the stove burners, his eyes wild. "Get your shoes, Angel. Alex says they might have something."

I didn't even ask questions, rushing upstairs to pull a pair of flats from my bag and palming my phone off the nightstand.

I put the shoes on as I ran, hopping on one foot and then the other and I was back in the kitchen in record time.

Already, Noah was waiting for me, keys in hand, his face set in a hard, determined expression.

Noah drove like a bat out of hell and I hung onto the Oh Shit bar to keep from smacking into the window with every wild turn he took.

He'd reached across the space between us immediately after I clipped the seatbelt and squeezed my thigh, holding onto my leg as he drove and I wanted to protest, but I let him.

I looked up in surprise as Noah stomped on the brakes, and the tires squealed on the pavement in front of Alex and Lauren's house.

Alex was waiting at the edge of the driveway. Without a word he wrenched open the door behind me and threw himself into the truck.

"Station," he barked, and Noah floored it.

We tore through the residential neighborhood and out onto the highway, the scream of a siren drawing closer and closer behind us.

Noah swore angrily, flipping on his blinker and preparing to pull over when Alex reached over the seat to grip his shoulder. "Let him around you," he said calmly. "That's our escort. We're taking you to your son, Eve."

What in the hell was going on? Finally, my brain began to process what was happening and I whipped around in my seat to pin Alex with my eyes. I wanted to believe him, but I needed more. "Talk," I demanded, and he sucked in a lungful of air, letting it out with a big sigh.

Noah listened with obvious tension in his shoulders as Alex told us the FBI had accidentally picked up Jason trying to cross the border into Tijuana with a woman and four children she tried to claim as her own, but they didn't have a passport for any of the kids.

Jared didn't have a passport for that very reason: I was paranoid.

"Jason tried bribing one of the border guards to turn a blind eye, but there was an agent nearby who overheard the whole thing. The department had a couple people stationed there to investigate a child sex trafficking ring and when Jason couldn't produce any form of ID for any of the kids, it set off all kinds of alarms."

"Why?" I cried, my head in my hands. "Why would he do this?"

"I don't have all the answers yet," Alex said gently, reaching over the seat to squeeze my shoulder. "I'm sure there's a great deal that has yet to come out, and we *will* find out.

"One of the guards took the kids and Jared, who was terrified out of his mind--he thought he'd done something wrong and was going to jail--he told them they needed to call his mom."

I leaned back into the seat, a wave of nausea washing over me.

Jason could have slipped over the border and I'd have never seen my son again. An extradition agreement with the Mexican government meant nothing if Jason was never located again.

"I don't understand why he would run." I shook my head, trying to rattle the disjointed thoughts into some sort of order. "He was just approved for more visitation--he got what he wanted."

Alex heaved another deep sigh from the back seat. "He lost his job a while ago, Eve. Dishonorable discharge. I don't know anything beyond that, but that can't be good. My guess is that he was running from a deal gone bad, and since Jared knew more than he should have, he took him with."

"Jason wasn't a very careful person," I muttered, remembering the woman with the obvious drug habit who'd let the detectives into the house when it was searched. "He probably pissed off the wrong person."

He definitely had some illegal side gigs going on.

More than one questionable girlfriend.

Noah followed the squad car with the blazing light bar and howling siren.

"They're going to need to talk to you," Alex said quietly over my shoulder. "The FBI brought all the kids back; there should be a few happy reunions today."

I sat numbly, heart hammering as we screeched to a stop behind the squad car.

"Go," Noah encouraged. "I'll find you."

Alex jumped from the car and pulled open my door, yanking me out when my legs refused to cooperate and dragging me behind him as we ran into the station. He knew exactly where to go, hauling me with him, barking at several officers standing outside a nondescript locked door. They nodded, quickly unlocking the door, and we burst through it.

"Mom!" Jared jumped up from a chair, his face dirty and streaked with tears. I folded myself around him so tightly, he choked trying to take a breath, sobbing into my sweater as my own tears streamed down my face. I stood there, rocking him back and forth until I felt his small body relax.

Huge arms went around both of us and I gratefully rested my face in the curve of Noah's neck as I sniffled, trying not to openly sob. I felt his breath hitch in the same way, something hot splashing on my neck.

I pulled back slowly, shocked by the misery I saw on Noah's face.

"I'm sorry, baby...I'm so sorry. I didn't ever think it would come to this."

Something inside of me coiled at the new nickname.

Pulled up tight.

Hissed.

"What do you mean, Bear?" I asked softly, my words weighted, my expression definitely tense.

"Jared said something about other kids at his dad's place and I should have caught it. He said the other girlfriends were mean to him."

"You didn't tell me there was anything weird going on." My voice was cold.

Noah looked wrecked.

"Noah! You. Didn't. Tell. Me."

Shit, being lost. At warp speed.

He squeezed his eyes tightly shut, his nostrils flaring and his lips pressing into a thin line, and when he opened his eyes, I could see fear. "You have to believe that I meant to." He swallowed hard. "I didn't know what to do; thought maybe I was overreacting to think it sounded weird."

I pulled back, looking at him with incredulity written all over my face.

Jared's eyes were ping ponging between the two of us, his expression panicked. "Don't, Mom. Don't pick on Noah--it's not his fault."

"There is never a *right time* to tell me that Jared's father has a houseful of kids that aren't his. Are you crazy?" My voice was rising,

254

heading into Unhinged Territory, because I knew I was overreacting, and the two detectives in the room with us looked uncomfortable.

"Hey, man." It was Alex, stepping up next to Noah to take his arm. "How about we take you into the next room and get a statement from you, too? It could help."

He let himself be led away, looking back at me before the door closed.

Must keep it together.

I took a deep breath.

I'd cried enough in the last week to last me a lifetime. It was time to figure things out, and that included figuring out who I could trust.

Maybe it was unfair, but as of just now, I'd removed one more name from the list.

TWENTY-THREE

Noah

◄||►

Eve cut me out of her life like I was a cancer.

She wouldn't answer my calls.

My texts remained unread.

The flowers I sent were refused.

I tried to throw myself into completing the house as the summer bled into fall, but my heart wasn't in it.

Even Finn could tell when she called, commenting that my voice sounded flat. And she was right: it was, because all the joy had been sucked right out of my life.

The joy I'd just found.

Lauren felt sorry for me, checking in on me at least once a week, and Alex invited me out with his group of friends a couple times. I thought that was pretty big of him, especially considering he still acted a little suspicious when I was around his wife, but I started to think he was watching her more than me.

Maybe she'd said something to put him on edge?

There was a little press coverage about the case--it even made it to national news when it turned into a manhunt.

Somehow, Jason had slipped through the fingers of the border patrol when trying to sneak Jared into Mexico. It was more than dumb luck, that much I knew, and Alex was fairly certain several sympathetic blind eyes had been turned, allowing that piece of shit to disappear.

It seemed pretty unlikely he'd be able to hide for long. His accounts had been frozen, though he'd managed a sizable cash withdrawal, and records showed he'd been withdrawing routine amounts--like a fuckton of money--over the past few months.

There were forensic accountants at work, and the IRS moved in when it was discovered that Jason's multiple bank accounts did not--hardly shockingly--match up with the Army's payroll numbers.

The guy had been just smart enough to keep the government's fingers out of his ill-gotten gains--and avoid child support--for years. But he hadn't been smart enough to cover all of his tracks, and it resulted in a few more arrests locally--but still no Jason.

Turned out he was dabbling in the distribution end of a drug ring, and for serious money he and some of his smarter buddies were producing porn for the dark web. (I don't mean your standard stuff, either. The guy was seriously fucked in the head.)

A general court martial was issued, which was no joke, and last I'd heard several bounty hunters had picked up the ticket. But that was when media coverage stagnated. Since there hadn't been any new development in weeks, Jason had fallen out of the news cycle and we were back to horrifying crimes committed by people we *didn't* know.

It had been a while since I'd last met up with Alex and when he called to invite me to dinner, I was relieved. I needed the distraction, because I was climbing the walls in my very large, very empty house. I'd kept myself busy with work for the most part, because downtime was a dangerous thing for me to have. The problem was that I was working myself into the ground and while it was great for business and my bank account, I was weary down to my bones.

When I walked into the little restaurant, a seriously authentic mom-and-pop Italian spot, it was Lauren who was waving at me from the back table.

I paused, looking around, suspicious of a set-up.

"Noah!" Lauren hollered, like I hadn't seen her, gesturing me over just as Alex stepped out of the kitchen with a bottle of wine.

"Nice spot," I said, sinking into the large circular booth on Alex's side.

He nodded at me like he approved of my seating choice.

"His parents'." Lauren gestured to Alex, who grinned and poured most of the bottle into Lauren's glass, and she raised her eyebrows at him.

"He's trying to get me drunk because he thinks I'll put out." She tried to pout, but she was on the verge of laughing because she knew what he hadn't seemed to figure out yet: She was always a sure thing.

"From what Eve tells me, you're pretty good about that even when you're sober." I couldn't help it--it slipped out--and Alex looked shocked.

Lauren didn't protest and she went quiet for a moment, digesting my comment, then a big smile broke out over her face. "So, Noah...Alex asked me to come with him tonight for backup."

Apparently I was still terrifying.

"He wants me to convince you that Eve is miserable and she's just being a stubborn shit. You're going to have to save her from herself."

"Is she, though? Doesn't seem like she *wants* saving," I said, a little irritable. Her avoidance had been so complete, so pointed, it was easier to think she hated me than that she was just being stubborn.

"She does." Lauren's voice was firm, and she rose from her seat to kiss the cheek of the older woman who appeared at our table with a fragrant, steaming dish.

"Grazie, Nonna."

I looked up in surprise. The woman presenting our food appeared young.

"Nonna?" I asked, and Alex grinned.

"My parents have aged well, perhaps thanks to the fountain of youth." He grinned, gesturing toward the bottle of wine sitting on our table. "My family has a vineyard."

"Damn straight they do," Lauren said very seriously, pouring until the wine reached the top of her glass.

Alex asked me to tell him about the conversation Jared and I had that summer, and though I tried to include every detail I could remember I knew it wasn't more than what was already known. I didn't have any new information for him. It had been an isolated experience, that brief "after school special" moment with Jared.

Lauren, clearly the more outspoken of the two, told me that I'd bombed the test. My face fell when she said that, because I knew she was right: Dating a single mom was a much bigger deal than I'd been ready for, because it meant I was also auditioning to raise her son. And if she couldn't count on me to keep her kid safe like he was my own, acting on the barest of suspicions to keep Jared safe, it was a pretty big black mark against my name.

According to Alex, Jared had been coming over after school on the days Eve was working. She was fearful of trusting anyone else with him and while he was a little too old for a babysitter, he was just a little too young to go entirely without supervision. It had worked out great to that point, since Jared was a natural at parenting the little ones, and it gave Alex an extra pair of eyes for Blake, who seemed to be trying to kill himself before he reached double digits.

"So…" it was Lauren, her mouth so full of Mama's garlic bread, she looked like a chipmunk. "You want to stick around just because of us? We *are* pretty awesome." She gestured between Alex and herself. "Or…have you been holding onto hope because my best friend is on fire in the sack?"

Alex swatted her under the table and she jumped, leaning over to him. "That part's important, baby."

"Both?" I knew it sounded like a question rather than a statement, and the truth of it was that I wanted to know the answer myself. I did know it was about more than sex. She'd given me a glimpse of what we could be the few days we had together, but since I'd been iced out.

"You know…" Alex looked thoughtful. "We've been meaning to redo the kitchen for a while now--my crazy woman wants to take down the wall and open things up."

There was some kind of spousal telepathy going on between the two of them and I watched Lauren's eyes light up with delight. "You are brilliant, baby," she cooed, and Alex's grin was devious.

"I know you're probably booked up," he continued, "but I think your way back in is through the kid. He's at our house between four and seven-thirty a couple times a week, if that window works for you."

I pondered it for a moment, knowing Eve would be furious with me, with Alex, with Lauren. She wanted nothing to do with me, which meant she sure as hell didn't want me having anything to do with her kid.

Snagging a piece of the fragrant garlic bread from the platter at the center of the table, I shoved the whole damn thing in my mouth.

"I'm in."

***

What I didn't count on, at least at first, was that those "couple times a week" days were all over the place. They weren't consistent from one week to the next and because I was trying to fit the job into a full schedule, I missed them again and again.

I had reviewed the plans for the kitchen and Lauren and Alex had drawn up a budget we'd agreed upon with a handshake. Then I showed up most days of the week and spent three or four hours each day working my way through demo, cleanup, filing the necessary permits and arranging inspections--you name it. It was exhausting to do on my own, and it was tedious in that I was only doing it a few hours a day, a few times a week. But more exhausting was that I never knew what I was walking into. I lived in the hope that Jared would be there and I would catch a glimpse of Eve--just a look. Just long enough to see whether her eyes had gone cold, or whether there was a tiny spark of tenderness left for me.

I was totally off booze. I couldn't afford the downtime and the hangovers, and if I was being honest with myself it was because I still prayed I had a chance. I needed to be stronger for Jared, if I had any hope at all, and more than anything I knew I was trying my hardest to be enough for both of them, even if they didn't know it yet.

The first time I saw Jared, just days after Christmas, his face lit up. He'd walked into the kitchen to find me installing cabinets and since I didn't hear him come in, I was startled when I looked over to find he'd squatted down beside me, grinning up into my face. It stopped my heart, something fierce and joyful squeezing my chest and I leaned over, scooping him into a hug he easily melted into. He was comfortable and at ease with me, something I knew he wasn't with many people, and the lump in my throat was hot and spiky, refusing to be swallowed down when I thought of how he could have been lost forever.

"I'm so glad to see you, buddy," I whispered and he responded quickly, his words muffled by the mouthful he had of my flannel shirt. I pulled back slowly. "What was that?"

"I've missed you, big guy. Probably as much as Mom."

Cold chills sprinkled their way down my spine at his honest, easy admission.

"Nah, little man, I miss her, but I'm not so sure the feeling is mutual. She was pretty mad at me the last time I saw her." This was unfamiliar territory and I didn't want to overstep my boundaries.

Lauren came bustling into the kitchen, her little belly just starting to show with baby number five, and her face lit when she saw Jared tucked under my arm.

"Now that looks right," she said with a smile and I caught a hint of something in her tone. Something that told me there might be something going on with Eve that *wasn't* right, and an old suspicion flared to life. I didn't give it a voice, but I gave it a seat at the forefront of my mind and let it nag at me for the rest of the day.

Blake kept trying to draw Jared away, but he stayed in the kitchen with me, very nearly an appendage of my own body. He observed as I measured and marked, mounted boxes and installed slides. He said little and I tried to keep my own conversation light and Eve-free. I didn't want to pry, even though I was dying for information about her.

There was a small station set up in the corner of the room where Lauren sometimes put together food for the family. More often than not, Alex brought home food from his family's restaurant, and the microwave and toaster oven were put through their paces.

"Jared," Lauren called from the corner, and reluctantly he drifted over to take the plate she offered.

It was early enough yet, but I knew her kindness wouldn't go unnoticed by Eve, who wouldn't have to worry about putting together dinner that night.

As the weeks ticked by, I began to notice a pattern: Lauren was typically at work once I arrived to start work on the kitchen, leaving Alex to wrangle the monkeys and put together meals. Jared's schedule became more consistent and he was there on Mondays, Wednesdays and Thursdays, and on Thursdays he was there quite late. I knew, because he stayed with me as long as he could and I didn't leave until after he did.

Alex was careful to have Jared packed up and in his coat, waiting near the front door when he knew it was time for Eve to arrive. Some nights, when Lauren wasn't working, he took Jared home himself. And as time dragged on, I began to suspect it was an overabundance of caution on their part, so that Eve wouldn't catch sight of me.

"You afraid I'll spook her?" I asked Lauren one night as she helped Jared into his jacket, and the wide-eyed look she gave me told me everything I needed to know.

Jared held a finger to his lips, a smile on his face. The little sneak was in on it, I realized, and I shook my head at both of them. "What are we playing at?" I asked, unable to keep a little anger out of my voice.

"Long game, big guy," Lauren said quietly and I set down the box of tiles I'd been hauling in from the garage.

The game was so damn long, I was going to be on a walker before I ever caught sight of Eve again.

"We're about to move on to Phase Two," she said, exchanging grins with Jared, who was clearly far more clued in than I was. "Just trust me: We don't want to rush our girl."

Jared shook his head at me, in something I thought might be agreement, and suddenly I wanted to sit him down and quiz him for all the details I *hadn't* been collecting for months.

It was another week before I saw Jared again, and I'd just had countertops installed. The kitchen was coming together, lacking only the tiling and finishes, and it was no secret I was starting to drag my feet.

Jared was hard at work at the kitchen island that night, a bottle of oil in one hand and a rag in the other as he worked the oil into the thick slab of soapstone.

I had my back turned, mixing the adhesive I needed to run tile across the long space between upper and lower cabinets on the far wall.

I didn't hear a door open or close, but the air changed in the room. There was an awareness, an electric presence, and I turned slowly when I heard Jared still.

"What are you doing here?" Eve's voice was cold and flat and Jared swallowed so loud, I could hear it from several feet away.

"Lauren!" Eve's voice raised to a level I'd have normally described as panicked, and she was *pissed*. "What the hell is *he* doing here?"

It took a long time for Lauren to saunter into the room, an easy, knowing grin on her face. The puppet master.

"I ordered the fixture that goes over the sink," she said breezily, looking in my direction, and I gave her a short nod without my eyes leaving Eve's face. She was still so beautiful, I couldn't get enough. I stood staring, drinking her in like a fool.

"Should be here in a couple days." Lauren must have been talking the whole time. She seemed completely unperturbed, finally turning to face her friend.

"I asked you a question," Eve hissed, and her beautiful bronze hair was very nearly standing on end.

I wanted to reach over and cup my hand around the back of her neck, but I was rooted to the spot.

"Get your panties out of a twist," Lauren snarked. "As you can see, he is here doing a damn fine job on my kitchen." She spread her arms out, forcing Eve to break my gaze and look around the room, "And it just so happens that while he's been working on my home, your little man has been falling in love with him."

Jared blushed a violent shade of red, ducking his face quickly. What an embarrassing revelation, and my hand shot out to squeeze his shoulder and draw him back under my arm. This kid had become my buddy and I really wasn't eager to lose the easy friendship we had.

"You should hear the two of them," Lauren laughed breezily, ignoring the glare from Eve that should have buried her. "In here, talking and laughing all afternoon...you're learning to tile next, right Jared?"

Jared nodded slowly, bringing his eyes up to meet his mother's.

"I can't believe you went behind my back." Eve was looking at me when she said it, but I knew the words were meant for both me and Lauren. "You knew I wouldn't allow it, so you went sneaking around."

Her eyes suddenly filled with tears and I itched to step closer and crush her to my chest, squeezing all the anger out of her until only the hurt was left. Because that was something I knew how to fix. I'd learned slowly, with Jared, over weeks spent together, watching him bloom with patience and attention and kindness.

How Eve hadn't noticed the change in her son, I couldn't begin to imagine.

Jared set the tin of oil and the rag on the stone, turning wordlessly into my side to wrap both arms around me and, not caring what anyone thought, I brought both arms up around him and dropped my face to my chest.

The thought of losing the kid who'd become my buddy was suddenly and intensely painful. I had looked forward to our afternoons together and loved the way he learned to trust and joke with me.

"I gotta go, Bear," Jared said softly and I quickly wiped away the tear that was trailing down his cheek.

I felt Eve go rigid at Jared's use of the name, and I searched my brain for something--anything.

"He's a good worker," I said quietly, directly to Eve. "I always need someone around to help me out with odd jobs. When he's out for the summer, I could pay him to help out. You know...train him in some useful stuff."

264

Where was this shit coming from? I hadn't even asked Jared if he was interested in learning what I did.

"Beats laying around playing video games with Blake," Alex's deep voice drifted into the kitchen, and I realized he'd been giving us a little time and space, not wanting to contribute to what was already a volatile environment.

"Thanks a lot." Eve held her hand out to Jared, summoning him to her side. "You're all ganging up on me now, acting like you know what my son needs more than I do."

"I have some idea, and it involves a great male role model."

It was Alex.

"And don't forget we know what you need, too."

That was Lauren.

"I don't need anything," Eve hissed. "Or anyone. I can manage just fine." But there was weariness in her words, like she was hoping someone would step in and prove her wrong. Challenge her.

Without another word to any of us, she spun Jared toward the front door and marched him out. The house was silent when the door slammed and across the room I could see Blake's huge eyes peering over the back of a sofa.

"That went about as well as I expected." Lauren's voice was breezy and carefree, completely unlike the knots in my trachea that kept any words from getting past.

"Better, actually." Alex looked equally unconcerned. Downright pleased with himself, in fact, and I wanted to bash their heads together. So much for their idiotic plan, because all I was feeling right now was a sensation of deep, terrible loss. I knew just how much I'd come to depend upon seeing Jared. The kid had given me hope.

"Give her time," Lauren soothed, her small hand squeezing my arm firmly.

"Time." I croaked the word and I sounded awful. I'd already given her so much time, I knew more wouldn't fix things.

"Planting the seed, my friend," Alex announced with a grin, and he snatched a longneck out of the fridge, cracking the cap off before reaching back in and handing a root beer to me. I took it without a word, setting it on the counter in front of me while Lauren pulled several huge takeout containers from the fridge. "Noah," she said gently, and I knew then she could see I was suffering. "Dinner will be ready in ten."

And because I didn't trust myself to be alone, I stayed.

TWENTY-FOUR

Eve

Class had let out early tonight, which was why I'd been early to pick up Jared.

Alex and Lauren had been wonderful the last few months, stepping in and parenting Jared where I fell consistently short. They made sure he had a place to go every day after school, while I drove to the university for several hours of class that often ran late into the evening.

Something had changed since I'd been to Sonoma with Noah. Something that had nagged and irritated and prickled until I addressed it, something that had eaten at me for years and I'd always managed to shove down and keep buried. And now that I'd opened up one void in my life, I had to address another: I didn't love what I was doing with my life. I was good at my job. It was safe. And every day I had to push myself a little harder to go to work, to a place that gave to my bank account but took from my soul.

Seeing Thomas's grief and being largely unable to help…that had been my catalyst. Seeing how much it tore up those close to him and how hard they worked to get him the things he needed...it all made me wonder if I had been right all those years earlier, when I switched majors to study Nursing. I'd wanted for years to pursue counseling, and spending some time with the Atholton family made things click into place: I wanted to study grief counseling, with a strong emphasis on the destructive nature of substance abuse. I wanted to learn how to help; how to help others overcome, because I knew it would finally give my life meaning.

The hospital gave their full-time employees a modest education allowance annually. It was the unspoken understanding that it would be used to further one's current career, but my direct supervisor had signed off on my plans without more than a knowing smile. It was then that I noticed she started scheduling me in a consistent three-day block, almost always the same days each week, and she mentioned I should keep her updated on any scheduling changes when it came to my classes.

Largely, I could build off my existing career, since I had my Bachelors of Science in Nursing. But still, there were credit hours to complete and hours and hours of training to log. It was going to take time and dedication, and while I had a lot of the second, I had much less of the first.

Why was I doing this? I'd asked myself more than once, going with the answer that I'd always wanted to. I didn't want to wonder *what if*. Life would be more fulfilling if I felt like I was *truly* able to help people, in a way that wasn't just physical. And, more honestly, that I needed something to fill the little time I had to myself now that Noah was no longer in my life. Because without him, my days were empty and the nights brutal.

Such a short period of time. I had so much of him for such a small window, and in that brief time I had begun to feel alive and hopeful in a way I hadn't known before. He'd made me consider so many possibilities, and the way he adored me filled my heart in places that had been empty and aching for years.

I hated that.

I hated that I let him in and let him ruin me all over again.

But when I was really honest, late at night when I couldn't sleep, there was a tiny voice in my head that whispered to me none of it was his fault.

I did it; the fault was mine. I had chased someone I had no business going after. He was confused and broken and I put myself in his way, giving him no choice.

When I looked at it like that, I hated myself. It made me feel guilty and dirty, like I'd manipulated a situation to my benefit.

Jared had been quiet and withdrawn since the day I lost my shit on the people I loved most. The feeling of betrayal when I'd walked into my

268

best friend's kitchen to see the person I struggled every day *not* to seek out, standing there working quietly alongside my son, was like a sharp knife to the gut.

He wasn't supposed to be there. Seeing him opened up something inside my chest that bled messily all over my insides, and it had come spewing out of me as anger and hate.

I'd worked so hard to protect myself from him; to keep him at a distance. Because I felt guilty over the way I'd treated him, and the last thing I could do seemed to be to take full personal responsibility for what had happened to Jared. It was easier to share the blame with someone else, rather than to accept it for what it was: all mine.

I should have been the one keeping tabs on what was going on at Jason's place.

I should have insisted a social worker stay involved.

I should have pushed harder; asked more questions.

I should have dropped Jared off and picked him up, rather than relying upon Jason for any of it.

It had been months on end, and Jason was still on the run. By now the dirty details had come out, and they were even more sordid than any of us had expected, far-reaching and horrifying, and one by one the various members of an enormous drug and sex trafficking ring were being picked up during late night raids. Several had pointed the finger at Jason as occupying a place of mid-level authority and it made me sick to think of the things Jared had probably witnessed.

He was still seeing a therapist, though with Jason's absence his attitude had improved remarkably, and we'd been able to cut down our visits from three times a week to just one.

Not surprisingly, I was immediately awarded full, irrevocable custody in light of "recent events," said the judge. Daniel had hauled me into a huge hug right there in the courtroom, lifting me up off my feet. Even the judge smiled, having presided over years of my personal struggle.

That was when Daniel asked me out again.

Said he wanted another chance, because he felt like we'd gotten off to a bad start.

Maybe he hadn't shown enough interest, when all he was, was interested.

Said he knew he could win me over, if I just let him try again.

I hesitated, and I knew he could see it on my face. I had to be honest with him. It was only fair to let him know that I wasn't sure there was a chance, ever--not for anyone.

That was the entirety of the problem, really, that Noah had completely ruined me for anyone else, and I hated that.

"You're not still seeing that beast, are you?" Daniel asked, and for the first time ever, I heard disdain in his cultured voice.

Surprised to feel anger rush over me at his words, I snapped back, "There's nothing about him that makes him a beast."

A snort from Daniel told me he disagreed and I leaned back against the brick wall, folding my arms, waiting for his explanation.

I didn't get one.

Instead, Daniel went whiny and placatory. "You know I'm right, Eve. He's just some overgrown, jacked up guy who makes women's brains go soft with all those muscles." He rolled his eyes. "He's obviously blue collar. A tradesman." He scoffed. "Works with his hands. You deserve more than that."

Oh, did I ever remember what he could do with those hands, those huge callused fingers so incredibly gentle.

"He's all muscle. No intelligence and no class."

"You're right," I said slowly, and Daniel's face lit up victoriously. "He *is* all muscle." I struggled with the feelings. "He has the biggest heart of anyone I've ever met."

The biggest something else, too, but I managed to keep those words to myself because nobody but Lauren needed to know about that.

Daniel's face fell again. It was clearly not what he'd been hoping for.

"In fact," I continued, "he's offered to let Jared start apprenticing for him during the summers and I think I might let him do it." I was shocked by the words that tripped out of my own mouth. I had been considering no such thing until this very moment.

Lauren left me alone to stew for a while, and when I finally broke down and apologized to her, she was uncharacteristically quiet. Somehow, this pregnancy had mellowed her. She was quieter, more patient, and she'd developed the disconcerting ability to see right through me like my thoughts were being scrolled across my forehead in real time. Zero effort. She'd turned into an Italian grandmother.

She showed up at my place unannounced a few weeks later, a grocery bag in her arms and a knowing look on her pretty face. I was surprised that Alex let her out of the house, as he was protective of her on a normal day, but when she was pregnant he was like a caveman with a compulsive disorder. And several months along already, her belly starting to round just to the point it was noticeable, she had her pregnant glow back. My beautiful friend was stunning, and I couldn't blame Alex for wanting to constantly knock her up when it made her look like this.

She leaned in to kiss my cheek when I opened the door, and wordlessly, I let her in.

I hadn't been expecting her and she made no excuses, just sailed in and deposited the paper bag on the kitchen island. Then she reached in and pulled out orange juice and champagne, fetching a champagne flute from the cupboard and filling it with more bubbly than orange juice before handing it to me.

Jared giggled from where he sat on the sofa, a manga book in his hands--those things drove me insane--as he watched Lauren try to get me sloppy. She was a bad influence.

I took the flute suspiciously. I owed her a much larger apology and we both knew it, but there was a bad taste in my mouth and I filled it with bubbly orange juice in hopes I could wash it right back down.

Gesturing toward the small table in the corner of the kitchen, she crossed the room and sat carefully, her eyes not leaving me as I followed her and sat across from her. It was disconcerting. Lauren was always talking a million miles a minute, full of stories and exclamations, loud laughter and inventive curses. And the woman was dead-silent. Patient. Absolutely freaking serene.

"Alex invited Noah over for breakfast this morning," she finally announced casually, taking a sip of her own plain orange juice. "He has these ridiculous plans for the tree house, since he's convinced this is Son Number Five." She gestured toward her stomach. "So Noah's being conscripted into Alex's crazy construction army this morning." She rolled her eyes. "He's got some of the guys coming over to help...I expect to find the kids running around in their underwear, all hopped up on ice cream, and the kitchen counter covered in beer bottles by the time I get home."

I made a very noncommittal noise and took a large swallow of the drink I held in my hand. The thought of Noah building things, his muscles straining as he hauled heavy pieces of lumber, made my lady parts quiver in an unnerving way.

"How long has it been?" Lauren asked casually, and my eyes snapped back to her. Apparently I'd been daydreaming about shirtless Noah for long enough that she'd noticed.

"A while," I said quietly, and I wondered if I should tell her about Daniel asking me out again.

"A while," she led slowly, her eyebrow lifting, and I knew the expression on my face turned into something bitter.

I could see it reflected on her face: pity. People had looked at me like that my whole life, and I hated it. But this time? Well, I'd probably earned it.

"For the record," she said casually, reaching back into the crinkly bag and pulling out a fruit tray. She popped the lid and shoved a strawberry into her mouth. "He's got a real bromance going on with my husband. I'd almost be jealous if it wasn't so damned cute."

I made a face. "Better not tell Alex it's cute; that's the last thing your super-manly man wants to hear."

She grinned. "Know what else is cute?"

Uh-oh, here it came.

"The way that one looks at him." She gestured casually toward the sofa, where Jared was engrossed in his book. "Hero worship, if I ever saw it. The man can do no wrong. Thick as thieves and all that, always giggling together." A soft, sweet smile crossed her face. "They're adorable."

Pushing up from my chair, I pulled a box of muffins from the fridge and set them out. Lauren had a good appetite to begin with, but she ate like a locust when she was pregnant and if I put food in her face, maybe she'd shut up.

Also, I needed a moment when she couldn't see my face.

"So, babe…" she sat back in her chair and smoothed her shirt over her belly. "What's the story?" Oh boy, she was settling right in.

"What story?" I kept my face down so she couldn't see my eyes.

"The one where you're punishing him because you let him get too close."

Shit, that story.

"I'll have you know," she wagged a finger at me and I had no choice but to look up. "I have spoken to Noah and to…" She pointed across the room toward Jared. "And you're making everything out of nothing. If that man had even an inkling *he* was in trouble, there is no way he'd have let it continue."

"He didn't *say* anything, Lauren." I could feel flames licking up my neck.

"Because there was nothing to tell, woman! It's not like he had any clue our boy was stuck in a den of iniquity." She lowered her voice a little, toning it down considerably for Jared's sake.

"I failed him, Lauren. I should have known. It was my job." The guilt swam back up to meet me.

"Oh…" She leaned back again, understanding dawning in her eyes. "Oh, so that's what this is."

I sank down into the chair across from her again.

"You're punishing *you*."

The air between us was thick with something I couldn't name, but it felt an awful lot like regret, and it was coming from me.

"Seriously, Eve. You're one of the most intelligent people I know, but sometimes you really are a dumb shit."

My head snapped up at the insult. Lauren was always very forthright, but this didn't feel like tough love. It hurt to hear her say it, even though I knew every word was true.

"You made *one* mistake, Eve. You trusted the wrong man for a split-second, and he's spent years failing you. Why you think that's your fault--or your job to make up for that--I'll never know.

"Shit happens, woman. It happens to all of us. Do you know how many years I've spent unwinding all the mistrust woven through my husband's brain because of his stupid ex?"

I did know a little of that, as Lauren had spent a few drunken nights on my sofa when she and Alex were dating. Usually in tears. When she had too much to drink, she was almost unbearably emotional.

"Bathroom." Lauren jumped to her feet, her eyes wide, and I smirked. That was the part I didn't miss about pregnancy, since Jared had always played soccer with my bladder.

I put fruit and a muffin on a plate for Jared, who took it with a sweet smile before going back to his book.

Thanks to hours and hours of therapy, and Jason's absence from our lives, I almost had my sweet boy back. We were still dealing with fluctuating hormones, and we still had our moments, but largely he was kind and thoughtful, back to being the boy I knew before Jason twisted him up. Better, somehow, and it dawned on me that perhaps I had Noah to thank.

"Whew." Lauren's relief was evident as she came back down the hall. "This one is trying to kill me...that's why I say it's a girl."

I grinned. "Are you ready for what that'll do to your husband?"

"Lord save us," she groaned, lowering herself back into the chair. "The sun will rise and set on the princess who can do no wrong."

"That's right," I agreed, handing her another glass of orange juice. "And for the first time in your marriage, that princess will *not* be you."

Her eyes didn't widen in surprise, like I'd expected. Instead, she waved a hand at me. "Psssh, fine. I'm ready to pass that baton." She grinned. "It's exhausting business, anyway."

She helped me clean up once we finished eating, and before letting herself back out the door she pulled me into a tight hug. She put her lips close to my ear, so that only I could hear her words: "For the record, babe, he's punishing himself far more than you are--and it hurts to watch."

Then she slipped out the door and left me to my boiling thoughts.

TWENTY-FIVE

Noah

◄❙►

Alex had no idea what a lifeline he'd been the days, weeks and months since I'd last seen Eve. I'd counted every single one of them as some sort of sick exercise.

Already, it had been over a year since I'd held her in my arms and it probably wasn't a big surprise that I wasn't eager to fill the hole she left. I didn't want to try to replace what I'd lost, because no one else could come close.

Eve had actually allowed Jared to work with me over the summer. She dropped him off each morning and drove away without coming inside, and I took him home each evening, waiting until I knew Jared was safely inside but not walking him in because I couldn't handle seeing her. Feeling her disappointment.

It was getting cold again, the holidays right around the corner, and still Jared came to see me every weekday. Alex picked him up from school on his way home from his shift, dropping him at my place since I lived all of five minutes from their house.

I was in a weird work lull, which sometimes happened between big contracts, and I'd taken the time to put finishing touches on the house. It was almost done, finally, after countless hours of work put in by an army of men. It was finished, painted, largely furnished, and the grand old girl was a warm, beautiful home.

Just empty.

Coming up the driveway each day, I couldn't help but notice how deceptive it was: The house glowed with light and warmth, like it was hiding a sweet secret, welcoming me back like I was about to walk into laughter and love and the smell of delicious things baking. And stupidly, I always psyched myself up for it--just a little bit--always disappointed when I walked in to find the house empty.

Jared had found two tiny kittens nestled under one of the hydrangea bushes a couple months ago, and while the two of us raised the tiny kittens with bottles and an electric blanket, he set out to tame the suspicious mama cat. It took him a while, since she'd obviously been mistreated by humans in the past. She gimped around on three legs, one hanging uselessly from her side, and Jared named her Paws.

So now the three of those damn cats roamed my house, finding warm sunshiny spots to sleep in during the day and pouncing on me at night.

The runt was a champion at the sneak attack. She was a pretty little calico Jared had named Patches and she was my guard dog. That little shit was forever under foot, following me from room to room to see what I was doing. The instant I sat down anywhere, she was in my lap, purring so hard that her whole little body shook with the effort.

Alex had shaken his head at the scene when he'd come to pick up Jared a couple weeks earlier. It was late and I knew Jared was spending the night at Lauren and Alex's place because Eve had something going on, but I didn't know what.

Honestly, I didn't want to think about it too much because I knew it could have been that she was working late, but it also could have been that she had a date.

Jared and I had been working in the garage together, making a Christmas present for his mama, and we were covered in wood shavings when I opened the door.

"You got something here, man," Alex laughed, nudging my shoulder where Patches rode like a parrot. She squeaked a greeting at him and he shook his head back and forth, blowing out a breath as he rubbed her ear. "Time to get a dog to even things out here. Nut up."

I grinned at him. "Best way to keep the chicks away that I know of."

"Like they're hammering down your door," he shot back with a grin of his own. He knew very well that I had no interest in getting out there again, and he had joked time and again that he was going to create a dating profile for me and upload a picture of me with Patches, just to see what kind of crazy it attracted. Because the sane ones? Those ladies stayed the fuck away when a man said he was a cat lover. He said it was guaranteed to get me some wild action, probably of the mentally unstable variety, but I wasn't even a little bit up for it.

Alex followed me back out to the garage and Patches hung on for the ride, chirping her greeting to Jared when I opened the door to let Alex into the space where we were working.

"Wow." He sounded impressed as he took in the expanse of smooth wood we'd cut and sanded, notched and pieced together. "No way she's gonna think J made this all on his own."

I blushed guiltily. When Jared had come to me with his idea of a Christmas present for his mom, I'd been all over it. A nice desk, he said, because she needed space for her things. She spent nights with her books piled up on the small kitchen table, hunched over a space that was too small and too short. And I'd wanted to ask why--what was she doing? But I didn't. As hard as it was to keep my curiosity to myself, I wasn't going to stoop to pumping her kid for information.

"Gonna need an intermediary," I said to Alex as Patches purred in my ear. I reached up to pull her off my shoulder, scratching her tiny belly before passing her over to Jared, who cuddled her to his chest.

"Think I could bring this over to your place and set it up in your garage? Can't very well take it to her place."

"Sure you can," he answered easily. "Let me know when it's finished and I'll help you one afternoon."

I didn't know how I felt about that, sneaking into her space even if my intentions were pure.

"Not sure she's gonna feel real positive about that," I said, noticing a quick grin exchanged between Jared and Alex.

"J-man, whatta you say give us a couple minutes?"

Jared jumped up, taking Patches with him as he let himself into the house through a side door.

"Stop the bullshit." Alex looked mad.

"I'm...what?" I felt my forehead collapse into a deep furrow.

"The two of you are being dumbassed kids about this. She thinks she fucked up and she's punishing both of you for it, and all you gotta do is go make her see that she's wrong."

"Easier said than done," I scoffed. "The woman wants nothing to do with me--and have you met her? She doesn't *do* 'I was wrong.'"

"She wants everything to do with you, though." The corner of his mouth tipped up slowly. "But my girl *does* have a real hard time admitting when she's been wrong. She's stubborn as fuck--sorry if you just figured that out."

I shook my head. "She cut me out, Alex."

"And yet here you are," he gestured toward the nearly finished desk. "Obviously still all tied up in knots over her. A smart guy would have moved on. He'd have given it a couple months and gone out and forgotten all about it by getting balls-deep in a trashy blonde. But nope, not you...bet you haven't gotten laid since." He said it like he couldn't believe it even as it came out of his mouth.

"That what you did?" I asked, knowing I was punching below the belt.

The air was so still, it positively crackled with an electric charge as he stared at me stonily. I had crossed the line and I knew it, because one did not joke about his precious Lauren. Not ever.

"Let me tell you a little something about my wife," he said, his voice deadly calm. "When I met her I was pulling an Eve, all wrapped up in self-pity and keeping people at an arm's length. I was scared to let her in, because I was sure if she saw how weak I really was, she'd turn around and run. But you know my woman. Takes no prisoners and she damn sure wasn't about to let me get away with it.

"Don't get me wrong, she gave me a minute to think on my sins. Made me miss her like hell. Then she got tired of waiting and bulldozed her way right in." He slapped one big hand over his heart. "Not gonna say it's been one hundred percent sunshine and unicorn piss, but that woman is my miracle. She doesn't let me be an asshole, and every time she sees that stupid self-pitying, doubting shit start to build back up inside my head, she chases it all away again."

I didn't want to ask, because I had a pretty good idea of how Lauren chased away Alex's demons. I also knew that he had more than most, having been married before he met Lauren, and it had ended in spectacularly bad fashion. He'd told me something about it in the months since we'd waged a cautious truce; his way of drawing me out, I guess.

He'd said his piece, planting the seed inside my mind that he wanted to, and he left me standing in the garage by myself to think things over.

***

It was two weeks to Christmas and according to Alex, today was the day. He said Eve had exams most of the day and as much as the curiosity burned inside of me, I didn't ask a single question. Just nodded like an idiot and motioned for him to follow me to the garage.

Jared and I had stained the pretty wooden desk and added vintage hardware, then he had wrapped it up with a soft blanket and I taped around the perimeter to hold the cloth in place.

Alex and I loaded the piece into the back of my beat up old truck and the three of us crowded into the cab to drive downtown.

There was no way to leave the truck on the street, so I pulled into the parking garage across the street and Alex and I struggled to lug the piece across lanes of active traffic, sweating and cursing as we went.

"How the hell did she get all her shit in, in the first place?" I wheezed and Jared rolled his eyes at me for my use of the s-word.

"Duh, Bear. Service elevator in the back."

"Now you tell me," I grunted, sticking my tongue out at him as he held the door for us to shuffle through.

Alex punched a code into the smart lock, swinging open the door to her place and I tried my damndest to look disinterested. Like I wasn't taking in every detail; like her possessions might tell me something more about who she was.

I could smell her here, and the realization that I could remember her scent even a year later almost knocked me over. It was something warm and clean and comforting I wanted to bathe myself in it.

Get lost in it.

Drown in it and never resurface.

Alex whistled at me to snap me out of it, shaking his head at me. "You got it bad, man. Stop mooning and get yourself together."

Yeah, I did have it bad--even after all this time--even for a woman who couldn't stand the thought of me. That was the part I tried not to think of often, because I knew I'd spent more time grieving the loss of a woman I'd barely had than I'd spent grieving the one I'd had for decades. That revelation alone probably presented enough billable hours to pay off a therapist's car.

The third bedroom in the condo was the smallest of the three, obviously used for storage. Jared had cleared just enough room for us to fit the desk against the wall with the window, and once we unwrapped it I stood there looking around. "Too bad we don't have a little more time," I said, and Alex nodded like he knew where my thoughts were going.

"No time for painting and organizing, my man. Don't think we wanna tell her you were in here in the first place," he said gently, and I nodded, moving a couple boxes aside. I was still persona non grata, and this was as close as I could get.

We drove back to my place in silence, not totally weird for a truck filled with dudes, but it was a little weird that Jared wasn't filling the empty air with words. It was something he'd started doing lately, like he'd been storing up all kinds of questions for years, and lately they'd been pouring out faster than I could answer them.

Lately he'd been asking me an awful lot of questions about relationships, and it was easy to see that he was struggling with things. He was a smart kid and it was obvious that he loved and wanted the best for his mom. The problem was that his little heart was completely transparent and I knew his brain was spinning, trying to pull a Parent Trap setup between me and Eve, and there was no way in hell she was gonna go for that.

Jared promised to keep our secret until Christmas morning, and Christmas came and went without a word from Eve. I hadn't been expecting rapturous thanks or to find Eve at my door praising my craftsmanship, but that she remained silent hurt a little because I had really poured myself into the creation of something beautiful for her.

Alex and Lauren invited me over for Christmas dinner and since none of my family had managed a cohesive celebration this year--too much family turmoil--it was the bright spot in what had been a very bleak season.

I showed up with a bottle of wine for Lauren, well aware she couldn't drink it just yet, but soon. She was due any day now--a girl, she still insisted, though they had decided not to find out beforehand this time.

The noise when she opened the door was insane. Her four little boys were enthusiastic soldiers in the Army of Chaos, charging through the house with squeals and screams as they chased one another with their Christmas gifts.

Alex appeared behind his wife as she leaned up to kiss my cheek-- something that took real effort since she was so tiny. He held a glass of amber liquid in his hand and he lifted it toward me in an unmistakable gesture. "Coping mechanism," he said, his other hand coming up over his wife's shoulder to hand me a glass, and out of the corner of my eye I thought Lauren looked like she was in pain.

"Drink fast," he instructed. "You'll need this more than I do--and I need it pretty bad."

I took the glass from his hand, a little fearful of sliding back down that slippery slope, and he nodded at me like he'd read my mind. "I won't let you go there. Trust me," was all he said, and that was something I could do, so I took a sip of the fiery liquid. It burned and warmed and dulled ever so slightly and I tipped the rest of it back in a quick, molten shot.

A sweet laugh drifted out from the kitchen and I froze in my tracks, my eyes widening.

"Told you," Alex whispered, and my eyes swung immediately to Lauren, who had a wicked grin on her face. She held up her hands, her eyebrows wiggling mischievously.

"You are the devil," I whispered softly, and her grin stretched wider.

"No, Bear," she whispered back and her use of the nickname startled me. "You should know by now, I'm Mother Teresa." Her eyebrows wiggled again and her husband snorted, rolling his eyes.

Eve's back was to me when I walked into the kitchen and I felt her register my presence without seeing me. I saw it in the way her back went rigid and she drew in a deep breath that pulled her shoulders back.

Jared sat at the island, his mouth full of something as he chewed, and he gave me a thumbs-up. What it was for, I wasn't entirely certain.

"I'm an idiot," Lauren announced loudly and Alex and Jared grinned at the same time. "I completely forgot to mention that we have an additional dinner guest." Her voice was forced and bright. The woman knew exactly what she'd done: set both of us up.

Eve turned slowly and I expected her expression to be angry. Furious, maybe. But instead, all I saw was hurt. I didn't know whether it was directed at Lauren or myself, but it was something visceral. She wrapped her arms around herself, affording me a single curt nod. "Noah."

"Angel." I swallowed hard. I hadn't meant to say that, but it was *her*. I couldn't help it.

She looked like I'd slapped her when I said it, and I ducked my head guiltily, aware that Lauren's face was about to split, she was grinning so hard.

"Oooh, hey…" Lauren winced, poking a finger into her stomach and I could see the movement in her belly. "You settle down in there, princess. Mama is *not* going into labor tonight."

Eve's lips lifted just slightly, into a soft smile, and she reached over to touch Lauren's belly. "You should sit," she said gently. "Everything is under control and we can get dinner on the table from here."

Lauren winced and nodded and Alex sidled up to her, dropping a kiss to her forehead before pulling her across the room to sit. He made sure her feet were up and covered her with a blanket, then removed the cork on the wine bottle I'd brought and poured a small portion into a glass.

"Not a bad idea." Eve was smiling at him like she knew something I didn't.

"May as well take the edge off; she's gone this long," Alex said, and I watched as he crossed the room to hand the glass to Lauren. She looked up at him, her eyes widening as she took it and he kissed her again before coming to stand near me. "Stubborn little shit," he said under his breath. "Insists she's fine, but the damn woman's been in labor all day. Killing me to watch her like this, but we won't go to that hospital until she's good and damn ready." He gritted his teeth. "She'll be much more agreeable after a glass."

"Man, you should have told us." I clapped him on the shoulder, simultaneously overjoyed for him and overwhelmingly jealous. *What would it be like to be in his shoes?*

"No way." He shook his head. "That tiny terror has been masterminding this for weeks, and she's not about to let my kid steal her thunder."

Eve and Alex pulled dishes from the oven and I carried whatever they handed me to the dining room table, setting things out as best I could and filling glasses with wine, water and juice, Jared working quietly at my side. My little helper, as always.

Alex slipped from the room halfway through the meal to make a phone call and I knew reinforcements, in the form of his parents, would be showing up shortly. It would take the both of them to wrangle the four unruly boys while their mother pushed another one into the world.

"So Eve," Lauren called across the table, her face twisting as she fought another obvious contraction. She sucked in a few deep breaths, always in control of the situation even when she wasn't. "Tell us about what you've been up to lately. Get Bear all caught up."

Eve had been stealing furtive glances at me the whole time and I'd hardly been able to eat, my guts all twisted up in fucking knots. I just wanted the meal to be over, so I could escape. I couldn't stand to be this close to her, yet feel like she was miles and miles away. It was easier to play pretend when I didn't have to see her sitting right across from me.

"Just...work and classes," she said quietly and my eyes focused on hers so that she couldn't look away.

"Classes for…" Lauren led, breathing heavily. I had to hand it to her, when she set her mind to something she really worked hard to see it through.

"I'm studying to become a grief counselor, and I'm focusing largely upon the destructive role addictions play in that recovery process--how to get a person over one thing so they can get over the other."

Understanding bled through me. It had been the time spent with me and my family that pushed her to it. She'd seen our brokenness, our dysfunction, and in her own way she'd set out to fix it. I swallowed hard, because it felt a little like a recrimination. *You were all so broken, you forced my hand.*

"You'll be wonderful," I said around the thick feeling that was crawling up my throat.

"I just want to make a difference," she said hopefully, and my eyes locked onto hers.

"You already have," I said, pushing myself slowly away from the table. Because every adult in the room knew what that meant.

Lauren winced again and the huge smile almost left her face. "Excellent," she said, squeezing Alex's hand in a death grip. "Now, you two work on mending fences while I go push this monster out." She rose, and Alex spoke to me with his eyes as he scooped an arm under his wife. Eve made a motion as if she was going to follow and Lauren shook her head. "No baby, I got this. Get your little man home for a good night's sleep; this will be over soon."

"Go, man," I said to Alex. "We'll wait for your babysitters."

We didn't have to wait for long, and thank God, because Eve went completely mute once Alex hustled Lauren out of the house. I could feel her eyes on me, watching me, and I didn't know what it was she expected me to say. That I was sorry? In her mind my transgression had been far larger than in reality. It had been stupid on my part, a careless ommission, and God knew how dearly I'd been paying for it. But never, ever would I have ignored it if I'd thought Jared was truly in danger.

"See you at the hospital tomorrow, little man?" I asked Jared as the three of us left the house and splintered apart to head to our cars. He lifted a hand to give me a fist bump, and for the first time I realized he wasn't so little anymore. He'd turned twelve and in the past year he'd started to shoot up. Kid was going to be tall.

"Gonna collect on my bet with Uncle Alex," he grinned, and I looked to Eve for clarification. She rolled her eyes, an indulgent smile on her lips.

"Alex insists this is Son Number Five," she explained, and I nodded at the obvious inference that Alex was wrong and he was about to be a girl dad. It made my heart twist in a fist, jealous of what I'd lost and would never have.

I nodded to the two of them and tore my gaze away from Eve. It was like ripping off a limb, walking away from her, and I staggered to my truck. I dropped in behind the wheel and turned over the engine, waiting for it to warm while she backed her car out of the driveway and disappeared down the street.

I was pretty sure she hadn't looked back at me at all.

TWENTY-SIX

Eve
◄II►

I could hardly handle the idea of seeing Noah again the next day, but I was sure of one thing: If I wasn't there when he arrived, he would sit there and wait. He would wait until he saw me, because it was the purest form of torture I knew, and since I'd refused to talk to him last night I deserved the punishment.

I had tossed and turned in my bed, which wasn't anything new, and I couldn't get Noah's anguished expression out of my head.

Jared knew when I was fishing for information about the big man he spent his afternoons with, and my own son was a locked vault. He protected Noah's secrets more closely than he protected his own. I hadn't been able to get anything out of him the night before, and I'd tried like hell the whole drive home.

Every time I rolled over and closed my eyes again, all I could see was the hurt in his eyes and the guilt crawled up my throat, hot and acidic. Because I had done this to him. I had known he would be deeply loyal, even if I hadn't expected he would be loyal to *me*. We hadn't been together long enough for him to attach himself to the idea of an *us*. But somehow, I knew that was exactly what he had done. Because that's who Noah was, and when he'd told me he was a one-woman man, he'd been telling me the truth.

The problem was that a big part of me feared that one woman was still Avery, and I knew better than to try to compete with the dead.

Alex called me late that morning, his voice strained with exhaustion. Labor had been hard, he said, and when I heard his voice catch I knew it had been worse than all that.

"Is she ok, Alex?" I asked, sitting straighter in my chair, pins and needles rushing across my skin.

He was quiet for a long time and when I heard the sharp intake of breath, I knew. The man could hardly get himself back under control.

"The monitors started going crazy," he said finally, and his deep voice was thick with tears. "The doctor panicked and kicked me out--shoved me out the door and said they needed the room, and thirty seconds later they went flying out of there screaming things at each other...there was blood *everywhere*, Eve." His breath shuddered in and out and there was a pain in my right hand. I looked down to realize I'd had my fist pressed so tightly to my teeth that I'd drawn blood.

"I didn't get an update for an hour...the longest hour of my life."

I dashed at the tears that had started streaking down my cheeks.

"I'm telling you, for the first time ever I was staring at what it was going to be like to parent five kids all on my own. And I couldn't do it. I couldn't..." There was a low sound.

"A hemorrhage?" I asked softly, my heart hammering erratically in my chest.

He made a sound that seemed affirmative, sniffling a few times before he could answer with words. I heard a deep voice then, close, and I dropped my head to my chest in shame: Noah was there, holding Alex up.

"She's not out of the woods yet," he said finally, "but she's stable at least. Barely."

"The baby?" I finally asked, fearful of the answer.

"Chiara," he said softly, and I couldn't help but smile.

"She was right."

"I'll never doubt her again."

We sat quietly for a moment and something dark and painful started to churn inside my chest. *Loss.*

"Is there anything I can do?" I asked softly, and Alex drew a deep breath.

"Yeah," he said quietly, and I waited for the rest. "Don't be stingy with your love, Eve, because a fight--a disagreement--a grudge--isn't worth it. Tomorrow might be too late, and think of all the time you'd have missed. Memories you won't have."

I sat with the phone in my hand for a long time after Alex was called away to check on Lauren.

Alex was an emotional guy, but not with me. Lauren was the only person who saw the softer side of him, and for a long time I'd remained unconvinced the man didn't have a heart made of granite. (According to Lauren, another part of him was of similar construction and no lie, I'd been a little jealous.)

"Jared?" I hollered, tossing my phone to the side on the sofa and rushing down the hallway.

"Mom?" He stumbled out of his room, rubbing his eyes and I knew it was because he'd fallen asleep reading one of those stupid manga books I'd gotten him for Christmas.

"Babe, I need to go to the hospital--Auntie Lauren is..." I paused then. There was no easy way to explain this. "You have a new honorary cousin, but Auntie is not well."

His face went pale. He loved Lauren, maybe more than he loved me. And rightly so, since she'd been his real mother for the past year I'd been working and going to school.

"I'm coming with you," he announced firmly. "Uncle Alex will need my help."

He probably wasn't wrong about that. In my own experience, women were much more accepting and capable of coping with grief, loss and hardship than most men. Like it was a birthright, to shoulder the heavy loads on their own.

I rushed through a shower and threw on the first clean pair of clothes I could find. (They sort of matched, so that was a win.)

Jared was standing near the kitchen island, ready to go when I finally rushed back down the hallway. He had filled a go-cup with coffee for me, and his clothing *actually* matched, a skill he hadn't gotten from me, apparently.

"Mom," he panted as we dashed across the street to get to the parking garage, and the sideways look I gave him was all I could manage. "If Bear is with Uncle Alex, it's gonna be ok."

I clicked my key fob, my forehead wrinkling a little, because I had no idea what my son meant. Noah couldn't fix this any more than I could.

I didn't exactly drive like a bat out of hell, but I did put the poor little car through some undeserved paces as I tore out of the garage and toward the hospital. (And thank God traffic was light.)

Jared was almost as familiar with the hospital as I was, and he ran ahead of me as we rushed through the wings, leading the way to the ICU, where he knew we'd find Lauren.

Bursting into the waiting room, we were both surprised to find it empty. And Jared, wise beyond his years, pulled a long face. "Frickin' figures no one else came," he muttered, and he definitely felt the look I gave him.

"Come on," he said, leading me in the direction of the nurses' desk and I knew then that he'd spent entirely too much time in my hospital.

"Please." His baby face went all soft and sweet, and I watched the three women sitting behind the counter go all maternal. "I'm looking for my auntie, Lauren Antolini. Can someone help me find her?"

All three of them were on their feet, murmuring and gesturing, one of them slipping out from behind the barrier to lead us down a quiet hallway. She smiled at my son, resting a hand on his shoulder, and I followed behind, not willing to interrupt.

"Thank you." Jared threw his arms around the woman when we stopped outside one of the rooms, and she smiled down at him and patted his head. He wasn't much shorter than her.

"I know you're family," she said quietly, and she winked. "Try to keep very quiet, and no more than ten minutes."

Taking a deep breath, I followed Jared into the room to find Alex on his knees beside the bed, his face pressed into the blankets as a respirator whirred and monitors beeped.

I sank into a chair near the door while Jared edged up to Alex, dropping beside him and huddling into his side.

Without looking up, Alex put his arm around my son and drew him close, and I pressed the heels of my hands into my eyes.

This was wrong. All wrong. Lauren was young and healthy and fit, and yet here she was, barely hanging on, her husband beside himself while he waited for fate to decide whether or not his children would be raised by their mother.

When he raised his head, Alex's eyes were swollen and bloodshot, and he let me give him a brief hug.

I dropped down beside him, grasping her limp hand in mine and it took everything I had not to start sobbing into the blankets.

"She'll come back to us," I whispered to Alex fervently. "She's got way too much attitude to let something like this take her down."

One side of his mouth pulled up into something that might have been a grimace, or a smile.

"Alex." A sudden wave of panic washed over me. "What about Chiara?"

"She's in good hands," was all he could say. He leaned back into Lauren's side, his lips on the back of her cool hand, and I knew he was lost, unable to think beyond what was right in front of him.

"Babe," I whispered to Jared. "Stay with them, ok? I'm going to check on the baby."

I rushed to the elevator and hit the button, climbing four flights at a pace slower than I could have walked them.

Because I knew what Alex meant, and I knew where I could find him.

I didn't stop at the desk. I rushed to the nursery and peered through the glass to see an enormous man, swathed in a gown and covered with all manner of hair nets, sitting in a rocking chair with a tiny bundle held to his chest.

My heart stopped beating and I choked on a breath.

He rocked her gently, his lips moving in what I thought was a lullaby, and my ovaries clenched even as my heart started beating again.

Slowly, he stopped rocking. He adjusted the baby gently in his arms, and then he looked up, his eyes meeting mine through the glass.

I was done.

His.

Tired of fighting and hurting, and hating what I'd done to this man.

Very carefully, he got to his feet, moving toward the glass that separated us, and my eyes filled with tears when he held the little face before me so that I could see she had Lauren's nose.

Warm fingers curled over my shoulder and I looked down to see a friendly face smiling up at me. "That beautiful man in there says you're a nurse here," she smiled up at me. "Just want to let you know now that the general consensus is that we're going to keep him, and good luck convincing us otherwise." Her smile was sweet and warm.

"I need to talk to him," I said softly, having a hard time projecting my words. "I need to tell him I've made a terrible mistake."

Her expression folded a little, in sympathy and understanding, and she gestured to him through the glass. He shook his head at me, looking back down at the sweet bundle in his arms with an awe and reverence that made my heart twist. The way he was looking down at the tiny little girl in his arms made my heart splinter and quake in a way I hadn't known was possible, seeing the depth of this huge man's love for something so new and small and helpless--something that wasn't even his.

The nursery was quiet, a few small snuffles and mewls. Most of the babies had just been fed and were sleeping through sweet, milk-fed dreams, and when one of the nurses approached Noah with her arms out, he handed the baby over with obvious reluctance.

Kissing her tiny forehead, he placed her gently in the nurse's arms and swallowed hard before his eyes met mine, and he made his way slowly to the door.

I took his wrist when he came through the door, swiveling the barcoded band to read *Baby Girl Antolini*. It made me smile softly, because today he was an honorary brother and uncle. I was sure Lauren had somehow arranged this--there was no way this was standard operating procedure.

"This is what I missed out on," he whispered softly to me, and I looked up into those warm brown eyes to see the loss and regret swimming there.

I swallowed hard, because I wanted to fix the pain I'd caused and the pain I hadn't, and slowly I leaned forward so that our foreheads touched.

"I've been wrong, Bear..."

His forehead moved against mine and I looked up to see his eyes wide with shock. He hadn't been expecting my apology. "Yeah, you've been fuckin' wrong," he retorted, his voice hushed but filled with anger and hurt.

"It was unfair, and I'm sorry." I sure as hell couldn't stop it now, and it poured out. "I blamed things on you that weren't your fault. I made you suffer for things you didn't do, and I'm...I don't deserve to be forgiven."

Oh, the words tasted *so* bad.

"You hurt me, Eve." He'd taken a step back. "You hurt me real bad. You finally let me in, let me see what I could have with you and Jared, and then you just ripped it all away--didn't even give me a chance to explain my side. Just cut me out." His big shoulders heaved with the exertion of his breaths and I reached out a hand to touch his cheek, but he caught my wrist mid-air.

"It's not like that anymore," he said thickly, and a cold wave of panic washed over my body. *It's too late.* "You don't get to touch me and get me all twisted up inside anymore. I know you got trust issues, but I don't need 'em too." He paced a short distance from me, turning back, his long legs eating up the short hallway in only a few steps.

"But..." My protest was almost as weak as my voice. "You have Jared now." Because he did, almost every day during the week, and for that I was incredibly grateful to him. I had seen the change in my son, the way he'd become more responsible and focused. The way he treated me with more thoughtfulness, and there were things he said that sounded just like Noah.

"I can at least do right by him," he ground out, and he turned so I couldn't see his eyes. "At least I can be something to him--a part of his life when he needs a man who will help train him up right."

I caught a glimpse of myself in the nursery glass and it startled me, how flat my expression had gone. There was something awful happening

293

inside, like the extinguishing of a pilot flame. I sank down into a nearby chair, because I knew what it was: My hope was dying.

Noah stalked off and I stayed sitting there for a long time, trying to sort through the mess in my own brain. There was so much useless junk in there, like I'd taken all the things I hadn't wanted to deal with over the years and just tossed them into a room and locked the door. Now someone had opened the door and shit was spilling out all over the place, demanding I deal with it all at once.

I had to remind myself to breathe, feeling perilously close to a panic attack as I remembered every tiny detail of the moments with Noah. It was knowing I couldn't have that anymore--that I'd been the one to throw it away--that made me think I might need a tranquilizer.

One of the nurses observed my struggle, as I sat rubbing the heels of my palms over my jeans and angrily wiping at my eyes with the sleeve of my sweater. Maybe she'd overheard our conversation, because finally she knelt next to me with a paper cup of water in her hand and she pulled my hair back over my ear before setting a warm hand on my shoulder, her eyes earnest when she looked up at me. "Honey," she said gently, and I knew my face was a red mess of emotions. "Fate doesn't make our decisions for us."

With that she stood, patting my back before disappearing back into the nurse's station, and like a bolt of lightning to my brain, I knew what I needed to do.

TWENTY-SEVEN

Noah

◄II►

I stayed at the hospital most of the day, but I made sure to steer clear of Eve. I could feel everything she was feeling--the things I'd felt for so long, all by myself--and I couldn't deal with it any longer. It was time to let her go, because hanging on was just fucking with my head.

The problem with letting someone go is that it's a hell of a lot easier said than done. All the resolve in the world sometimes isn't enough to keep that person out of your thoughts and those stupid dreams that creep in at night.

Jared didn't come back to my place for the rest of Christmas break and I knew it was because Eve didn't have school until after the New Year. I suspected that on the days she worked, Jared was going to Alex and Lauren's place. And while I wasn't going to call Eve and ask about it, I missed the kid. A lot.

Finally, figuring I'd given Alex and Lauren long enough to settle after what had been a pretty big scare, I went over with a basket of diapers for the baby, chocolate for Lauren, toys for the little boys, and a bottle of something old for Alex.

It was Alex's mom who met me at the door, looking a little tired, but her face lifted into a friendly smile as she looked me over. "Mr. Noah," she said in a lyrical accent and she leaned up to kiss each of my cheeks twice. I fucking loved that tradition, since gestures of affection were totally my way of communicating. My whole family was that way; we were a touchy, kissy bunch, and it drove some people crazy. Not this one, though. Her giggle was adorable when I gave her two big, sloppy smacks on each cheek. None of that air-kissy crap, totally fake shit.

Lauren was lying on the sofa, wrapped in a blanket, the sweet baby bundled in with her and lying on her chest. She smiled up at me, her cheeks still a bit pale, and I dropped down to sit on the floor beside her. "Gave us a scare, little lady. I expect that will never happen again, if you don't mind."

Her smile was tired and she shook her head slowly, careful not to wake the baby. "Nope, my man is a big believer in signs and he said that means this is it." She looked a little sad when she said it. "Time to close up shop."

"No Italian soccer team?" I asked, just teasing a little, and she rolled her eyes.

"You and Eve, on about that nonsense." She didn't even bother correcting me, like I'd been expecting her to do.

Alex drifted into the room with one of the twins draped across his shoulders like a scarf, the other one tucked under his arm. "Atholton." His voice was friendly and he carefully set down both boys, swatting their backsides playfully as they ran off, and he reached out a hand to help me up.

"Buon Dio," he grunted as he hoisted me to my feet, and he pulled me into a big, backslapping hug. "Always forget you're a gorilla," he grumbled over my shoulder, and I had to chuckle.

"Don't go being jealous now, some ladies like a beast," I teased and Lauren's subdued voice called out from behind me.

"My husband's plenty beast for me, and I've been told my bar is high."

I grinned over my shoulder at her. *There* was a spark of the old girl.

"Speaking of some ladies and their beasts…"

Uh-oh, here it came. Apparently despite all that blood loss, Lauren's ability to meddle hadn't drained out of her.

"It's over, Lauren," I said quietly and Alex's jaw dropped at the same time hers did. "I'm just hurting myself hanging on, not lettin' myself get over things, and that's not fair to anyone."

"Oh shit, you didn't," breathed Lauren, and I sucked in a big breath. "Baby," she hissed at Alex. "He went and got a shrink."

I chuckled, and Alex startled at the high-pitched noise, but admirably he kept further commentary to himself.

"Yes and no," I said. "My stepmom is a therapist and I've been talking with her lately. A lot. She's been helping me to sort out the things that are keeping me from moving on, and me hangin' onto something that's never gonna happen is one of those things."

There was a soft rustling from behind me and I looked back to see Jared, his eyes wide and solemn. Kid was quick, and he wouldn't have had to overhear much to know exactly what--who--I was talking about.

"What about me?" Jared's voice was filled with hurt and I swallowed hard, turning my body so that I could face him like a man.

"Doesn't change anything about us," I said, and my throat felt scratchy because those stupid allergies were about to make an appearance.

"Does too," he said flatly. "It means that my mom will start seeing that stupid lawyer again. He's after her like a dog and I don't like that. If I have to have a new dad, it's not gonna be him."

Lauren's eyes went wide and Alex folded his arms over his chest as he nodded thoughtfully. "Who would you choose, then?" he asked the boy gently, and Jared dropped his gaze to his feet.

"You already know, Uncle Alex."

"I do." Alex's voice was uncharacteristically kind. "But I think there's someone else who needs to hear it."

I stood completely still as Jared squared his shoulders and walked over to me, putting his arms around my chest and holding on like he was afraid I'd disappear. "I choose Bear," he said softly, his head tucking right in under my arm. "And mom does too, but she's being stupid right now."

"*Right now?*" A snort rocketed out of Lauren.

"Understatement of the year, my man," Alex said with a grin, reaching across to high five the kid.

Jared whispered something into my side and I looked down into his eyes with the question written all over my face.

"Please don't give up on us," he whispered, so quietly I knew I was the only one who heard it and I felt like the kid had a vice around my heart, squeezing it with those big blue eyes of his.

I had to swallow real hard and when I looked over at Alex, there was something brewing in the air between him and Lauren. Those two were damn near telepathic, communicating with glances and smiles and raised eyebrows. It was fucking annoying.

"Well," Alex led dramatically. "Know what I think? I think that when J's mama comes to pick him up, she'll have *forgotten* that I was taking him over to help out Noah today."

Lauren's smile was so big, I thought she might need stitches later.

"But baby, everyone just got their wires crossed." She picked the thread right up, holding the baby up so I could cuddle her to my chest as she sat up and swiveled her little body on the sofa. "Because by the time she gets to Noah's place, I'll be calling her to apologize...Alex was planning to take the boys to dinner so that Mama and Chiara could get in a little nap."

The two of them looked positively smug. I wasn't sure I liked it.

"Don't worry, babe," Lauren pitched her voice a little higher, like she was talking to someone else. "Alex can bring Jared by when they're done with dinner--not a problem."

"It's a shame everyone forgot Jared was sleeping over tonight," Alex finished for her, and Jared narrowed his eyes at me from where he stood at my side.

"Is that secret code, guys?" he demanded, looking suspiciously from Lauren to Alex and back.

"Can't hide anything from him," Lauren sighed, but she was still smiling. "Yeah, J. It means putting your mama in a situation where she *has* to talk to Noah, and maybe they can work some things out."

"And have a sleepover?" he asked pointedly, looking around suspiciously, and I couldn't help but burst out laughing.

"I think your mom would burn my house down before she'd sleep over, but either way, I'm happy to make pancakes in the morning." I ruffled his hair. He'd been asking me questions about things related to adult sleepovers lately, and I'd answered him carefully and honestly. The kid absolutely knew an adult sleepover didn't involve a pillow fight.

"I'd hurry home," Lauren admonished, holding her arms out for her daughter and I was reluctant to put the sweet little bundle back in her arms, dropping a kiss on the tiny forehead before I did.

"You probably have some tidying up you want to do," she continued, settling back on the sofa, and Jared grinned up at me. Totally here for this.

"You'll need this." It was Alex, hurrying back in from the kitchen with a reusable bag in one hand. I couldn't resist peeking in and my expression must have been funny, because Jared giggled.

"Pizza and wine," Lauren explained. "Eve's idea of the best date night ever. A sure tool of seduction."

Alex was across the room, covering his mother's ears, protecting her from the blasphemy that was frozen pizza, while Jared stood next to me with his hands over his own ears. Apparently he'd checked out right around the "date night" part.

"I'm not seducing anyone, and I'm sure as hell not begging," I practically hissed at Lauren. "I'll make the pizza and pour the wine, but if she wants me, it's her turn to do the work."

Lauren wiggled her eyebrows at me in a way that suggested she had no doubt someone would be working.

I gave Jared an extra squeeze and rolled my eyes at the two meddlers before I left, then I set the bag carefully on the passenger seat before turning over the engine and tearing toward home. Because yeah, I needed to do a little tidying. But mostly? Mostly I was real fucking nervous, because I had no idea what was coming.

TWENTY-EIGHT

Eve

❮❙❯

By the time I pulled up in front of Noah's house I was a sweaty, angry, nervous wreck. I called bullshit on the excuse Lauren fed me, but if Jared was at Noah's place, that was where I'd go to pick him up.

I was tired. Since school didn't start again for a few more weeks, I'd been pulling some pretty long shifts, and the last thing I had was the energy to put on a happy face and pretend around Noah that things were fine, great, happy, sorted. Whatever. All I wanted was to go home and crawl into a hot bath with the largest glass of wine I could manage.

Today had been hard. I'd lost a patient right up at the top of my shift, a homeless man who came in often, always completely strung out. But Gerald, one of the sweetest little old men I knew, had a horrible story of loss and rejection and when he was sober-ish, though it was rare, he told me bits of it, as he'd done for the last six years.

"I always feel better after seein' you, Miss Eve," he always said as he was being discharged. And I knew he meant it, because all he needed was to be heard and I always gave him both ears.

He needed to be recognized.

To see a friendly, smiling face even though he was in one of the most depressing places on earth.

I drew a deep, shaky breath and climbed out of my car on sore legs. Everything hurt, but today what hurt most was my heart and here I was, about to walk in and face the man who would surely smash it to smithereens with just a few more bitter words.

"Angel."

Surely I was imagining things.

There was the huge man, standing on the front porch, waiting for me in the cold as I trudged up the steps.

Arms wide open.

I walked into them, sinking into the wall of hot muscle, my face pressed into a soft flannel shirt that smelled like my dreams.

His heart thundered beneath my ear and his arms went tightly around me, one hand wound up into my hair, his thumb brushing back and forth over my ear.

I couldn't move. I was glued to the man, and as he patiently held me, I felt the stupid waterworks welling up behind my eyes.

No, no, no.

"Tough day," he said softly when he heard me sniffle and I didn't even have to nod. He already knew.

Tough life.

"Come on in." His voice was kind. "I have dinner ready."

Like I was coming home to him.

He led me through the entry and into the dining room, which was right up at the front of his house. It was a room I'd never actually seen him use before, and when I exclaimed over the beautiful dining set he hung his head and blushed.

Told me my son had helped him make it.

The table was set for two and when I looked over at him he looked quickly away, probably to avoid the suspicious glare.

"Nothing fancy," he said with the grin I'd missed so much. "Just pizza..." He left the room.

"And Lauren thought you could use some of this." He reappeared with a bottle of wine, pouring until one of the glasses was filled to the brim. He gestured I should sit then, raising his own glass to mine with a little shrug. "Just water for me."

I didn't even ask him where Jared was; two place settings confirmed this had been a setup from the start and I was too tired to fight with anyone.

"I had an interesting conversation with the little man today."

I stared down at the slice with two bites in it. Apparently we weren't going to waste any time.

"He asked me not to give up on the two of you."

He hadn't touched his pizza and I looked back down at mine, suddenly unable to take another bite. Instead, I lifted the wine glass and took several large chugs.

"I told Lauren and Alex that I wasn't going to beg," he said quietly, dropping his eyes to his own glass. "If there's even a chance you want this, it's something you gotta figure out, Eve. I don't have the energy anymore, 'cuz I can't just wish this into being."

When I didn't answer he pushed back from the table and the floor shook as he thundered past me, rushing toward the kitchen.

I sat there for a moment longer, trying to sort the tangle of thoughts that refused to unravel and organize in my brain. A few more sips of wine didn't help that process either, and when I stood to go after him, all I knew was that I was my own worst enemy.

He was standing at the sink when I walked in, his arms stretched wide on either side of him as he leaned forward, his head dropped down between his shoulders.

Coming up behind him, I hesitated for just a second. He could feel me in the room I knew, I had seen the prickle of awareness ripple across his back: my heart calling to his.

There were no words for what I'd put him through, and I moved carefully behind him and slipped my arms under his, up over his chest, and he straightened slowly as I pressed myself into his back, my face between his shoulder blades as I held on for dear life.

His hands came up to cover mine and I felt a deep sigh leave him, either resignation or relief, and I desperately hoped it was the latter.

We stayed like that for a long time, until he gently pried my fingers from his chest and turned to face me. His expression was sad when he did, so different from the smiling, silly man everyone else saw, and it hurt my heart. This was my fault.

"I'm so sorry," I whispered, the words not even close to all the things I needed to say.

"Me too," he answered, his voice rumbling, my cheek vibrating where I'd pressed it to his chest. "Mostly sorry for myself if I gotta be real honest, 'cuz I couldn't be enough for both of you."

That was what he thought? That was what I'd *made* him think?

"That sounds more like a me problem," I answered against his chest, and it made him chuckle just a little. That stupid little girl chuckle of his that I had to admit I'd actually really missed.

"Can I request a do-over?" I finally asked softly, pulling back just a little and lifting my eyes to his. He had grown in a beard again, and hesitantly I lifted a hand to run my fingers through it. He caught my hand when I did, spreading out my palm and pressing a kiss into it before putting it back on his face and leaning into it.

"I love it when you do that," I said shyly, pretty sure he'd just let me off the biggest hook ever.

"I recall you loving a couple other things I can do, too," he answered cheekily, his handsome face pulling into a straight, white smile. There was my silly man. "You need some reminders?"

"Just this," I sighed contentedly, burrowing back into his chest. A piece of me had been missing ever since I'd left California and I'd just found it again.

"Not putting up much of a fight, Ryan," he smirked into my hair and I shook my head just slightly.

"This last year wasn't enough for you, big man?"

"Too much, Angel." He pulled back and looked down at me again, hooking a finger under my chin so I had to meet his eyes. "Way too damn much. And you need to tell me something right now: Are you in this with me, or am I on my own?"

I lifted up on my toes, curling the fingers of both hands into his beard to pull his face down to me, and I shivered when his warm lips met mine.

"In," I sighed into his mouth, and his arms banded so tightly around me, I couldn't breathe.

He scooped me up and I wrapped my legs around his waist, hanging onto his shoulders while he bumped his way through the house. He felt his way along the walls, pushing hard off the balls of his feet to carry me up the stairs.

He carried me past all the empty bedrooms, the hallway bathroom, the tiny nursery, and into the large space that smelled like him: warm, familiar, comforting.

When he set me down his kisses turned gentle, and I felt a hesitation inside him. I looked up just as he captured one of my hands to hold over his heart.

"My sister always says that when the Atholton boys fall, it's like taking down a sequoia." His words were deep and rumbly. "There's a lot of crashing and shrieking and everyone better get the hell outta the way, 'cuz there's about to be a huge mess." He grinned. "We're real good at fucking things up in a big way."

"This wasn't you," I said quietly, toeing off my shoes and unwinding my hair from the tight coil at the back of my head. I watched his eyes flare when he understood I was undressing. "I didn't deserve you, and I found a way to push you away and tell myself it was your fault. I've always been scared of not being enough, and it's even more complicated when you have a child because you're asking so much more of that other person."

"You coulda just asked," he said, his fingers sifting through my hair, a small smile on his face.

"Nope." I reached down to grab my sweater by the hem to pull it over my head, watching as his eyes lit up. "Come on, Bear. You know me by now. When do I ever ask for help?"

"Damned woman," he grumbled, but his expression was sweet and he leaned down to kiss me again, his tongue insistently sweeping through my mouth while his big hands kneaded my backside, bringing me up tight against his body.

I shivered. I'd missed the raw power of this man, able to toss me around like a ragdoll though he treated me like I was something delicate and precious. The look in his eyes at that moment, though, told me he wasn't feeling particularly gentle, and I. Was. Here for it.

"You done toyin' with me, Angel?" he asked, and my forehead wrinkled in confusion.

"Noah, I'm not...I don't..."

"Oh, I know you don't mean to." The corner of his mouth lifted and he leaned over, stripping off my pants with a single yank. I don't know how he did it, my feet still under me, but when he stood again he pushed down my underwear and snaked a hand behind me to rip off my bra, the hook popping when he tore it from my body. "But see, you got an unfair advantage." He grinned wickedly down at me, his hands coming up to cup my breasts, and I felt a violent shudder run through him. "Because once a man's had a taste of this..." He hitched me up so my chest was tight to his and I felt completely ridiculous, stark naked while he remained fully dressed. "No, no, no..." He murmured as he lifted my face again, his thumb brushing against the pink rising in my cheeks. "There's nothin' else that'll do." His thumb rubbed back and forth. "Wrecked me, woman." He was dead serious.

He lifted me suddenly and with a squeal I went flying through the air, bouncing when I hit the middle of the bed.

"Don't suppose you missed anything, did you?" he led, standing at the foot of the bed and staring down at me as his fingers started to work slowly through the buttons of his shirt.

"Um," was all I could manage, my jaw hanging slack as I watched the slowest, most painful striptease of my life. He was watching my eyes as he peeled his clothes off an inch at a time, waiting to see something in my eyes before he dropped his shirt to the floor and started on his pants. I might have groaned then, and I pushed up on my knees to lean forward and help him along.

"Nope," he chided, purposely slowing his movements. "This show's all mine, sweet thing. You had me all twisted up and crazy; you can handle a few minutes of your own medicine." His eyes twinkled as the button on his pants finally popped and I bit my lip so hard, I winced when I tasted blood. He was enjoying torturing me.

"Now..." He stretched purposefully, spreading his wide arms, every muscle in his stomach straining, his arms bulging and popping and I made a needy sound. "What was it, exactly, that my Angel missed the most?" He grinned mischievously.

The shoe was *so* on the other foot.

"I recall a certain someone enjoying the view…" He finally dropped his pants and my fingers curled into fists at the sight of his muscular thighs, the tight black boxer briefs doing nothing to conceal what I'd felt against my stomach earlier.

Who was this man? This wasn't the bashful, tentative man I'd steamrolled in bed. This one was self-assured, aware of what he did to me, and he was enjoying watching me squirm; making me wait for him.

"Somethin' you're gonna need to know, Angel," he said, finally crawling up the bed toward me like a huge, predatory cat. He pushed me back and I stared up at him as he caged me in with those huge arms. "This is your spot," he whispered, something gentle coming over his expression as he patted the pillow next to my head. "Want you here with me every night. Wanna wake up to this every morning." He sifted fingers through my hair. "Want our sweet boy sleeping down the hall from us, and we can work on filling up those bedrooms with some little angels." His eyes searched my face, waiting for my reaction. "You with me on that?"

"Bear," I begged, reaching for his shoulders and he grinned down at me.

"Gonna take that as a yes."

Then he lunged, the force of his mouth on mine launching me up the bed and with each brutally hard kiss, his hips snapped against mine, the rhythmic sound of my skull bumping the headboard as our bodies ground together.

"Last chance, Angel," he growled down at me and something bright and hot cracked open inside my chest.

"You're the first chance I've ever had," I whispered back and his body stilled, one of his hands moving to cup my face.

"Only one you're ever gonna need," he whispered back with the smallest smile, reaching between our bodies to peel his underwear down his legs and when his hips dropped to mine I kept my eyes open, watching him as he joined our bodies.

This was his wheelhouse, the communication of his feelings through touch and physical demonstration, and I watched the emotions play across his face as he struggled to say all the things he needed to without words. And when we fell apart together, I could feel the fluttering of something in my chest that I knew meant I'd fallen without wanting to.

The whole time, this man had been waiting to catch me.

Epilogue

One Year Later
⬥

The last twelve months had been a whirlwind of activity.

Eve sold her condo in the spring and she and Jared moved in with me just a few months before we flew to California to be married on the edge of the vineyard at Thomas's place. It had been Eve's request, since she said that was the place I first became hers, and there was no fucking way I was letting my woman down.

Jared had started high school in the fall and he was young for it, but he was no longer struggling with school. I wondered sometimes if he hadn't been challenged enough in school before, or whether his struggles had been more emotional--mine sure had. But in any case, the kid was brilliant. He'd settled right into his studies and joined a couple clubs, too, and sometimes his friends would come over to play video games all night on the weekends.

Jason seemed to have disappeared from our lives forever, and I sometimes wondered if he ended up in a shallow grave thanks to the unsavory company he kept. Seemed to me that with several bounty hunters after him, someone would have scooped him up.

Eve had been working really hard to get through school and I'd told her to cut back on work and let me carry the load for a while. That way she could focus on finishing her schooling and logging the insane number of supervised hours she needed.

As for me, things had finally fallen into place. The house was finished and filled with people I loved, and my days took on a steady rhythm that grounded me. I didn't have to search anymore to find things to keep myself out of trouble, and my hard drinking days were over now that I'd found something worth more to me than mindless oblivion.

Da had asked me if I wanted to go into business with him over the summer and after careful consideration and drafting several contracts and partnership agreements, we merged our ventures and I started to hire on full time guys to handle the projects that were coming in faster than we could staff and handle them.

It seemed like my family was starting to get their shit together too.

Finn was living in northern California with her baby boy toy, as I called Mateo teasingly, since I knew Finn was extra sensitive to their age gap. But honestly, that shit didn't matter to me. What mattered was that she was happy--beyond happy, glowing with the joy she and my nephew Griffin found with Mateo in their new home.

There was a new family member coming soon, too. A new nephew, and I was just a little jealous when Finn called me to breathlessly relay the news. Eve and I had been trying for a couple months, but I really couldn't blame her--girl was exhausted all the time. She couldn't get enough of me, though. All I had to do was give her a certain look and she was rushing up the stairs, dragging me with her.

My life with Eve was nothing like my life with Avery, and had the worst days of my life never happened, I wouldn't have discovered the best days of my life.

Looking back, I still suffered a little guilt. I realized that making Avery my wife hadn't been important to me because she had never demonstrated she wanted me to be her husband. Was it just a bunch of fancy words and an official piece of paper? Maybe. All I knew was that I didn't take the first full, deep breath of my life until the minister told me Eve was my wife.

The best days of my life were spent with a woman who loved me with her whole heart, joyfully, her face lighting up each time she saw me. She couldn't get enough of me, and that was something that soothed me, giving me a confidence my brother Thomas said I hadn't had before. That either meant he saw the change or he was totally jealous, because I was pretty sure he was still clawing his way through some similar insecurities now that he was finally getting over Lydia. Not that he wanted to talk about it, of course. The man was ridiculous.

I'd been out to visit Thom much earlier in the year and I'd finally met the top-secret source of his suffering. It was something he wasn't willing to admit, but one look at the little Marilyn Monroe lookalike he just couldn't seem to stay away from, and I knew he was done for.

Me and Natalie got along great, and she gave all my joking and teasing and stupid right back to me. Little spitfire, that one. Thom was a lucky man, if he'd just pull his head outta his ass long enough to see it.

The last five or six years, the siblings had been trying with some success to gather for Christmas and spend a few days together just being thankful for each other. We always had a good time, there were generally no injuries, and to this point no one had been hospitalized.

This year Finn was hosting in her new home, and word on the street was that Aaron was bringing a woman with him. That blew my hair back, tell you what, since I'd decided a long time ago my next younger brother was a monk, totally married to his Army career. He'd kinda gone into an emotional lockdown when his wife cheated on him, and I knew that while he'd been overseas their divorce was finalized.

One by one, my siblings were starting to settle down and when Finn saw Aaron walking across the yard from the guest house with a gorgeous brunette tucked under his arm, she grinned at me. "Timber," she mouthed, making a slashing motion over the cinnamon rolls she was icing at the kitchen counter.

Thom was being a surly fuck, and that was nothing new, sitting over on the sofa and brooding by himself while poor Mateo tried desperately to keep up in his second language with my equally irritable baby brother, Asher. He'd already given up on Thomas.

Something had crawled up Asher's ass lately too, and historically, when it came to our family, it had to do with something he wanted but couldn't have. Definitely a woman.

My girl fell right into step with my sister, doing the washing up while Finn cooked and baked like a maniac.

Jared and my nephew, Griffin, were thick as thieves. When they weren't chasing Griffin's new rescue dog Jet across the yard--for the record, that dog loved every second of it--they were in Griffin's huge new room playing video games, Jet sprawled out over their feet.

When it came to Christmas, I was a much bigger kid than most. I had been snooping around for weeks trying to figure out what Eve had planned for me so I could outdo her. Damn straight it was a competition, and I was gonna find a way to one-up her if it killed me.

For my part, I'd planned something a little more elaborate than was my usual forte. Since Eve had been all wound up in schooling, we really hadn't taken what one would call a proper honeymoon and after all the rush of moving and selling, settling Jared into a new school and a new routine, the late nights merging my business with Da's, and the steady stream of teenage house guests we seemed to have, I wanted a couple weeks with my girl all to myself. So I'd booked tickets to an exclusive resort and spa in the southwest over Eve's spring break. Nothing but sun, food, the pool and a helluva lot of naked.

The woman would not give me a single clue when it came to my gift. She was secretive as fuck, giggling and whispering with my sister and Aaron's girlfriend, Harlowe, but the instant I walked into the room she'd go totally silent. I'd tried sneaking up on her more than once; eavesdropping--nothing was working.

I fell asleep on Christmas Eve with my angel in my arms and dreamed sweet dreams of warm sunshine and my wife rolling me over to have her way with me. (Must have been part Christmas wish, because when Eve woke me in the early morning hours and nudged me over onto my back, that wish came true. Twice.)

"He can't even sit still," Jared giggled to Griffin as he watched me impatiently waiting for Mateo to get his coffee and sit down in the living room. It was just us, Eve and me and Jared, and Finn with Mateo and Griff, since no one else was up yet. The kids were dying to open their gifts and I was dying to give mine to my wife.

"Let the man go first, before there is an explosion," Mateo teased, rolling his eyes at me and both kids shook their heads as I dove under the tree for the envelope I'd put there with Eve's name on it.

"Bear!" she exclaimed, a huge smile on her face as her eyes scanned the paper. Both boys were giggling like Eve's pet name for me was the most disgusting thing they'd ever heard. On their good days, girls still had cooties and it needed to stay that way for as long as possible.

"Pack your sunscreen, Angel," I teased, leaning in to nip her earlobe with my teeth. "Ain't gonna have *no* tan lines." I leaned back to lick my lips suggestively.

The boys were already ripping into their gifts and Griffin had taken to throwing things from under the tree to Finn and Mateo. I tried to wait patiently, but it was absolutely eating me alive.

Eve was watching me out of the side of her eye, and she was sucking in at her lips, trying desperately not to smile.

"So," I led, wiggling myself closer to her and kissing her temple. "What did you get me?"

"You'll see," she said, and I saw her and Finn exchange looks. "I think it got buried under everything else. Shouldn't take long, but you have to be patient." If the woman knew anything about me, it was that I had absolutely no patience, and I heaved out an irritated huff.

"Trust me, Bear," she whispered finally, leaning over to kiss my cheek. "It'll be worth it."

Finally I heard a triumphant shout from under the tree and I looked over to see Jared clutching something tiny to his chest. It was a small box, so small it could have held nothing larger than a pen, and I turned an unamused look on my wife. "That better be the key to an awesome sports car."

Her smile was positively wicked. "Don't worry, big guy, it'll be just as expensive."

I shredded the paper so fast, I almost mangled the thin box and when my big fingers struggled to open it, Eve slipped an index finger into the tiny tab to pop it open. Something slipped out into my hand, sealed in a

Ziploc bag. It was lightweight and plastic and there was a bright pink plus sign on the face.

I sat there staring at it and the room went completely silent. Eve shifted next to me, slipping something into my lap and I looked down to see a photo of the nursery I'd made so long ago, with a scrolling letter H hanging above the white crib.

"What...I...Angel, what is this?" I asked, feeling hot and panicky and there was something prickly happening in my eyes that told me this was going to be an epic attack of allergies.

"It's almost ten weeks," she said quietly, dragging one of my hands out of my lap to rest over her stomach. "You can call it a woman's intuition if you want, but I'm almost certain it's a girl."

I looked down at my hand, then back down at the picture, then at the pregnancy test in my hand. "H?" I asked stupidly, the wheels finally starting to turn in my head. You could almost hear them.

"Hope," she whispered softly to me, and that was when the dam burst. Holy shit, did it burst. I couldn't control what was running down my cheeks or the fact I was wailing like a baby, and I hauled Eve up from her spot on the sofa and absolutely crushed her in my arms.

"What the fuck?" Aaron had chosen that moment to drift into the house, and I left everyone else in the room to explain to him what was happening while I covered my girl's face in big, wet kisses. She squealed and squirmed and laughed with her whole self, and when I could finally stop sobbing like a damn toddler, I kissed her hard before leaning back to look at her. She was radiant, glowing with happiness and what I now knew were probably an insane amount of pregnancy hormones, and I wondered if that was why she'd been waking me so much in the middle of the night lately. (I was not one to complain.)

"Hope," I mumbled to myself, trying out the sweet little name in my mouth. I liked it.

"It was something you gave me," she whispered and I could hear her clearly despite all the happy noise in the room. "And now I can give it back to you."

313

I wrapped my arms around her and pulled her close, so I could press my nose to the heartbeat in her neck.

Because I'd been wrong.

I sucked in a deep breath, inhaling the warm, sweet scent of her skin and the promise she'd just given me.

Now I could take the deepest breath, because my life was just beginning.

The End.

Keep turning to read a sneak peek of "The Things I Can't Say," Asher and Olivia's story!

The Things I Can't Say

Asher

◄II►

"You might wanna get something on that."

Molly winced sympathetically from where she sat behind the desk, eyeing up the angry red mark around my eye: The impending shiner I'd just earned because I'd underestimated my opponent. He'd jabbed and I'd ducked, but I'd miscalculated, punching his fist with my face instead. Hardly the way it was supposed to work, and a really fucking great look.

I was presenting at a conference tomorrow, and now I'd be doing it with a black eye. Made me look like a powerful leader in the free world, showing up looking like I'd gotten my ass handed to me in some back room brawl.

Which was pretty much exactly what it was. I knew the risks–had known the risks for years–but I loved cage fighting entirely too much to give it up. It was brutal, vicious and completely unforgiving, which suited me just fine.

It was also a great way to keep myself in shape while pushing myself to exhaustion.

It took the edge off.

Filled up a hole that my demanding day job couldn't, and made up for what wasn't happening when I was off the clock.

Kept me out of most trouble and took up almost all of my "free" time.

Today I'd knocked off a little early because I couldn't stand to be in the building anymore. The hot, itchy feeling clawing at my throat told me I should go to the gym and train, so rather than stay and bark orders at my terrified assistant, I told her I was out for the rest of the day and left.

Operating at a high level on the administrative diagram helps with shit like that: No one questions you.

It had started like any other day, decent enough. Breakfast was ok and coffee was passable.

My stocks were up and, a bright spot, my biggest enemy was testifying before Congress for something underhanded his company had tried to pull. That part was very satisfying, watching him all pale and stuttering, groveling on C-Span as he was grilled by the junior senator from Kentucky.

Guy landed a couple good ones.

Max had it coming. He knew his business model crossed every line there was, and he wasn't sorry. (He was only sorry he'd gotten caught.)

Undue influence over the election process, the conservative press was calling it.

The other guys? They weren't even covering it, choosing instead to downplay it and focus on a developing public health crisis in China.

Truth was, Max and I had always been at each other's throats. In fact, you could almost say our animosity was predestined, attending the same college and then the same graduate program.

Chasing the same girls.

The difference between the two of us was that he was the Have and I was the Have Not, and he had never let me forget it. I'd scraped and clawed and worked and fought for everything I had, landing a full ride to Stanford by some inexplicable miracle. (Or maybe my brother Thomas was the miracle, considering it was his alma mater and he had serious clout. I'd never asked.)

Since Max's daddy came from money–and was an ex-senator to boot– Max sailed into Stanford with straight C's.

After six years and what was probably a million dollars in tuition later, he walked out with a graduate degree.

Now he waltzed around Silicon Valley with that proverbial silver spoon shoved so far up his ass, he was insufferable.

Max had been raised to believe the sun rose and set on him and when it sometimes didn't, he didn't know how to handle it. He turned into an angry, whining little bitch when he didn't get his way, and since he had money and connections, he almost always got his way.

If fate had been kind, Max would have been an ogre and a thirty-five-year old virgin.

A troll living in his very wealthy mother's basement.

But as luck would have it, all of his ugly was on the inside and the outside was this tall, blond, arrogant Viking god.

I fucking hated that.

Because, me? Well, let's just say that when Max and I went toe to toe for a woman's attention, there was no competition. He won the prize every damn time.

Then again, the girls he pulled in weren't usually looking for the sort of action I had to offer. They were after money and power, influence and name dropping, and it took me a while and some frustration before I figured that out.

There was a single time Max hadn't been able to work his magic on a woman, and he wasn't about to forgive me for that.

I was no slouch, but there was no mistaking me for Scandinavian royalty, either. I was shorter, darker, and considerably less pretty than Max. My nose had been busted up a couple times and, thanks to always getting into fights with my much older, bigger brothers, I had a number of interesting scars.

I'd added to that collection over the years in the ring.

After graduation, I'd done a quick stint overseas before hiring on with a tech company in San Francisco.

With nothing in my life to demand my time or hold me back, I'd slowly clawed my way to the top of the food chain.

Max had started his own company right out of grad school, funded with the money from Daddy's bottomless pit of wealth and influence, and he attracted all the best talent because he paid crazy salaries. It allowed him to build an empire on a new concept, and before we were thirty he'd surpassed the billion-dollar mark several times over.

As the Chief Product Officer for IntrinoTech, I was pretty far up the ranks and I had a very comfortable salary to show for it. It was nothing that put me in the same field as Max, but with some aggressive investing I was building a very comfortable cushion in case I ever decided to explore Plan B.

It also meant that I had no life to show for it, and some nights I didn't even bother making the short drive home, opting to crash on my office sofa because it wasn't like there was anyone waiting for me anyway.

Most nights, I could be found at the gym. That sometimes kept me out of the gossip columns some of my coworkers found themselves in, and probably saved me innumerable cases of drunk driving.

But today? Well, there was really only *one* thing that could have taken what was a pretty ok day and flipped it on it's ass, and when I rounded the corner to my office I was kicked in the gut by that one thing.

A blonde stood with her back to me, her posture ramrod straight, her body something straight off a runway.

Stopped me in my damn tracks, because I knew that hair…that body.

In a tight black pencil skirt and red-soled heels, long, silky legs and even longer, silkier hair, the demure blue button-up blouse only emphasized the fact that Olivia Fucking Mattingly was still sex on a stick.

Damn it.

Swear my knees knocked.

Get it together, boys.

"Asher." It was Taylor, our CEO. The Big Man. "I'd like you to meet Ms. Mattingly."

I watched her work to turn her neck my way, her deep blue eyes stealing my breath the way they always had.

I hated that.

Hated her.

"Ms. Mattingly is joining us as our new Chief Technology Officer."

I didn't move a muscle, frozen to my spot, my mouth suddenly so dry it felt like I'd swallowed sand.

Taylor was looking back and forth between the two of us, like he couldn't understand why we needed to maintain a distance.

The polite thing to do was shake hands, but I'd never been described as polite.

My face froze and the few angry thoughts bouncing around in my brain screeched to a halt.

"Really," I said, the irritation painfully evident in my voice.

No one had bothered to tell me Joshua, our previous CTO, was leaving.

Had left.

Whatever.

I was going to have to work directly with this woman every damn day? God help me, my life could not get any worse. Starting right now.

"Asher and I went to school together," she said smoothly, aiming a charming smile at Taylor, who was obviously already under her spell.

I couldn't tell if he wanted to mentor her or hump her leg, but the way he watched her was making me uncomfortable: hot and itchy and all kinds of angry.

I felt my fingers curling in, my thumb sealing the fist.

"That so?" Taylor asked, but he didn't look terribly interested in my part in that story.

We'd done a hell of a lot more than just go to school together, but certainly nothing Taylor needed to know about.

Excusing myself, I mumbled something about having a packed schedule, because just being near her was like being burned by a thousand suns, every stupid nerve ending in my body on fire.

The one who didn't want me.

It took serious effort on my part, but I stayed away from her the rest of the day.

After ten years without her in my life, in any capacity, I hadn't been prepared for the sudden and unexpected reintroduction, and to say it knocked me sideways was being pretty damn generous.

I sure as hell hadn't been prepared to see her and it had thrown me for a loop. It left me reeling, pulled up short and disoriented.

It still fucking hurt to look at her, after all this time: Another case of Time not doing her damn job, because Olivia was gorgeous. She was more polished and professional than she'd been when we were in school–more contained and aloof–and still the most breathtaking thing I'd ever seen.

I hated her for being so calm and possessed and beautiful, because today hatred was the only emotion I was capable of expressing.

That's how I ended up at the gym that afternoon, angry and distracted, getting my ass handed to me because I couldn't keep my head in the game.

Bryson, one of the trainers and my semi-official-sort-of-coach, disappeared into the staff room and reemerged with a bag of frozen peas. He slapped it over my eye, none too gently, and I grunted my thanks. "Gonna bleed on your veggies, man."

"Eh." He grunted back at me. "Been in the freezer for years--nobody eatin' 'em anyway. Smaller problem than whatever it is you got going on up there." He twirled an index finger over his head.

He wasn't wrong. The guy could read me like I had a teleprompter spooling my thoughts out across my forehead.

He gestured that I should follow him, leading me back through the door marked "Staff Only."

There was a plain formica table and seven mismatched chairs, and I threw myself into one as I leaned into my fist, holding the bag of peas to my eye.

I was irritated.

"You gonna tell me what's got you so off track today?" he asked, digging through the cupboard hanging over a small counter and sink. He pulled out a package of ramen and my nose curled up, but dude was only twenty-six; supposed he could still get away with eating like a college kid.

"That shit'll kill you," I rasped out, and he threw a grin over his huge shoulder.

"Probably slower'n takin' punches to the face, my man."

He had me there.

"And?" He was leaning against the counter, those disgusting plastic noodles already in the microwave, the low hum filling the room.

"New hire," I ground out.

"Asshole?"

"Worse."

"Boss?"

"May as well be."

He hummed, lifting his chin before he turned to pop open the microwave door.

"Hot, then."

How in the hell did he do it? My jaw sagged just in time for him to turn around and bark out a laugh when he saw the look on my face.

"That's what I thought. Such a hardship, man."

He had no idea how much a hardship it was going to be. It was going to be a trial each and every day I went into the office, and with the visibility of my job, I wasn't logging a whole lot of remote hours from the comfort of my sofa.

I'd have to see her; smell her; be in the same room as her, every damned day. And already I knew that would compromise my focus.

On the job, I was a machine. Nothing and no one got in my way. I wasn't derailed for anything, and I'd prided myself on that the last ten years I'd spent clawing my way up the ladder.

Everybody move.

Get out of my way.

At thirty-four, I'd held the position of Chief Product Officer for the last six years, which meant I'd landed a C-level position at a young enough age.

But while I was young in the tech world, I was old in the ring. My days as a cage fighter were limited, since most of my opponents were getting younger and younger. Most of them had been training since they were in the single-digits, whereas I'd only been training since my late teens. I was a dinosaur by their standards and despite the considerable time I devoted, I would never make it as big as I wanted.

I didn't lie to myself. I knew that making it this far was part hard work, part miracle, and I wasn't guaranteed anything.

I trained religiously and fought a couple times a year–would have done it more if I could have managed, but my day job was a bit of a kink in those plans.

If I'd gotten the call from the UFC when I was a kid, no doubt I'd have jumped at it: a few thousand dollars per fight with no guarantees I'd fight more than once. There were probable medical bills and recovery time...the idea slightly less attractive now than it had been when I was eighteen.

My dual focus hadn't left much time for anything else, and much of my success could be measured in things: I had the multi-million dollar home on Santa Paula Avenue and the three-stall garage filled with expensive cars.

My closet was full of expensive suits, silk ties, custom-made shoes and watches that retailed for the GDP of third world countries.

On the surface I had it all, but I wasn't so shallow as to think I had everything. Because I knew the truth: the expensive house and the nice cars, the fancy clothes and the stupid parties I attended...all of it was empty.

I didn't have what really mattered.

The one thing that would give my life meaning had been missing for ten years. Something I could ever consider a possession, because I'd tried that once and I'd paid for it every damned day since.

Lost her.

Lost a huge piece of myself when she walked out.

I probably deserved it then, but I'd definitely deserve it now.

Instead of becoming more worthy, I was decidedly less.

"You have no idea," I sighed, handing him the bag of peas and pushing to my feet. I needed to get home and eat something, then deal with the fact I might need stitches. I could handle that part on my own, though: I'd been stitching myself up since I was a kid. (I'd practically sewn my own leg back on after my brother Noah pushed me out of a tree when we were kids.)

Bryson crossed the room to set the steaming bowl of noodles on the table, a small smile on his face. "Chicks, man...they absolutely know when they've got us all wound up."

I shook my head. "You just don't even have the first idea. This one...she's been fucking with my head for years."

Even though she didn't know it.

I leaned a little and clapped him on the back, wincing when he returned the favor and I felt the movement in the split skin around my eye.

Hoisting my gym bag onto my shoulder, I snapped off a salute to Molly as I passed the desk and let myself out into the parking lot.

Clicked my key fob, bringing the AMG immediately to life, her lights a pretty welcome.

I heard a car door slam at the other end of the lot and looked over to see a shiny new Mercedes.

Laughed to myself: What a poser.

Sobered for a second. Probably couldn't throw that stone, looking at my pretty girl parked right there...also a Mercedes.

Damn glass houses.

A swish of blonde hair and tight, toned legs in sleek black leggings.

My mouth watered as I watched her cross the parking lot, oblivious to my lustful stare as she yanked open the door to the gym and let herself into the raucous noise: death metal, always Molly's first choice.

Karma, that bitch, was messing with me. It was enough that I had to see Olivia every day, but now I had to share *my* gym with her?

Dropping my bag into the passenger seat, I crawled in behind the wheel and groaned at the throbbing that was setting up on the right side of my face.

I threw the car into reverse.

This was nothing a whole lot of scotch and an evening with my willing fuck buddy Kristyn couldn't fix.

Acknowledgements

Thanks to my family for their patience while I disappear for days at a time to write out the characters in my head, so they'll shut up.

Thanks so much to friends who offer encouragement and support and get all excited when I tell them what I've been doing. The pursuit can be frustratingly solitary sometimes and though I enjoy it more than anything I've ever done, it's good to get out and commune with real people!

And thanks to my bestie, who's been working her way through all of it, trying to save me from myself!

About the Author

Erin's a fan of big trucks, strong-minded men, grocery delivery services and happy endings.

Years after studying Journalism, she's returned to writing the kinds of stories she's been penning since she was ten years old: sweet stories of love lost, won, broken or regained. Her characters have seen some things and they tend to be a little older, a little broken, and just redeemable enough to get their shit together, usually after a few seriously stupid missteps. (Because life is hard, but the mistakes can put us on the path we're meant to travel, right?)

Erin's family relocates with some frequency, thanks to her husband's career. For now she lives with her very own Alpha male and two children in the Metro D.C. area.

Most days you'll find Erin trying to write--anywhere will do, even if it's doing edits in her head--while wrangling hungry kids, three demanding cats and big, hairy Mastiffs.

You can find her at erinfitzgeraldwrites.com, Facebook, and Instagram at erinfitzgeraldwrites.

Other Works & Coming Soon

The Atholton Series

Forsaking All Others - Book One

The Battle Back Home - Book Two

The Things I Can't Say - Book Four, Coming January 21, 2022

When I Had Nothing - Book Five, Coming February 21, 2022

Men of the First Brigade

Unexpected (Jack & Daphne), 3/21/22

Unforgiven (Scott & Mia) TBD

Unwelcome (Brandon & Giulia) TBD

Undeniable (Adam & Madelyn) TBD

Made in the USA
Middletown, DE
01 February 2022

60173512R00186